Dear
Sue,

[handwritten cursive note, largely illegible]

Remember Matt 18:21-22

YOU'VE GOT A

man!

*Within the inner circle,
how much do we really
know each other?*

Gloria P. Pruett

PURE PRAISE PUBLISHING

All Scripture is taken from the King James Version (KJV) of the Bible, unless otherwise noted.

CREDITS
Editing and Proofing
www.thesoundproof.com
Email: info@thesoundproof.com

Cover Design and Layout
Pure Praise Media

Published by
Pure Praise Publishing
www.purepraisemedia.com
Email: designer@purepraisemedia.com

Printed in the United States of America

ACKNOWLEDGMENTS

First and foremost I'd like to thank the "movers and shakers" in my life who constantly encourage me to do what I think I can't: God my Father, Jesus my Savior and Friend, and Holy Spirit my Helper and Comforter (The Man). These Three Men saw something in me that I never saw in myself. They encouraged me to do what I thought I couldn't. I'm so glad to have You Three in my life.

Trying to thank everyone who played a part in this endeavor is a very daunting task because I'd never want to leave anyone out. So if perchance I make a mistake, please accept my apologies and know that it's certainly not intentional. So with all my heart and much gratitude, I thank…

My children, Charles III, Carlton (Tosha), and Kelli, for loving me unconditionally, for making me laugh at my mistakes, and for godly counsel. Some people think they can't learn from their children, but I can testify that children can teach you things. You've helped me be a better mommy and person.

Carlton Jr., Cariel, and Camaran, my grandbabies, you provide the spark when my natural fire is running low. Your drawings are special, and the hair rubs relax like nothing else.

Pastors Larry and Sylvia Jordan, you have helped me publish what God has put on the inside of me. You've helped make the vision a reality, and I'm truly grateful to you and your ministries.

My spiritual parents, who have fed me the Word and opened up Scriptures, allowing me to see and experience the love and character of God. Locally, in Southfield, Michigan,

Pastor Andre Butler and his wife, Minister Tiffany Butler; Pastor MiChelle Butler; and Minister Kristina Jenkins, Esq. In Dallas, Texas, Bishop Keith A. Butler and Pastor Deborah Butler who for over 20 years richly sowed the Word into my life before relocating to Dallas. You've truly blessed me to love and acquire a taste for the Word of God.

Before I could get up enough nerve to have professional editors read my manuscript, the following friends read to confirm that the book made sense and provided feedback. They were Stacey Hanks, Mrs. Rosemary Collins, Ms. Brenda Jackson, Mrs. Rhonda Wright, and Mrs. Michelle Stephens.

The real editors sent by God whose hard work, counsel, patience, and anointing amaze me, none other than R. and J. Johnson. You have not only blessed me with the gifts God has given you, but He has knitted our hearts together. I love you like family.

Margo Collins, your extra eyes helped complete the project. You're a true blessing.

Ollie (Linda), James (Diane), Malcolm (Charline) and John (Nicole), my real brothers, I love you; Denise and Jackie, my sisters, I just wish everyone had sisters like you. We not only love each other as sisters, we really like and enjoy each other's company—and that is a blessing. Aunt Barbara, Aunt Marie, and Dot, can't leave you out—thanks for being a friend and confidant.

Pastor Raymond and Minister Andrea McClintock, I miss you so much. You hooked me up with Dr. Orlena Merritt-Davis, who provided the inside scoop—Orlena, you're the best. Ministers Nathaniel and Lois Vaughn, you provided the Natchez experience, along with Mrs. Thelma Stancel and Mrs. Ella (Chunk) King. Allowing me to use you as fictional characters in my book makes it all seem so real.

Berlinda Wilcox and Patricia Johnson, you both are living examples of a Divine gift. You have been there for me and my ministry on numerous occasions. You always come through for me with my last-minute requests. You're a wonderful blessing to my ministry. To Carol Couch, what can I say? You bless me in so many ways—can't name them all, but I must put a plug in for the home-cooked meals. To my cousin Donald Smith, he knows how to work you, but he also knows how to love you—and that he does very well!

Brenda Smith, Daphne Adams, Annie Coakley, Carole Waldowski, Carmelita Badia, and Monique Dumont, too bad you don't have a dollar for every time I came to you talking about this book; you'd have a lot of money by now!!!

My GM Gospel Group, you keep me spiritually sharp, you pray for me, and you bless me in many ways. I'll not name names because I'll get in trouble if I leave someone off. You're all so special to me.

Last but not least, I want to thank **each person who will purchase this book**. It's one thing to write a book, but if no one reads it—what have I accomplished? As you read, may Holy Spirit be the "Man/Buddy" in your life. He will help you be the friend as well as the person God has called you to be.

REVERENTIAL DISCLAIMER

To my readers…please know that I am by no means trying to put Holy Spirit on my level or take away His Deity by referring to Him as my Man. It is an endearing term that He has allowed me to use, but I use it with respect and awe. The God of the Universe, our Great God, and His Son, My Lord and Savior Jesus, has given you and me an awesome Gift, in the Third Person of the Godhead, Holy Spirit. He is with us daily to help us on this journey of life. He is my/our Friend. It is a special relationship that allows us to interact with Him on a personal level. So with the respect that's due Him, I'm honored to call Him my Man and Buddy.

—Gloria P. Pruett

*FRIEND, n. frend.

1. One who is attached to another by affection; one who entertains for another sentiments of esteem, respect, and affection, which lead him to desire his company, and to seek to promote his happiness and prosperity; opposed to foe or enemy. *"A friend loveth at all times"* (Proverbs 17:17).

2. One not hostile; opposed to an enemy in war.

3. One reconciled after enmity. Let us be friends again.

4. An attendant; a companion.

*According to *1828 Noah Webster Dictionary*

A man that hath friends must shew himself friendly: and there is a friend that sticketh closer than a brother.

Proverbs 18:24

Something's got ahold of me
And it's something I cannot see
Something's got a hold on me
And it's bothersome you see
It messes with my mind
Tells me I don't measure up
It tugs at my heart
Makes me keep my head low
Thinking no one will ever love me
What's this—that's got ahold of me
It's something I cannot see
I stay up late, and can't sleep when I lie down
I get up tired, 'cause I fought with it all night long
It's taken away my joy, and stolen my song
I eat when I'm not hungry; my smile has been replaced with a
frown
Something's got ahold of me—and it's pinning me down
This thing has got me going—my decisions no longer sound
I do what I feel—not what I want
I speak and don't think
I hurt those I love
This thing has got to go
We can no longer cohabitate
I need to come clean
I need to be straight
But how can you fight something you cannot see
Something's got ahold of me

—Gloria P. Pruett
11/9/06

Chapter One

September 26 turned out to be a picture-perfect day. The temperature held steady at seventy-five degrees—with no humidity and just a tint of chill in the air. With eyes closed, that day easily could've been mistaken for the end of August. Summer mixed with just a cup of fall. Weather-wise, Lenda couldn't have picked a better day to get together for dinner with the girls. Mentally, however, perhaps another day would have been better.

Sandwiched between the Detroit River and the towering Renaissance Center, the quaint, luxurious restaurant reeked of money, influence, and power. Lenda arrived at a quarter to six, which gave her plenty of time to park. She knew she'd be ahead of the other three, too. Walking from the parking structure to the restaurant, she caught a glimpse of the enviably peaceful water outside. Inside, fine china graced the white starched tablecloths. The black linen napkins made a stark contrast on the decorated tables. The table settings alone made most women feel like the princesses they had always longed to be.

Lenda heard glasses clinking and waiters placing silverware on the tables. Given her day, it all sounded like a well-played symphony. She exhaled and thought: *This is just what I needed, Lord.*

"Reservations for four under the name of Lenda," she announced.

"What time were your reservations for?" replied the hostess.

"6:30 p.m."

"Our policy is not to seat a partial group. Please have a seat and let us know when *all* parties arrive."

Lenda heard her loud and clear. But she looked at the hostess's name badge, put on the best smile she could muster, and began to speak in a voice that *appeared* calm but was a few minutes from explosive.

"Angie, can you please allow for an exception this time? I really need to sit and gather my thoughts before my friends arrive," Lenda asked.

"I'd like to, but management…"

"May I speak with management?" Lenda interrupted.

"Just a moment…I'll have to find the manager because I believe she stepped away," smirked the hostess.

"Do that, please," Lenda asserted.

Lenda felt borderline offensive, but she didn't care. That day, just once, she wanted what she wanted! Knowing her friends, she knew she would have *at least* fifteen minutes to compose herself. And she needed every second of that and more. Lately, it seemed that everyone wanted a piece of her, and she felt that soon nothing of substance would be left. Why couldn't people leave her alone? Her mother, her siblings, her ex, her co-workers, and yes—even the girls sometimes! The only person who truly gave her the space and unconditional love she so needed was her son, Matthew. Oh how she loved that boy!

While Lenda waited for the manager, she realized that

she needed a vacation. That was the problem. All work and no play made Lenda a very touchy woman. But she knew she didn't have any vacation funds, as she had lent all of her money to her mother for a lawyer to represent her brother— and he still went to jail. Family! She desperately wanted get away from them. Then as usual, the guilt came. She shame- fully thought: *How could I even think about them, especially Mom, like that? My mother has done so much for me; she can't help it that she's older and not aware of the demands that she puts on me. We can't really talk about our relationship because she always takes what I say the wrong way, which forces me to keep quiet. Any relationship that constricts you from being honest is not healthy. You should be able to talk.*

By that time, Lenda was wondering where the hostess went. She could sense the panic button rising higher and higher. She focused again on all that had been going on: bills ate up her checks, and family buzzards had devoured her nest egg. When she reflected on how her savings had dwindled to almost nothing, she could hardly keep it together.

Then, the divorce weighed in. It, too, had really drained her financially. She could never share any of this with the girls. They'd never suspect anything anyway. Still, Lenda wished she had enough courage to tell her best friends all about it. She quickly shoved that thought aside. Meanwhile, Lenda didn't even hear the manager approach her about the table.

"Ma'am, I'm Heather Green, manager on staff," she said.

As she snapped out of her daze, she couldn't help star- ing. This woman looked more like a model than a manager, which made Lenda feel a little self-conscious. And she felt like an idiot just standing there. Somehow, she managed to start talking and explained her case again. To her surprise, the manager treated her like the Queen of England, quickly insisting that she be moved to the best table in the house.

The new seating far exceeded Lenda's expectations. She couldn't wait for the hostess who seated her to leave so she could give a victorious fist pump under the table. Then she whispered to herself, "Yes, thank You, Holy Spirit, for sending someone with sense and *real* customer service."

Even though she was happy about the restaurant choice, she started thinking about whether she'd made a selfish decision by choosing it. She knew the girls, with the exception of Quintella, might complain about it. But she didn't really care. For the most part, she usually kept quiet about where they ate. But this time she stood her ground. While she enjoyed being with them, the compromising had become too much for her to deal with anymore. That day, Lenda planned to be totally pampered on the outside, because on the inside, she felt like she was falling apart, little by little.

Just then, Lenda quietly asked the Lord to allow His peace to prevail during the dinner. She really wasn't up for any questions from anyone about anything. She could just hear them all: "Girl, what's wrong with you? You can tell us. We're your inner circle. You know anything you say will stay right here!"

She didn't want to hear anything like that, so she knew she had to pull herself together. But before she could do that, out of the corner of her eye she saw two of the girls approaching. *So much for peace and quiet.*

Chapter Two

"Hey girl, how are you?" Quintella asked, approaching the table.

"You look simply gorgeous," Karen followed, as she hugged Lenda and gave her a kiss on the cheek.

"You know you're the gorgeous one," Lenda said, as she returned Karen's hug and offered her a genuine smile.

"We're just waiting on one person," sang Karen.

"Why is Claudette *always* late?" sighed Quintella.

"Girl, we've been *friends* for fifteen years, and she's been *late* for fifteen years. Why do you keep asking the same question year after year?" Lenda seemed annoyed. "Let it go—for real!"

"Friends for fifteen years? Wow, that's a long time to put up with foolishness. She's late for every function," Quintella continued.

"It's not like we're sitting here doing nothing," Karen chimed. "After all, we can have a good time with each other, right?"

Lenda couldn't help but see the sincerity on Karen's face. *She's always been so gullible.* Lenda cupped Karen's chin in her hand and pretended to give her a kiss, "Yes, my little Po-Po, we can have fun."

Karen playfully slapped away Lenda's hand, "Go on, girl… don't be trying to get on my good side. You know how much I love you, so just stop," laughed Karen.

Lenda knew how much they all loved each other. She couldn't believe that fifteen years had come and gone. God really had blessed them all. Lenda always prayed that they'd continue to love and honor one another. So why did she feel like they were drifting apart instead of getting closer? Correction, Lenda felt closer to Quintella, while Claudette and Karen seemed to have a clique of their own. An inner circle was definitely forming within the circle.

Despite her feelings, Lenda also knew they all shared so much. She couldn't imagine anything that they didn't know about each other. Yet they didn't know a thing about her brother being in jail. Lenda immediately attached shame to that thought like two-sided tape. Then, the ring of Karen's cell phone jolted her back into the present moment.

"Hey, can't talk now—I'm out with the girls. Not now. I'm going to hang up," Karen giggled like a sixteen-year-old, even though she was forty-seven. She paused to give the girls a "just a minute" look, as she scooted out of the booth.

"Great. Now we have one on the phone and another who's late," Quintella quipped.

"Don't let it get to you, Queen," Lenda said nicely.

Karen skipped back to the table, only for the phone to ring again. Making an about-face, Karen vanished with the phone snug to her ear. Quintella and Lenda looked at each other with rolled eyes and laughed.

"I'm beginning to hate cell phones," Lenda said.

"Where did that come from?" Quintella asked.

"They're an interruption. Tell me why you can't turn it off for an hour to be with friends. It doesn't make me feel important when someone keeps jumping up and down to answer the phone. How's Ken's firm?"

"Things are good, girl!" Quintella laughed. "He's not traveling as much, so you know I'm loving that—'cause I love my man! But…is something wrong with you? You seem edgy." Just as Quintella gave Lenda a smile, Karen reappeared once more, grinning from ear to ear.

"You can get that surgically removed," snapped Lenda.

"What?" said Karen, feeling all over her body like she was looking for some abnormal growth.

"The cell phone!" Quintella laughed.

Karen playfully frowned while sliding back into the booth. The small talk continued, but Karen wasn't listening. Her thoughts rested on the previous phone call. She couldn't quite shake the conversation. Then suddenly, she noticed two fingers snapping in her face like a hypnotist trying to bring someone out of a trance.

"Where did you go? You clocked out on us. Earth to Karen!" Quintella demanded.

"Sorry ladies, I was just thinking about us," Karen rattled off.

"You're lying. You're thinking about that phone call and the man on the other end!" Lenda professed.

"It *was* a man, right?" Quintella curiously demanded.

"Why?"

"'Cause I'm nosy," Quintella confessed.

"Now that's the truth," Karen said in a matter-of-fact way. "How's Ken?"

"See, if you sat still long enough, you'd know the answer to that question because I just asked about him. But you were off somewhere on a phone call that couldn't wait!" Lenda said.

"Queen, when I get married, I'm going to treat my man like you treat yours." Karen chose to ignore Lenda's comment. "I admire you. There is not a woman alive who respects and honors her husband more than you. So personally, I give you the Wife of the Year award."

"Thanks, honey," Queen said, waiting to see if there was a punch line coming. When one didn't come, she asked, "So, what time is it?"

"Five minutes later than when you asked five minutes ago," Karen snickered.

"You think it's funny that she's late, don't you?"

Just as Karen was about to respond, all eyes were fixed on the woman standing in front of them with her arms outstretched as if she was leading a praise service. You couldn't help but notice the warm smile and eyes that glowed like candles, not to mention the red dress that looked like someone tailored it to her body.

"Here I am to save the day!" Claudette proclaimed.

On cue, all three spoke out: "She's here!" Laughter exploded as Claudette settled into the booth.

"Why are you always late?" Quintella couldn't let it go.

"Tutt, tutt, tutt—always is an absolute, and you should stay away from those…" Before Claudette could finish her sentence, the waiter approached the table. He looked like he was in his mid-thirties. His dark hair was neatly cut, with pearly white teeth peeking through a wonderful smile. As soon as he took the order, all eyes checked out his physique when he walked away from the table.

"Now that's one fine brother," Karen lusted.

"Yeah, he's a keeper," Claudette sang. "But before I wrap him up and put a red bow on him, let me check out the ring finger to see if he's taken."

"What, you can't look 'cause a man has on a ring?" Karen asked.

"You can look, but it should be quick!" Claudette responded.

"Hey, did you guys see that fine white boy over in the corner looking like Yanni?" asked Karen.

The rest of the ladies turned.

"Don't everyone look at the same time. He'll know we're talking about him," she warned.

"Guys, we should change our vocabulary. I detest referring to Caucasians as *white people* and African Americans as *black folks*," Lenda said quietly.

With a puzzled look on her face, Claudette innocently asked, "What do we call them?"

"I'm glad you asked," Lenda perked up, like a little kid who had just been given a triple scoop of ice cream. "We should say, 'Did you see that fine man over in the corner—the one dipped in the vanilla batter? He looks like Yanni.' Or, 'Did you know Mary's boyfriend is dipped in the chocolate batter?'" Lenda patiently waited for a response from the girls, hoping it would be positive. After all, this was a great idea to her, even if she had come up with it.

"Who is Yanni?" Claudette asked.

"He's a pianist, and you would love his music *and* his locks!" said Karen.

"What's the purpose?" Claudette shrugged.

"Purpose of what?" Karen asked.

"The purpose of replacing white and black with vanilla and chocolate batter," Claudette replied.

"I'm just tired of the white-black thing. We all need to get over it and just love each other. We all bleed red blood, and we all cry clear tears. We make too much of a fuss about the color of the house we live in, and I think what I'm proposing just softens the ethnic thing. After all, do you see all black dogs running together and all white dogs hanging out? Humans are the only creation of God struggling with the color thing. It's ugly, and I'm tired of it."

Lenda had never seen so many mixed emotions. Quintella was looking at her like she was a visitor from another table who had just sat down and started eating someone else's food without asking. Karen had the palms of both hands on top of her forehead, with her elbows resting on the table as though she had instantly gotten a migraine headache. And Claudette was slumped in the booth, shaking her head in wonderment.

"Can't we at least try it? My goodness, I'm not asking anyone to donate a kidney!" Lenda began.

"How about we take a vote?" Claudette sarcastically asked. "All in favor of using chocolate batter and vanilla batter instead of white folks and black folks take the ring out your noses." Hysterical laughter erupted, with one exception— Lenda.

"Y'all act like a bunch of teenagers," Lenda pouted.

"It does have a nice *ring* to it!" Karen quickly added.

Quintella decided not to counter because Lenda was acting strange.

"Let's just change the subject," Lenda pleaded.

"How's business, Claudette?" asked Karen.

With that, the girls began to catch up on all the latest news. Then the waiter returned to the table to see if anyone needed anything while they waited for their food.

"What are you doing after the restaurant closes?" Karen flirted and batted her eyes.

The waiter simply smiled in embarrassment. Lenda was thankful he hadn't responded to Karen. And even though Karen purposely didn't make eye contact with anyone else around the table, she could feel the stares of disapproval. Karen thought: *I don't even care what they think. Lenda has Holy Spirit, Quintella has her husband, and Claudette is in denial. A fine brother needs to know that he is fine.*

The waiter hadn't taken five steps away from the table before the girls were all over Karen. She put her hand up as if she were a police officer stopping traffic, "Remember, I'm grown. I'm at dinner—not church. I don't feel like being politically correct, spiritually speaking, if that's OK with you, Queen James. Now where were we?" Karen asked, adding her teenage giggle.

"Karen, that stuff is not funny. But right now, I'll pretend what we just witnessed didn't happen." Claudette continued talking, hoping the girls would calm down.

The salads and drinks arrived. "Thank you" echoed like the chorus of a song. Then silence blanketed the booth while everyone checked out their orders. And without any discussion, they all held hands, looked at Karen, bowed their heads, and closed their eyes.

Karen thought: *Here we go again.* She knew it was her time to pray. Since they made it a point to get together formally four times a year, they established early on that everyone would take turns praying. But after all these years, Karen still felt uncomfortable praying aloud in public. She didn't understand why, but she knew they would sit until Jesus came if she didn't pray. She knew no one would come to her rescue. That's why she had prepared ahead of time…if only she could remember what she had written and studied.

"Father, in the Name of Jesus, thank You for Your Word that tells us in Exodus 23:25 if we serve You, then You will bless our food and water and take sickness away from us. So we say that this food is sanctified by Your Word and Your Blood. Should there be anything harmful in it, that we know not of, we thank You that it will have no effect on our bodies, in Jesus' Name."

In unison, all the girls said, "Amen."

"Go on, Karen, with your bad self!" Lenda joked.

"What happened to the 'Lord, we thank You for this food' prayer?" Claudette teased.

Karen wasn't paying attention to any of them. She was thankful and proud that her study and preparation had paid off. She felt good about the prayer and was happy Holy Spirit helped her remember it all. She had to admit that she felt a bit like Lenda…she had a "Man," and He came through for her that night.

"What's this?" Claudette innocently asked, holding up a yellow object with a ribbon wrapped around it. "Do they give you little gifts with your tea?"

Lenda couldn't help but chuckle, while Quintella stared in amazement.

"Girl, what gift?" Quintella asked, daring Claudette to answer.

"This!" Claudette shamelessly pointed to the yellow object.

"That, my friend, is a lemon in cheesecloth. Finer restaurants do this so the seeds won't get in your tea when you squeeze it. The little ribbon tied into a bow is known as *presentation*."

Lenda and Quintella immediately burst into laughter, while Karen raised her index finger in her usual "just a minute" fashion.

"See, y'all snobs. Why you gon' make us feel bad because we didn't know it was a lemon in cheesecloth?" Claudette huffed.

"No one is trying to make you feel bad, Miss Jeopardy! I can't believe you've never seen it in some sort of lemon category on the show," Lenda said.

"Girl, can we forget about the cheesecloth *and* Jeopardy? We're jumping all over the place. We never did hear how Claudette's business is doing."

"Long story short," Claudette continued, "I'm tired of people writing checks that bounce, so I had to stop taking them. I don't like it that people take my clothes, wear them, and then I have to hound them for a bounced check."

"Do you still take plastic?" Lenda wondered.

"Plastic still works, even though I had another *Christian* come in one day to buy a dress, and it took four tries on four different cards to ring a hundred-dollar sale. I wanted to tell her that she needed to cut those cards up and stop shopping."

"Why didn't you?" Karen inquired.

"'Cause I needed the sale," Claudette growled, as they all gave each other high fives.

"I'm just curious," Quintella questioned, "why did it take four cards for a hundred dollars?"

"Well, the first two didn't go through. The third one only had, I think it was forty-two dollars and some cents. So the difference was put on the fourth card," Claudette explained.

"See, that's what makes Christians look bad to the world—what did this woman look like?" Quintella asked.

"Forget what she looked like. I want to know what the dress looked like. It had to be one gorgeous dress to go to those extremes," Karen offered.

"What's sad is, it really wasn't all that; she was going out and wanted something new to wear," said Claudette.

"See, Reverend Smith would say that girl was caught up in the lust of the eyes! I can hear him now: 'The lust of the eyes got Eve kicked out of the garden, and it's still kicking our blank every day 'cause we still fall for the same old tricks of the enemy!'" Karen pretended to preach.

"Girl, I know Pastor Smith don't talk like that in the pulpit!" Lenda was appalled.

"Yes, he does. What's wrong with that?" Karen challenged.

"He said the real word? The 'A' word in the pulpit?" Lenda shrieked.

"Well," Karen continued, "you know when you and I had this discussion about Pastor Smith a couple of months ago, I told you that he rarely has us use our Bibles. So I was grateful he had us turn to something. But then he told us to turn to First John 2:16, which talked about the lust of the flesh and eyes. Do you know it took the people forever to find First John 2:16? That's 'cause some folks was over in St. John, Chapter 2. You know, the John that comes after Luke. Until I looked at the lady next to me, who reminds me of you, Queen James, and when I saw her all the way in the back of the Bible, I knew I had the wrong Scripture. Pastor had to tell some of the people that First John was before Second John, and somebody hollered out: 'That don't help us, Rev!' Then he said, 'Go to Revelation and go back three books.' Well, we finally found the Scripture, but by then he had to explain all over again why we were even looking for the Scripture. That's why sometimes I don't even take my Bible. We never use them, so why carry it?"

"Karen, I want to say this with all the respect I can muster. Why do you continue to go to a church that does not feed you spiritually?" Lenda asked while shaking her head in disbelief.

"Girl, that's where my grandmother went. If I left that church, I'd probably get a visit from the grave," Karen warned with an attitude.

Lenda wanted to change the subject before she said something she would regret. But Quintella couldn't let it pass, and she was quick to express herself. "Look Karen, I hope you take this the right way, 'cause I just want us to be correct when we talk about God's Word. Let me ask you this: how can we all say we believe in the same God, when even amongst us there are so many differences—how can that be? I don't understand it! Let's just get off this whole subject."

"Queen James!" cried Karen while slamming her fist on the table. "That's why I want to be just like you when I grow up. You know the Bible like you know the back of your hand. I know the Lord is going to tell you: 'Well done, My good and faithful servant.' Listen, I tease you a lot, but I really admire you and the way you know God's Word. I'm serious. You and your husband have got to be God's shining example of what real Christians should look like."

At that moment, each one of Quintella's friends began to tell her in their own words why they admired her. It was too bad Quintella didn't hear them. She was busy thinking about her past. If they only knew the secrets that were buried deep down inside, she knew they wouldn't want to have her as a friend—let alone their best friend. Quintella was so thankful that she didn't have to worry about telling everyone what she and her husband had done.

Changing the subject, Quintella asked, "Lenda, your birthday is coming up in a couple of weeks. What are you doing?"

"I'm having a day at the spa; then I'm going home to flop on the bed!

"Girl, that sounds wonderful. Take me with you!" Karen exclaimed.

Things were winding down. And they all agreed that dinner had been wonderful.

"OK, how much is the tip?" Lenda asked.

"Look at the bottom of the bill. The last time Ken and I went out to dinner they had precalculated a fifteen, eighteen, and twenty percent tip. They don't even consider ten percent anymore," Quintella said.

"Hold it—I have my tip card," Karen proudly proclaimed. "Let's see…the meal was $147.56, so the tip is $23.13. Let's round it off to twenty-five dollars—he was a fantastic waiter."

"You know what intrigues me about people? They will go out to dinner, eat, and never hesitate about paying a fifteen percent tip to someone they have never seen before. They will even round off the tip 'cause they fine, but some of those same people struggle to give God His ten percent and an offering. They don't ever think about rounding off their tithes; they calculate those to the penny—yet God has been *soooo* good to them. I mean, Karen just made the comment that the waiter was 'fantastic.' Well, God has been all that and more to folks, and people *still* struggle with this issue of the tithe. Why?" Quintella wanted an answer.

"Queen James, you never cease to amaze me. You preach everywhere you go. First of all, I don't have an issue paying my tithes, *and* I give generous offerings. Aren't you tired of practicing without a license? Why don't you just go to ministry school? Graduate and get a real license to preach; then we can at least take up an offering for you," Karen said.

"No, I mean it; people have their priorities mixed up," Quintella said. "They forget about God until something happens. Then it's: 'Oh God, help me!'"

"Yeah girl, we live in a messed-up world. I told you, Queen—put in the time, go get trained, and then you can legally save the world. But in the meantime, we've got to go because a line is forming for this booth. And in all seriousness, you really have a heart for God, and you're sincere about your commitment to Him. I really believe you have a call on your life. Before we go, can I ask you something?" Karen's voice got low. "It's personal."

"Oh my, Karen, what is it?" Quintella asked.

"Can we settle the tip first, ladies?" Lenda begged. "All agree on fifteen percent, nod your head."

All heads nodded.

"So what did you want to ask me, Karen?" Quintella said.

"Well, you and Ken are about the holiest couple I know. I only ask this because I want to know what to expect when God blesses me with a man and I get married," Karen said.

"Do we really want to hear this?" Claudette interrupted.

"Come on. Let's let her have her say," Lenda said.

"When you and Ken want to be romantic, do you listen to music?" Karen probed.

"Well, I don't know where that came from. Ladies are the only ones who have enough nerve to talk about the bedroom business. If we were men, this conversation would never come up," Quintella said.

"Queen, I'm sorry. This is something I've been wanting to ask you for years, but I was afraid. I mean, you guys are always talking about the Lord, and I just wondered—I felt like I could ask you."

"To answer your question, we do listen to and enjoy music. We don't listen to it all the time, but we do. We dance together sometimes, and we just have fun."

"Y'all dance, by yourselves?" Karen asked in awe.

"Yes…" Quintella's voice trailed, wondering what was coming next.

"What kind of music do you play?"

Without losing a beat, Quintella said, "I like to hear 'Blessed Assurance,' and Ken loves to hear 'Bringing in the Sheaves.' That really gets him going." Before she got it all out, Quintella began laughing hysterically—and the girls giggled.

"Why are you guys laughing?" Karen demanded.

"'Cause that's about the stupidest thing anyone could ask a married person," Claudette said.

"What's so stupid? I just wanted to know—y'all so holy and all. I really didn't know. And I vowed I never wanted to get that saved, where when I get married I can't listen to music," Karen said.

"OK, let me set the record straight. I was just teasing. Depends on the mood. Sometimes we listen to jazz. I like Tim Bowman, and Ken enjoys George Howard—he plays the saxophone. We like Ben Tankard. We enjoy all types of music," Quintella stated.

They were all still looking at Karen like she was the biggest fool.

"Well, I didn't know. I bet I'm not the only person who wonders. When you see people who really love God, you just don't know. I mean, you guys seem very loving; you hold hands and show affection. But you also lift your hands a lot and shout Hallelujah. I've just always wondered, so I thought I could ask. Now I know, and it came straight from the horse's mouth!"

"That's OK, honey. People have formed opinions about Christians and intimacy. But we have to remember who created intimacy, because we know everything God created is good. OK—one more thing before we leave, what are you guys doing after church on New Year's Eve, since technically we won't get together again until January?"

Lenda was first to respond: "After church, I'm going home and jumping in bed; I'm always so tired after the service."

"You have what you say. If you say you're always tired, you will always be tired. Why don't you begin to say you have energy? It only has one more syllable, so you won't use up a lot of strength saying energy instead of tired," Quintella added.

"You little Jeopardy wannabe," Lenda declared.

"I'm going to a Christian club. This new comedian is going to perform, and I hear he's really good," Claudette added.

"That sounds like fun," Quintella chimed. "How about you, Karen?"

"I'm not going to church. I'm going out to a party, non-Christian, before you ask," Karen said.

"Going out!" all three said simultaneously.

"Yes, going out. Listen, I've been in church for the last fifteen years of my life, and I think I'm overdue for a change."

The booth was silent.

"My friend and I are going to a party—a secular party. Don't look at me like I just robbed a bank. It's one out of all these years, OK?" Karen said firmly.

"Karen, why don't you go to church first, and then go to the party if you still feel led?" Lenda offered.

"Lenda, that's double-talk. You're led to church; you saunter to a party," Karen responded.

"Won't you feel funny not being in church on New Year's Eve?" Quintella pressed.

"Well, it's the first time in fifteen years. So, once again, I don't know how I'm going to *f-ee-l*," Karen said.

"Girl, I bet your mom is kicking up dirt from her grave. Why would you not go to church, but go partying? I don't understand that," Lenda cried. "We're supposed to get wiser as we get older."

"Lenda, you know what? If my mother kicked up as much dirt as everybody tells me, I'd be ordering more for her grave, because she would've kicked all the dirt off by now." Throwing her napkin on the table, Karen motioned for Claudette to let her out of the booth.

"No, we said we would never leave mad, and I'm not going to let you out," Claudette said.

Quintella's mouth was still open in astonishment at what she had just heard. She wasn't so surprised anymore that Karen was thinking about going to a party instead of church. From where she stood, the "poor baby" wasn't being fed the Word of God, so she probably didn't know any better. She kept her mouth closed on that subject, however, because she would never put her mouth on a man of God, even if she disagreed with what he did. Instead, she decided she'd have a private talk with Karen later about visiting her and Lenda's church.

"Don't get mad, Karen. We're just surprised about

what you told us. We just assumed, like other years, you'd be in church. Hey, why don't you come and go with us? CeCe Winans is ministering in song, and then you can party after if you want to," Lenda urged.

"Now if that's not being a hypocrite, what is? Why would I go to church and then party? Everybody don't go to church on New Year's Eve, ladies. Y'all live in this Christian bubble, and you're detached from the real world," retorted Karen.

"Excuse me, but I thought everyone at this table was a Christian. And we *do* party; we just do it differently. Ken and I always have couples come to the house after church, and we fellowship and play games. But at some point, real Christians don't party like the world," Quintella challenged.

"Oh, so you think there are no Christians who party on New Year's Eve, and that I'm the first? You better get your head out the Bible, Queen James," Karen said.

"Hey guys, we're getting loud. Let's calm down," Lenda reminded the group.

"See, that's why I wasn't going to tell y'all; you judge people too much. You know what? We can't be real with each other. We can't take the truth, and that's why we all hide our deepest secrets from each other. Sometimes I wonder if we're really friends," Karen snapped.

"You hiding secrets from us?" Lenda innocently inquired.

Karen chose to ignore the question. "Even if you felt like I shouldn't go—and it's none of your business—you could've responded in a kinder fashion. I'm a grown woman, as you stated earlier. I'm not a kid. It's reactions like I just witnessed that make people not want to open up to *Christians*. I'm sick and tired of y'all thinking that you know everything. You need to re-read, once again, First Corinthians 13.

"Oh no she didn't just quote a Scripture," Quintella mocked.

"See what I'm talking about? Queen James thinks she's the only one who can quote Scripture. I bet you think you're the only one God talks to, right? Wrong. Just like this morning, when I was having my time with God, Holy Spirit told me that you were going to make me mad at dinner. And He said, 'Forgive her now, and you won't have to do it later.' So I forgave you this morning. See, the Word is true. Holy Spirit is The Man, and He will tell you things that are going to happen in the future," said Karen.

As she looked around the table at the women who were completely stunned, if only for a minute, that one moment gave her more satisfaction than eating four Oreo cookies with ice-cold milk. They all regained their composure at the same time, but Quintella spoke first.

"You got up and had Bible study this morning?"

"See, Queen. I told you that you were a hypocrite. I remember once, you told me to never assume that God has had no influence in people's lives…yada, yada, yada… Well, you just assumed that God has had no influence in my life. I mean, all of you were surprised to hear that I got up this morning and had Bible study. That tells me you felt God certainly had not moved in my life and brought about a change in me," Karen said.

Silence.

Lenda took Karen's hand, only to have it pulled back abruptly.

"No, I don't need your sympathy. Every single one of us at this table has issues. So while I'm at the party, popping my fingers and shaking what God gave me, you three can press yours together, make praying hands, and pray for me, OK?

But I tell you what, after I go to the party, I'll still have my name written in the Lamb's Book of Life, and I'll still go to heaven when I die. One party will not make me hellbound," said Karen.

"Karen, we didn't say you were going to hell because you're choosing to go to a party instead of church. It's just a shocker. May I ask who the fellow is?" Lenda probed.

"Yeah, who *is* this mack daddy?" Claudette asked facetiously.

"Mack daddy? That's so old, girl! You're stuck in the seventies, and you're hating because you haven't had a date in five years," Karen said.

An uncomfortable silence came over the table. Eyes were wide with shock and disbelief. It seemed like an eternity before Quintella spoke. And when she did, her tone was low and deliberate. "Karen, that was a low blow. Come on, apologies are in order."

Karen looked slowly at each of them. But when she got to Claudette, the hurtful look in her eyes made Karen even more ashamed.

"I'm sorry. What I said was mean, and I'm *truly* sorry Claudette." Claudette's eyes softened as she looked at Karen. "That's OK. I forgive you, love," Claudette whispered.

"Claudette, I'm really, truly sorry. I know you're trying to live the committed Christian life. Christians shouldn't hurt each other and when we stoop that low, we become just as carnal as the world. I love you too much to hurt your feelings and again, I'm truly sorry. What I said was spoken out of anger, but I lashed out at the wrong person," Karen whispered. "You've been like a sister to me, always there when I needed you. And you've never judged me, even when I told you things that I swore I'd never tell anyone else. I admire that you made a commitment to God and have been faithful for five years. I am truly remorseful. And I repent, girl. Please, Claudette, charge it to my head and not my heart. You know I'd never hurt you. I think it's awesome that you keep your body and remain celibate, like Lenda, until God sends you a man. I had no right… I-I…"

Before Karen could say anything else, Claudette put her index finger to her own mouth to motion Karen to be quiet; then she spoke in a hushed tone.

"It's OK, girl," Claudette lied. She was hurt, immensely hurt that someone she loved and trusted would cut so deep emotionally.

"Girl, don't tell her it's OK. Let her grovel some more—I didn't know the girl had it in her to be so remorseful. Keep on, Karen. You left off at the I-I… What were you about to say?" Quintella said.

Lenda could not believe what she was hearing. As she took her cloth napkin and pretended to strike Quintella, she said, "Queen, that's not becoming—not from you."

Just then, the manager came over to the table. "Is everything to your liking, ladies?"

They all replied, "Yes!"

"Is there anything else we can do for you?" the manager asked.

"No, but that's kind of you to ask," Lenda replied. As he walked away, Quintella reminded the girls that they had been sitting, laughing, and talking for three hours, and that was the manager's way of saying he needed their booth.

"See, at Red Lobster we can sit and holler all night, and the manager will never come to your table," Claudette reminded Quintella.

"Girl, don't worry about that manager. I know the real one. If he messes with us, I'll just call her," Lenda announced, remembering her short-but-sweet quiet time, which seemed so long ago.

"Hey, before we leave, how are your fine brother-in-law and his wife doing? Are they still together?" Karen inquired of Quintella.

"Girl, we would be here another two hours, but that's a testimony, if ever. It's been about five years, and their marriage is stronger than ever. They've been attending church. He's moved up the corporate ladder, and their marriage is solid. To see them together, you would think they're newlyweds," Quintella bragged.

"Well, since we're on the subject, did they ever find out who the girl was—not that it matters?" Lenda asked.

"Never found out who it was—I just hope she got saved. Nothing but a whore would go with a married man and try to break up his home. I'm glad they never found out who she was, because I believe I would've paid her a personal visit myself," Quintella admitted in disgust.

All eyes were now on Karen, whose head was bowed; she was praying only loud enough for her ears to hear.

Lenda broke the silence. "What are you doing?"

"I'm praying for Queen. She just cussed," Karen said.

"What did I say?" Quintella looked perplexed.

"You said the 'W' word," Karen answered.

"Whore? Read Proverbs 23:27. It talks about how the whore's ditch is deep. And it warns men that she lies in wait for her prey, which in this case was my brother-in-law. And like the Bible says, she snatched him right up. But praise be to God." Quintella lifted her hands in praise and closed her eyes in genuine thanks. "She was not able to break up what God had put together. Hallelujah! So I said it then, and I'll say it now—she was a whore!"

"Girl, shut up! Are you serious? Is what you said really in the Bible?" Karen asked with all sincerity. This time, no one said anything. Lenda and Quintella were staring at Karen like she was a dog with a red feathered hat. As they stood to leave, Karen inquired again.

"Come on, y'all. Is that in the Bible?" Karen earnestly inquired.

"Tell you what," Quintella snickered, "tomorrow morning when you get up to do *your* Bible study, read Proverbs 23. Or do you do Bible study two days in a row? Well, even if you skip a day, read it the next time you sit to do your Bible study," Quintella said.

The manager was watching from afar and to his chagrin, all the ladies sat back down again.

Quintella couldn't let it go. She turned and gave Claudette a suspicious glance. "You got anything to say?"

Claudette had drifted off into her own world. Quintella repeated her question.

"Hey, I said, 'You got anything to say?'"

"Got anything to say about what?" Claudette asked.

"About my brother-in-law and his little tawdry affair," Quintella said.

This conversation was old—really old. Claudette told them then, and she would repeat it to them now, "I have nothing to say about your sister and her husband. We need to stay out of their business."

Quintella still wouldn't let it go. "I still think you know something. Even though the details never came out, we are almost one hundred percent positive that it was someone he worked with. I said it years ago, and I'll say it again. That company may be big, but gossip gets around. And I know you heard something while you were working there. But I accept your answer that you were not going to get in their business. I still say, as *my* friend, you should've told me what you heard."

"Back to you, Miss Thang," Lenda eyed Karen. "Bible study is a personal choice; you either decide to spend time with God or not. It has nothing to do with going to church on Sunday. When you have a personal relationship with the Lord, you talk to Him and study His Word. I for one am glad you're doing more of it."

"Amen, sister," Quintella slurred.

"Did you go to sleep that fast?" Lenda wondered. "You're talking like you're drunk."

"Girl, you know when you eat, you get sleepy." With that, they finally got up to leave, just as the manager was approaching their table for the second time. They all looked at him. His face said, "Yippee," without muttering a word. He squeezed past them and began taking the tablecloth off the table. It was his way of assuring himself that they were leaving for good. The waiter removed the dishes half an hour ago, but that didn't seem to work. This time, he made sure they got the message that dinner for them was officially over.

The girls kissed each other on the cheek and hugged as they made their way to the door. When Quintella hugged Karen, she couldn't help but leave her with these parting words: "Sometimes I forget you're a forty-seven-year-old woman."

"You're just jealous that I'm younger than you," Karen teased, as she playfully stuck her tongue out at Quintella.

"Yeah, by three whole months! Whoopee!" Quintella shot

back.

They stood in the parking lot for another ten minutes, talking. Right before they parted, a familiar sound was heard—all talking came to an abrupt halt. Lenda broke out in prayer.

"Father, in the Name of Jesus, we ask that wherever the destination of that police car, we pray that You will bring calm to chaos. Lawlessness will be apprehended, and justice will prevail. Thank You for protecting those who are endeavoring to protect the citizens. We pray that You give wisdom to those in authority answering the emergency call. Protect not only the police officers but any innocent bystanders, as well. We pray that if anyone has been injured, they will be healed and an ambulance will arrive quickly. We also pray that You will soften the heart of the perpetrator. If a crime has been committed, may the person be brought to justice, in Jesus' Name. And all in agreement with that prayer, let's say, 'Amen.'"

"OK ladies, got to get home to my husband, or he won't let me out next time," Quintella said.

Karen blew kisses as she said, "Bye, y'all."

"See ya," Lenda said.

"Te veo después," said Claudette. And before the girls could respond, she added, "That was the final question on Jeopardy the other night…how to say good-bye in Spanish. See, if you'd watch the program, you'd learn something."

"Will that be one of the prerequisites for marriage, that your husband-to-be is a Jeopardy lover?" Karen shouted from her car.

"You got that right," Claudette playfully replied. "I'll never marry a man who does not watch Jeopardy."

"No wonder you're not married," Quintella snickered.

Even though they all were joking and laughing, Lenda couldn't help but feel grieved—like something wasn't right. She couldn't help but notice how quiet Claudette had been. She made a mental note to talk to her about it later. She couldn't put her hands on it, but something definitely wasn't right.

Chapter Three

As Karen backed out of the parking lot, her immediate thoughts went to the police sirens and Lenda's prayer. Then she smiled. Her relationship with the girls did wonders for her spiritually. She had grown by leaps and bounds. She could still remember the first time she was with them when a police car went speeding by. She was in the middle of a conversation, and it was as if she wasn't even there. Quintella, Lenda, and Claudette bowed their heads, and Quintella began to pray as Lenda did tonight. Karen was floored back then because all of a sudden, it was as if she hadn't existed. Once Quintella stopped praying, Karen's look told them she hadn't understood what took place. Quintella's response was as clear to Karen now as it had been fifteen years ago.

"Karen, God's Word says that we have not because we ask not. His Word also says that we need to pray for those in authority so that we may lead a quiet and peaceful life. Whenever we hear a fire truck, ambulance, or police car, it signals trouble, so we pray for the people involved in the situation and ask that God intervene. My mother taught me that, and I've been doing it ever since. When I met Lenda, I told her. She bought in, and it was the same when we met Claudette. Iron should sharpen iron. We tailor the prayer for ambulances and fire trucks, and we believe it makes a difference."

Karen thought: *I was so naive back then. I still can't believe I came back with, "Do you do that every time? Just stop in the middle of conversations like you did just then?" Quintella's response made such an impact on me. I guess that's why I've been doing it for fifteen years, too. Maybe it was the tenderness when she said, "Karen, perhaps the people who are being attacked don't have anyone to pray for them. Some may argue that people shouldn't pray for the person responsible for the crime; I pray for them because if they aren't caught, we could be their next victim. And you know what? God's Word says He rains on the just and unjust. We need to be quick to pray and quick to forgive."*

Karen knew how important her friends had been in her spiritual development thus far. Still, sometimes she felt it was next to impossible to measure up to their standards.

"Wow God! I know they get on my nerves sometimes, but they really have taken me to another level in You, Lord. I so depend on their counsel. Thank You for giving me friends who love You and care enough about me spiritually that they will help me grow.

"Like Quintella said earlier, Lord, I just don't understand how we can all say we're Christians when we are so different. I feel like I don't know anything when it comes to the Bible. Quintella and Lenda were born with a Bible in their hands. I'll be fifty before I know it, and I still feel like I don't know anything, compared to them. Help me, Lord, to get the strength and courage to leave the church I'm in. They don't teach me about You, and I know that's what's missing in my life. But it seems like I'm more interested in pleasing people than You.

"I want to have the relationship that they have. I never

thought at forty-seven I'd look at my Christian walk and want more. I've been so satisfied for such a long time, but every time I get in Queen's and Lenda's presence, I feel like I don't know anything. How can I have been in church this long and still feel like I don't know anything? Help me, Lord, to get to know You better."

Karen's thoughts shifted, and she picked up her cell phone.

* * * *

When the phone rang, Lenda knew it was Karen. She could bet money. It always happened like that. Whenever the girls had an evening out and there was a disagreement, they would leave pretending all was well. But when they got home, each one would call her, seeking guidance about the rift. So Karen's call didn't surprise her; it was the request that caught her off guard.

"Lenda, can I come over? I really need to talk."

Karen sounded anxious. And a talk with Karen was the last thing Lenda needed; she just wanted to go to bed. They had already been together for three hours eating dinner. Lenda couldn't imagine what could be so important that it couldn't wait until the next day at least.

"Girl, do you know what time it is? Go home, and go to bed," Lenda said.

"I know it's late, but I really need to talk. And I want a face-to-face—please!" Karen begged.

Lenda was never good at saying no, even when she knew she should. But this wasn't the time. "Come on, girl. Be as aggressive with your foot on the pedal as you can without going over the speed limit."

"I'll see you in fifteen—bye," Karen said, before Lenda could change her mind.

Lenda snickered to herself: "When did I become Counselor? I thought that was your job, Holy Spirit." *And why does Karen want to come over to my house? Her home is much nicer, and it's right around the corner from the restaurant. Why didn't she just ask me to come to her house? Probably because she knew I wouldn't,* she thought. Lenda began looking over her house to see if things were in order for a visitor. She tried to keep it looking nice, but she had too much clutter on this night. When she was awarded the brick bungalow after the divorce, she wanted to sell it and leave behind all the memories of the past. But she was smart enough to know that she couldn't go anyplace else and pay what she was paying. And she knew she couldn't hide from her past. The only way to get rid of the past was to take it to Jesus and let Him do it. Moving to a new house would only change her surroundings.

No, she was glad she had kept the house. While she and Matthew had their bedrooms downstairs, the upper level was furnished like an office and sitting room for her. She could go up there to work on her consulting business, and it was like being away at a real office. Matthew knew it was off-limits to him. That's why she didn't have one of those front rooms that no one could sit in. Her living room was comfortable with a white sofa and loveseat that visitors could actually sit on. They had a TV in the corner and glass end tables to match the coffee table. She long gave up asking Matthew to keep his feet off the coffee table. "Ma, it's only so much room." He would protest. "Let's just make a big family room out of the upstairs and put your office in the basement," he cried. And she gave him the "nice try" look.

She didn't know why he would complain anyway; he had a TV, computer, and comfortable chair in his room. Lenda went to great lengths to make sure he had a very nice teenage room. It looked like something out of a magazine. The elegant linens that covered his queen-sized bed were masculine. She wanted him comfortable in his room because the house lacked space overall, so she had Karen help her decorate it. They went to IKEA and found a really nice wall unit so the room wouldn't look disorderly. His desk folded down so that when not in use, it didn't take up any space. His room looked better than hers. The only thing she regretted in the house was the small kitchen. She couldn't fit a table in the kitchen, so the dining room was used quite well. But it was so close to the kitchen that it didn't make much of a difference. The dining room set still looked good, even though it was ten years old. She was so glad she got the darker wood set with light chairs. Yeah, her home wasn't as beautiful as Karen's condo, but she loved it. Karen must have loved it too, because she always found herself in it—and tonight was no exception.

It didn't surprise Lenda that Karen, or any of the girls for that matter, wanted to talk about tonight. "We act like twenty-year-olds when we're all in our forties, closer to fifty. Wow God, do we change at all? I can see why men sometimes shake their heads in exasperation at us. We have nonstop conversations. One woman can't wait until the other woman stops talking before she starts talking about something else. Yakety, yakety, yak! What did we really talk about?" Lenda laughed. "I guess we talked about nothing, but we sure had a good time doing it."

* * * *

The knock on the door told her it was Karen without looking at the clock or through the peephole. Karen had a patent on her knock—two regular beats, two quick beats, one regular beat, pause, and then two additional quick beats. How original. But this time her knock didn't appear urgent—it was quiet, almost as if Karen was afraid to disturb those on the other side.

Lenda opened the door and had to laugh in spite of herself. Karen was one beautiful, gullible, sweet child. She had a body that most women would buy. At her age, she looked thirty—a perfect size 8, beautiful legs, and one of those protruding butts that spoke loudly: "Eat your hearts out, ladies!"

Karen kept her hair cut short. One would think at first glance that she had just got up from the hairdresser's chair. She was blessed with light hazel eyes and was always asked if they were contacts. It didn't help that she wore designer clothes and kept her nails and feet perfectly manicured. The only thing she lacked at times was brainpower and confidence.

Without hesitating, Karen kissed Lenda on the cheek and didn't stop until she was in the kitchen raiding the cookie jar.

"We just had dinner, and you ate dessert. You don't need cookies."

"Where are the Oreos?" Karen demanded. "These are dollar-store cookies," Karen moaned, with her mouth full.

"What do you know about the dollar store? You're eating them, aren't you? I buy Oreos on the fifteenth and the thirtieth. If we eat them all, I buy dollar-store cookies in between because my son doesn't care. He just wants cookies. Now you can feel free to bring some Oreos with *you*. I didn't put a gun to your head and say eat those cookies or else," Lenda mocked.

"What's that?" Karen's voice followed her eyes down Lenda's legs.

"What's what?"

"That!"

"That, my friend, is a new color in ladies' pants—it's called brown sugar."

"You're not funny. Are you going to put on some clothes? I don't want to look at your naked butt!"

"I have on clothes. It's called a baby doll nightgown. I am *not* naked. All you see are legs, and nice ones I might add. I've had a long day, which is going to be longer thanks to my wonderful friend. So I've decided if I must stay up all night, I may as well be comfortable. If my legs bother you…suck it up and get to talking!"

"Thanks a lot! What would I do without you?"

"You would make use of the Best Friend anyone could have—Holy Spirit."

"See, there you go again—you know I'm not as spiritual as you."

"I wish you would quit saying that. You choose not to be as spiritual. That's a cop-out, and you know it. So what's so important that you had to come over here tonight?"

"Did the timer go off and I didn't hear it?" Karen asked in agitation.

"Don't get huffy, Miss Thang. It's after ten o'clock now, and it takes you an hour to get started telling a story, let alone finish. We're already looking at midnight. So again, what's so important?"

"Tomorrow is Saturday. You don't have to go to work!"

"I may not have to punch a clock, but I do have to work."

Karen just sat there and didn't respond to Lenda's last comment. Even though she said nothing, her eyes said it all.

"It's about the guy you met, right? The one you're going to the party with, right?" Lenda asked.

With eyes lowered, Karen spoke with a whisper, "Yes."

Lenda put her arms around her and apologized for the hurried approach. She comforted Karen by telling her to take as much time as she needed. Silently, Lenda wondered if she would regret the generosity. It seemed like forever but when Karen finally spoke, she was very pointed in her speech.

Nervously, Karen began, "Lenda, when can you tell if you've gone too far without going too far?"

As Lenda looked at Karen, she listened to her spirit to see if Karen could handle the truth. Lenda had learned the hard way that she couldn't say what she wanted to say all the time, even if it's the truth, and even if people ask for the truth. She knew to check with Holy Spirit to see if the other person could handle the truth, especially if it would hurt.

"Karen, you really don't know when too far is too far?"

"I really don't." Lenda and Karen both knew she was lying.

"It's scary to think you're almost fifty, and you don't know when too far is too far." This conversation had a teenager tag on it, not a mature-woman label, but Lenda decided to play the game. "OK, more details are needed."

"Well, we were *kis-sing* the other night…"

"Kissing! I can tell by the way you stretched out the word kissing, it wasn't a cheek thing. You're kissing someone you just met?"

"Don't forget that I'm forty-seven, girl! I'm grown, and I didn't just meet him!"

"Oh, I'm sorry. My fault—let me rephrase that. You kissed him. But the relationship is still in its infantile stage?"

"Lenda, I didn't come over here for you to poke fun at me."

"I'm not poking fun. I'm surprised. But I should let you finish—go on, girl. Or I should say, 'Miss Forty-Seven and

Grown.' Why did you come over here anyway?"

"I'm going to ignore that, Lenda. Look—when I kissed him my toes curled, and it was like I lost consciousness for a while. But we didn't do anything, so I guess it wasn't too far or I wouldn't have been able to stop, right?"

Lenda just looked at her friend. She was trying to figure out if Karen in fact was that stupid, or if she was just playing stupid. This really was scary. "Karen, you can't be that naive, can you? Stop kissing, and watch cartoons 'cause toes don't curl when you watch cartoons. Blackouts or near-blackouts are *not* the norm. Come on, who are you fooling? Your toes don't curl with one quick peck on the lips. You know you went too far, and what you experienced was God's grace—big time."

"You think so?"

"I think so," Lenda mimicked.

"What church does he go to?" Her following silence spoke volumes. The fact that Karen got quiet was all the answer Lenda needed. Without waiting for an answer, Lenda fired another question. "Is he saved?" More silence. *Lord, how is it that instead of getting older and wiser, we just get older and more stupid?*

"Do you know his name?" Lenda teased.

"That's not funny," Karen quickly responded.

"It wasn't meant to be!" Lenda continued, more determined than ever before to help her see the light. "How can you date a man that does not even go to church? Does he at least go on Easter, Mother's Day, and Christmas?" Still no answer was needed—the blank stare said enough. Lenda could only moan three words, "Why, Karen, why?"

"Lenda, he is such a classy guy. I have *never* met anyone like him, and he wants me."

"Who in their right mind wouldn't want you? You're a successful woman. You're beautiful—gullible, but beautiful inside and out. You have a heart of gold. You really love God. You just need to be more committed, but you do love God. Who wouldn't want you?" Lenda all but yelled. "What makes him so *classy*?"

"Well, he's got a really good job, and he makes six figures. He dresses in designer clothes. He wears designer shoes. We go to nice places, *and* he's got friends in high places. He's really nice, and he has a good heart."

"Listen at you, Karen. You don't even sound like yourself. Everything you just said is so fleshly. OK, you say he's classy. Tell me if you can answer yes to any of these: Does he open the car door for you? Does he respect your time and call before 10:00 p.m.? When you go to a restaurant, does he pull out your chair? Does he let you order first? Better yet, do you decide together what you will order, and then he orders for you? When he comes to pick you up, does he come to the door? Or does he blow the horn? Does he say grace? Do you even know if he washes his hands when he uses the bathroom? And that's the teenage list for classy, not the adult version.

"He may wear designer clothes and know a lot of people. But he probably has a designer bottle with imported pabulum. I *know* he wears diapers by the mess he's asking you to put up with. But that's OK with you because his diapers are designer diapers! Woohoo!

"Karen, you are too wonderful to settle. Listen girl, don't compromise. You deserve better. I know none of us thought we would be almost fifty and still single. But the truth of the matter is, we are. We can't turn the clock back, but we can still have our dignity. I came down hard, but you…you are BETTER THAN THAT!

"I've told you before, and it bears repeating now. All you need is a good dose of confidence, and you can only get that from God, Karen. Have confidence in yourself, and you won't settle for anything less than God's best. I'm not saying all church men are perfect, but it should be a starting point for you."

As expected, the tears were forming and Lenda thought to herself: *Lenda, don't give in. Let her cry! She needs to grow up. You've had too many of these talks. The information is the same—only the name changes.* But she refused to be the one to break this silence. It was time for Karen to act her age.

"But I really like him."

"Do you? Do you? Or are you tired of being by yourself?"

"Honestly Lenda, that's not it. It has nothing to do with being by myself."

"Then answer me this—remember when we had a similar discussion, and I asked you to write down the ten things that were most important for you in finding that special some-one?"

"I remember."

"How does he fair? Does he have five out of the ten?"

As they both stared at each other—Lenda in anger and Karen in defiance—once again, no answer was needed.

"You don't even know where the notebook is with the list, do you? It's all flesh, isn't it?" Lenda's questions were met with a surprising look from Karen. Was she reading her right? Did she have a smirk on her face? Lenda chose to ignore the look momentarily. Determined to win this round—Lenda threw a curve ball. "Tell me, does he like Jelly?" Karen's change in expression told Lenda that she had hit the jugular. "You're dating a man who does not like your dog? You have lost your mind!"

"Since when did you become a dog lover? If my memory serves me correctly, you don't care for them at all. So why are you now so concerned about whether someone I'm dating loves my dog?" Karen asked.

"To answer the first question, I haven't become a dog lover. But I know how much you love Jelly. If I'm not mistaken, you told me, 'Girl, I'll know that he's from the Lord because he'll love Jelly like I do!' Remember that conversation, girlfriend?" Lenda now had her hand on her hip, and her neck was moving. It was on; she was on a roll!

"I remember when we were developing our relationship, and I came over your house for the first time with my son. I asked you if you could put your dog in a room and lock him up—you looked at me like I had crawled out of a hole. And in no uncertain terms, you told me, 'Do I tell you to lock your son up when I come over to your house?' I was stunned, but I said, 'No, he's my kid. Why would I lock him up?' Then you said, 'Jelly is my kid, so don't ask me to lock him up when you come over my house!'

"Are you not that same woman? So tell me—do you put Jelly up when Mr. Classy comes over?"

Karen could only laugh, because she knew Lenda was about to go ballistic. "Karen Renee McDonald, get your coat and go home! I have nothing else to say to you this night. You have lost what little mind you have left!" Lenda moved toward her door, waving to Karen, "Let's go." But Karen didn't move; she just sat, defiantly wrapping her hands around the chair.

"Lenda, I'm not through!"

Lenda stood with her hands on her hips and said, "I am."

"Please, ten more minutes?" Karen pleaded, releasing the

vice grip from the chair.

"I can't take ten more minutes—I can't take another minute!" Lenda moaned.

"Lenda, you know how you always tell people 'I've got a Man'?"

"Yes," Lenda replied, while holding her head as if a migraine suddenly attacked her body.

"Is that just the thing to say, or do you really believe it?" Karen tiptoed.

"Karen, I don't believe it. I know it," Lenda said, continuing to hold her head.

"Then tell me again, why do you say that?"

Lenda could see that Karen was genuine in her request.

"Because Holy Spirit is everything to me—I know you don't understand that, but He is. The Bible says Jesus gave Holy Spirit to us as our Comforter, Teacher, Helper—you name it, He is It. Holy Spirit takes good care of me. I don't lack anything. I'm very happy where I am, and it's because of my Man, Holy Spirit.

"Don't you know the life I lead hasn't been easy? It gets easier, but it's not easy. I've learned to protect myself from people, and that's a difficult thing to do. Without the Lord on my side, I couldn't..." Lenda's voice trailed off as she mumbled, "...'cause if I had sought His counsel when the phone rang, you wouldn't be here now asking me dumb stuff."

"What are you mumbling? I can't hear you."

With the shake of her hand, motioning Karen to continue, it worked without having to give an answer.

"But how can you call Him your Man? Isn't that disrespectful?" Karen asked.

"Why do you think it's disrespectful? Is God a man?"

"Yes."

"Didn't Jesus say that He was leaving to go to the Father, but that He would give us a Comforter?"

"Yes."

"Didn't He say that the Comforter, who is Holy Spirit, would be everything we would need?" Karen's eyebrows tightened, and her nose squinted as if to say, "Huh?"

"Karen, I'm paraphrasing it, but He can teach us all things. That means if it's motherly advice we need and we don't have a mother, He'll be that mother. If you need a counselor, like tonight, He'll be that counselor, 'cause I'm only giving you secondhand info. And much is my opinion, based on what you're telling me and my mood, which is not good right now. Being a single mom, I've had to be a father to my son, and He's helped me with fatherly advice. Holy Spirit knows everything. He is our Helper. You're still squinting. Do I need to give you chapter and verse?" Lenda regretted the question as soon as it rolled off her lips. It would only generate more dialogue.

"Could you?"

"John 14:26 and while you're in John, back up to verse seventeen. He's also called the Spirit of Truth, which you really need right now. Ask Holy Spirit to reveal the truth about this man to you. But you know what? I don't even think you want to know the truth. For you, it's convenient to play dumb!

"Do you even read your Bible Monday, Tuesday, Thursday, Friday, or Saturday? For real, do you?" Karen lowered her eyes to avoid Lenda.

"OK, I forgot you told us tonight that you now have a regular study. Karen, you and Claudette accuse me of being super-spiritual—I'm not. Because of all I've been through, I endeavor to DO what God says because without the Word, I would be lost. The difference between the two of us is, I know my life would be a mess without a close relationship with God. You don't have that revelation yet, so you keep hitting your head.

"You may be reading your Bible, but do you meditate on the Word? How will you ever build spiritual muscles if you aren't consistent? Our physical muscles are built by exercise. Our spiritual muscles work the same way as our natural muscles. If we don't use our faith, we never get to the spiritual level we desire."

"I just don't understand it like you," Karen confessed.

"Do you try?"

"Yes, I try."

"Why don't you let me help you? I've offered before. But every time you get in trouble, we have these talks, and nothing comes of the offer for Bible help. I would love to help you, Karen. I would. The Bible comforts me. Do you read a sentence, stop, and ask yourself, 'Did I understand what I just read? What is God saying to me?' You need to do that before you continue."

Karen thought for a moment and said, "I will try that— well, it's late. We'll pick this up later."

"Karen, cut the relationship off now," Lenda warned, continuing to plead her case. "I say do it before it's too late. Or is it already too late? Leave Mr. Classy alone. Tell him it's over. He'll be OK. If he starts to whine and cry, buy him a designer pacifier to go along with all of his other designer duds. Then wait on God. In the long run, it'll be worth it. Do it while your heart is still in one piece."

"Lenda, can I just say one more thing?"

"Go ahead, Karen. You're going to say it anyway."

Karen frowned, but it didn't stop her from continuing the conversation. "He's so knowledgeable about everything."

"Knowledgeable?" Lenda echoed. "About what, Karen?"

"Everything," Karen repeated, as if she was stuck on stupid.

"You're sounding like those high school girls that you counsel. How much Word does he know?" Lenda challenged.

"Lenda, I'm not talking about the Word, even though he knows that, too."

"How does he know the Word if he doesn't go to church?"

"There are a lot of people who don't go to church who read the Bible."

"Karen, God never created us to be alone. Church is where we learn how to rightly divide the Word of God. You can't just read and never submit yourself to a pastor. So back to your statement—what is he knowledgeable about?"

"He's knowledgeable about life."

"So where did this *intellectual* get his schooling from— Shysters University?" The glare from Karen said it all. "Listen, if you're happy with a man who knows nothing about God, if you can be satisfied with a man who doesn't submit himself to God, go and be happy. But don't ask me to cosign the relationship."

"Can I ask you something, Lenda, without you getting mad?"

"I'll probably get mad. But sure, go ahead. You're out there anyway."

Lenda could sense that Karen was choosing her words

carefully. "Are you anointed to be celibate, because it seems like it doesn't bother you to be by yourself and not have intimacy with a physical man?"

"Well, you asked two questions, so I'll answer them. No, I'm not anointed to be celibate. However, having control of my body and deciding to live holy before God is a decision. No one is anointed to be celibate. It's been ten years, and I'll continue to practice it because it allows me to lead a peaceful life. I will not allow my body to control me. Even if you took God out of the equation, factor in all the diseases out there and the emotional attachment that comes from being intimate with someone who is not your husband.

"Put it this way: think of all the guys you dated that you gave up the dessert to before you were married. When the relationship was over, you probably never regretted going to the movies with that person. When you thought about all the dinners the two of you shared, they didn't make you cry. But if you're honest with yourself, the thing you regretted most was giving your body to someone who had moved on to someone else. Karen, the difference between you and me is not that I haven't made that mistake before, because I have. The difference between the two of us is, I learned quick that I don't need the extra baggage that comes from sleeping with someone who is not my husband. I choose not to deal with it, and I've decided that I'm better than that, Karen. But that's a lesson you must learn for yourself.

"Your second question—does it bother me to be by myself? I'm not by myself. Again, I have Holy Spirit as my Friend—He's great company. He doesn't keep me up at night when He knows I should be sleeping. *Hint! Hint!* He helps me have a well-rounded life. I go places. I treat myself. I'm never bored.

"I can thank Him that my vocabulary is more than, 'Girl,

he's so fine. Listen, did you see so and so on TV last night—chocolate delight walking? He asked for the seven digits.' I'm sorry, Karen, if I disappoint you by talking about my Man.

"I enjoy discussing world events, sports, and the Bible. Excuse me, but I get sheer pleasure out of seeing a sunset—by myself—'cause I'm never alone. Forgive me because I love to travel and enjoy visiting ministries that I've seen on TV. Museums, plays, and musicals—girl, I don't know why I enjoy those things. Call me weird, but I like myself. You see, *my Man* wants me to have a global view 'cause He's a Global Man, and I just love Him for it."

"Why you have to go off on me, Lenda?" Karen snarled.

"Why do I have to be *anointed* to be celibate, Karen? I'm so sick of hearing that, and you know it. People who fornicate—are they anointed to fornicate?"

"That's stupid—how could you say something like that?" Karen barked.

"It's about as stupid as asking me if I'm anointed to be celibate. Listen, please listen, Karen. If you can't remember anything else from our conversation this evening, please remember this: I am not judging you. You came over here and asked my opinion on a matter. If you left my house right now and slept with multiple men at one time, God would still love you. He'd be disappointed, but He would still love you. Remember when the woman was caught in the very act of adultery over in John, the eighth chapter, verses one through eleven. I think that's it." Lenda thought for a moment. "Yeah, that's it." Silence. "Just shake your head yes, Karen, so I'll know you're still listening."

Karen shook her head.

"Jesus didn't get angry. Didn't even raise His voice. First of all, He addressed her accusers and told them, 'Listen, anybody here without sin, you throw the first stone.' And one by one, the accusers left. Then He looked at her and said, 'Where are your accusers?' There were none and Jesus said, 'And I don't condemn you either.' But He gave her some parting words. He said, 'Go and sin no more.'

"Karen, I'm not judging you. I've got my own life to keep clean. I know I have issues, so I try to work on them daily. But I don't ask you to counsel me on eating chicken. I don't come to you and say, 'Girl, I found this designer chicken, and I can't stop eating it…I eat ten pieces at a time…it's so good it makes my toes curl…you think I went too far eating eight pieces?' Do I do that? But if I told you right now that I was going to rob a bank, wouldn't you discourage me?"

Karen gave another blank stare.

"Just shake your head yes again, Karen."

Karen shook her head again.

"Why? Why would you discourage me? Because you don't want me to have to face consequences that could last a lifetime or be deadly enough to kill me. I don't want anyone to experience hurt, disappointment, or betrayal. But those are just some of the paybacks of sin. Not to mention diseases. Jesus loves the sinner, but He hates the sin.

"Never forget, there is a huge difference between sin and practiced sin. Doing something over and over because you don't want to discipline your body is practiced sin. That's willful disobedience and no matter what the label, God hates practiced sin. He'll forgive you, Karen, when you fall into sin. But when we sin, we also need to repent, turn around, and not do it again!"

Karen was thinking.

"And don't forget, Karen, you work in a school with girls.

You're a role model to many of those girls. The Bible says that we, the older women, are to guide the younger women so they won't be drunks and they'll know how to love their husbands and children, be virtuous and pure, and keep a good house, because we are the example."

"Where you find that?"

"Oh Karen, I don't know. I think it's in Titus, the second chapter, verses three through four. Wait a minute." Lenda quickly retrieved her Bible from her bedroom. She looked in the back and turned some pages. "That's it, Karen. It's Titus, the second chapter, verses three through four. So how are we going to tell them not to sleep around if we're sleeping around? What hope will young girls have if they have no role models or examples?

"Karen, I'm trying to live this Christian life just like you. I have my issues, but you know what one of my daily confessions is? 'Lord, I'm determined to be holy as You are holy— holy in my conversations, holy in my thought life, the places I go, and the things I watch on TV.' Look Karen, just about every week, I quote that Scripture in First Peter 1:16. I know I need to be holy with what I eat. Not there yet, but I will get there. Watch me."

"So you would forgive me if I slept with multiple men?"

"I said God would. Get out of here, Karen!" Lenda said, playfully pulling Karen from the chair.

"Wait a minute!"

"You've used all your minutes. Bye, Karen!"

"Bye! Hasta la vista, amigo," Karen shouted as she grabbed her purse.

"Sayonara. Hockey, hockey," Lenda said in a hushed tone.

Karen turned and rolled her eyes as she put her hand on

the door. "What the heck is 'hockey, hockey'?"

"I don't know. I couldn't think of anything else to holler." Both friends rolled their eyes at each other and laughed loudly. "Call me when you get home!"

Karen yelled back, "Are we still talking to each other?"

More laughter erupted as Karen pulled out of the driveway. Once the taillights of Karen's Cadillac SRX turned the corner, Lenda closed the door and leaned against it, exhausted. "Why me, Lord? Why me?" Whenever she asked that question, God didn't answer.

* * * *

Karen's head was swimming by the time she put her key in her front door. The fifteen-minute ride seemed so much longer than usual. It had to be her angels who got her home, because she didn't even remember getting off the express-way—not to mention the aggressive manner in which she was driving.

She really loved Lenda as a sister, but she was convinced she was out of touch with reality, with her "global" self. Karen thought: *She is so black-and-white—nothing is gray. I think Lenda is one of those people who is too heavenly minded to be any earthly good. And she's the only black person I know who has more white friends than black. Oh forgive me, Lord—they're not white; they're your kids dipped in the vanilla batter. How can I poke fun at her when she's my friend? It's not right.*

Dialing Lenda's number to let her know she made it home safely only brought guilt. Lenda had already fallen asleep, but she was able to catch the call. "I'm home," Karen announced.

"I'm sorry I went off, Karen. I'm here for you, girl."

"I'm sorry I kept you up and asked so many questions. Forgive me?"

Lenda yawned and weakly said, "I'll think about it."

"The Bible says, *'Don't let the sun go down on your wrath,'*" Karen proudly recited.

Lenda abruptly pulled the phone from her ear. That comment woke her up somewhat. As she stared at her extended arm, phone in hand, she frowned at the headset. *What the heck is she talking about?*

Karen on the other hand was smirking while waiting on a response. *I got her this time. For a change, I gave* her *some Bible to think about.*

Ever so slowly, Lenda put the phone back to her ear. "I hate to burst your bubble, Miss Thang, but the Scripture you're talking about, in context, is referring to a husband and wife. But yeah, I guess it could be used for friends, as well! Just go to church on Sunday and Wednesday and get some Word, Karen Renee McDonald!"

"Hey, don't hang up—just wanted you to know that I called my nail tech, and she can take you tomorrow at ten."

"What are you talking about? Why did you call your nail tech to get me an appointment?"

"'Cause your nails asked me to! They said, 'Girl, can you help a nail out, 'cause this girl don't have a clue?' So I called my nail tech, and she can take you at ten."

Lenda looked at her nails. They *were* long overdue. "You're being funny, aren't you?"

"Yes, I am. But you do need to go handle your business. Bye, Lenda Pearl!"

"No you didn't call me Pearl. Good-bye." Lenda playfully slammed the phone down. She couldn't help but chuckle as she looked at her nails, murmuring, "No she didn't go there." Looking up, she began talking to her Man. "Holy Spirit, there are too many crazies in this world. Why does God put up with us? Was it like this when God wiped out the world during Noah's day? If I were God, I would've started over again. Why did He promise to never wipe out the earth with water again?"

This time, Holy Spirit's voice was clear in His reply: "Because of love." Lenda smiled, turned out the lights, and went up to her room. She felt like she had been in an emotional boxing match for hours. She couldn't wait to put her head on the pillow. *Funny Lord,* Lenda thought, *I always looked at Karen and wished I had a body like hers. Thank God I don't have her brain!*

Lenda heard a gentle voice say, "That's not nice, Lenda."

"I know, Holy Spirit. I'm sorry. Please forgive me. I repent according to First John 1:9."

Chapter Four

Lenda couldn't go back to sleep. She thought about the conversation with Karen and shook her head, looking at her nails once again. She could only shake her head when she thought about the events of the day, and then Holy Spirit gave her a reminder: "You forgot to call your mother."

"Oh my goodness, Holy Spirit. This is only the third time today You've reminded me. Why am I so hardheaded? How come I don't do things the first time You tell me?"

Lenda looked at the clock—it was way too late. "Well, I have something to look forward to tomorrow—Mom telling me how my word don't mean anything. I deserve whatever I get. If I'd only listen to Holy Spirit when He talks to me, I wouldn't stay in trouble."

* * * *

Dinner just wasn't what Lenda expected. So many things ran across her mind when she thought about her friends. While she and Quintella embraced the Word and ran toward God, she thought about how the other two were at another place in their Christian walk, especially Karen. In all fairness, Claudette seemed to be growing up spiritually, but Karen appeared to be going in the opposite direction in her eyes.

"Lord, while I'm sitting here looking at other people, I

need to focus on me. I need to come clean with You about some things, and there's no better time than now, while my son is visiting his father, to have some uninterrupted time with You."

Lenda got out of bed and looked in the mirror. She didn't tell Karen earlier that her baby doll nightgown was what she put on when she wanted to talk to Holy Spirit about something special. Karen already thought that she was weird when she would say, "I've got a Man." The term was never used out of disrespect for God. She had a special relationship with the Lord. Yes, she saw Him as holy. Yes, she looked upon Him with reverence and awe. But for her, their relationship was one where she could refer to Holy Spirit in that way and not be disrespectful. She liked looking special for Him.

Lenda looked in the mirror again. Unlike Karen, who had the perfect butt, hers was flat and wide. She wondered as she looked at herself: *Why do I keep squeezing into a size 14 when a 16 would feel and look better?*

Looking intently into the mirror, she smiled when she looked at her skin, "Lord, You've blessed me with beautiful skin and nice hair and even though it turns into an afro during late spring and summer, I'm still thankful for my hair!"

She loved this time of the year because her hair always behaved. Fall was her favorite of the four seasons, despite the fact that it had felt like summer earlier that day. "Lord, why is it that during the summer months my hair sweats out before I get out of the beautician's chair? Why can't my hair always be like this? I get so many compliments on how beautiful it is. That's why I refuse to cut it, no matter how often everyone else tries to persuade me to."

Interestingly enough, she found that folks always wanted to tell her what to do with her hair. It was so easy for her to put it in a ponytail when the humidity and temperature would rise. She knew she couldn't do that with short hair. If she had a dollar for everyone that told her, "Girl, when you get past forty-five, you need to go short—that long hair makes you look old." She thought just the opposite. Her long hair made her look young, and she felt good about herself—that's all that mattered.

Snuggling into her "prayer chair," she decided to pray for Karen first before praying for anyone else, because she felt Karen needed prayer the most. Sixty minutes later, after praying for everyone else, it was her turn to pour her heart out to God about her issues.

"Lord, I've been in Your presence for an hour and for the most part, it's been sweet fellowship until I read a passage of Scripture in First John that challenged me. In verse twenty of the fourth chapter, it says we can't say we love You, whom we haven't seen, yet hate our brother.

"I know You're not just talking about our blood brothers and sisters—I know You're talking about other people as well, but my blood brother and sister are included in this Scripture. Lord, I loathe the relationship I have with my natural brother and sister. It's so fake. I enjoy my friends and fellowship more with them than I do my own brother and sister, and this should not be. After reading Your Word, I've come to grips with a horrible truth—I really haven't tried nor wanted to reach out to them before.

"Yeah, that's the truth. I've never owned up to the truth before. I'm tired of people telling me how wonderful and compassionate I am. 'Girl, you're a saint.' 'I wish I was like you.' On and on, people bestow accolades on me that I don't deserve. Lord, what good is it for people to believe that you've got it all together when you know you don't? I have issues, and I need help.

"Lord, please help me be the person people believe me to be because right here, right now, as I lay before you emotionally naked—I feel like someone who's living a double life. On one hand, I am the Christian who strives to study my Bible and be what You've called me to be. But on the other hand, I wrestle with evil thoughts and harbor feelings of unforgiveness and feelings of superiority. I like other people, and I tolerate and love other people more than I do my own flesh and blood. And I'm ashamed.

"Overall, You've blessed me with five wonderful friends in Quintella, Karen, Claudette, Arlene, and Nancy. But I really want to restore my relationship with my younger brother and sister. I've allowed the enemy to steal the joy and intimacy that brothers and sisters share. Lord, I want it back. I so want back what the enemy has stolen. Help me to reconnect with them. Help me, Holy Spirit, to reach out to them. I will do anything to rekindle the relationships so that we can once again enjoy each other's company.

"I wonder how many people I work with, or how many people I pass on the streets, have great outside relationships with everybody else but can't even love their own brothers and sisters. How many people are like me, who can forgive everybody else, but can't forgive their own flesh and blood?"

"It's not about everyone else; it's about you, Lenda," she heard Holy Spirit whisper.

"You're right, Holy Spirit. It doesn't matter about anyone else; this is all about me and You."

As tears flooded her eyes, Lenda thought about all the tears she had shed over the years over her family. She thought: *Enough already! Get it right and stop crying.* Her eyelids were heavy, and she could feel sleep blowing in like the wind on a breezy, summer day—so gentle and refreshing.

Lenda welcomed the much-needed sleep, which had eluded her for the past two nights. After crawling into bed, she drifted off—and her thoughts went to a happier time when she was nine years old, her brother was eight, and her sister was seven. These thoughts rested on one of the many days her mom would wake her up for church, which seemed like only yesterday.

* * * *

"Cocoa, Cocoa! Wake up, baby! Time for church," Mom called.

"I'm sleepy. I don't want to go." Mom shook her head in dismay and continued to pull me feet first out of bed. A better description would be *snatch*. That Sunday was no different from the others. The tug-of-war began, with Ethel Mae on one side and me on the other.

It was as if someone was yelling, "Get on your mark!" Mom came into the room. "Get set!" I heard her and tightened my fists about the covers. "Go!" Mom began pulling, and I held onto the covers as though they would save me from the obvious. It never worked; Ethel always won. The tug-of-war ended with pillows and covers on the floor, along with me as I succumbed to defeat. Oh the warmth of a nice comfortable bed! No school, no chores, just complete rest! However, the ending was always the same. This particular Sunday was no different. I *had* to get up.

I always had to get up first and my baby sister Annie got to sleep late all the time. My mom said it was because it took longer to get me ready. Well, my version of the story was very different, but no one cared. Annie always got preferential treatment because she was the baby.

It was the same old story every Sunday, and I hated it. Church in the morning, church in the evening. Why couldn't we miss church sometimes? The only way I could miss church was to play sick, but there was too great a price to pay. I didn't even think about telling a lie.

It's like this: if we played sick on a Sunday, my mom would go to the medicine cabinet and take out the cod liver oil. She would then take a tablespoon out of the drawer and instruct us to open wide. Then she would make us go to bed and forgo the best dinner of the week, which was always served on a Sunday: fried chicken, greens, macaroni and cheese, candied yams, fried corn, and corn bread with sliced tomatoes. We always had a great dessert—chocolate layered cake or pound cake or sweet potato pie.

Why did my grandmother have to be a preacher? To make matters worse, the church was in the basement of the house! Yes, that's right—in the basement of the house. We didn't even get a snow day. If nobody else came to church, my sister, my brother, me, Grandma, and Reverend McDonald—our piano player—were still there. We just walked down into the basement after we dressed up in our Sunday best. My friends all had normal lives. They got up, got dressed, and *drove* to church. *So much for being normal.*

After Mom successfully snatched me from bed, she would drag me into the bathroom and begin to scrub my face until I could feel my skin peeling—one layer at a time. See, my mother believed that your face was not clean until your nose shined like a new penny. Even though I didn't enjoy the face scrubbing, I loved it when Mom would cup my chin ever so gently into her hand, tilt my head toward her, and plant a soft kiss on my lips. She would then laugh as she continued to hold my chin to prevent me from getting away from her. Then she would tell me how much she loved me, in spite of our early morning tug-of-war. I'd look into those eyes and see that smile. And before I knew it, I'd have this wide grin on my face that said, "Kiss me again." And she would.

The bathroom was a special place for us. We didn't have to share these moments with anyone else—just Mom and me.

She was so pretty, my mother. She had the face of an angel. Her eyes were chestnut brown and as large as saucers. They were as clear as a glass of water, and they sparkled like the stars. Even sadness couldn't drown the sparkle from *her* eyes. Her smile reminded me of the sun—bright and warm. Her hair, which fell in her face, was soft as silk.

After scrubbing my face, Mom began the long process of combing my hair. Let me say up front—I wasn't a crybaby. While someone from the outside would have invariably formed that opinion, there was always the other side—mine, of course.

Just seeing a comb and brush in Ethel Mae's hand would cause me to go into fits. Mom didn't enjoy combing my hair because I always made such a fuss. It didn't help my cause any, considering the length of my hair. It would only anger Mom that we'd start in a sitting position in the chair and within minutes, I'd be on the floor withering like a snake and yelling at the top of my lungs. See, I'm one of those persons they call "tender-headed."

It was at these precise moments when I'd picture the comb as a bloody sword attacking me with a vengeance. And my beautiful soft-spoken mother became a vicious and violent villain. Sometimes I'd be screaming at the top of my lungs, only to look in the mirror to see that she didn't even have the comb in my hair; she would just be sitting there holding my hair with one hand, and the other hand was in the air holding the comb. Her eyes would be fixed on the mirror and if they could speak, they would say with that sparkle, "See, I'm not even touching you, and you're still acting a fool!" Then we'd start all over again, with our eyes locked once more. And this time she'd say, "Shut up and sit still."

Did she feel sorry for me? Did she console me? No was the answer on both counts. She'd tell me I'd better be quiet just as she'd grab a hunk of my hair and shake it like someone with a bag of chicken and Shake 'N Bake. She would then tell me, "If I really wanted to, I could hurt you and hurt you bad!" This behavior of my mom only came out when she had to wash or comb my hair. She hated both tasks and told me on several occasions that she'd do anything to avoid messing with my hair.

"Go put on your clothes," she demanded. As I looked in the mirror again, I could hardly see my hair for the barrettes.

"I need to blow my nose," I cried, hoping for some sympathy. "Do what you need to do. Then get your clothes on so you won't be late for church." How could you be late for church when all you had to do was walk downstairs to the basement—oops, I meant to the church?

Like every Sunday, I stopped on the landing of the basement and peeped around the corner to see who was there. All outsiders used the side door. That's one argument my dad won. He told my grandmother, "Momma, if you're going to continue having church in my house, your folks will use the side door!" And that they did. My dad didn't win many arguments, but he won that one.

I didn't understand as a little girl why my grandmother had to live with us. She and my mother didn't get along. But it was an unwritten rule that as long as Daddy was alive, my grandmother could live in his house.

I really didn't hate church—I just didn't like the fact that it was in our basement. Most of my friends played or watched TV in theirs. None of them had a church in the basement.

So here I was on the steps, taking in the view, when I spotted him in his gray suit—hubba-hubba. One day I'd let him know that I was his girlfriend and that one day he would be my husband. The time hadn't come yet. He wouldn't understand that we were meant to be together. Even though I was only nine years old, I knew who my husband was going to be.

I don't know how long I'd been on the landing—it obviously was too long because I looked behind me to find my mother with her hands on her hips and that look again. My legs told me I'd been squatting longer than I'd planned because as I tried to get up, I lost my balance and had to grab the wall before I fell. Mom didn't even try to break the fall; she just kept staring as I proceeded to church. I kept my head turned backward to keep an eye on her just in case she tried to hit me. Then I could perhaps run and miss the hit, but I thought better.

As I landed on the bottom step, I noticed the seat next to Wilbert was still empty, but I knew not to try to sit in it. Grandma would kill me for sitting next to a boy. Girls who did that were called "fast."

"Good morning Pretty Gal. Don't you look pretty." "Well, look who's here, none other than Pretty Gal." On and on they chanted. I hated all the attention as much as I hated the name Pretty Gal. The kids in the church hated me because my grandmother was the pastor, and they thought I thought I was something when in reality, I hated that my grandmother was a minister. I know I used the word hate a lot—but that's how I felt.

If left up to me, I would disappear into a crowd. So it was worse when people would single me out or single out one of my siblings by saying something nice. I knew I didn't look cute all the time. People would say that to get on my grandmother's good side. I never really knew if people were my friends or if they just liked me because they were trying to get close to the preacher, who happened to be my grandmother.

To tell the truth, I never thought I looked cute. I always thought that my eyes were too big and my nose too pointed. My hair, though thick, long, and curly, reminded me of dangling black hot dogs. And I hated the stares. It always felt like I was in a circus with a spotlight on me. While in that spotlight, people either threw tomatoes or kisses at me.

Where was I going to sit? There was a seat behind Wilbert. I decided to sit there so I could stare at him all Sunday without anyone ever knowing. As I walked past his row, I didn't dare look at him because then he would know how much I loved him, and it certainly wasn't time for him to know that.

Footsteps jolted me from thoughts of my husband-to-be—footsteps that were all too familiar to me, the steps of *Grandma*. I loved my grandmother. It was her rules that I didn't like. We could do *nothing*. If you were a visitor to our house, you would have thought it was Grandma's house and not my mom and dad's.

Grandma should have been the mom, and my mom the grandmother, because whatever my grandmother said was law. While my mother was soft-spoken, my grandmother was something else. She was firm, assertive, and demanding. No one messed with her.

I remember when she once overheard me talking about Wilbert, and how I thought he was cute. She snatched me by my hair and told me to go somewhere and sit my "fast self down!" I could never understand how saying a boy was cute made you "fast." She also added that if she so much as saw me look at a boy, she would beat me until "kingdom come." I still haven't found out how long that is.

It was the Wilberts in my life who kept me sane while

growing up, because living with my grandmother…let me put it this way: it wasn't easy living with her, even though I loved her very much.

My grandmother traveled a lot as a pastor, and she took me everywhere. I remember we would take the train to Cleveland, Chicago, Philadelphia, and Kansas City. To me, it was like traveling around the world. My grandmother was really smart. The problem was that she knew everything about every subject.

She would always tell us that "God was going to get us." No matter what, "God was going to get us." I think it was in those early years that I formed my opinion about God. It was an unfair opinion but my opinion nonetheless.

God got mad if you wore pants and if you chewed gum in church. He really got mad if you talked in church, and you could be assured that He'd get you. It didn't take much to make God mad. I wondered if He ever had any fun.

Coming from upstairs, I could smell the chicken frying. But the shuffling of the offering plates kept me focused. My dad gave us money every Sunday for the offering plate. I always put my money in, and so did my sister. My brother, on the other hand, was a different story. This particular Sunday, I saw him when he put his money in the plate. I couldn't wait to tell Daddy so he could get in trouble and get a whipping.

I never disappointed Daddy! Maybe that's why my brother called me Motor Mouth. It's interesting all the names people gave me. It's a wonder I kept up with them all. Back to the offering plate. There was a special way I knew my brother put in the wrong amount. Every Sunday, Daddy gave us $1.75. The dollar was for church, and the seventy-five cents was our allowance. One day, he called me to the side and sat me on his lap. Daddy had straight black hair, and it shined like new pennies. See, our family is part Indian, and everyone always told us that our hair came from the Indian side of the family. Well, I loved sitting on Daddy's lap. He had strong knees, and he was handsome.

Daddy said, "If you hear change drop when the offering plate comes along, tell Daddy. I've told Ernest time and time again that Grandma gets tired of counting change and that he better put the whole dollar in." So when the offering plate came past that day, I heard change, and I couldn't wait to tell!

Daddy didn't go to church. It had something to do with his mom, my grandmother. But he always made us go, and he gave us money. He told me to tell him when my brother or sister misbehaved and didn't put the right amount in church.

* * * *

Lenda smiled thinking about the past. It felt so good. She wanted to continue her journey. But sleep was winning the battle, and she was too tired to fight. Perhaps at another time, she would dream once again of years gone by.

Hours later, Lenda was awakened by the phone. She wondered how long she had been asleep. She let the answering machine get it, figuring someone had to be out of their mind to call her at 6:00 a.m. on a Saturday. It had to be the wrong number and from the message she heard recording on the machine, it was. She vaguely remembered what she was thinking about when she fell into semiunconsciousness, so it seemed. One minute she was in deep thought about her past, and the next minute she was asleep. Her latest trip down memory lane only propelled her even more to seek the relationship she so desired with her siblings.

As Lenda stared at the ceiling, she realized that she couldn't go back to sleep. Maybe the phone ringing was a Divine Appointment because she needed to talk to God some more.

"Lord, You mean everything to me. I never want to disappoint You. Jesus, You, God, and Holy Spirit are the Men in my life for right now, and I like it that way. Help me to have a better relationship with my sister and brother. Help me to love them unconditionally without judging. Yes, we've chosen different roads, but they all lead to You. Restore what the enemy has tried to destroy.

"Mom never says anything, but I know it hurts her to know that my siblings and I have little interaction. Help me to change all of that. I'm tired of being convicted in their presence *and* Yours. It's so overwhelming.

"Lord, I believe that today You're wiping the cobwebs and polishing the dullness that has prevailed between us for so many years.

"I look forward to a bright, restored relationship with my brother and sister. Holy Spirit, You are "The Man." God gave You to me to help me on this journey, and I love You. Thank You for illuminating this part of my life that's been dark. I leave Your presence with hope, knowing that with Your help, I'll no longer be held captive in this situation. I will begin to reach out to them. I'll stop judging, nagging, and believing that my way is the only way. I thank You for helping me to do this. And Jesus, please, please Jesus, I need a financial breakthrough, a miracle. I'm a tither and a giver, and I thank You for unexpected income in the Name of Jesus. Amen.

"Now one last thing—Holy Spirit, please tell me why I was so weepy yesterday. When my ex came over to sign some papers and get our son, why did old feelings surface? I felt anger that he and his new wife are doing so well. He's even found You, God. I didn't want to hear about his vacation in Hawaii and how much fun he and his wife had. What's up with *that*? When we were together, he didn't want to travel at all! We didn't even go to the grocery store together. When will I get over it? Since the divorce, it seems I've been piecing my life together like a complicated puzzle. And frankly, I'm having a hard time of it. It's been years, and I'm still asking myself how someone I was so in love with ended up on the other side of the room in divorce court with me.

"Divorce is so ugly. Everybody suffers emotionally and financially. My son is growing up without a dad in the home, and it hurts to see him watch football without a male to slap hands with and ask questions that I can't answer. That's what happens when you put someone in a place they should never be. It's like I forgot about You. Before my husband, You were first. After I got married, it was like I threw You to the curb. My focus was only to please my husband. I didn't even pray consistently anymore. I was totally out of balance. Funny, like so many people, I put a lot of trust in earthly things. And when the people I made gods out of left, who was there to wipe my tears and hold me in their arms? The One I kicked to the curb.

"God, You never left me. You've always been there to hold me in Your arms when everyone else let me down.

"No one ever gave me a manual on marriage. It's like playing house, until reality kicks in. I am only anchored by Your love and in knowing what the Scripture tells me, You will never leave nor forsake me. Never would I have imagined that my life would be as it is now."

Lenda fluffed her pillow, laid on her back with her arms stretched to her sides while she stared at the ceiling. "Holy Spirit, I'll not get out of bed until You answer me. I need You to help me make some sense of this." Lenda was determined to wait on an answer. And wait she did. Unfortunately, she was later startled by the familiar sound of the alarm clock, and she would have to get out of bed shortly—even though she still didn't have her answer. She pressed snooze.

As she tried to get a last bit of sleep, she couldn't help but feel confused by the fact that once again, God had not answered her. She didn't know what was going on. She felt she deserved to know how her marriage crumbled like a house of cards.

All of that thinking ate up her final minutes of sleep, as the snooze alarm once again began blaring incessantly. Lenda made no attempt to get up.

"I guess we'll never know the answer to some things."

As Lenda's eyes adjusted to the sunlight, she said, "I have got to get some of those room-darkening shades." Once the sun popped through—sleep was history.

Lenda was due to go out of town next week, and she had not packed nor finished her presentation. She thought about her schedule—she had several trips planned, all within an eight-week span. It looked like a good day to get ahead of the game and prepare herself. Just as she started to get in motion, the phone rang again. The caller ID wasn't visible. "Hello," Lenda whispered, hoping the caller would feel responsible for interrupting her sleep.

"Lenda, how are you, baby?" her mother asked.

"Mom, I'll be fine as soon as I wake up."

"Are you still taking me to see your brother?"

Lenda totally forgot that she had promised her mother that she would drive her to see her brother. Her eyes rolled just thinking about the long trip where he was incarcerated. "Mom, I did forget. Do you still want to go? After all, Baby Sister went to see him last week, so it's not like he hasn't had a visitor in a while."

Her mother's voice was a whisper, "You know I want to go."

"I'll be at your house in an hour." Before she could hang up, the question was popped.

"Are you going in this time?" her mother asked.

Silence was not golden—it was ugly and uncomfortable.

"Mom, I'm taking you, right?" Lenda's voice softened. "Let's talk about that when I get there, OK?"

First the sigh, and then her mother's reply, "OK baby, whatever you say."

Lenda hung up the phone and jumped out of bed. "Ugh! Ugh! Ugh!" Lenda yelled and stomped like a kindergartner who was told she could never have candy again.

With fists clenched, she began prancing like a cat about to chew its prey. It was a good thing she had a house. Neighbors would have kicked her out a long time ago if she lived in an apartment. It was then that Holy Spirit impressed upon her that only hours ago she was before Him confessing that she wanted to make it right with her siblings.

"Well Lenda, now is your chance to get it right," she heard Holy Spirit gently say.

Lenda quickly filed the thought that she needed to be careful what she asked God for.

Chapter Five

Karen wasn't sleepy, and she didn't have to go to work the next day. So she decided to put on her gown, cut out all the lights, open her blinds, and look out of the window at the Detroit River and Windsor across the water whose lights lit-up the city.

She needed time to think about the evening—not just dinner with the girls, but her conversation with Lenda. She wasn't sure if she'd ever find a guy they would approve of. No guy was good enough. "Yeah, I know as a Christian I'm supposed to date Christian men, but where are they? Hello! Of course, Claudette swears they're out there. She's waiting for one—God bless her—but I'm not! I'll get the man first and if he's not saved, I'll get him saved," Karen blurted.

She remembered something Lenda told her a long time ago; she said, "Karen, low self-esteem is the silent killer of confidence. It has done more harm than some drugs because it tends to mask problems, especially when it comes to relationships. I question your self-esteem. It seems whenever a man comes along and pays attention to you, you end up 'falling' hook, line, *and* sinker. Why?" Karen couldn't answer Lenda then, and the question bothered her now. Did she have low self-esteem?

She was so confused. One minute she felt her new relationship was right—the next minute, she was sure it was all wrong. It wasn't that she didn't think she could find someone. She believed her real issues stemmed from her mother, rather than men. She always thought: *When your mother doesn't love you enough to hang around, why would someone else love you?*

As she continued to enjoy the view from her window, she couldn't help but talk to herself a little more about her true feelings. Shaking her friends' opinions about her love life was no easy task. "Why am I allowing what the girls said tonight to bug me? I know Queen has her man, and he sure is a good one. He's the complete package: saved, fine, nice, *and* rich. I'm beginning to think that's the exception more than the rule. I'd be happy with saved, fine, and nice. Claudette, on the other hand, will probably never get a man—she's so messed up because of a mistake she made. And Lenda, well, she's 'got a Man.'"

As soon as she said that, Karen looked up like she was acknowledging someone in the room. "Holy Spirit, I'm sorry. Some things you don't play with. I understand why she says that she's got a Man. You're always available to talk to us—I just don't go around saying what she says…telling everybody she has a Man like You're alive and in person. You and I have a different relationship. I believe a man is a man and God is God—I don't mix the two.

"Let me back it up. I know You're a real man, Holy Spirit. But I have issues seeing you as my 'Man' like that! You know what I mean? I love my friends, but we all grew up so different. I really love them, even though I know I'm the 'spiritual black sheep' in the group.

"Finding them was a good thing. They have really helped me come up in my faith. I always thought I was a good Christian until I met them. Lord, You know I never knew anyone who actually read their Bible until I met Quintella,

Lenda, and Claudette. I knew a lot of people who carried one to church. But to have actually read it, I didn't know of anyone. So I'm so thankful for how they have helped me grow.

"Before I met them, church once a month was acceptable. Now I go just about every week. I'm not quite there for the midweek, but I do go every now and then. I recognize I need to work on the personal study. So they've been good for me, but it's like I can't really tell them about my life and how I really feel. Like tonight when I asked Quintella the romantic question, they laughed at me. When people act so holy, you don't know, so I thought it was safe to ask. But it's the kind of reaction I got tonight that makes me want to clam up and not ask or share things that are close to my heart."

Walking through her condo, Karen acknowledged that the beauty of it never wore off. "Lord, thank You for helping me find this—my view is breathtaking." The condo always reminded her of New York City—at two in the morning it was as bright as two in the afternoon because of the lights. When she would turn off all her lights, the lights from the Ambassador Bridge and the casino on the Windsor side lit her place up like the lights in Times Square on Broadway and 47th Street. "Thank You, heavenly Father—thank You for taking care of me when I felt helpless."

Then Karen's thoughts went to that negative space. Angrily reminiscing about her past, she couldn't forget that her condo was bought with "blood money," as she liked to call it.

* * * *

Being underage when Momma died (and that's a nice way to put it), the insurance money was put in a trust fund. Later, when I became of age, I remember telling my aunts that I didn't want the money. I had so much hate for my mother. But I'm so thankful for my aunts, who took the money and invested it for me. They could have used it, but they didn't. After moving to Michigan, I was blessed with a good job, and I invited them to come see me in my first place. It wasn't anything elaborate, but it was mine, nothing like this condo.

When my aunts finally came for a visit, I didn't know how much my life would change. They came, but they didn't come empty-handed. They brought this money, huge sums of money, and made me promise to take it and put it up. If I didn't want to use it myself, they urged that I put it in a bank and give it to my kids—whenever I had some. Reluctantly, I took it and called my financial adviser. He told me to invest some of it in real estate.

It took me six months to check out this place called Riverfront Condos. I always admired Riverfront, but it wasn't until I actually took a tour of the place that I decided it would be a good investment. After looking at my options, I decided on the two-bedroom condo with the panoramic view of the Detroit River. Since it had a den, the total square footage was 2,300. *Take that, Momma!* I picked the seventh floor because I knew seven was the number of completion! And with the panoramic view, it didn't matter what room I sat in, a tranquil scene was viewed from every window and every angle.

The amenities were more than I could imagine. A gated community, covered parking, a full-service health and fitness center, tennis courts, a signature grill and bar, dry cleaners, a private marina, on and on I could go. But it was the Fourth of July festivities that were always special.

* * * *

It had been ten years since Karen moved into her condo, and she was still in awe of the view and all the perks. "Things have not changed, nor the views. I celebrate every time I open the blinds. I could never see myself moving to a stuffy old subdivision," Karen marveled aloud. "Nope, this is the place for me! You can't see the Ambassador Bridge with all its lights in a subdivision." The evening sunsets that calmed her state of constant anxiety definitely couldn't be found in a subdivision. "Even though my mother's suicide will haunt me for the rest of my life, this place is the closest to heaven on earth for me."

Yes, there were moments of peace, especially on Sunday after church. Sometimes it was days of peace, but the life-altering experience always came back to trouble her. If it had not been for Aunt Thelma and Aunt Chunk, she would have lost her mind. They both called her at least once a week, ever since what Karen viewed as her mother's oh-so-selfish act. She thanked God for them often, and she always looked forward to talking with them. It was also why she insisted on giving them a big portion of her insurance money.

In hindsight, the money didn't matter. Karen had a good job as a counselor with the Detroit Board of Education, and she was a saver. So she didn't need anybody's blood money. And if it hadn't been for her aunts, she would have given it all away. She could hear Aunt Thelma's voice in her head as if it were yesterday: "Yo' mammy was always selfish. Take that money and spoil yourself, girl, because she certainly didn't spoil you. Ol' heifer! Buy something that you wouldn't normally buy yourself. You deserve to be spoiled. We can't pick our mommas, and you certainly got cheated with yours! So take that money and use it! Pamper yourself…make up for all the times when she acted like the fool she was!"

That's Aunt Thelma. She's a "tell it like it is" type of person— no matter what, she thought. It was a good thing Karen didn't like her mother, or Aunt Thelma's words probably would've hurt. But in Karen's estimation, if she liked her mother, it would've probably meant she was a good mother, and there would've been no need for harsh words.

Once again, Karen became aware of Holy Spirit's presence. She acknowledged Him, saying, "Holy Spirit, am I the only person—sane person—who hates her mom? I know there are twisted folks in the world. But I'm pretty sane. I just got the raw end of the deal for a mother. I mean, the 'Leave It to Beaver' mom is a far cry from the mom that I grew up with. The 'Leave It to Beaver' mom would never commit suicide knowing her daughter would find her. A good mother does *not* do that. And since we're talking, can you give some preacher somewhere the courage to stand in his pulpit on Mother's Day and acknowledge the bad mothers and send us someone who will help us? I'm tired of always feeling like there are no bad mothers in the world. Yes, that needs to be addressed. I know you're supposed to wear a white flower if your mother is deceased and red if she's alive—I think I'm going to wear a black one just so someone can ask why mine is black. Then I can say, 'This is for all of us who were unfortunate enough to have a mother from hell!'"

Karen laughed at her dark humor, but she knew Holy Spirit wasn't finding her conversation very funny. Sick as it all sounded, it was sort of a relief for her to talk about it to God. After all, He *was* the only One she could bare her soul to, except Claudette. Claudette was a good friend. Someone else would think she was crazy. Heaven forbid that she'd say anything bad about "Momma."

"I know the Scripture says to honor your parents, but just what if you had bad parents—are you supposed to honor them, too? Maybe there's a Scripture that will let me off the hook. Perhaps just somewhere in the Bible it will say if your parents are bad, you won't have to honor them."

Karen's thoughts turned back to Quintella, who had it all by her standards. "Now I would give all my money to have the relationship that Queen has with her mom. They go shopping together. Her mom is almost seventy-five, and she looks sixty. She buys Quintella clothes, even though she doesn't have to, and continues to spoil her to this day. I'd give anything to have what she has. By the way, Lord, why does it seem like some folks have everything? I mean, Queen has the most wonderful parents. I love them. They treat me like a daughter.

"Then she has Ken, the husband every woman wants. I say that a lot, but it's true. You know I mean it in a nice way. He looks at her like they just fell in love yesterday, like he could eat her up, and they've been married for over twenty-something years. She has it all. Why? Why?! WHY?!?

"And you know what else, Lord? Queen could lose some weight—she's not big, but she's not skinny either. And her husband doesn't care. He's fine, and I've never seen him even look at other women. His eyes stay glued to her. How do you get a man to love you like that? People say I'm cute and have a good figure but in all these years, I've never had a man to look at me like Ken looks at Queen. Is *that* what I'm searching for?

"I know the girls laugh at me and wonder what my problem is, but if they knew half the story. The girls can talk about church and being holy all day long—that's because they've led such sheltered lives. All of them have good relationships with their mothers. I guess I should say Lenda and Queen. Like me, Claudette's mother is dead. They don't know what it was like to be the daughter of the Wicked Witch of the South. Claudette knows my story. It was easy telling her because our stories are kind of similar. Her mother just drank herself to death. But I'll never share my story with the other two. They will never know how you died, Momma, nor will I talk about our stormy relationship when I was a child. They could never relate, and they'll never know. I'll go to my grave with this secret.

"I just know when I have a daughter, I'll never treat her

like you treated me—MOMMA!" Karen spat the word out with a vengeance. "I'll love her with all of my heart. I'll take her shopping…paint her little toenails soft pink. I'll hug her and kiss her. We'll dress up together and dress down together. I'll buy us matching nightgowns and house slippers and every day, I'll tell her how much I love her. I'll allow her to wrap her arms around my neck, and I'll shower her with kisses. You wait, I'll show you how to treat and protect a daughter."

Chapter Six

When Quintella pulled into her subdivision, even though it was dark and secluded, she could make out every house—their custom designs were forever etched in her mind. She absolutely loved her neighborhood. She could trace most of the trees with her eyes and knew every turn on the numerous winding streets because they had become friends over the last twenty years.

Before she and Ken found this house all those years ago, they had grown so tired of house hunting that Quintella almost suggested they put house hunting on hold. Then one of the new partners in Ken's law firm told him to check out Wabeek, an exclusive subdivision in Bloomfield Hills. When Quintella drove through the lush community, she was struck by the beauty of its landscape, which was hilly with lots of trees, greenery, and winding streets. She instantly knew one of those houses would have their name on it.

Surrounded by lakes, there were plenty of spacious contemporary homes that also had character and personality. Not one house looked the same. No cars were parked on the streets. It wasn't until after they bought their home that Quintella found out that street parking wasn't allowed unless a resident was having an event. Fences were even prohibited.

The house they settled on had an elegant white foyer, with

floor-to-ceiling windows on the whole lower level. The living room was large enough to put their entire first apartment in it. And the kitchen was every woman's dream, with an island and plenty of cabinets. Four bedrooms, four full bathrooms, and two half baths filled their house, which was nestled in a quiet cul-de-sac. Its finished walkout basement and three-car garage were also desirable features. Still, compared to the other houses in the neighborhood, their house was one of the smaller ones. They didn't find out until after they signed the papers that there was a North Wabeek (Wabeek Ridge to be exact, which is where they ended up) and a South Wabeek, which contained the Wabeek Golf Course and Country Club. Quintella was happy that they had chosen Wabeek Ridge.

She and Ken immediately fell in love with the house and couldn't wait to sign on the dotted line. Back then, it seemed to cost so much money. But in the long run, it was worth it to find a home that still gave her great joy after so many years, and the neighborhood really hadn't changed much either. Property values were at an all-time high, but they had no plans of moving.

She and Ken had to pinch themselves because they never thought in their wildest dreams that they would ever own a home like this one. Right before they purchased it, Quintella's realtor warned them that they had to use neutral colors if they ever decided to paint the exterior since loud colors weren't permitted in Wabeek Ridge. And on the day they got the keys, they went in the house and ran through it, hollering like little kids: "It's ours! Can you believe it? It's ours, all ours!"

It took three years for them to fully furnish it. In the early days, they were just happy to sit on the carpet, looking out of the windows and thanking God for all He had done.

Initially, they imagined their home would be filled with kids, so this community was perfect because it had a good school system. It was unfortunate that they hadn't taken advantage of that perk—yet. They still remained hopeful, even though age was not on their side. They were confident that God could do anything.

When the garage door opened, Quintella was startled to see Ken standing by his car, staring into space. Her face must have revealed her concern because Ken gave her the smile she's loved for over twenty-five years and assured her that everything was fine. He was looking for some documents for a case he was working on when he discovered that he had somehow misplaced them.

"Did you ask Holy Spirit to help you find them?" she asked, returning a knowing smile.

"You know I didn't. It's a man thing—we don't ask for help until we've wasted hours trying to find it on our own."

"Well, let's ask Him to help you find them so you can come in the house with me."

That's one of the reasons Ken loved this woman. He knew he got on her nerves at times, but she always had his back. Ken grabbed her hand and with their heads bowed, he called on their Helper. "Holy Spirit, forgive me for wasting so much time trying to do things with my own strength. You know where those documents are. Please locate them for me, in Jesus' Name. Amen."

Ken wrapped his arms around Quintella's waist while simultaneously asking her about the evening with the girls. "Same ol', same ol'—we fussed, laughed, and almost came to blows. We so love each other." They began walking in the house, and Quintella asked Ken if he bought more water. Ken's eyes lit up like he just got a bright idea.

"My briefs are in the trunk of your car with the water. Remember when I went to gas up your car yesterday?"

Quintella nodded while Ken continued talking. "I took the briefs out of my car so I'd remember to bring them in the house. I put them in the trunk and when I got home, the neighbor called me to look at something. I got distracted, and I came right in the house after we talked and left the briefs and the water in the trunk. Thank You, Holy Spirit!"

"I think I had something to do with that, too. Don't I get any thanks?" laughed Quintella. Ken promised to thank her big time, "later." She rolled her eyes up in her head and smiled as she mumbled, "Men." She knew what "later" meant.

Quintella opened the door while Ken got the water and put it in the kitchen sink.

"Did you have fun tonight?" Although he already inquired, Quintella knew he didn't want to hear details. He was trying to be kind. She almost called his bluff, but she decided to be nice.

"Yes, I had fun." He saluted her, glad he escaped the loaded question, and disappeared into his office. Quintella took off her shoes and exchanged them for house slippers and decided it would be a good time to wash the water bottles. As Quintella made some mild dishwater, she began to unload the bottled water from the grocery store packaging to start her signature task of washing off each bottle. People often laughed at this seemingly odd ritual, which she'd been doing for years. Most think it's just added work. But she knew the value for *her* house, thanks to her father-in-law, and that's all that mattered to her.

When she and Ken were newlyweds, Ken's dad once came over to visit and witnessed Ken bring some water up from the basement. It was still in its packaging, and she opened the water and began to put some of the bottles in the fridge. His dad abruptly said, "Hold it, missy! Don't you wash those bottles before you put them in the fridge?" Startled, she shrugged her shoulders and shook her head no. Ken's dad took that opportunity to tell her a story she's never forgotten.

When he was working his way through college, her father-in-law was a stock boy at a large grocery store chain. He worked the midnight shift in a warehouse. He said, "I didn't have to worry about people at night—it was the rats and mice that ran around like they were training to be store manager that I worried about." He saw them running all over canned groceries and bottled water. And when he would move stock, little puddles would be on top. When he asked one of the guys what the puddles were, he was told they were the urine from the mice. "Ma and I never put up groceries without washing them off. So the next time you don't wash your water and you open that cold bottle and put it up to your mouth, I'll let your imagination tell you what you're drinking other than water."

Quintella never forgot that story and has washed not only water but her groceries and milk, as well. The milk gets washed before it goes in the fridge, and she's trained to wash any cans before opening them. While she's converted some, others think she could use her time more wisely.

When the last bottle was washed, Quintella stopped to enjoy her kitchen. She loved to cook, so she was adamant about what she wanted in a kitchen when they got their house. The mahogany cabinets with brass handles still looked as good as the day they moved in. The island in the center of the kitchen was used very well.

God had been good to them. Ken had a successful practice with a lot of high-profile clients. They entertained frequently and whenever the opportunity presented itself, they were quick to share their faith. People always complimented them on the beauty of their home. But they never took all the credit—they wouldn't hesitate to give God the glory!

As she thought further about things, Quintella remembered that she had to prepare their tithe and offering for Sunday. Before reaching for the light switch, she turned once again to look at her kitchen. She smiled and hit the switch.

Quintella loved the fact that she had her own office and Ken had his. Those rooms alone kept the "intense fellowships" at a minimum. She didn't have to touch his stuff, and he didn't touch hers. Unlike most families, Ken was the neat freak, and she had some growing to do in that area. Her space was described as controlled chaos—at best.

As she began to write out the check, she couldn't help but think about the night's events. She played with the idea of inviting Karen over for Thanksgiving dinner. If all went well, maybe they could find a nice single guy from church and invite him, too. Ken frowned on such ideas, saying, "No, because if it doesn't work out, we'll never hear the end of it." Quintella, on the other hand, always saw the brighter side: "Suppose it does work out?"

While she desperately tried not to think about the dinner conversation, she couldn't help herself. And her thoughts wandered over to the subject of having children: *How is it some people have tons of babies that they can't afford, but here we are, a couple who can afford children and give them a nice home, and we haven't had any?* Quintella's hard-to-forget mistake from long ago ran across her mind like an old movie. Shaking her head as if it would cause the memories to disappear didn't work. The old film continued to play. Quintella ran and turned on her favorite CD and began to sing along:

Say the name of Jesus

Say the name so precious

No other name I know

That can calm your fears and dry your tears and wipe away your pain

When you don't what else to pray

When you can't find the words to say

Say the name...

She loved "Say the Name." When Quintella first heard the song, she thought it was by a black artist—not that it mattered. After finding out that Martha Munizzi was white when she went to buy the CD, she was shocked. Of course, Quintella found it interesting that she, like many people, tried to fit someone into her own little mold. The fact was, Quintella knew that woman could *sang!* She was anointed, and color didn't have a thing to do with it.

Her thoughts went back to Lenda's comments at the restaurant. "Excuse me, Holy Spirit. She's not white. She's dipped in the vanilla batter. I kind of agree with Lenda—that does sound better."

The music in the background was so soothing. "Lord, thank You for Holy Ghost-anointed music." Every time the enemy tried to attack her, Holy Spirit always provided a way of escape. She tried to remember what she was doing before the mental attack came. The pen in her hand and checkbook on the desk quickly jogged her memory. She resumed writing out their tithe and offering. Ken always insisted that they do it on Friday, which was payday. He consistently reminded her that tithes were written *before* other bills. God came first.

She pressed the intercom button to get her husband's thoughts, but she knew what he was going to say before he said it. Sometimes he'd surprise her and give an amount, but most of the time he left it up to her. Tithes were easy to calculate; it was the offerings that they discussed. Ken was very generous when it came to giving to the Lord. He always told Quintella that because they were one, she had his heart. So whatever she was led to give, he'd agree—most of the time.

"Yeah, babe?" Ken finally answered the intercom page; she wondered what he was doing.

"I'm writing the check for the tithe and offering. Did you get a figure for the offering?"

"Just be led, babe. Whatever you do, make sure you put something in for missions, too."

"OK, I'll be down once I'm finished."

"I'll be right here."

Quintella finished and reached for the glue stick to seal the envelope. That's another thing she stopped doing a long time ago. Licking envelopes was a thing of the past. Just like the mice story, she didn't know what germs were lurking on the paper and glue.

As Quintella ran down the steps to Ken's office, she was thankful that they had multiple floors in the house. Sometimes the only exercise she got was running up and down the stairs.

The scene that was about to play out was so familiar, but one Quintella still enjoyed. When Ken saw her, he turned in the swivel chair. Without saying a word, he grabbed her hand with the envelope in it, they raised their hands toward heaven, and Ken began to pray.

"Heavenly Father, in Jesus' Name, we join our faith as husband and wife. We thank You for an opportunity to give into the Kingdom of God. We are thankful for all that

You have done for us, and we're thankful for every blessing You've given us to enjoy. Father, we pray that as we give, men, women, boys, and girls will hear the gospel, receive You as Lord, and get snatched out of the hands of the enemy. We pray that marriages will be restored and made whole. We pray that children who may be separated from their parents will return home, and families will be healthy, loving, and living examples of Your goodness. We thank You that laborers are sent to all nations so that people from every race can hear the good news of Jesus. We also thank You for the promises You've attached to our obedience and the harvest that will come back to us so we'll have more seeds to sow. We thank You that the enemy is defeated in our finances, and we pray this prayer according to Malachi 3, verses eight through twelve, and Luke 6:38, in Jesus' Name. Amen."

Like clockwork, Ken turned and went right back to the computer without missing a beat, and Quintella headed back upstairs. No additional words were needed between the two of them.

She loved to hear Ken pray. It was sexy to her. And it was something she'd never discuss with the girls, but she wondered if anyone else felt that way. "Holy Spirit, why does praying draw me to my husband like that? Am I the only lady who feels that way? I'd like to know."

Climbing the steps, she couldn't help but think about how far God had brought them. Everyone who knew them always commented on how "spiritual" they were. Comments like, "I wish we were like you guys." "Y'all need to be in ministry." "I wish I had a husband like yours." Or men often told Ken, "Man, you can tell your wife really loves God." The girls weren't the only ones who teased them and called them King and Queen James. If they only knew…

As she passed the kitchen, Quintella thought about

making a stop to the cookie jar, but she dismissed it. When she returned to her office, she located her Bible and put the check in the pocket of her Bible cover. She had to laugh as she remembered the earlier years of their marriage. Ken's church attendance was sporadic, and hers was nothing to write home about. Even when she went by herself, she didn't feel like anything was wrong with Ken staying at home. Ken's Sundays were just another workday at home in the morning, and a spot in front of the TV to look at sports in the afternoon.

They both grew up in church, but they went out of tradition more than anything. They never, ever prayed together unless they were eating—even then it was more like a children's prayer: "Lord, we thank You for this food, in Jesus' Name. Amen." They never prayed that the food was sanctified by the Blood of Jesus and good to eat. And as far as tithes, they couldn't even remember what they gave and called tithes. Whatever was left over when the bills were paid is what they gave, and sometimes that decision wasn't made until Sunday morning.

When sitting in church by herself, Quintella would wait until the preacher said it was offering time, reach in her purse, fill out an envelope quickly before the pan or bucket got to her, and toss it in. On the rare times Ken would be with her, half the time he wouldn't even fill out an envelope. He would just pull something out of his pocket and drop it in. What mercy and grace God had on them and their ignorance.

It didn't help that the church they attended at that time never taught them the importance of worshipping God with their giving. It wasn't until she met Lenda and began going to a church that taught the Word that she learned to never just throw money in a bucket. Once Ken started coming with her, he liked the fact that they were encouraged to bring their Bibles, and he began to attend regularly with Quintella.

It was at this church that they were taught about prayers of agreement. One Sunday a year, the minister always taught on the proper way to give offerings. He did it once a year because there were always new people joining. Also, each Sunday when offerings were received, the pastor would briefly talk about offering time being a time to worship. Quintella still remembered when she and Ken decided that they would begin to pray over their offerings at home. It was very awkward at first. Ken would say, "You say it." She would say, "No, you say it." It was so uncomfortable. She would wait for him, and he would wait for her. And for almost a year, she would end up saying "it."

They continued being faithful in church attendance, but Ken still wasn't ready to lead in prayer. The good thing was, they eventually stopped calling prayer "it." They also didn't go back and forth on who would pray. Ken told her flat out that he just wasn't ready to pray and if they were going to pray together, she would have to be the one to pray. If she couldn't agree with that, he said there would be no prayer at all. Quintella of course agreed, not wanting to stop the momentum, so she prayed every Friday for that next year.

That's also when Ken gave her the responsibility of preparing the tithes and offerings without any input from him. Ken's rationale was, he didn't tell her how much to pay on the bills—he trusted her judgment on that—so why should he have to give input on the tithes and offerings? Besides, he once explained, if he were to do it, his giving would be more on the conservative end; he knew Quintella would be more generous, and he was OK with that.

Then one Friday, out of the clear blue, Ken told her he was ready to pray. As they held hands, she could feel him shaking, and her eyes filled with tears as he opened his mouth. His first prayer was nothing like what he said tonight. It was more like,

"Lord, please accept our tithe. We thank You for all You've given us, in Jesus' Name." He was talking so fast that it was as if he was trying to hurry up before he changed his mind. That was a huge step in their spiritual journey. From that prayer, they began to pray about other things. They would take turns praying for protection over each other. They prayed for Ken's law practice, their parents, and Quintella's time at home. Even they couldn't believe the growth that came from practiced prayer.

After Ken's breakthrough, he decided that as head of the house, he would take the lead on praying over the offerings. He didn't mind asking Quintella if she wanted to pray from time to time. But for the most part, he preferred to pray over the money. And they normally took turns praying when it came to other topics.

Daily devotion started a few years after that, and everything had pretty much become second nature. Even though people looked at them and thought it had always been like that for them, it hadn't; it was a journey. There was no mistaking that they had come a long way in the things of God, and life was better for them because of it.

Chapter Seven

Claudette was momentarily calmed as she pulled into her subdivision. She had moved to Southfield over ten years ago. Her home nested on a cul-de-sac beautifully located on a tree-lined street just thirty minutes from downtown Detroit and ten minutes from her shop in the Northland Mall. People who didn't pay her bills said that the house was too big, but Claudette thought it was just right. Even though it was 2,000 square feet, it didn't seem large. Impressive from the street, it was even more striking on the inside. The automatic garage door opener reminded her of a game she used to play as a young girl: Open Sesame. Voilà—the massive door opens, and all she had to do was drive in.

She decided as a child that her home would be a reflection of the princess who was on the inside and with the Lord's help, it was all that. She loved her entrance. The hardwood floors looked like mirrors when they were clean. On any other day, they just looked like hardwood floors.

Claudette also enjoyed the living, dining, and family rooms, which were covered with plush carpeting and decorated luxuriously. The kitchen is what sold her on the house. The open layout with dark, rich cabinets and the island in the middle of the floor, which helped her prepare meals, were everything her heart desired. The huge master suite with an adjoining four-piece bath, which included a soaking tub, allowed Claudette to relax after a long, hard day. The other two bedrooms and bathrooms served as closet space for the clothes, jewelry, and mannequins that she couldn't keep at the store.

She promised herself that one day she'd keep everything in the basement. After all, that's why she got it finished. But it was easier to bring everything upstairs, because that's where she spent most of her time. Whenever company came, she'd quickly hire the young girl next door to take everything in the basement and lo and behold, once again, she'd have three beautiful bedrooms and bathrooms!

Walking into her bedroom, the brief calm that she felt moments ago vanished. A feeling of heaviness was all that was left, and it felt like a 300-pound cloak of sadness.

Claudette couldn't stop thinking about what Karen said at dinner. It was true that she hadn't had a date in five years. And if she had anything to do with it, another five would pass before she would allow herself to be used again. Truthfully, it wasn't the man's fault; she walked into her situation with her eyes wide open.

At one point, Claudette blamed him. But she soon realized that when the relationship is consensual, no one can do anything unless you allow them. Controls must be in place in order to be a successful single. She lacked those controls five years ago—but not anymore.

The lesson was costly, but she promised herself and God that she would not pay that bill again. As Claudette began to go over the dinner conversation, she couldn't get over Quintella calling her a "whore." And when she said it, Claudette could feel the venom leave Quintella's mouth. But Holy Spirit gave her a timely reminder: "She didn't call you that—she called the woman who had the affair with her brother-in-law that name."

"But Holy Spirit, You know and I know, I was that woman. If she ever finds out—I'm dead meat. No one could've ever convinced me that I—Miss Goody Two-Shoes—would have an affair with a married man. It wasn't planned; it just happened. So for her to call me a whore and act like her brother-in-law was just seduced by this evil woman is far from the truth. My prayer is that she'll never know.

"God, You've been my 'Secret Keeper.' Please don't let Quintella find out. Our relationship will go up in smoke—not to mention that it will take Lenda along, too. I could live without Quintella, but Lenda—she's so dear to me. Lord, please continue to hide me. I believe that Karen will still love me if she finds out—but Queen, that's another story. I mean, I haven't judged her for her and husband's mistake."

It was during the affair that she found out some unbelievable news about Quintella and her husband. She didn't ask for the information, but it was aptly volunteered when she happened to mention that she thought Quintella and her husband were the perfect couple. Quintella's brother-in-law couldn't wait to tell her all about their "dirty little secret." She couldn't fathom why he would tell her something like that other than he was so miserable in his own life. And it was extremely hard for her to believe what he told her.

"Maybe next time she gets in her pulpit, I'll just throw in a hypothetical about that subject and watch her response, since holy—not blood—runs through her veins. Maybe she won't be so quick to start calling people whores," Claudette rattled off.

"Let it go before you find yourself right back in the pit where you were a couple days ago," interjected Holy Spirit.

"Remember, she doesn't know that you were the one, so don't take her comments personally. You've been forgiven—receive the forgiveness."

Claudette ignored the voice of Holy Spirit and began to think back on the day she met Clay. They were working on the same project and because of their work schedules, they hadn't been able to juggle their calendars to meet. And the deadline was approaching. So they decided lunch was the best alternative. Bad move.

If Claudette was ever in a position to talk to up-and-coming young females, her advice would be to keep two-person meetings in workplace conference rooms, with the door open. And if at all possible, she'd urge them both to take another co-worker along. This all started when she had a business lunch with a married man who talked about his personal life, which wasn't going well. She didn't have adequate safeguards in place to make sure their conversation remained businesslike. Once they began to talk about his husband-wife relationship, they were set up for a fall.

When she met Clay, there were so many signs that she ignored. From that very first business lunch, she couldn't help but think: *He's kind of cute.* That was a sure sign. Then she thought about how she never stopped their conversation when he said, "My wife just doesn't understand me or my job. I try to explain how it drains you." She could've easily redirected the conversation and said, "We'd better get back to work." But she didn't. She was so concerned about not hurting his feelings that she gave a sympathetic reply: *"Real-ly?"* And from that point, barriers were broken that should've remained off-limits, and one word of sympathy led to another lunch and then another.

Before long, she was talking about *her* private pity parties. That led to dinner. Through it all, Holy Spirit was warning her,

"Enough—cut it off. Don't see him again." But no, she overrode the warnings and thought that Holy Spirit was overreacting. She hadn't valued His counsel or recognized that He was The Man in her life. He was the One who would've kept her from making that mistake, and she would've avoided ending up in a sordid relationship that never should've happened. It was hard for her to understand why she thought she knew more than Holy Spirit.

She always promised herself that she'd never make the mistakes that her parents made. But just saying it didn't make it happen. She wished her grandmother had been a pastor like Lenda's grandmother. Maybe she would have found Jesus at an earlier age. Maybe she would have been spared some heartache. But no. Her grandmother ran numbers, and her mother went through men like she was trying to make the *Guinness Book of World Records*. Claudette began to reminisce heavily about her childhood.

* * * *

When I thought of all the men my mom went through, I decided to set my sights on having only one man in my life, my husband. The only reverence my family had on Sunday was imposed. They didn't sell liquor on Sundays; that's the only reason my mom didn't buy it. But she made sure she bought enough on Saturday so she wouldn't run out. I hated when my mom drank, and I told myself that I never would. It had nothing to do with the Bible. I just saw what it did to her, and I was having no part.

I really loved my mom. She did her best. I never doubted that she loved me because she told me often. She showed affection. But when she drank, it's like she became another person. Not only did she show me affection, she showed affection to everybody. It made me so sad. My younger sister, on the other hand, never seemed to be affected by what my mom did. She didn't care.

We were so poor, and I never found out why. I just knew my mom didn't work. How well do I remember the times I had to go to the corner store with food stamps; she never sent my sister.

This one particular time, I waited until the store was empty before I took our milk, bread, and other items to the counter. While I was waiting for the store to clear, I just pretended I was looking around. It was all so embarrassing. To spend $2.30, I had to watch the man tear out a two-dollar stamp and a one-dollar stamp, and then give me a seventy-cent due bill on a sheet of paper. Just as he was writing the due bill, other customers *had* to come into the store. They all stood there while he asked my mom's name again. I had to repeat our address, only to have him find it and say in a very nice voice: "Don't forget to tell your mom she had a balance last month. She's a good lady. I know she'll pay—let's see, her balance is $5.50. Should I put this seventy cents on the bill? Then she'll only owe $4.80." I could only shamefully shake my head yes.

After that, Mr. Brown handed me the brown paper bag. I squeezed past the people with my head down, wishing I could just disappear. That day, I determined that my life would be different. I vowed never to be on welfare, and I would never make my daughter go to the corner store every day of her life to buy cigarettes and pop and milk, while I just sat on the porch and smoked.

I shouldn't have disliked Mr. Brown. I don't know what we would've done without him. It seemed like our food stamps ran out every month. Mr. Brown was a kind man, and he didn't have to keep accounts for the people in the neighbor-hood. He could've just told everyone no. He and his family kept food on lots of people's tables during the lean years.

After that incident, I had to go back to the store without money, and I was dreading asking Mr. Brown to put it on my mom's bill because we still hadn't paid the $4.80 we owed. Just as Mr. Brown pulled out the book to write my purchase down, Ruby, the girl who lived two doors from me, walked up to the line. Up until that day, we never talked. I think it had something to do with the way my mom lived.

Ruby was the last person I wanted to see me getting food on credit. Mr. Brown pulled out his shoe box. As usual, it seemed like a lifetime before he found my mom's name. He obviously didn't have them listed in alphabetical order. And it took him forever to add and post what we owed. I was so nervous with Ruby standing next to me that I began to put one foot on top of the other, fidgeting like a toddler who couldn't keep still.

Ruby's mom was known in the neighborhood as a "churchgoing woman" who didn't hang around with the unruly crowd. She and Ruby went to church every Sunday. They would pass our house and on the days I would be up on the porch, our eyes would meet. But I would drop mine before I could read hers. She always looked nice. It was like they didn't belong in our neighborhood.

Finally, Mr. Brown told me I could go and then I heard a voice say, "Wait for me." It was Ruby calling out to me. I nodded and wondered if she was going to ask me how I was able to buy groceries with no money. As I stood trying to come up with something, I heard her say, "Mr. Brown, my mom wants you to put this on her account."

I thought to myself: *What? Ruby and her mom have an account, too? Naw, not Ruby. They couldn't have an account— could they?* I guess my eyes were still wide in disbelief when

Ruby came and put her arm in my arm and propelled me through the door. "Don't you just hate coming to the store having to ask for credit?" Ruby laughed.

"Yes, I would've never known that you and your mom got food on credit."

"The whole neighborhood practically has an account with Mr. Brown."

"It doesn't bother you?" I replied.

"Nope! 'Cause when I grow up, I'll be paying for other people's food. When you have hope in God, you know this is only temporary. That's what my momma tells me. Our pastor also says that we shouldn't allow our current state to define our future."

"I wish I went to church."

"Come go with us on Sunday."

"Your mom won't mind?"

"What? Mind—she'll be happy you're coming."

That was the beginning of my turnaround. I went to church, got saved, and never missed a Sunday until I graduated from high school. I tried to get my mom and sister to come with me, but they wouldn't have any of it. Thank God my mom didn't stop me from going.

I accepted Jesus as Lord when I was fifteen, thanks to Ruby and her mom. I'm forever thankful to God that He sent Ruby along. What I thought would be one of the most embarrassing times in my life turned out to be the best.

After I graduated high school, my mom died of cirrhosis of the liver. In other words, she drank herself to death.

I went to live with her sister when she died, and my younger sister went to live with my grandmother. I immediately found out why my mom and her sister never got along. They were like night and day.

It turned out that my aunt was like Ruby's mom. She went to church on Sundays and in the middle of the week. My grandmother and my aunt didn't get along either. I later found out that it was because my grandmother was more like my mom.

Thank God my grandmother felt she was too old to be tied down with two granddaughters—especially me, because I had just graduated from school.

I tried to keep in touch with Ruby for a while, but nobody had a phone. So I only saw Ruby when we went to see my grandmother, which wasn't often. Then Ruby's mom got a really good job and moved out of the neighborhood. I never saw Ruby after that, but I found myself praying for her often because I was thankful that she introduced me to Jesus.

My aunt got me a part-time job at Crowley's Department Store. I worked twenty hours a week, and she made me enroll in Wayne County Community College. Although I never told anyone—and I was ashamed just thinking about it—my life got better after my mom died. Most people that I talked to who lost their moms would cry and say that their quality of life went down. Not me. I learned how to be a lady through my crisis and contrary to what I thought, Ruby's mom wasn't the only woman who didn't drink. Lots of women didn't drink. But living in a situation where I was surrounded by a particular group, I just thought that was the way the whole world lived.

It was my aunt who began to talk to me about family curses. She said alcoholism and unemployment were curses in our family. Because my grandmother ran numbers, my mom was never motivated to work. My aunt moved away from my grandmother right after high school. She knew she didn't want to live like they did. She quoted Galatians 3:13 to me, which talks about being redeemed from the curse through Jesus. I really do thank God somebody had some sense and broke the curse! After staying with my aunt for a year, I made a decision to be more like her than my mom.

* * * *

Looking back on those times, Claudette made peace with how her mother raised her. But she acknowledged that her aunt helped her to get on a better path in life. And although she didn't feel it was a story worth repeating, somehow she did—in her own way. History often can be unkind, and for Claudette it was.

She hated what her mother did and was able to be redeemed from it, but she couldn't figure out why she did the same thing. It was a mystery to her how she could fall in a trap that she loathed coming up. Through her experiences, she learned that the Word of God is true. But the possibility of overriding His Word and the counsel of Holy Spirit also factored in—she did both.

If only she had been brought up like Lenda and Quintella—maybe she would've made better choices. To her, they had it made. But as bad as Claudette perceived her life to be, she saw Karen's as worse. Some of the things Karen had shared with Claudette made her jaw drop. Deep down, she knew that was the reason she got along better with Karen— they simply had more in common than Quintella and Lenda.

So she also picked up on the circle within the circle of their close-knit friendship—Karen and Claudette, and Lenda and Quintella. Since *she* noticed it, she wondered if they did, too. She even wondered if she gave herself away by getting quiet when they talked about "the affair" at dinner.

She was so tired of hiding the truth. And her thoughts continued to reflect that notion: *You would think if we were really as close as we think we are, we could share something like this with one another. I guess we really aren't as close as I thought. How can you say that you're friends but hide things from one another?*

Claudette, you're thinking too much—go to bed.

Chapter Eight

Lenda was really irritated, and she didn't trust herself to talk. Everything was bothering her. She was mad at her brother, again! She longed for this cycle to be over. In annoyance, she thought to herself: *Some day off! A trip to Jackson Penitentiary.* She had just prayed for God to restore the relationship, but driving out there when she had plans to get organized for her trips was bothering her more than in the past. Not to mention she was going to have to call and cancel the nail appointment she made for herself after Karen's comment because she forgot that she wouldn't be back in time.

"He needs to know he's loved," her mother reminded her days prior. But Lenda's thoughts went in the opposite direction: *No, what he needed to know years ago was to stay away from troublemakers 'cause they cause you to ruin your life and others, as well!* That's what Lenda needed him to know.

This day found her in an unforgiving mood. *My son also needs to know that he's loved,* Lenda thought. She was feeling like his dad always had him when she wanted to spend time with him. Holy Spirit quickly reminded her that she should be glad that her son's dad was taking an active part in his life. "Besides, he's at that stage where male influence is key. He'll be fine; it's you who needs a touch right now," she heard Holy Spirit say.

It wasn't just her brother that was bothering her. Her mother's perfume didn't help. It smelled like she paid two dollars a gallon for it. And on this day of all days, she put on half a gallon. Lenda cracked the window, trying to breathe. Her mother's response was predictable, "Baby, it's chilly outside. Let yo' window back up."

Lenda contemplated going off. She wanted to tell her that if she could wash the smell of the perfume off, then the window would go back up! The more respectful reply won her mental battle. "Sorry Mom, I don't want you to be uncomfortable."

Some obvious sarcasm remained in her tone, and her mother came back, "Is everything OK, baby? You seem irritated. Have I done something wrong?"

Lenda lied because if she told the truth, it would be like the surge of a Category 5 hurricane. She knew the intensity of her anger would knock her mother over. If she had her way, she'd say, "Yes, you've done something wrong—you've made me bring you to this godforsaken place today and all the other days. I'm sick and tired of driving you up here to see yo' son who decided to break the law! And while we're talking, can you ease up on the perfume, because I can't stand the smell?" She also wanted to tell her mother how selfish she was for monopolizing her Saturdays. But once again, she bit her lip.

"Sorry Mom, I've had a rough week. They've let so many people go that it's hard on those who are left to do all the work. I'm really tired and irritated—not at you, just about work. I'm sorry!" she lied again, but she surprised herself by managing a real smile.

"Lenda, guess who I saw yesterday?"

"Mom, I haven't the faintest idea. Who did you see?"

"Whatchamacallit's daughter!"

Lenda's mind was reeling: *Here we go again! Not only do I have to put up with unwanted banter, now I have to play Guess Who? Get a grip, Lenda; this is what happens when you go days without your Bible study and time with God.* "Mom—who is whatchamacallit's daughter?" Lenda asked in a surly voice.

"You know, whatchamacallit who lived across the street from us when we lived on Hunt Street."

"Mom—do you know how long ago we lived on Hunt? I don't even think the houses are still standing."

"Yes they are. I had your sister take me over there the other day when we left the grocery store, and houses are still there. The one we lived in looks bad—but it's still standing. You still didn't answer my question, baby."

"Let's see, whatchamacallit! I'll do what you used to tell us to do as children—let me put on my thinking cap. I know who you're talking about—that's whatchamajig's cousin—the one who lived on that street about five blocks from us." As soon as she said it, she wished she could've taken back the words. She didn't know why she was being so mean to her mother; it was so unlike her.

"I won't bother you anymore, baby—I see you don't want to talk."

"That's not it, but I don't know who whatchamacallit is no more than you know who whatchamajig's cousin is. I only said that to prove a point, and I'm sorry." Reaching over, Lenda grabbed her hand and lovingly squeezed it. Ethel was too sweet and loving to get the brunt of her frustration. "Lord, I've never talked to my mom like this. What's wrong with me?" she silently asked Holy Spirit.

Trying to lighten the mood, Lenda started again, "Listen, I have this CD that I got from church; I think it'll bless you. This was a Sunday I missed, but everyone was talking about how good it was. Shall we enjoy it together?"

"I was looking forward to talking with *you*. We haven't talked in three days," her mother whined. Wisdom told Lenda to be quiet on that because if she opened her mouth, she would probably regret anything she said.

"Mom, we'll talk coming back. I really want you to listen to this CD; I think you'll like it."

Lenda was such a hypocrite. But the only thing she knew was that it would substitute for small talk, which she had no desire to engage in. So in went the CD.

The minister's voice was instantly soothing. Yes, this was what she needed. Every now and then, Lenda could just look in her mom's direction and smile. This would make everybody happy—not!

About fifteen minutes into the CD, something caught Lenda's attention. She reached for the knob on the dash to slightly turn the volume up. "So you see, my brothers and sisters," the pastor pleaded, "many of us are quite familiar with this verse, but we lack the discipline to do it. The Word says that we are supposed to forgive seventy times seven. *Ahhhhh*, y'all don't believe me. Turn in your Bibles to Matthew 18:22. We want and expect God to forgive us, but we don't want to forgive anyone. That's not Bible. Everybody knows Mark 11, verses twenty-three and twenty-four, but you play dumb when you get to verse twenty-five, which says, *'And when ye stand praying, forgive, if ye have ought against any: that your Father also which is in heaven may forgive you your trespasses.'* This tells me that if I can't forgive my brother, help me y'all, God won't forgive me!" he bellowed.

Lenda went to reach for the knob to turn off the CD. Perhaps talking would be better, but her mother grabbed her hand. "No, baby. Don't turn this off now. I'm really enjoying it.

I think I'm going to like this CD."

"I thought you wanted to talk?" Lenda asked. She could feel the smirk on her mother's face, as she obviously chose the wrong CD. She had no idea that the pastor was going to be talking about forgiveness. She guessed that her plan was backfiring and that God had a sense of humor. Here she was, thinking the CD would help her not to deal with idle chitchat from her mother; she clearly hadn't bargained for a lesson on forgiveness.

Sitting in the seat next to Lenda was a grateful mother. She hoped the message would be the tool God used to soften Lenda's heart. "Lord, she needs a touch from You," she prayed silently under her breath. "Soften her heart toward her brother, and please work on the sister relationship while You're at it."

Lenda could hear her mother praying under her breath. She decided to let the CD play.

Forgiveness. It wasn't a subject Lenda wanted to hear about, because she still struggled with forgiving her brother for the pain he caused—not to mention the mental and physical toll it was taking on their mom.

It was a long ride to the prison. The hour drive felt like triple that, but she could feel herself calming down. God's Word has always had that effect on her.

* * * *

Against Lenda's will, she decided to go in when they arrived—the pastor's message had done a job on her. Prison security always made Lenda feel violated. The search, the questions, and the atmosphere—she hated them all. She could drone on about how she detested the process, but she knew there was no point in doing so.

Lenda didn't know what was worse—the sight of her brother in prison garb or sitting in the visitor lounge being forced to listen to unsolicited conversations, many of which would certainly be X-rated if ratings were required.

Her heart ached for the men who filled the jails. Good men gone bad. In that moment, Holy Spirit said, "You can sympathize with other men, but not extend that same support to your brother?" Lenda was convicted. *I guess I just expected more from my brother.* She thought about First Corinthians 15:33, which talked about how evil associations corrupt good character. This was a Scripture she made her son memorize at an early age. The last time she had him recite it, he playfully told her, "Ma, I got it. Can we move on to some other Scriptures now? I'm not going to hang around with people you wouldn't want me to—I promise!"

Ernest had so much going for him. He had a heart of gold, which is why he was behind bars. He just didn't know how to say no, and he couldn't let go of his childhood friends. Even though they had grown apart, he still continued to go see them on a regular basis. Their last joy ride proved to be the final straw, landing him behind bars.

Lenda heard the familiar sound of iron hitting iron. She didn't have the heart to look right then; she was still dealing with the message on forgiveness. She glanced inconspicuously at her mom out of the corner of her eye and decided the trip was well worth the smile on her mom's face. That's the thing about mothers—no matter what their children have done, they seem to stand by them.

Past visits only brought contempt when Ernest appeared. But this time was different. When he entered the room with his usual smile, tears began to fill Lenda's eyes. This was her baby brother. The one she would tattle on. The one who tried to protect her. The one who would give her the last bite of his

Popsicle. The little boy she took back and forth to school and made sure no one messed with him. This was the teenager who made birthday cards for her, expressing his forever love.

Before she knew it, memories flooded in and the dam of her emotions broke, causing Lenda to let out all the tears that she long held inside. She didn't care that she was being stared at. Nor did it matter that her mom was crying, too. Her brother only stood by her, rubbing her back and repeating over and over, "Sis, it's OK."

The only thing Lenda remembered was her plea to Holy Spirit to help her get control of herself. As she stood and wrapped her arms around her brother, she managed a pitiful "I'm sorry" between the heaves and tears.

Usually, Lenda clock-watched when they came to visit. Not this time. Once her emotions were in check, she sincerely wanted to know how her brother was really doing.

"So, how are they treating you?"

Ernest was shocked, but he tried to conceal his feelings. He wasn't used to his big sister coming in anymore. And when she did, she just sat in the chair and glared at him as if to say, "I hate you." This person in front of him was somebody else.

"Well, I'm being treated better than I treated myself."

"How's the appeal going?" Lenda asked, with true concern.

"I'm waiting for the legal process to work."

The rest of the visit was quite pleasant. For once, they talked about old times and when they were little kids. As they talked, Lenda held Ernest's hand and rubbed it. She couldn't remember the last time she had touched her brother.

And Ernest couldn't believe that his sister touched him. If she only knew how much he needed her touch. He so loved her. He thought to himself: *A lot of people think people who are locked up don't have feelings. Well, we do. We hurt. We cry. We beat ourselves up for past mistakes. And we yearn for a touch.*

"Hey, before y'all go, I've got to tell you this. The other day they served us chicken, right? They never serve chicken, and I thought about Mom."

Before Ernest could complete the story, he and Lenda were laughing until tears were running down their faces. Their mother wasn't laughing. It's never funny when kids remember something their parents did that was totally embarrassing now that they are grown. Parents do the best they know at the time.

"Lenda, to this day, when I tell people that story, they don't believe me."

"I know. I can see the scene replay as we speak."

More laughter.

"You know Mom was mad at you, and you knew that was a girls outing! She told you more than once to leave, but nah, you had to keep asking for some chicken."

"Y'all was sitting at the table throwing down on fried chicken, so why not throw a brother a bone?" Ernest said, as the laughter continued.

"See, that was the problem. When you yelled, 'Can't you throw a brother a bone?' Mom told you to leave her alone."

"But I wanted some chicken!" Ernest laughed.

"You got some chicken alright, didn't you?" Lenda could hardly finish the sentence without laughing. Their mother could only painfully sit as they retold the same story; she wanted to disappear.

"Yeah, when she started yelling, 'YOU WANT SOME CHICKEN…YOU WANT SOME CHICKEN?!' I should've known nothing good was about to happen," Ernest said while laughing.

"Ernest, when I saw her go to the freezer, I thought she was getting some ice or something for the Kool-Aid. When she started throwing frozen chickens out the door at you, I thought: Mom has *lost* it!"

"Look sis," Ernest sat on the edge of his chair, and his body language said it was on. "All I heard was 'YOU WANT SOME CHICKEN' and instead of following my instinct and running, I was stupid enough to walk toward the house, thinking she was inviting me in to eat some hot chicken with y'all.

"When that frozen chicken came flying past my head, just missing me, I thought: You better run, fool. But before I could turn, here comes another frozen chicken, and she was still hollering, 'YOU WANT SOME CHICKEN—HERE'S SOME CHICKEN!' Listen, I started running, and I didn't stop until I couldn't see our house anymore."

Hysterically laughing, Lenda said, "Ernest, we tried to stop her, but she was like a possessed woman, determined to empty the freezer on your head."

Though Ethel was uncomfortable watching them make fun of her, she was filled with joy because for the first time in years, her children were actually talking and laughing. What a sight for sore eyes!

* * * *

The ride back home was good. Lenda couldn't remember when she had enjoyed visiting her brother. Normally, she was depressed. But it was the best visit she had since he had been incarcerated. Lenda looked at her mom and really felt bad about the earlier perfume thoughts. She was glad she could smell her mom. So many of the people she knew had already lost their moms. She was blessed to have hers. She made a mental decision to work on that critical spirit when it came to other people—especially her family.

"You OK, Mom?" Lenda asked, with a genuine smile.

"Couldn't be better! This is the first time you and your brother had a real conversation—and that picture warms any mother's heart."

Lenda smiled in agreement with her mom because she knew deep down inside that she was telling the truth. The rest of the ride home was enjoyable, as they both shared memories and talked about the wonderful future that lay ahead for their family. The only way was up for them! The curse was broken. Hallelujah!

When they got closer to home, Lenda stopped at Boston Market and got carryouts for both of them. After getting her mom settled, Lenda kissed her good-bye and began the short ride home.

* * * *

Lenda loved her home, but the neighborhood was changing. A couple of people had lost their homes, and the city wasn't doing its job on the outside upkeep. Other neighbors weren't as conscientious as most, so their homes weren't kept to the standard she was used to. But she couldn't move—not now—it wasn't the time nor was the money right. Besides, she was close to her mom and if needed, she could be there in ten minutes. That meant a lot, and it gave her comfort.

Once the key was in the door, she paused to check the mailbox. The food, mail, and paper were too much to juggle. Something had to fall, and it wouldn't be her food. As the mail scattered in the foyer, Lenda used her foot to close the door.

There she made it to the kitchen counter where she unloaded the bags. The extra gravy she asked for on her mashed potatoes now covered the bottom of the bag. *Better in the bag than on my hips,* she thought, looking at the mess.

She found herself standing in the middle of the kitchen and forgot for a moment why she was standing there instead of making her way to the dining room to eat. *That's it—something to drink. Iced tea.*

She had made some iced tea earlier in the week. As Lenda opened the door to the fridge, she stared in disgust. "Why does he do that, Lord? Why does my son drink all the iced tea and leave three drops in the pitcher so I can't say, 'You drank it all.' WHY?"

She was determined to keep her joy; after all, this was one of the best trips to see Ernest, and she was not about to let iced tea, dropped mail, or anything else steal her joy. And the mail—she decided to go pick it up. She thought again—it could wait until she ate.

After eating, she remembered the mail but stopped in the bathroom to run a bubble bath. As she looked at her various bath gels, she was having a hard time choosing between Trésor by Lancôme or Japanese Cherry Blossom from Bath & Body Works. She turned on the hot water and poured in some Trésor; then she stopped and began to lavish the Japanese Cherry Blossom. She took a deep breath. The smell was sweet. *Yep, that's it—Japanese Cherry Blossom mixed with Trésor wins.* She laughed and continued on toward the front door.

As she bent down to pick up the mail, Holy Spirit told her, "You left your keys in the door." Mouth opened, Lenda bolted to the door, not even questioning her Best Friend. There in the cylinder were her keys. She had been in the house for thirty minutes or more. Lenda looked up and raised her hands, "Thank You, Holy Spirit, for protecting me. What would I do without You?"

"Just doing My job, which I love," was the response she heard.

* * * *

The scented bubble bath was just what she needed to top off what turned out to be a great day. As she got under the covers and began to think about the events that took place, she was pleased. Her prayers were being answered, and she felt like the healing had begun. But then her thoughts turned again to the broken marriage that continued to bother her. She still couldn't grasp why she couldn't let it go. She wasn't bitter. She just didn't understand how two people who really loved each other ended up divorced.

"Lenda, don't go there…" she heard her voice warn. "Enjoy what happened today. You can tackle this issue another day." But as hard as she tried, she couldn't avoid going there.

It was love at first sight.

Love?

What did love have to do with it? She never asked her ex if he loved God. That never crossed her mind. She was only interested in him loving her. However, she did ask if he believed in God. When he said yes, that was all she needed to hear. Well, she found out too late that the devil himself believes in God. *No, next time around, believing will not be enough. "Are you submitted to God?" will be the question.*

It never crossed her mind to ask, "How often do you go to church?" Not Lenda. Her marriage was one of those founded on the following principle: "He's so fine, and he wants me." In retrospect, she wondered why she thought someone wouldn't want her. Simple—low self-esteem and worrying about not finding someone else causes a person to settle. Had she really, really known God, she would have known that she was a good thing!

She didn't know the Scripture back then that talked about being unequally yoked. Lenda wondered out loud: "What's that Scripture in Hosea? Help me, Holy Spirit. Where is it? Oh yeah, Hosea 4:6 says, *'My people are destroyed for lack of knowledge…'* Yep, I lacked knowledge 'cause I didn't even know a Scripture existed about being unequally yoked. But I BET I KNOW IT NOW! I EVEN MEMORIZED THE AMPLIFIED VERSION!" Lenda began to recite the Scripture (Second Corinthians 6:14–18) with rhythm, while her fingers pretended to be feet dancing:

> *Do not be unequally yoked with unbelievers [do not make mismated alliances with them or come under a different yoke with them, inconsistent with your faith]. For what partnership have right living and right standing with God with iniquity and lawlessness? Or how can light have fellowship with darkness? What harmony can there be between Christ and Belial [the devil]? Or what has a believer in common with an unbeliever? What agreement [can there be between] a temple of God and idols? For we are the temple of the living God; even as God said, I will dwell in and with and among them and will walk in and with and among them, and I will be their God, and they shall be My people. So, come out from among [unbelievers], and separate (sever) yourselves from them, says the Lord, and touch not [any] unclean thing; then I will receive you kindly and treat you with favor, And I will be a Father to you, and you shall be My sons and daughters, says the Lord Almighty.*

Lenda said it once, she said it twice, and she was going to say it a third time when she heard a voice say, "Alright already, give it a break." Funny thing is, she didn't know if it was her voice or the voice of Holy Spirit!

"Well, that tirade felt good!" she went on. And as hard as she tried to avoid it, her thoughts took her into full-fledged remembrance of her relationship with her former husband.

* * * *

But we *were* unequally yoked, and the marriage was destroyed. We both were professionals with good jobs and seemingly good heads on our shoulders. Now that I look back, I married thinking I could change my ex. But it didn't happen.

As the pastor said on the CD today, "Nobody can change anybody but God." Mistake number one. Then I ignored so many warning signs—mistakes two, three, and four. I loved the movies—he hated them. I liked going out to dinner—he didn't. I was a tither—he wasn't, and that was a bone of contention from day one. Oh the list mounts. He wanted his money, and I wanted to put all the money in one pot. After all, we were one—why separate the money? We had a laundry list of issues.

Yes, Holy Spirit. You tried to warn me that he was not the one. But love will make you do foolish things. Mom tried. Grandma tried and Daddy tried, but I decided that I knew more than them all, so I thought. I remember when Daddy first met Edward, his final words to him were, "You mess with my daughter, and I'll walk through hell with gasoline drawers on to find you! And when I find you, I will kill you!"

I think that's what made me run toward Edward rather than away from him. He wasn't scared of my father like the other boys. Most of my boyfriends were afraid of my dad, but Edward's reply to the hell thing was, "Baby, he won't have to kill me; I'd kill myself if I did anything to hurt you. I love you too much to hurt you. And if I was ever that stupid, I deserve to be killed." I feel like throwing up just thinking about that "tired" conversation.

So there I was, five years into the marriage, with one son, and the verbal abuse began. I've never been called so many names by someone who was supposed to be in love with me. He treated me like the wife he hated rather than the women he loved. He found fault with everything. He began to drink, stay out late—and at times, he wouldn't come home. It was like someone threw an atomic bomb in the middle of my marriage. While my son and I survived the attack, we're still feeling the effects years later.

But then I had my faults, too. I felt like if he wasn't giving respect, he shouldn't get it. Two wrongs never make a right. As I look back, I was too independent. No man wants to feel like he's not needed. But what do you do when a man does nothing? He refused to clean. He didn't take out the garbage. He was always too busy to shovel the snow. I'd shop, and he would be home when I returned. But he never came out to help me bring in the groceries. So I did everything myself. It was like I was a single mom. I never wanted a divorce. But at the time, it seemed like the only answer.

Just then, Lenda heard a voice, and she knew it was the voice of Holy Spirit: "Let it go. You just received healing with your brother—enjoy the victory. Salvage the rest of this day— allow peace to prevail."

You're right, Holy Spirit! I need to move beyond this! If I can mend fences with my brother, why am I allowing a dead relationship to control me? Holy Spirit, how can I move beyond this? Why do I keep thinking about this foolishness? Why can't I forgive myself for a mistake I made years ago? Well, at least it doesn't hurt any longer. It just seems like I can't shake thinking about it sometimes.

What...it's been ten years and counting since I took the

vow of celibacy, and it's one of the best decisions I've made thus far. Yeah, I learned the hard way that a nice, fine man with a good job does not equal a good husband and father. He'd better *know* and love Jesus. He better beat me going to church every Sunday. Forget this "picking up a guy" madness. Let him be hungry for God. And at some point in his life, he should've volunteered at church.

Yeah, I got knowledge now. I refuse to be destroyed again!

Chapter Nine

Claudette didn't want to get up, but she knew staying in bed was not an option. "Lord, if this wasn't one of the biggest shopping days in October, I would crawl right back in bed and pull the covers over my head," she grumbled.

It had been some year for her. Claudette would cry all the time whenever she was home. It was no wonder that she enjoyed reading about David in the Bible. He reminded her of herself; she could identify with him saying that his tears had been his meat day and night, while continuing to cry out to God and ask, "Where were You?" Upon rising, she got her Bible to find that very Scripture. Claudette remembered reading it just a couple of days ago; she had dog-eared the page.

She went right to Psalm 42:3. "I feel you, David. The tears don't stop. Salty as chips—no nourishment—but I've been eating them for breakfast, lunch, and dinner," she wallowed.

After reading, Claudette made her way into the bathroom. She shuddered to think about what she must look like in the mirror. Well, now she knew. Facing herself, the mirror was unforgiving. Her red hair was all over her head. That's because she didn't take the time to wrap it the night before—she just fell into the bed. Her eyes were swollen with circles. She was a mess. Skin indentations were all over her shoulders because she was so exhausted that she had slept in her bra—she couldn't remember the last time she had done that.

Looking at her reflection in the mirror, she uttered, "I just couldn't stop crying last night. Lord, I don't know when I've bawled so. What's wrong with me? I feel like I'm coming unglued—please help me get it together. I bet Lenda and Queen don't sit around crying about something that happened in the past!

"God, no man, money, or friend can bring me from this pit but You. I've asked for forgiveness thousands of times. When will I ever feel like You have forgiven me? All it takes is for someone to bring up the past and I just lose it. I need You, and I need You right now. I don't want to go to work. I don't want to see or be near people. Please help me."

The tears began to flow once again, and Claudette felt sheer hopelessness. Before she knew it, the toothbrush that was in her hands had fallen into the sink, along with the toothpaste. As her arms dangled in the sink, her body began to heave once again, while the tears continued to fall like confetti at a wedding.

Then she mysteriously felt the sensation of a person's hands under her armpits, tangibly pulling her up. Startled, Claudette looked in the mirror to see who had come into her house—but no one was there. Just when she was sure she had lost her mind, a voice spoke to her and said, "Claudette, you were forgiven five years ago. Why don't you let it go?"

Claudette couldn't explain it, but the peace that had escaped her gradually began to return. It was like someone was pouring warm soothing oil over her, and it was streaming ever so slowly down her hair along her neck, gently rolling down her spine. She thought: *Oh God, can we put this on pause because I don't want to move?*

Her eyes caught another glimpse of herself in the mirror.

This time, she wondered where the woman was whom she had seen only minutes ago. The reflection that stared back at her had a slight smile, one that said, "I have a wonderful secret. The love of my life is here, and I only want to share this moment with Him." The presence of the Lord was so strong in that bathroom. Yes, she had a Man, and His Name was Jesus. And that smile turned into a full-grown grin.

The clock on the wall told her she still had plenty of time, so she jumped at the opportunity to bask in the presence of God. She could feel the loving tug of Holy Spirit. Claudette laughed and said, "Let me at least get my teeth brushed and a shower, please." She felt the impression of Holy Spirit saying, "Hurry up, woman—don't keep Me waiting."

While brushing her teeth, she wondered how she could experience so many emotions before 8:00 a.m. If someone had told her that recovery would come so quickly, she wouldn't have believed it.

The last swish of mouthwash wasn't out of her mouth before she felt the tug again. "Come on, Claudette. We have things to talk about." She hurried to get showered. After drying off and putting on her robe, she allowed herself to be led, as if by the hand, into the bedroom and over to her favorite chair. It sat alongside her little side table that had her Bible and prayer journal on top. This was *their* spot, and she so loved being there. Claudette tried to remember the last time she sat in her special chair to be with the Lord. It seemed like so long ago. But after taking a look in her prayer journal, she saw where it had only been four days.

Claudette was pleasantly surprised. She thought about how weeks used to go by before she would remember to write in her prayer journal. It wasn't that way anymore. She started feeling spiritually dry after a few days. She thought: *What would I do without my prayer journal?* This was Claudette's fifth year faithfully using her journal.

Journaling was therapeutic, and it allowed Claudette to chart her spiritual growth. If she didn't have that record, she would've surely thought more than four days had passed by. But this was one of the many things she could thank Lenda for. She didn't know anything about journaling until Lenda shared with her that she had been journaling for ten years. Claudette could still hear her voice: "How can you keep track of your time with the Lord unless you *journal?*"

What Lenda didn't know was that Claudette didn't need a journal to keep track because she didn't spend time with the Lord—except for at church. But she finally fessed up. Claudette could still see the shock and horror on Lenda's face, despite Lenda trying to hide her feelings about the matter.

Claudette learned right away that Lenda was someone whose eyes and facial expressions always revealed her true thoughts. She could say yes with her mouth, but her eyes would say, "Why did you ask me something so stupid?" So she knew that if she wanted the real answer from Lenda simply to look at her eyes.

The day Lenda challenged Claudette to get a prayer journal was the day she embarked on a remarkable ride—and Claudette loved every minute of it. Though she still wasn't where she wanted to be, Claudette's walk with God was beginning to escalate. Underneath it all, she knew that was to be expected since she had been enjoying the company of Holy Spirit. It also didn't hurt that she had Lenda, a good, Christian friend who was further along spiritually, because that even helped to take her higher in God.

Turning to her Scripture for the day, Claudette chuckled as she read the text because it was so like Holy Spirit to take her to First Peter 5:7: *"Casting all your care upon him; for he careth for you."* Claudette repeated the Scripture three times. She spoke it, sang it, and then did a dramatization of it. All this so that she could recall the Scripture at lunch and then again at dinner. If she was successful, she would print it on a five-by-seven card when she got home and file it in her box of "remembered Scriptures."

Claudette's box of remembered Scriptures usually got pulled out once a month. If she couldn't remember a Scripture, she would take its card out and put it in a "learn-again box." It gave her much pleasure to file away a card. It was her way of saying, "devil, you no longer have me by the throat. I am slowly putting God's Word in my heart and one day, I will have the whole Bible memorized! Glory to God!"

It blew Claudette's mind to see God's love. Her whole study was about forgiving herself. She was reminded of how His Word declares in Psalm 103:12: *"As far as the east is from the west, so far hath he removed our transgressions from us."* And like a little child, Claudette approvingly began to pump her fist in the air, making circles while yelling, "Yes!" It felt so good to memorize Scripture. At least for her it did. Those Scriptures brought healing and peace when the enemy attacked her mind. She understood why God wants His children to hide the Word in their hearts.

Her thoughts went to Lenda and Quintella. What she was doing was probably no big deal to them. She figured that they must have recited chapters of the Word when they got up in the morning. She thought about how she didn't grow up with a silver Bible in her mouth like they did. Until she met Ruby, she hadn't seen the inside of a Bible or a church. So for Claudette to actually sit in the presence of God and enjoy it brought her much satisfaction.

"Holy Spirit, give me my high five!" Claudette said emphatically, raising her hand to give a high five to that certain Someone in the room. Like Lenda, that Someone was her Man, her Friend, her Confidant, her Everything. And He was now trying to get her moving so she wouldn't be late for work.

Claudette was glad she finally listened to Holy Spirit and disconnected from her past. If she hadn't, it was clear she was about to go to the very place emotionally where she never wanted to visit again. Her previous bout with despair had done enough damage.

"Yes, Holy Spirit, I can go to work now," Claudette said with a smile. Being in God's Word and His presence had the power to make her go to work when she really didn't feel like it. "But before I leave Your presence, Holy Spirit, I must tell you again that You are a special Man to me!"

As Claudette began to dress, she reminded herself to wear comfortable shoes. She knew it was going to be a busy day, but a great day, because all day long she'd hear the cash register ring, "Cha-ching! Cha-ching!"

She quickly checked the time and realized that she was probably going to be late. Without wasting another moment, she reached for her black pants and thought again—she decided to be predictable and put on her red pants with the red tweed turtleneck. After all, it *was* Sweetest Day—and it was going to be a "sweet day!"

Chapter Ten

The mall was on jam, and Claudette made up considerable time on the freeway. Lights were in her favor, so she didn't end up being too late.

"Shoot! Somebody got my spot. I'll just have to find another one," Claudette said in disappointment. She parked in the first space she saw and then took a slight jog to her store. Since the mall had already opened, she decided to go in through the front of the store. As she got closer, she squinted her eyes. Claudette thought: *Is that man waiting for me? God, I hope he's not here to start some mess. It's too early for all that.* Drawing even closer, not only did she know the man who was waiting for her, he was one of her favorite customers. If no one else bought his wife a Sweetest Day present, she could depend on Mr. Lee.

"What you doin' comin' to work late?!" Mr. Lee demanded.

"What happened to 'Good morning Miss Howard. How are you?' Don't have to be those exact words—just something similar," Claudette teased. "And just why are you out so early, Mr. Lee?"

"'Cause I wanted to beat all of your other customers who'll be closing the mall today, trying to make up for bad behavior.

You still didn't answer my question. Why are you late for work?"

"Is that why *you're* here, 'cause you've been bad?"

"You know better than that. My Rosetta has a good man, and my daughter's got a good father. What's wrong with your eyes? Look like you been crying all night!"

"Mr. Lee, you don't miss anything, do you?" Claudette said, as she fumbled with the lock on the security grille.

"I don't miss much. What's wrong, you can't get it unlocked? Y'all lock this place up like Fort Knox."

Claudette chose to let that last comment pass and decided it would be in her best interest if she got him in and out. The less conversation, the less time she'd have to spend explaining her eyes, because she knew Mr. Lee was going to fire questions at her like a machine gun.

After looking around for a bit, Mr. Lee ended up spending $857.39. Once his sale was complete, he looked at Claudette with the concern that a father would have for his daughter.

"You never answered my question about your eyes. You been crying?"

"Mr. Lee, I really need to get ready to assist my other customers. I thank you for your support *and* for your concern. May you and Mrs. Lee have a ball this evening!"

"In other words, you're not going to answer the question?" he continued to prod.

Claudette slightly turned her head, pretending she was assessing the store to see if anything needed her attention. She then turned back to Mr. Lee, and she smiled without saying anything.

"So, you have a date tonight?" he asked.

"Yep," Claudette replied.

"Is it with Jesus again this year?"

"Nope."

"Oh," he said, seeming surprised. "You got a real date?"

"Yep."

"Can I ask his name?"

"What if I said no?"

"I'd ask anyway."

"Mr. Lee, you don't bite your tongue, do you?"

"Why bite my tongue? When I want to know something—
I just ask. What's his name?"

"His Name is Holy Spirit." Mr. Lee rolled his eyes up in
his head as if to say, "Girl, you need a life." And Claudette
continued, "I'm going to pick up my favorite Chinese food
after work, go home and pull out my beautiful dishes, light
a candle, put my Chinese food on my plate, and sit up and
enjoy Holy Spirit."

"Miss Howard, can you step over here for a moment?"
Claudette was thankful that he wasn't spreading her business
by allowing incoming customers to hear their conversation.
When she stepped over to him, Mr. Lee continued, "I've
been coming to your store since you opened it almost five
years ago. I believe you know by now that I truly like you as
a person. And would you agree that we have a relationship,
somewhat?"

"Yes, Mr. Lee."

"Look, you're a nice-looking young lady. How old are you,
about forty-five?"

"Yes, Mr. Lee—forty-five exactly."

"I'm a religious man myself, but I don't believe God meant for you to be by yourself. You haven't had a date in all the years I've been coming to your store. It's time for you to get out and meet people."

If this was anyone else, Claudette would be fuming. He didn't know anything about her personal life, so there was no way for him to know if she got out or not. But he was a nice man and his intentions were good, so Claudette decided to share some details of her personal life with him. As a rule, she wouldn't tell anyone who wasn't close to her anything personal.

"Mr. Lee, Holy Spirit is a wonderful Friend of mine. He helps me to put up my displays. He tells me what looks good together and what doesn't. I enjoy His company, and He enjoys mine. See, I'm not like some ladies. I have a Man, and He's good to me. So when I say I've got a Man, I really mean it! The two of us will enjoy the evening just fine."

What was so surprising to Mr. Lee was that she really believed what he thought was crazy talk.

"Mr. Lee, let me ask you a question. Do you believe in Holy Spirit?"

"Of course I do!" he indignantly answered. "I love God. I love Jesus, His Son, and I'm well aware of Holy Spirit and His job as our Helper. He's also our Intercessor and Comforter. But you take it to another level, calling Him your Man like you intimate with Him!"

"We do have intimate fellowship—but not the type you're talking about. Do you talk to Him?"

"Of course I do—I asked Him just this morning if I had to spend all this money on my wife."

"What did He tell you?"

"He said, 'Yes.' And He said, 'If you ask Me again, I'll double the amount.' See, I left out the part where I asked Him several times because I didn't want to buy anything this year. Holy Spirit and I just had a long talk a couple of days ago when I told him about my wife acting up. He then ignored what I said about my wife and began to address the things I was doing wrong. You'll like this one—He even told me to come here to buy her clothes, because I was going to Nordstrom—they're having a sale. But He told me to come here 'cause you needed the sale, not Nordstrom. What you got to say now?!"

"I'm glad He told you to come here," Claudette laughed, while gently touching him on the arm. "Don't you see what I mean? You have a Buddy to talk to, and I have a Man. That's all I'm saying. I so enjoy His company, and He enjoys mine."

"Well, when you put it like that—I guess it's OK. I'm still going to pray that He sends you a real man. I'll also pray that my sale will be the lowest sale of the day!"

"Oh Mr. Lee, what would I do without you?" Claudette gave him a playful hug and walked him to the front of the store. "Now I have other customers vying for my attention. See you next time."

Mr. Lee couldn't leave without some parting words. "You never answered my first question, but I just want to leave you with this: God's Word says in Psalm 30:5 that *weeping may endure for a night, but joy cometh in the morning.* Your morning is coming, and the tears that only God sees will dry up. Enjoy your dinner with yo' Man." He let out a laugh and yelled to the rest of the store, "Hey ladies, y'all husbands and boyfriends told me to tell you to spend it all. And to the husbands in here…spend it like you want her to share it!"

Laughter broke out in the store, and Mr. Lee left, continuing to laugh to himself. Claudette looked somewhat embar rassed, but it soon passed.

Once things quieted down, she thought about Mr. Lee and how perceptive it was that he talked about her tears. She scanned the shop to see who she would approach next, but she couldn't help but laugh to herself. People were funny. She knew they would rather see a woman with any man, no matter whom—unemployed or not—as long as she had a man they could see. Holy Spirit doesn't count; if she brings up His Name, she's weird. After all, He's not a real date. "Well, You are to me," Claudette whispered.

As her eyes continued to rove the store, she set out to offer some customer service to those she had neglected. Claudette's eyes landed on another one of her regular customers, Mr. Davis, who was admiring a coat. "Happy Sweetest Day, Mr. Davis. May I help you?"

Chapter Eleven

The last customer finally exited the store. Claudette couldn't remember when business had been so great. She thought: *Folks are lying when they say men don't go all out for Sweetest Day.* Claudette had more men than she could count to come into the store that day. And these were men who talked glowingly about their wives. She was happy to see that love was alive and well.

Claudette smiled, waved good-bye, and couldn't wait to go home. Her feet were screaming "off me, off me."

Not only had it been a good day for her business, it had been a good week, starting with Ken. He had visited the store about a month ago and told Claudette that he wanted to buy Quintella something really special for Sweetest Day. He asked her to contact her buyers and come up with something nice. She sent him some emails of outfits, with jewelry to match. He picked out a gorgeous ensemble.

When Claudette called to say everything was in, he told her, "I'll be there bright and early Monday morning." Being a man of his word, he was her first customer. When he came in to pay, he even gave Claudette a large tip. And she would always remember what he told her. Their conversation was still fresh in her mind.

* * * *

"Good morning Ken—when you say early, you mean it," Claudette said as she gave him a hug.

"Got to get to work, and you know I don't want to be in this store with a bunch of ladies," Ken said.

"Here is the outfit. What do you think?"

"I think my baby will wear it well, and I just might fall in love with her again for the thousandth time."

They both laughed, and Claudette couldn't help but feel a pang of jealousy. But it was a good jealousy. Quintella wasn't superfine, and she was a size 16—not a 6. But her husband adored her! She didn't know many men who came in early to put in special orders for their wives for Sweetest Day.

And Ken seemed to be unaware of the stares he got from other women. Everyone thought he was fine. Women would look at him like, "Who you belong to?" But he never seemed to notice. He truly seemed oblivious to the stares.

It was then that Claudette recommitted to only having a man who would treat her like Ken treated Quintella, like she was the only woman alive. Yeah, Ken set the tone for the week, because his sale alone totaled way more than $800— and he didn't seem to mind spending the money.

Claudette laughed to herself because Ken told her point-blank: "You will never see me in this store on Sweetest Day. If I don't have it by then, she won't get it until later. I'd rather suffer the wrath of Quintella than the last-minute rush for outfits and peace offerings!"

* * * *

Looking around the store and thinking about the day, Claudette could understand why Ken felt the way he felt. "Lord, I'm tired. It's been a good day, but I am tired." She couldn't bear to straighten another rack of clothing. She was such a perfectionist. Anyone coming into the store wouldn't even see what she saw. Everyone always told Claudette what beautiful displays she had.

She looked around the store one last time. *I should change that rack,* Claudette thought. Instead she chose to get her coat, lock up, and leave. "I'll change you tomorrow," she said as if the rack could hear her.

* * * *

From the looks of the parking lot, someone would have thought it was Christmas. Cars were everywhere—Sweetest Day definitely spelled "big business." Unlike some stores that stayed open an extra hour, Claudette closed her store at the regular time. The money wasn't worth the wear and tear on her body.

My car could really use a good wash, she thought. One look at the door on the passenger side told Claudette that she had left the doors unlocked. *I guess I lost my concentration since I was running late.*

After throwing her bags in the car, it was safe to yell, "I'm ready to roll—food, food, here I come! Lord, I can't take another minute, and I'm ready for a hot bath."

"Why is this key not turning?" Claudette asked aloud, shocked that the ignition would not move. She tried turning it from every angle. Still no movement. "What the heck?" After several minutes of trying to turn the ignition on, Claudette gave up.

The parking lot had thinned out a lot. It was no use sitting there any longer. She went back to the mall to call a locksmith.

When Claudette reached the door of the mall, it was still open. "Thank God for small miracles," she mumbled to herself. Routinely, when only a handful of stores were open, mall security would lock all the exterior doors, with the exception of the main one, which was clear on the opposite side of the mall.

She heard her footsteps echo as she walked back to the store. *That's what happens when no one is in the mall but you and security,* she thought. Claudette could see the security officer looking down the corridor and could tell he had yet to identify who she was. The change in his body language let her know that he had made the identification. "Well missy, what you doin' back here?"

"Something's wrong with my car—the key is not turning in the ignition."

"What you do, missy? Sounds like you jammed it."

"I don't think so, sir."

"What you gon' do?"

"Call a locksmith."

"Aw missy, they gon' charge you an arm and a leg."

"Well, I'm thankful I can pay for it."

"Listen, let me call the security patrol first—maybe they can do something."

Claudette hadn't thought of that. "Sir, that's a great idea—would you?"

"But of course for you, missy." The security officer got on the walkie-talkie and radioed security patrol. With great pride, Claudette watched as he barked orders for help. It worked. Someone was there within ten minutes, ready to solve her problems.

As Claudette walked to the patrol car, she could not believe this was happening to her. Her long day was becoming longer, and she could feel her pleasant temperament shrinking.

The security patrolman seemed nice enough, but this wasn't the time for small talk. All Claudette could think was, *Get my car started so I can go home.*

She sat and watched the patrolman struggle just as she did, and all hope drained. "This is the darndest thing...this key is not budging...you must've jammed the steering wheel. Sorry to tell you—but you're going to have to call somebody," said the patrolman. With that, he turned to the security officer, waved good-bye, and left the two of them to work it out.

"Can you recommend someone to me?" Claudette inquired of the security officer, who mumbled something about a mall list that was outdated. "Then who would you suggest?" Claudette snapped.

"I didn't jam the steering wheel—don't get all huffy with me, young lady," he quickly snapped back.

Claudette instantly felt ashamed. *He's right. It's not his fault; it's mine,* she thought. "I'm sorry. Please forgive me, sir. I'm just irritated because I'm tired, my feet hurt, and I just want to go home."

"I feel you. My feet hurt, too. And *I* want to go home. But neither of us can, so no use in anybody getting mad about it," the security officer said. "Do you want me to call a tow truck, 'cause a locksmith won't help? I know a good one," he added.

"I don't have a choice, do I?" Claudette sulked.

"You keep getting smart, and you'll be out here in this empty lot by yourself," the officer said.

"I'm sorry."

"You said that last time."

"I really am. It's just that…"

"You're tired, your feet hurt, and you want to go home—I know."

They both instantly broke out in laughter, and it felt good to break the tension that was building.

The security officer called for the tow truck. Then she and the security officer sat and waited, and waited. Claudette thought: *Christmas will be here before this tow truck.* As she looked around the now-empty lot again, she spotted the amber light circling, resembling a police car. *Now he wants to drive like a maniac because we see him. If he'd driven like that when he first got the call, I'd be home by now.*

"I told you—here's my boy."

Even in the dark, Claudette could see the proud smile on the security officer's face. If you didn't know any better, you'd think it was actually his son. Claudette wondered if it was. That would be all she needed—a family reunion.

Once the tow truck driver got to her car and acknowledged her with a polite "Hello ma'am," he proceeded to give five different handshakes to the security officer, who stood grinning as if he were a five-year-old who had just been told he could eat as much junk food as he wanted for the rest of his life.

After what seemed like a century, with the temperature continuing to drop, the tow truck driver was right in the middle of another version of "Good looking out for me, man," when Claudette began clearing her throat. It seemed to work because the driver looked at her with a smile that said, "Alright, I'm going to get to your car." Lucky for him, she acted on the Word because she *wanted* to holler and say, "ENOUGH of the handshakes—let's get this show on the road! You can small talk after you finish with me!" But she didn't, clearing her throat had been just as effective.

God had done a work in Claudette. She had learned to tame her tongue somewhat, and she got the victory over speaking what was *really* on her mind.

As she stood and watched the driver examine the car, she couldn't help but notice that he had a small gut. She wondered why she always focused on the negative instead of the positive. *It's that sin nature,* she thought. If she wanted to focus on some positives, one would have been that he came out on Sweetest Day when he could've been home getting ready to serenade his wife or girlfriend. All of a sudden, she felt guilty about zeroing in on his gut. He seemed like a nice man.

"Can I see your car key, please?" the driver asked. Claudette handed him the set of keys while telling him, "It won't turn."

He turned to her and smiled, "That's what *you* say, but I have to check myself." She returned a smile that said, "Do whatever."

After the tow truck driver adjusted the seat, he repeated the same steps as Claudette and the other long-gone security patrolman. Claudette noticed, however, that he had a funny look on his face.

"Is this the right key?"

Claudette got angry, "Of course that's the right key. Don't you think we had enough sense to check for the obvious?"

"Put down your rocks, ma'am—I'm just asking a question. Well, if this is the key, and I don't believe it is, but you say it is, I'm going to have to tow it because something is jammed. Is there anything you'd like to get out of the trunk before I hook it up to my truck?"

With a long, disappointed sigh, Claudette acknowledged that she would need to retrieve some things. "Do you know how long it's going to take to un-jam the steering column?"

"Depends, ma'am—I won't know the real problem until we get it to the shop."

"I was just curious because if you think they'll need it for more than two days, I'm going to need to get quite a bit out of my trunk."

"Sounds like it's a second closet."

Claudette ignored the sarcasm, even though he was right. "May I have the keys, please, to open the trunk?"

"Why don't you let me do that for you—is this the key?" he offered.

As Claudette looked at the keys, she noticed the ring that they were on, and she instantly felt like an idiot. How was she going to tell the man that those were not the keys to her car after all? She didn't know how she could be so dumb. After what seemed like a very long time, the driver asked, "Is something wrong, ma'am?"

"Please call me Claudette. I don't know how to say this, but none of those are my car keys."

The security officer blinked in disbelief. "Missy, we've been out here in the cold trying to start a car with the wrong key! Only a woman! Only a woman would have you..." he was suddenly interrupted by the tow truck driver.

"Don't be so hard on her, Pops—the last thing she needs right now is someone teasing her."

"Who's teasing? I'm for real. That girl…"

"Pops, what's done is done—not now."

Claudette was thankful for his intervention; she definitely didn't need to be scolded. She wasn't feeling that.

The tow truck driver asked if he could help with anything else. It was then that Claudette actually looked at his face, and she was taken aback by his compassion-filled eyes. She didn't want to stare. But she realized that in all of the mass confusion, she didn't even know his name.

"Excuse me, what's your name?"

"Christopher."

"Christopher, thank you for being so kind about this whole thing. I feel bad enough." The grunt coming from behind Claudette reminded her that someone else was standing in the cold with them.

"I know one thing, this incident right here is all I needed to let me know that I got to find another job!" the security officer griped.

Claudette didn't even turn to respond to that comment, but she was thankful that the crunch of his boots in the trash and debris in the parking lot confirmed that he was on his way back to the building, leaving her and Christopher alone.

"Under normal circumstances, I wouldn't take up more of your time. But as they say, 'Confession is good for the soul.' I am physically and mentally exhausted and yes, I would love to have you help me with something inside so I can go home. Follow me."

As they walked back toward the mall entrance, silence that

would usually make Claudette feel uncomfortable was clothed in an unexplainable peace. It was like they didn't need to talk to be together. *Snap out of it, girl—what are you thinking? "Be together?" You don't even know this man,* she thought.

When they got to the mall door, she was sure the security officer had left it open so they could get in. Claudette was a few steps in front of Christopher. She instinctively reached for the handle when a strong hand playfully slapped her hand away.

"When walking with a gentlemen, allow him to get the door," Christopher stated. His finger went up to his mouth to silence her words. "If you don't know if he's a gentleman—allow him the benefit of the doubt and just stand there. If you find out he's an idiot and he's looking at you like, 'What's the matter? Open the door,' turn on your heels, click twice, and find another door far away from him and run through it, losing him."

He bowed. With one hand, he opened the door; and with the other, he extended it as if he were allowing royalty to pass.

Claudette couldn't help but laugh. She liked him! He looked at her with a sheepish smile that said, "You really don't know whose company you're in."

As they walked through the door and down the hall, the security officer was waiting at the end with his arms crossed. And the disgusted look he had in the parking lot was now frozen on his face.

Claudette didn't know why, but while Christopher was waving at the security officer, she peeped at his left hand.

No ring.

For the life of her she couldn't explain why his ring finger meant anything to her. There were lots of men who didn't wear rings, even though they should.

"What's his name, Christopher?" whispered Claudette. *Interesting, I can remember his name, and I just met him. But I've been interacting with the security officer for almost two years and I can't remember his name. That's strange,* she thought.

Christopher whispered back, "Ned. And why are we whispering?"

"Well, he's been assigned to this side of the mall for two years, and I'll tell you the rest when we get to my store."

"What y'all whispering about, like you old friends or something?" grumbled Ned, as they continued to walk toward him.

"We didn't want to disturb the peace you're feeling now that the mall is closed and everyone has gone home," Christopher lied.

Claudette kept silent until they were safe inside her shop. "Why did you tell that story?" she asked.

"What story?"

"You know what story. I'm trying to be nice and not say lie. 'We didn't want to disturb the peace,'" Claudette mocked Christopher.

"How about I repent and go tell him the real deal that you didn't know his name, even though he's monitored and watched your store for the past two years—want me to do that?"

"Very funny."

"I didn't mean to be humorous. I've got to confess it to God tonight anyway—so confessing to Ned is the least of my worries."

"You're a Christian?" Claudette said in amazement.

"Why are you surprised?"

"Who said I was surprised?"

"It's all in your tone. 'You, a Christian—a tow truck driver,'" Christopher taunted with a high-pitched voice, emulating a woman. "Yes, I'm a Christian—been one all my life."

"How old are you?"

"Forty-seven," Christopher declared with no hesitation. "How old are you?"

Claudette answered with her eyes. She just looked at him, daring him to ask her again.

"Women! Who cares about age? Most times when guys ask, they don't care. It's just a 'you asked me, so I'll ask you' thing. When you asked, I didn't hesitate when I said forty-seven—I ask you, and you trip." He shook his head playfully and somehow felt the hesitation women had in sharing their age had something to do with men, even though he really wasn't sure why.

Christopher started looking around Claudette's shop—it had class. He noticed how the mannequins were decorated with style and eloquence—accessorized to perfectly bring out colors the natural eye wouldn't typically see. Christopher thought it was clear that she wouldn't be interested in a man who had a tow truck business. He thought she'd probably want someone from Wall Street.

"Christopher, I hate to ask you this, but I have a box in my office that I need to take home. Can you help me, please?"

Christopher agreed and began walking with her to the back of the store; he was even more impressed with what he saw. But as they went through the curtain, which doubled as a door, he was surprised to see that the office space was so small. And it greeted them with clutter, a far cry from the immaculate showroom out front. His eyes, which always told what he was thinking, soon made Claudette self-conscious.

"Messy, huh?" Claudette laughed.

"How about 'trying to make the most of every inch'? Does that sound better?" he replied. They both laughed.

As Claudette pointed to the box, Christopher slowly navigated through the other boxes, plastic, and papers on the floor to get to it. As he bent over to pick it up, he couldn't help but notice the beautifully framed sign that hung on the wall. In the midst of the mess, it stood out like a dressed-up pig with pearls, a hat, and high heels. He decided that he wanted to remember the sign.

"Chris, don't hurt yourself."

Claudette wasn't prepared for the response she got. His whole demeanor changed, and he was emphatic when he looked Claudette straight in the eyes and said: "Do me a favor—please don't ever call me Chris again, *OK?* I don't mean to get all 'Dr. Jekyll and Mr. Hyde' on you, but that's a no-no, *OK?*"

"Ohhhh-kay," Claudette repeated slowly. *So much for the*

nice meeting. His voice went up two octaves when I called him Chris. He was polite about it, but he still freaked. Thanks for showing me that side, Lord—I was actually thinking he would be nice for someone. Better leave him alone—the evil twin is not one to play with.

Shortly thereafter, Christopher seemed to read Claudette's mind because he locked eyes with her and said, "My ex-wife was never satisfied with what I gave her. She belittled me every chance she could. She hated the relationship I have with my mother because we are extremely close. She constantly called me a momma's boy and said that Chris was a better name for me because I acted like a woman when it came to my mother. So whenever we would argue, she'd start calling me Chris, and from Chris she would escalate the situation by calling me Chrissy with a hiss. I never forgot that, and I vowed that I'd never allow anyone to call me Chris. I'm still believing God for healing from her. I'd say I'm ninety-five percent there. But a few things still push the wrong button, and Chris is one of them.

"When a man is disrespected after he does everything within his power to only bless his woman, it leaves a wound. And every time the wound is opened, it's as if it never healed—almost like picking a sore. I said all that to say—you just picked my sore and if I didn't tell you that it hurt, you could do it again. Now you know." He turned and started walking to the door. He stopped midway and came back to the office, poked his head through the curtain, and asked for the key to the car. Dumbfounded as to how she could have turned something that seemed so nice into what now seemed to be an intense interaction, Claudette handed Christopher the same set of keys as before without even looking at him.

His instincts were sharp. He used his knee to brace the box and held it with his left hand. Without permission, he gently took his right index finger and lifted up Claudette's chin. Speaking softly, he whispered, "I'm taking liberties that I normally wouldn't. I'm touching you because I want you to know that what just happened here is not your fault. It was an innocent slip of the tongue, but it still hurt. If I thought I would never see you again, I probably would've let it roll off. But because I was firm, you'll remember this little encounter and it probably won't happen again, which would be wonderful. So don't feel like you have to walk on eggs. I'm OK, really. Now can I have the key to your car—the right one?"

They both chuckled—the atmosphere was still somewhat strained, but far from intense. After finding the right set of keys, Claudette handed them over by holding her car key between her thumb and middle finger, and off he went to take the box to her car. Claudette didn't even hear Christopher return to the shop because she was so engrossed in her thoughts. She didn't realize that she was still standing in the same spot where Christopher left her, gazing into the distance.

"You OK?" Christopher asked.

Startled, Claudette managed a smile, which indicated that she was, and asked, "How do you know Ned?"

"Long story for another night, but he's like a dad—we'll leave it at that. Your closet was too full for the box, so I put it on the backseat."

"What closet?" she asked, puzzled. Then she remembered what he had said in the parking lot about her trunk being a closet. "Oh—when you're in the clothing business, you never have enough room for the clothes you have."

"How were you going to pick up that box—it was heavy by my standards, and I used to lift weights." Claudette thought: *I'd like to see those arms under that coat.* And then she mentally slapped herself for thinking something like that. *It's amazing. You have to work on holiness twenty-four/seven.* She hadn't thought about a man's arms in God knows how long, and now she wanted to see something that had nothing to do with anything.

"So, how were you going to pick up the box?" Christopher gently repeated himself.

"Oh—I wasn't. I planned on taking several trips to the car until the box was empty, so I thank you very much…" Claudette was interrupted by banging on the window of her shop—she didn't have to look to know that it was Ned. "That's Ned—we're way past closing and locking doors for merchants. He's about ready to strangle me."

"I'll tell him I kept you," said Christopher.

"That's about the only thing that'll save me—he seems to be quite fond of you." Claudette motioned to Christopher to leave, implying with her body language that she was right behind him. As they were walking through the shop, she began to turn the lights off. Sure enough, Ned was standing there as if he was ready to arrest them both.

Ned waited for Claudette to walk out first. He completely ignored her and spoke right to Christopher. "What the heck are you still here for?" Ned asked in an agitated voice.

"Just trying to help Claudette with a box," Christopher replied.

"Help her with a box for what?" Ned asked.

Claudette looked at Christopher and smiled, "I see where you get your chivalry training."

Christopher refrained from commenting and gave Ned a man hug, the kind where they pat each other on their backs so hard that it seems like they might need back surgery, and he said, "Good-bye." Claudette locked up the store, with Ned waiting anxiously for her and Christopher to be on their way.

As Christopher and Claudette strolled leisurely down the hall, they could feel Ned's stare. They both turned and looked at him at the same time, and he had a baffled look on his face.

In the meantime, Claudette and Christopher talked not only as they exited the mall, but they stood outside talking until Christopher finally said, "You're shivering. We better call it a night. Besides, I got to get home and watch Jeopardy."

"Jeopardy! You watch Jeopardy, too?"

"Love the show!"

"It's late. How are you going to watch Jeopardy?"

"I DVR it every day 'cause I work late. While most people watch the ten o'clock news, I watch Jeopardy."

"Interesting, I DVR it and watch it when I get home, too. I hardly ever miss it!" They both laughed and stood for another fifteen minutes talking about the show and Alex Trebek.

They finally made it over to the driver's side of Claudette's car and just as she reached for the door handle to get in, Christopher gently tapped her hand. He gave her a look as if to say once again, "Don't try to open the door when I'm around." Claudette laughed and smiled at him. Suddenly she noticed his eyes as the light from the sky hit just right; they were beautiful.

"Thanks, Christopher! Please forgive me for trying to open the door; I forgot I was in the presence of a real man."

After she got in the car and drove away, Christopher just stood there, with his hands in his pockets, not knowing what to make of the evening. Then he remembered something and without thinking, he started running after the car and calling her name. Claudette was already looking through the rear-view mirror, so she saw him running before she even heard his voice. She quickly put on the brakes, wondering whether she'd encounter the evil twin again or the real Christopher. She was hoping he would ask for her number. *Silly girl, you don't even know him,* she thought.

She put the car in reverse to back up some. After stopping again, she rolled down the window and turned her head to see what he wanted.

"I just wanted to remind you—don't try to lift that box. I know I'm not your father, but do you have a covered garage where you live?"

Claudette laughed. "Yes. But why do you ask?"

"Because it's too late for you to be going back and forth tonight from the street to your house."

Claudette thought: *If you were that concerned, you would follow me home and take it out for me.* Instead, she replied, "That was very thoughtful of you."

You could tell by the look on his face that what she said wasn't the reply he wanted. He just stood and looked at her. She couldn't tell if he was irritated or if he was waiting for another answer.

"Since I do have a garage, it's OK. But just because you

brought it up, I'll wait until tomorrow," she offered.

"Thank you!" he replied with a grin wider than Miss Piggy.

Claudette was glad the parking lot was empty when she was leaving because she really wasn't watching the road while she was driving. She was busy looking at him through the rearview mirror—staring at a man she wanted to know more about. With the exception of the "Chris" outburst, she thought he seemed like someone who would know how to treat a woman.

Claudette was taken by Christopher's tender touch—but she was hurt that he didn't ask for her number. That thought sent sadness through her body like an electric current.

Meanwhile, Christopher continued to stand in the empty parking lot, watching her silver Bonneville disappear into the night. He didn't understand what had just occurred between them. All he knew was that his stomach was in knots, and he didn't feel the brisk chill that was in the air. He loved the fall, and this particular night felt sublime. *Boy, you too old to be feeling like this,* he thought.

Claudette continued her journey home. Both of them were feeling some emotions that they had been putting on the shelf for a long time.

* * * *

Unbeknownst to Claudette and Christopher, someone else was watching everything that had taken place in that last half hour—Ned. And he wasn't sure if he should be pleased.

Ned didn't have anything against the woman who owned the fancy shop. Claudette seemed nice enough to him. Ned thought she was a nice-looking woman, and he never saw any men hanging around her store. Everyone he talked to only had good things to say about her. But he didn't want his boy hurt again. Ned knew the last woman Christopher had was a pistol— he didn't even think *God* liked her.

Ned watched her take Christopher to the cleaners— mentally and physically. It hurt him to watch her rip way his self-esteem like someone quickly pulling the hairs of a mustache off with a strip of hot wax. She had absolutely no concern for his feelings.

Thank God no children were born of that union, Ned thought. He reflected on a conversation he'd had with Christopher almost ten years prior. Ned told him it was time for him to find a nice lady. Christopher told him he was just going to be satisfied serving God and making a difference in the community. When it came to women and relationships— Christopher was through with them.

Ned didn't know a lot, but he knew the look of a man who saw a woman he wanted. And he knew the woman who owned the fancy shop had him hooked. *Funny,* Ned thought, *I don't even know her name. I heard Christopher say something, but I was so busy trying to figure out what was happening that I didn't hear him. I could've sworn she called me by my name tonight, and it would be embarrassing if she knew mine and I didn't know hers. I have to remember to ask Christopher the next time I see him 'cause as sure as my name is Ned, he will see her again.*

Chapter Twelve

Claudette looked at her watch. *Impossible,* she thought. She couldn't believe that she had already been sitting in her chair over thirty minutes. But it was easy to do because it felt like someone was on her lap, preventing her from moving.

In her mind, she scrolled through all the men who tried to talk to her in the last five years. It wasn't that she wasn't interested in any of them. She just couldn't move past the hurt of what happened with Clay. She didn't even want to try again; she had become satisfied with Jesus. But Christopher did have an effect on her.

Claudette managed to get up from the chair and begin taking off her clothes. But she had trouble deciding whether she should take the time to wrap her hair. It was in that moment that Holy Spirit brought something back to her remembrance: she was crying her eyes out early in the morning. *What a difference a day makes with God. Now I'm daydreaming about a man I've only seen one time—go figure,* she thought.

She quickly stopped herself to dwell on how he didn't ask for her phone number. Then she got hit over the head with another thought: *I haven't paid him for his services.* She didn't know what was wrong with her. But instead of panicking, she decided to ask Ned later for his number to call him. No sooner than she made that decision, she thought: *Wow God, is this a setup?*

* * * *

Claudette ran a hot bath and drank some green tea to take her mind off the events of the day, but it didn't help. Her thoughts kept going back to Christopher. As hard as she tried stop it, the evening kept rewinding in her mind. Just like anything that's reviewed over and over, the reviewer always sees something that wasn't seen before—and this was no different.

She eventually got in bed and reached for the lamp beside it. Then she replayed the comment Christopher made when he went off because she called him Chris. He said, "If I thought I would never see you again, I probably would've let it roll off." That statement got Claudette's mind going. "Holy Spirit, You know everything. Did he really mean something by that?" she asked.

As Claudette stared at the ceiling in her dark room, she couldn't help but ask God another question, "What ingredients did You put in Your love potion? 'Cause it's some strong stuff—makes people act crazy!" The mere thought of a relationship had an intoxicating effect on her. And while it was taking effect, she suddenly remembered that she didn't get her Chinese food and somewhere during the evening, her feet stopped hurting.

"You are one BADDD God!" she said aloud with a smile. "Good night heavenly Father, good night Lord Jesus, good night Holy Spirit." Claudette turned on her side and closed her eyes.

Then Quintella popped into her mind. She was the one who told her to say good night that way. It was during one of those intense fellowships where Quintella had gone on one of her tirades about people saying they knew God was alive, but their actions didn't line up. "If they really thought He was alive and was with them at all times, then why do they ignore Him so much, especially at night? I don't know about y'all, but I don't go to bed with my husband beside me without telling *him* good night. So if I know that God, the Father, is with me at all times, as well as Jesus and Holy Spirit, who lives with me daily—why not tell Them good night, as well!" she remembered Quintella hissing. Claudette didn't tell Quintella that she was right, but she knew in her heart that she was. She agreed that They all were alive and should be acknowledged.

Claudette closed her eyes again and tried to sleep, but she still couldn't get Christopher off her mind. She knew, however, that she had to get a grip on this now or she would be in trouble.

"Father, in the Name of Jesus, help me go to sleep. I don't want to be thinking about any other man but You right now. You've been good to me and my family. You've blessed me beyond measure. You're my hope when I have none. Now Your Word declares in Psalm 4:8 that I can lie down in peace and sleep and You, Lord, will make me dwell in safety. Your Word is true. I believe it, so I thank You for sleep and the peace that You've promised, in Jesus' Name. Amen."

* * * *

Christopher thought a long, hot shower would help him forget Claudette, but he was wrong.

He went over to the TV and started the recorder to watch the latest episode of Jeopardy. But he found himself sitting there, staring into space. When he finally looked at the TV again, they were on the final Jeopardy question. He hadn't heard a clue or an answer since he turned the show on.

He was feeling funny inside because a woman hadn't had

moved him like that in years. He could still smell Claudette's perfume. It wasn't overpowering, but it was light—and it smelled so good. He felt as if she were sitting right next to him.

"It's sad that I let one person have that much control over me all these years," he heard himself mumble. He knew his bad experience with his ex had caused him to miss out on a lot of opportunities. He was tempted to get in bed. His mind was racing like a man trying to win a 100-meter sprint, but he was reminded of what his mom told him in his youth, "When you get out the bathtub, put some lotion on those big, rusty feet."

As he sat to lotion his arms, legs, *and* feet, he remembered his promise to himself, and the fact that there was a Protector set in place to keep him from being hurt again. Inside, he knew that trying to avoid getting hurt was shutting out the possibilities that God had for him. If he never rode a bike because he believed he'd fall, he'd miss the wonderful experience of the ride.

Christopher stood to get his pajama bottoms and took a look at himself in the mirror. He couldn't help but chuckle at the spare tire around his waist. "Who wants to look at this?" he mumbled. It was obvious that he had let himself go; it was time to go back to the gym.

Any other night, his next move would have been to reach for the remote to watch ESPN. But he was mentally tired, so he opted to get some sleep. That was proving hard to do; his shower didn't soothe any of his thoughts. *Why would a woman like Claudette want a man like me? Let's look at this logically,* he thought. *She's a successful entrepreneur, and I'm a laid-off factory worker running a little tow truck business. That check mark will go under the one reason she wouldn't want me.*

She probably owns her own home, and I lost mine in the divorce. One more check mark against me.

I love God, and I have some money saved. One check mark for why she would want me.

I would treat her like a princess. One more check mark for me.

Wonder what kind of perfume she wears…she smells so good. No marks for that one.

Christopher felt like a teenager. And he continued his little check mark charade until he had convinced himself that Claudette wouldn't want him. He then said aloud, "Women!"

Like a child, he took his posture beside the bed on his knees. He began, "Lord, it's been a good day. I made some good money. I thank You for being my Friend. Lord, continue to take care of my mom. I pray for the president of the United States. I pray that he makes decisions that will please You. Surround him with godly men who will have Your heart. I pray for the nation, Lord, that people will come to honor and respect You as never before. I pray for my nephew and nieces, that they will never take a strong drink in their lives. Use them, oh God, in a special way. Help me to grow as a man You will be pleased with, and may I never leave Your presence. As I sleep, Lord, guard my thoughts. When I awake, may I continue to walk in the paths of righteousness all the days of my life, in Jesus' Name. Amen."

Christopher climbed in bed and laughed at himself. "Lord, I'm a grown man—a big, grown man—why do I still say my prayers on my knees like a little boy? I don't do that when I'm praying during the day. Is it tradition that makes me do that? Will my wife laugh at me?" he said and paused. He couldn't believe the word "wife" slipped out of his mouth. He thought he'd never utter that word again in life. *Where did that come from?* Perhaps the painful fortress he had built around his heart was slowly crumbling. If so, it was feeling good.

Suddenly, Christopher sat straight up in bed. "Hey Lord… that woman didn't pay me! Am I crazy?! She didn't look that good," he found himself yelling.

Despite his mini rant, it didn't bother him that she hadn't paid him. "Yep, she looked that good," he admitted and smiled. The clock said 11:00 p.m., and it was his turn to run the camera at church the next day. "I got to get up at 5:00 a.m. Let me stop fantasizing," he added. And as soon as his head hit the pillow and he pulled the covers over his head, he was asleep.

* * * *

When Claudette opened her eyes again, it was to slap the snooze button on the alarm clock. It was time for church, and she was ready to go!

Chapter Thirteen

Karen's thoughts were on the girls. She knew they'd freak if they knew where she had just come from. She wondered if she should rethink New Year's, since she couldn't seem to do right or say no. She just kept going further and further with things. As soon as Karen's mind went to New Year's, she got a funny feeling in the pit of her stomach, like she should definitely cancel going out. But she dismissed it. She figured it was probably the talks she had with the girls.

"It's not the girl talk," she heard a voice say. "You need to change your plans."

Karen ignored the voice, and her thoughts went back to her Sweetest Day. Where did that holiday come from anyway? It was sweet, but it only reminded her of what she had missed. Love, such a strong emotion or, as Quintella would say, a commitment. *Whatever! Nothing is more powerful than the smell of a man wearing the right cologne. It drives me crazy, Lord. It's like I lose control when I smell it. And he don't have to be fine...just smell good. I guess that's why I almost lost it again. But the touch of Oliver is driving me nuts...it's been so long,* Karen daydreamed.

Even though Sweetest Day was barely over, Karen's thoughts briefly shifted to Christmas. Christmas was by far the saddest time of the year for her. Her mom's selfish act of committing suicide was hard enough to get over, but doing it on Christmas Day made it impossible to see how her heart would ever recover. "Thanks, Momma, for a wonderful Christmas present. Because of you, every year of my life since then has been marred by what you did. Wherever you are, I hope you're happy. You never liked or wanted me and even in death, you found a way to ruin my life and what should be a wonderful time of year. You spoiled it for me forever," Karen ranted. She hated the holidays.

Thanksgiving with Oliver, Christmas in New York with Oliver, and New Year's with Oliver again. She was glad she had orchestrated filling those days so she wouldn't have to think about her mother. But that funny feeling in the pit of her stomach came back again. It seemed like she got it every time she thought about New Year's Eve. She wondered why. But the phone jerked Karen from her venomous thoughts. "Hello," she answered.

"I can't wait until our next trip," Oliver said.

"I haven't even unpacked from the last trip, and you're off and running to the next one," Karen said.

"That's what happens to a man when he finds a real woman like you. Are you getting excited about going?" Oliver asked.

"Thanksgiving is a long way away. But to answer your question, I'm getting excited," Karen confessed.

"Now that sounds like my Karen. Did you find a swim-suit?"

"Yes."

"Did you get a sexy black dress?"

"Did you get the two adjoining rooms?"

"What do *you* think?"

"It doesn't matter what I think. Did you get the two rooms?" Once again, Karen felt sad on the inside.

"Didn't I promise you that I would?"

"Yes."

"Have I ever done anything that would cause you not to trust me?"

"No."

"Then back to my original question—did you find a sexy black dress?"

"Yes, I found a dress. Stop being nosy." At that point, it seemed to Karen that Oliver's intentions were lower than low.

"I'm not nosy, just excited."

"What did you really call for?"

"Nothing. I just called to hear your voice and to let you know that I was thinking of you. And that I'm thankful to God for bringing you into my life."

"Bye, Oliver!" Karen playfully yelled.

"Bye...for now," he sultrily replied.

Karen hung up the phone and thought: *He does believe in God. I don't see anything wrong with going away with him, as long as he has his room and I have mine. Nobody's planning to fornicate. I know the Bible says to "flee fornication" in First Corinthians 6:18.* She knew that Scripture, if she didn't know any others. Lenda and Quintella had rammed it into her head enough. *But you know what gets me, Lord? The Bible also says don't lie, steal, gossip—people do those things all the time, and it's no big deal. But fornication, that's a big one! Well, I believe you forgive fornication just like you forgive those others.*

Though she had plenty of time, Karen *had* begun to get ready for their next trip. Her drawer was full of Victoria's

Secret lingerie, and she planned on taking some of her pretty pieces. Not for Oliver, but she wanted to feel good as she sat on the balcony overlooking Banderas Bay. She had already gone online to find out more about the hotel Oliver picked, and it was definitely a five-star establishment. The Sheraton Buganvilias Resort & Convention Center in Puerto Vallarta was one beautiful place. One advertisement said, "The enchanting views of the bay and panoramic sunsets are just waiting to provide you with the vacation of your dreams."

The palm trees are calling my name, and I'm going to enjoy this trip in spite of my mother and my friends, Karen thought. She paused to look at her favorite teddy. As she admired it, she fiercely proclaimed, "I believe God inspired the folks at Victoria's Secret especially for us Christian ladies. Are we supposed to go to bed every night with a long flannel gown just because we're not married? I don't think so! God wants us to feel good about ourselves just like married women. I refuse to sit and wait for some 'godly' man to decide to talk to me before I can buy some nice lingerie. If all Christian women did that, we would force them to have an 'Annual Dry Rot' sale. But I'm not doing that. I'm going to enjoy myself, and I'm going to wear some beautiful lingerie.

"I know one thing: if something happens, it happens. We're putting plans in place so we won't do anything. But to tell the truth, it's been a long time since I've felt the touch of a man, and I'm not going to try to live a life that I can't. I like the touch of a real man, and I want to feel it before I die. Besides, why would God give me a body like this for no one to see it but myself?"

Chapter Fourteen

The alarm went off, signaling that it was time to get up and get ready for church. Lenda yawned and pulled the covers back over her head. The covers felt warm and cuddly, but the breath that met her nostrils was another story. *Oh, I did have a Caesar salad last night—must be the garlic. Get up, girl!* she thought to herself over and over.

When her feet hit the floor, she thought: *It's bad enough to have to get up at the crack of dawn. Why must a freezing floor welcome my feet? These hardwood floors might look good, but they don't feel good. I must get some carpet.*

Looking up at the ceiling, Lenda told the Lord, "I really don't feel like going to church today—it would be the perfect Sunday to lie in bed and daydream about being rich! Besides, I really didn't sleep well on my back and since Holy Spirit didn't answer me again last night, I could stay home and pout." Lenda thought about it for a moment: *I wonder how many people don't go to church because they are mad at God, like that's hurting Him.* But as quickly as the thought came—she dismissed it. Nothing would keep her from serving God—nothing. Even if she was miffed because of unanswered prayer, she wouldn't use that as an excuse.

I wonder if God ever feels like He wants to take a day off. I wonder if He ever feels like getting away from everybody and everything. Lenda lifted her head and her hands, "Thank You, Lord, for being a loyal God. You're always available, and I thank You for it!" With slow, deliberate steps, Lenda made her way into the shower and prepared for the day. She wondered what her son was doing at his dad's house. She hoped they were going to go to church. However, she was thankful that she only had to dress herself and didn't have to wait for a sleepy teenager.

*   *   *   *

Why is it that I can park a quarter mile away when shopping at the mall, but I get irritated when I can't get a spot right in front of the church door? Lenda had five minutes before church was to start, so she picked up the pace and ran. *I hate being late for church. I will not be late.* But as soon as her hands touched the door, she heard the singing begin. "How dare they start early?" Lenda mumbled. She was so looking forward to the continuation of the previous week's message, "Praying Effectively."

Lenda smirked as the usher handed her a bulletin and pointed in the opposite direction of where she wanted to sit. She wanted to sit with Quintella and Ken, but that wasn't happening. "May I go this way?" Lenda asked.

"If you don't mind, ma'am, could you please step this way?" the usher suggested. Lenda obeyed with her feet, but on the inside she was as rebellious as a two-year-old. She didn't know why it annoyed her when the ushers directed her to sit someplace that she didn't want to. She knew they were only trying to keep order in God's house. But it still bugged her. With a fake smile, she continued to follow the herd of people who were late like she was.

When the pastor walked to the pulpit, he had a confused look on his face. He finally spoke, but he seemed unsure, contrary to his usual confident self. It seemed like minutes had passed when it was actually only seconds.

"Greetings, church! While studying this week, I was sure that God wanted me to continue with the series I started last week. As always, I got up this morning and began to pray. I told God that if He wanted me to change the message, I stood willing and ready. And you know what? He's changed the message. I guess somebody in this place has been praying. So if you've asked God some questions, know that God changed this message just for you—to provide some answers."

Lenda's ears perked up like a dog who suddenly heard someone unexpected coming.

The pastor continued, "Today, I'm going to speak on the subject of forgiveness. Some weeks back, I talked about you forgiving someone else. Today, I'm going to talk about forgiving yourself for past mistakes."

Lenda couldn't believe her ears—she looked up at the ceiling and thought: *No you didn't, God.* His answer was, "Yes, I did," and she could feel the smile on God's face. Words couldn't explain the anticipation with which she waited to hear this message. She just prayed that no one else saw her mile-wide smile, because they would never understand what she was smiling about. They wouldn't understand that it was just last night she and God had this same conversation. They could never understand that the pastor was talking directly to her.

Lenda came back to the present.

"Forgive yourself that you didn't finish school," the pastor commanded. "It's never too late to take classes. Forgive yourself for not saving for a rainy day. Start saving now…more storms are coming, and you'll be ready next time. Don't look at me like that. What I just said was not a negative confession.

That's Bible. Turn to John 16:33, it says, '*These things I have spoken unto you, that in me ye might have peace. In the world ye shall have tribulation: but be of good cheer; I have overcome the world.*' What are the things He's talking about? The things in the previous verses. Go home and read them. I don't have time to go there this morning, but God said you'll have tribulation in this world. I didn't say that…God did. He's trying to tell you something. He has your back! Do you know what tribulation means? Suffering, difficulty, pain, trouble—get it?! Stuff nobody wants, but He does not want you ignorant about the fact that this stuff is coming. He tells you to laugh at it—'cause He has already given you the victory. Can you say, 'Amen,' this morning?!

"So your marriage ended in divorce. You're not the first, and you won't be the last. I'm tired of the church making divorced people feel like lepers. God still loves you. He'll still use you. It's not the unpardonable sin. He'll bless you with a husband or wife who's on fire for God, and the two of you will do mighty things. But you've got to forgive yourself!

"So the lesson today will be focused on forgiving yourself. Turn with me to our opening Scripture found in Philippians 3, verses thirteen and fourteen. That other Scripture I gave you was a bonus. Philippians 3, verses thirteen and fourteen says, '*Brethren, I count not myself to have apprehended: but this one thing I do, forgetting those things which are behind, and reaching forth unto those things which are before, I press toward the mark for the prize of the high calling of God in Christ Jesus.*'

"I like The Message version; it reads like this: '*I'm not saying that I have this all together, that I have it made. But I am well on my way, reaching out for Christ, who has so wondrously reached out for me. Friends, don't get me wrong: By no means do I count myself an expert in all of this, but I've got my eye on the goal, where God is beckoning us onward—to Jesus. I'm off and running and I'm not turning back.'*

"How can you see Jesus reaching for you when your head is turned, looking back? You can't run looking back! Try it—you'll end up running into something. If you've ever watched a race before, you never see anyone looking behind and running forward. It won't work. You'll never…hear me now…you'll never go forward looking back; forgive yourself.

"Listen, early on in ministry, I would leave church, and I'd listen to my messages. I can't tell you the number of times I beat myself up because I forgot to say this, or I didn't explain that. I would forget a Scripture that I felt was important. If I stayed there, I would've never come back the next Sunday. No, I learned early in ministry that I've got to be quick to forgive myself and get right back up here the next Sunday and do my best. That's why I've been in ministry for more than thirty years."

The pastor's voice faded, even though he was still talking. It was like another message was being preached. Lenda was still in church, but God was preaching directly to her. Lenda was aware of the people around her, but it was like she was face-to-face with God. He was washing her with His love. He was stroking her with His grace and pouring the oil of mercy on her head. The oil was warm, and it began at the crown of her head and was slowly making its way down the back of her neck, to her shoulders. It felt so good. She never wanted to leave the place where she now found herself.

She was brought back to the present when people around her began to stand for the altar call. If asked, she couldn't quite articulate what she felt. To think that Almighty God loved her that much was overwhelming. And the crazy part was…she had almost stayed home.

* * * *

While waiting to get out of the church parking lot, Lenda allowed her mind to reflect on the message she had just heard. To have the pastor change his sermon just for her was amazing. "Thank You, God, for loving me. I believe You are going to send me that special someone and when You do, I will follow Your lead—and I won't make the same mistake again. I forgive myself, and I promise You that I'll run looking forward from this day on," she declared.

She went to turn on a tape, but decided that she would continue to bask in the glory. It didn't even bother her that she had only inched about three car lengths. She decided there would be no complaints today—God was too good!

However, Lenda had other things to tend to—there was a flight to catch the next morning, and she still had to finish packing. A smile came over her face as she imagined her nightgowns. *Which ones am I going to take?* This was the best part of taking any trip, even if it was business, because she would always have her nights with the Lord where she'd put on a beautiful gown and perfume, comb her hair, and sit and read her Bible. And since the Lord blessed her with the finances to buy all the nice lingerie that she had, she thought it was only fitting to dress up for Him in it.

Lenda was looking forward to the rest of her day—and packing. She was feeling mighty good inside and exclaimed, "Let's go out to breakfast, Holy Spirit, and get some pancakes! This is a great day, and I'm going to treat myself!"

Chapter Fifteen

Ken's immediate response to Quintella's tears was one of self-ishness. After all, why would a woman be crying uncontrolla-bly in church while the pastor was preaching on husband-wife relationships unless she was in an abusive relationship? Ken was so uncomfortable.

He leaned over and whispered, "Are you OK, babe?"

"Yes," she faintly spoke in between sobs.

The pastor continued, "Men, in Ephesians 5, verses twenty-five and twenty-six, God says to love your wives as Christ loves the church. I'm not going to just quote it to you—I need you to turn there this morning. While I'm out here, I may as well preach this thing."

Hearing the word "preach" was bad news for the brothers. Their pastor had gone from teaching to "hooping," which was rare. *We should've said, "Amen," while we had the chance,* Ken thought.

"I like The Message version; it reads: '*Husbands, go all out in your love for your wives, exactly as Christ did for the church—a love marked by giving, not getting. Christ's love makes the church whole. His words evoke her beauty. Everything he does and says is designed to bring the best out of her, dressing her in dazzling white silk, radiant with holiness.*

And that is how husbands ought to love their wives. They're really doing themselves a favor—since they're already 'one' in marriage.'

"Too many men aren't loving their wives. They aren't going all out for their wives. Love is no longer marked by giving—the men are only interested in getting. Can I get a man to say, 'Amen'?" the pastor continued.

"Amen," Ken replied, along with about five other men. He knew this message wasn't for him, but nobody else would know it. Quintella was heaving and crying like Ken had just beat her up before church. No one would have guessed that as a Sweetest Day surprise, he and his wife attended the Detroit Opera House and had dinner at the Cadillac Café, where they dined on Persillade Lamb Chops and Broiled Stuffed Chicken Florentine, not to mention the really expensive outfit. The icing on the cake was a night spent in one of the luxurious suites at the Marriott Hotel, where they made passionate love to one another. He thought all had gone well. But what did he know? *You think you've just done something nice and here you are with your wife openly crying in church like she's married to Frankenstein,* he thought.

"I need another 'Amen' from the men. I said, I need another 'Amen' from the men." Ken didn't say it the first time because he was so involved with trying to calm his wife. This time, about 1,500 men all over the sanctuary shouted, "Amen!" It was obvious they wanted the pastor to move on.

"Men, you need to go home and love on your wives. Give her some money and tell her to go buy whatever she wants. Tell her to take off those thick stockings that look like tights—'cause you too cheap to let her buy some sheer nylons. Give her some money to buy some sheer pantyhose. Y'all don't like this, but it's true anyhow."

In the midst of her anguish, she silently prayed that her pastor would give her something to go home with. As terrible as she was looking and feeling, she was grateful that Lenda was still out of town on business. She didn't want Lenda to see her crying like this in church. *Lord, I'm so sad, and I don't know why. Things have been more than great between me and Ken. Give me something to hold on to,* Quintella wearily thought. It was as if God heard her plea.

"Men, as I close..." the pastor continued. "I'm going to tell on my wife. She confessed to me the other day that when we pray together, holding hands, she finds that sexy. I was shocked! So men, if the money won't do it, if the shopping won't do it, if candy won't fix it, and if flowers don't quite cut it—grab her hands and start to pray!" The congregation roared with laughter but for the next few minutes, Quintella didn't hear a word the pastor said. She wanted to laugh, but the pain she was feeling was too great. Thankful that God heard her prayer from a few weeks ago, it was nice to know that other women found their men sexy when they prayed together, too. She wasn't weird after all. And to her surprise, the heavy burden she was feeling began to lift.

Ken was never so happy for the altar call. He was even happier to see the offering basket because that meant church was pretty much over.

Ken usually looked forward to fellowshipping after church. He enjoyed talking to the brothers, especially on a Sunday like this. There was a double-header in the NFL. The Lions and the Bears came on at one o'clock and then at four o'clock, it was Dallas and New York. But all he wanted to do was get out of church as fast as he could. He looked at Quintella, and she was still crying.

Trying to avoid a confrontation, he lied. Yes, right in the church, he lied. He told Quintella that he was going to get the car so she wouldn't have to walk. Exiting from the church, Ken avoided any brotherly love conversations that were the Sunday norm. His main objective was to get in his car as quickly as possible.

* * * *

The silence driving home was heavy. Ken just couldn't understand it. When they pulled into their subdivision, he looked over at Quintella and to no surprise, she was still crying. It was weird. It seemed like ever since Quintella went to dinner with her friends, she'd been distraught. While he encouraged her to continue her relationships with her single girlfriends, he wondered what happened that upset her. He really didn't want to ask, because he didn't feel like getting into a ninety-minute dialogue on why he didn't understand her. Yet he loved her so much. If there was a guarantee that he could resolve the issue in thirty minutes or less, he would probe. But the game was going to be on by then, and he didn't want to miss it! He decided to put off asking her for the day.

Quintella knew Ken was aware that something was wrong. She didn't understand why he hadn't asked her about it. *Men! You love them but at the same time, you could choke them.* She needed him to be more sensitive. Yet she also knew he wanted to watch the "stupid game," which is probably why he wasn't asking her what was wrong. *I bet when the game goes off and he's ready to be stroked, he'll want to talk then. But I won't talk. Stop lying to yourself, girl. You promised when you got married that you would never deny your husband or use your body as a weapon,* she remembered. The counsel of her mother, who was also happily married, always kicked in.

Quintella and her mom could talk about anything. When she got married, her mother told her, "Baby, marriage sometimes has to be viewed as 'supply and demand.' There are two things you never want to withhold from your man because there's plenty of 'em in the streets—and that's food and good old-fashioned lovemaking."

Most of her friends got squeamish when their moms started talking about sex. Not Quintella. She has always been comfortable with her mom talking about sex. In fact, her mom had recently confided in her that she and her dad were still very much sexually active. And they were both in their late seventies.

It didn't surprise Quintella, but what did surprise her was the "still very much" part. They were always pulling on one another, but Quintella just thought it was more affection than real "action."

Still, her parents' sex life was the least of her concerns at the moment. Quintella wasn't a happy camper. The pastor's message hit home; she couldn't stop the tears. And she could no longer hold back words: "Holy Spirit, I am surprised at Ken. He's always been so tuned in to what's going on with me. Have we been married too long? Thank God I have a Man that I can talk to—One who will talk to me no matter what. I never have to play second fiddle to basketball, football, or golf. This Man always reminds me that I'm loved—what a Man. Thank You, Holy Spirit, for always being here for me. People mock me by calling me Queen James because I read the Word and talk to You. But You've always been the Comforter that Jesus promised. You also help me keep my mouth shut when I want to say things to my husband that a wife shouldn't.

"You've helped me over the years to honor my husband, and I'm so grateful. So, even though he hasn't said he doesn't want to talk to me—I know by his behavior that he doesn't. So I'm going to go into another room and talk to You. Thank

You for not turning a deaf ear because You weren't my first choice to talk to. It amazes me that You're always open to listen to me, even when I desire someone else instead of You." Quintella went upstairs, pulled out her Bible, and continued to talk to Holy Spirit.

Meanwhile, Ken saw the first half of the game, but he didn't even know the score at halftime. He was being a jerk. He put the game before his wife. He did love her, but sometimes his actions didn't line up with his thoughts. They were so blessed as a couple. And he was still madly in love with her. There had never been any other women; he enjoyed making love to her regularly.

His wife wasn't like some of the wives of his friends and co-workers. What horror stories he had heard—men who hadn't been intimate with their wives in months. That's not God's best. But Ken had a wife who had never said no to him, and he chose a game over her. It was evident that he wasn't thinking straight.

"God, please forgive me for mistreating Your daughter," Ken prayed. Ken knew Quintella was probably somewhere praying and talking to God; that's why he had no peace watching the game. She knew how to get to him. Ken called it the "Sic 'em, Holy Spirit" call. If ladies only knew that nagging gets them nothing, but praying can move a guy faster than anything. It's almost like a woman goes to God and says, "Sic 'em," and the man can't enjoy anything else until he gets it right with her.

So much for the second half of the game, Ken thought. The only consolation was that the Lions were behind—no surprise there. As Ken reached for the remote, he decided to take a shower, fix himself up, and then talk to his wife. She always fixed up for him, wearing her sexy gowns and sweet-smelling perfume; it was time for him to return the favor.

* * * *

Quintella had just finished her study and was about to close her Bible. It had proven to be a good one—she realized that her time spent praising God was glorious. She was totally focused, and she praised Him from A to Z. The praise just poured from her mouth. It was sweet to her—she could only imagine what God was thinking.

At that moment, there was a knock on the bedroom door, which interrupted Quintella's sweet fellowship with Holy Spirit. As Ken stuck his head in, He noticed the smile and state of peacefulness on his wife's face. There was only one other Man who could make her look like that, and he couldn't even get jealous.

"I'll come back later," he said.

"No, honey. It's alright—come on in," Quintella lovingly urged. "I just finished my study time."

When Ken walked toward Quintella, she could see that he had done a little "somethin', somethin'" to himself. He had showered, brushed his hair, and he had on her favorite sweater. The color was called Volcanic Ash, and he had on his black baggy pants that fit like they were tailor-made. He smelled irresistible. He was wearing her favorite cologne, Issey Miyake for men. And he had on his black Cody Tassel Loafers by Allen Edmonds. Ken never wore street shoes in the house; she assumed he must be going somewhere. *It should be against the law for a man to be so fine. Where is he going? It must be important because the game has only been on a couple hours.* They usually lasted three hours. It was little past half-time, so he had to have only watched the first half. She had no idea what could be so important that he would shower and put on those clothes. Quintella had to look elsewhere because she was beginning to melt and was reminded that she was mad at him.

Quintella was determined to keep her peace. She had just been in the presence of God, and nothing was going to take away what she was feeling—not even her husband who looked like he just stepped out of *GQ* magazine.

"Where are you off to, honey?" the words rolled off her lips—no sarcasm attached. *God is good,* she thought. *He'll have you speak sweet things when you want to go off.*

"I'm off to make amends with someone I offended earlier."

Now she was really puzzled. Ken offended someone, and she didn't know about it? He decided to stop teasing her.

"Babe, I came to apologize to you—I'm so sorry for being a jerk and choosing the game over you. I mean, you were crying during the whole church service. You continued crying all the way home, and I didn't even ask why because I was being selfish. I didn't want to get in a long, heavy conversation."

Quintella was waiting for the punch line. She was still trying to figure out where he was going. She wouldn't ask again; she would just wait for him to tell her. As she waited for him to say something, he came over to the large chaise lounge located in the corner of their bedroom, where she was studying.

"Baby, I want you to know that I'm here for you and if you want to tell me what's bothering you, I'll listen for as long as you need me to. If you don't want to talk now, that's OK, too. But I'll be here whenever you're ready to talk." He slipped his loafers off and gently squeezed behind her and straddled his legs on each side of her body. He then scooted her toward the middle of the chaise until her head rested on his chest. He began to massage her scalp as only he could. If he was going somewhere—he knew how to get her on his side. While she really didn't want to break the moment, if he *was* going someplace, she wanted him gone because he was stirring something up. Reluctantly, she broke the silence.

"You know you better go and do what you need to do, because I'm not going to let you go if you keep doing what you're doing."

Ken only laughed that laugh she loved to hear as he whispered, "No, baby. I'm for real—I dressed up for you. I'm here to talk to you, or I'll just continue massaging your hair. Whatever you want to do—I'm here for you."

Quintella realized that he was serious and before she knew it, she had turned around to give him a hug, and the rest was history.

* * * *

Quintella looked at the clock. Only an hour had passed, but Ken appeared to be asleep when her tears began to fall on his chest. She tried unsuccessfully to wipe them because she didn't want to disturb him. Why was she crying? She'd just had a wonderful time with the man she loved. Yet instead of resting, she was allowing their past to disturb her again.

Her mind started spiraling down: *Where are the people*

from the abortion clinic now? It's been twenty-seven years. No one told me that the pain would still hurt after twenty-seven years. They don't tell you about the nightmares and guilt that will never go away. No one prepares you for the day that you'll see that baby in heaven. No, if the truth be told—they don't tell you all those things because they know if they did, you wouldn't make a decision to murder something so small, something so innocent, something without a voice. I feel so guilty because of this thing that I've been hiding. I would never confide in the girls—ever. It just hurts so much when I hear about someone else having a baby.

Karen seldom hit the bull's-eye, but even she wasn't aware of how on-target she was at their last dinner when she said that they all have "issues."

It turned out that Ken was wide awake, and he could feel the warm tears fall on his chest. "Babe, please tell me what's been bothering you. Since you came back from your outing last month with the girls, you've been distant and visibly upset; please—let's talk about it."

Quintella was ashamed that Ken was awake; he was so quiet that she'd thought he was asleep. "I found out one of our friends that we went to school with is having another baby. This girl has seven kids…"

Then Ken finished the sentence for her, "…and we don't have one."

"Ken…"

"You don't have to apologize; we need to talk about this. When are you going to forgive the mistake we made well over twenty years ago? Don't you think God has forgiven us? Neither of us were in church when we decided to abort that child. We were dating, not knowing where the relationship was going. We were in college; we couldn't talk to our parents. We felt it was the right thing to do at the time. When are you going to forgive yourself? I have run out of ways to tell you I'm sorry. If I could turn back the clock, I would. But I've got to tell you—it's painful to keep opening up old wounds. You keep picking a scab that's trying to heal, and every time you do that it hurts both of us when you reopen the wound.

"Maybe we should go to the pastor and talk to him. I don't know what else to tell you. If God says He forgives us, and He does, why do you keep bringing it up? You can believe God for other people. You're always telling people to confess First John 1:9, and that God is faithful to forgive. Does He forgive everybody but you? Do you even believe what you tell everybody else?"

"Yes," was all Quintella could whisper between the sobs that were now causing her chest to heave up and down.

"Then if you really believe it, you have got to let this one go!"

"Ken, do you think that's why I can't get pregnant? The doctors have been saying for years that nothing's wrong with us. Both of us have had every conceivable test you can get. There are no medical reasons. I just feel we're being punished."

"Queen, Queen, our God is faithful. He knew we were just kids. He wouldn't punish us like that."

Quintella silenced her fears and told Ken for the umpteenth time that she was sorry for bringing it up. Once again, she laid in his arms and finally fell asleep. But Ken was still awake.

* * * *

"God, I need You to help me help my wife. When she picks back up that sin, it tears at my heart because I didn't protect her. I allowed her to make a decision that has hurt her deeply. Help me as the head of this house to help her move on, in Jesus' Name," Ken whispered, unable to go to sleep.

He knew it was going to be impossible to get any rest, yet there was no way he could get up without waking Quintella, especially since she was asleep in his arms. But what happened next made Ken smile. His Buddy, Holy Spirit, heard him, because suddenly Quintella rolled over out of his arms and was comfortably sleeping.

Ken didn't waste time getting up. Once again, he showered and put on his PJs. He got out his Bible, took his position on the chaise, and began to pray.

His first thoughts were of Adam and how he didn't protect Eve—he allowed the serpent to approach her. Their situation was the same. When Quintella came to him and told him she was pregnant, she saw the disappointment on his face and brought up the subject of abortion. Instead of rebuking those words from their seed, he panicked and agreed.

"I never asked Queen to forgive me for allowing her to make a decision like that. I didn't cover her. I took the easy way out," he mumbled to himself.

Then Ken began to read one of his favorite passages of Scripture—Psalm 112. This time was different. He didn't confess verse two, as he had done so many times before. He paused and verbally made this request: "Holy Spirit, this verse says that my seed shall be mighty upon the earth. Please forgive me for destroying my seed twenty-seven years ago. I have asked You many times to forgive me for the sin—but I've never confessed that I destroyed my seed. I didn't know any better at the time. I am asking that You give me another seed, so that this verse of Scripture will be true in my life."

Ken instantly felt compelled to lay hands on his wife. Without hesitation, Ken went over and gently woke up Quintella. After sharing what happened during his time of fellowship with his Buddy, Holy Spirit, he told her the confessions he was compelled to make. He even asked her to forgive him for not protecting her and saying that abortion wasn't an option.

They both came into agreement once again that they would have a godly seed. And for some reason, they believed this time was different from times before. And Quintella didn't care that she was well into her forties. God could do this, and He would.

Their job was to be patient and do things that made babies. That was the fun part. It was up to God to open her womb, and Quintella didn't doubt anymore that He not only could, but He *would*.

Chapter Sixteen

The clock on the nightstand said 6:30 a.m. Only thirty minutes had passed since she last looked at its face. Karen would've loved to be peacefully lying in her bed, listening to rain tapping softly on the roof. Of course, if this was any *other* Saturday morning, her eyes wouldn't have popped open like they just did. Karen's Saturdays usually found her asleep until 10:00 a.m. or later, if someone didn't wake her up by ringing her phone first. This Saturday morning found her in a position that she couldn't quite understand.

How could someone who loves the Lord…stop Karen, rephrase that statement. I can't understand how I, someone who goes to church, can be lying in bed with a man that I'm not married to, she thought to herself. *That's better—because if I truly loved the Lord, I wouldn't be here. Funny, I can feel His disappointment. I can feel His presence now—how was I so immune to it last night?*

Karen wished the movies and TV shows that she'd seen contained *real* scripts. Perhaps if they told the truth, she and a whole lot of other people wouldn't fall into sexual sins. She knew if her situation was on TV, she'd slip out of bed, tiptoe into the kitchen, and start breakfast. While turning the bacon, Oliver would appear and put his arms around her. They'd smile at each other and turn the stove off before heading back to paradise. But she wasn't on TV, and she wasn't in paradise.

I want to puke.

I feel so used.

Why didn't I have Oliver take me home?

Why did I come to his house?

Why did I think I was in control?

I wasn't in control at all this weekend.

The thoughts of regret poured in, one after the other. She was sure that her testimony was ruined. In fact, she was the one who said, "I am not having sex until I get married!" No sooner than she remembered her broken promise, the rain began to come down with great force.

Karen imagined God crying—He and Jesus together. She determined that it probably sounded like what she was hearing outside. She could also hear Them saying, "My daughter, My daughter, you're so much better than that. Why?"

Another vision crossed her mind that was often missing in the movies or on TV: she really didn't enjoy what she had done. Karen was uptight and confused, but she was caught up in the moment. *What I would pay to turn back the clock—but I can't. One thing is for sure, I will not be here when he wakes up.*

As Karen attempted to slip out of bed, Oliver began to stir. Even though she was in volunteered sin, she still had enough sense to know that God had not gone anywhere, that He still loved her, and that He would not just hear her, but He would answer her. She prayed, "Dear Lord—let me get out of here— please just let me leave without having to face him."

* * * *

Karen wasn't home five minutes before the phone started

jumping. This was one time she was thankful for caller ID. Oliver had called several times. After the rings came the same message on her answering machine: "Karen, give me a call ASAP. I want to know you're OK."

"No, I'm not OK. I want to get a one-way ticket to the other side of the world, but I can't!" she yelled at the machine.

Suddenly every gesture and movement of Karen's body became unusually mechanical. It was as if she was a marionette, with someone else pulling strings to move her body parts.

Walking into the bathroom, she began to run a hot bath—without bubbles. This wasn't a pleasure soak; she had some business to take care of. The water was so hot that Karen's skin turned red as soon as she inched her way in. After feeling each sting as she submerged her body into the tub, she began to scrub with a vengeance. Harder and harder, more painful with each motion. She was sure she could wipe away the stench. But when reality took the place of her temporary insanity, the tears began to roll down her face, followed by all-out sobbing. "What have I done?" she silently screamed. "What have I done?"

*　*　*　*

Karen had been sitting in the tub so long that she lost track of time. The water that all but scalded her in the beginning was now cold enough to send shivers throughout her entire body. Stepping from the tub to dry off brought little comfort; she knew she'd have to face the music sooner or later.

Her answering machine was blinking with a bright red "F," indicating that it was full. "Good, at least it won't record more messages from him, which means I don't have to hear his voice," Karen murmured in disgust. *Oh how I want this day to end, and it's only one o'clock.* This was much different from the weeks prior, when she was running to the phone, ever so eager to press the button to see if he had called.

Karen's mind took a rest from her ordeal for a brief moment. But thoughts of her best friends began to wake her mind back up. *I wonder what they would've said if they had been flies on the wall last night. I guess we'll never know because this is one little tidbit they will never hear about from me. Only four other people will know about this: God, Jesus, Holy Spirit, and him.* Karen hurriedly tucked those thoughts away, desperately yearning to put everything behind her.

Repent and make a 180-degree turn, she thought in jest. Karen couldn't believe that she could find something to laugh at now. Her mind went to her friend James. He always had a listening ear. The last time she told him she had made a big mistake, he said, "Repent and don't do it again." Karen proudly agreed and said, "You're right. I'm going to make a 360-degree change." When James began to laugh at her, Karen asked him what all the laughter was for. James said, "If you make a 360-degree change, you'll be right back where you started from, doing the same thing. What you want is a 180-degree change, which means you've turned and you're going in the opposite direction!"

Karen remembered putting both hands on her hips and having a confused look on her face when she answered: "You know, you're right! How come I didn't think of that? No wonder I haven't grown. I keep doing 360s, which takes me right back to the problem, and no one else has ever checked me on that issue. Thanks, James."

Karen remembered James flashing his bright white smile and replying, "Anything for you, sis."

On some level, Karen liked James, and she knew he liked

her. But she only saw him as a little brother. *Too bad,* she thought, *because he'll make some woman very happy one day. It just won't be me!*

Chapter Seventeen

Karen finally decided to meet Oliver for an early dinner. She rationalized that at least she would be safe in a restaurant, and she could fairly surmise that she wouldn't end up in bed with him, at least today. As she approached the restaurant, a slight grin developed on Karen's face. The man sure had class—he knew she wanted to dine at this restaurant. She was on guard, though. It would be dinner and nothing more.

"May I assist you?" the hostess politely inquired.

"Reservations for Oliver," Karen barely whispered, as if someone knew what she was thinking.

The hostess glanced at the book in front of her, fingers slowly roving the page until they came to a halt. She looked up, smiled, and said, "Right this way, please."

As Karen proceeded to follow the hostess, she felt like she was going in and out of a maze. Around this table, behind that one, through another. It seemed as though they were running out of space. The only thing in front of them was the Detroit River and a wall.

They were about to run into a door when the hostess stopped, tapped lightly on it, and entered the room after hearing, "Come in, please." Beyond the door was a private dining room that overlooked the river. The room was intimate and beautifully decorated. Ambiance is usually at the top of any girl's list when rating a good "date restaurant." And the ambiance at this restaurant screamed "good mood, good feel, good everything."

Something told Karen to "flee, turn around, and leave now while you can still run." But like so many other times, Karen chose to ignore that still, small voice and charge full-speed ahead into the brick wall of a person named Oliver.

Dinner was difficult—the river, Oliver, the soft music playing. *Do it before dessert,* she told herself.

"Oliver, I need to tell you something," she dramatically began. Oliver grabbed her hand and began to massage it. *Stop him, Karen,* she thought. But she couldn't; she didn't want to. *God, why is this so hard?*

Gently pulling her hand away and allowing it to rest in her lap where she thought it was safe, she continued, "Oliver, after our little encounter last week, I don't think going to Puerto Vallarta is a good idea."

Oliver straightened up and his facial expression changed to one of uncertainty. "What did I do?" he asked.

"It's not what you did…it's what WE did!" Karen exclaimed.

"What did WE do?" he sheepishly teased.

"We fornicated."

"We what?"

"We fornicated."

"What's for-a-cake? Is that on the menu? You mean Black Forest Cake?

"You need to be serious, because I am."

"I know you are; that's why I'm trying to make light of things."

"Fornicate—First Corinthians 6:18 says to flee fornication. Fornication is sex outside of marriage, in case you didn't know. And instead of us fleeing, we seem to be running toward it. If I can't resist and control myself in Detroit, where I live west of Woodward and you live on the Eastside, when we get to Mexico and only a door separates us, how am I going to resist you then?"

"Well, what did Paul say in Romans 7, verses nineteen and twenty?" Oliver asked.

Karen had no clue what the Bible said in those verses. She looked at Oliver and stated, "You tell me." *Good recovery, girl,* Karen thought to herself.

"If I'm not mistaken," Oliver went on to recite, "it says, *'For I do not do the good I want to do, but the evil I do not want to do—this I keep on doing. Now if I do what I do not want to do, it is no longer I who do it, but it is sin living in me that does it.'* Verses twenty-four and twenty-five go on to say, *'What a wretched man I am! Who will rescue me from this body that is subject to death? Thanks be to God, who delivers me through Jesus Christ our Lord!'* That's the New International Version. I understand that better than the King James," Oliver said.

"Baby," he purred, as he somehow got a hold of her hand again, "even Paul understood human struggles—adult ones to be specific. And if I'm not mistaken, he wrote over two-thirds of the New Testament. If *he* struggled, and *we* fall every now and then, surely God won't toss *us* aside. He'll still use us like He used Paul."

Karen was amazed at his knowledge of Scripture.

Oliver continued, "God doesn't expect us to be perfect. He requires that we do our best. In a way it's His fault, 'cause He made irresistible women and you, my love, are one fine, or let me say it this way…" Oliver paused for effect. "You are one

190 | YOU'VE GOT A MAN

gorgeous specimen of a woman, and no man in his right mind could ever run from you. Nah baby, the only direction to run is straight into your arms. I am one blessed man."

He finished his sales pitch by kissing the tips of Karen's fingers. Her only thought was, *When did my hands get from my lap to his lips?*

Once Karen was able to speak, she added, "I just think it's a bad idea."

"Well, what do people do when they don't know what to do? They pray, so let's pray."

Dumbfounded that Oliver would pray in a restaurant, Karen asked, "Right here, right now?"

"Right here, right now; I'm not afraid to let anyone know I'm a Christian. Let's come into agreement that we'll become stronger in our areas of weakness," he said.

Oliver's behavior was difficult for Karen to read. Her *spiritual* weakness was allowing her to fall for his pathetic game of "I know my Bible; I told you I was a Christian."

He offered his prayer. If only he could've included, "Angels who are assigned to Karen, if I don't mean her any good, remove me from her presence, in Jesus' Name," when he prayed, Karen would have been better off. But he knew just what to say to keep his foot in the door. It was too bad Karen didn't know what to say to save herself from him.

After Oliver said, "Amen," the door opened and the server came in, walking softly. She said, "I'm so sorry to interrupt. May I say something, please?"

Oliver extended his hand, signaling for her to speak.

The server looked at Karen. She seemed like she was about to cry. "I wasn't eavesdropping, but I was getting ready to come in to see if the two of you wanted dessert and when I knocked and opened the door and saw the two of you praying, I was stunned. I've never seen a man pray. Girl, you are one lucky woman!"

Embarrassed, Karen nodded, "Yes, I am. Thank you for reminding me."

The server's eyes shifted to Oliver. "May I bring dessert, sir?"

"Please don't call me sir," Oliver pleaded.

"Oh, you do deserve to be called sir, sir," the server replied.

They all laughed.

Oliver decided on cheesecake with strawberry topping for their dessert. As the server was about to exit, Oliver stopped her, "Excuse me, Vanessa. That is your name, right?"

"Yes, sir, that's my name."

Oliver chuckled at the sir thing again. "When you bring that cheesecake, make sure you only bring one fork."

Both ladies looked at each other, but it was the server who spoke. "I'm scared of y'all," she said as she hurried and closed the door.

Karen turned to see Oliver's pearly whites, the smile that made her melt. It didn't help that the scent of his cologne was messing with her mind. She was in way over her head…it was going to be a long night.

"By the way, good news, our Thanksgiving trip has been moved up. I need to get out there earlier than we planned. It's next week. Can you get away?"

"Oliver, I'm a counselor. I can't just take off work like that!"

"It's Friday through Sunday. I thought your school was on

a four-day week. Didn't you tell me that?"

Karen thought she could get out of the commitment. Why didn't she just say she wasn't going?

* * * *

Sin can be likened to a snowball. It may start out small but when rolled around, it gets bigger and bigger and bigger. As Karen sat on the plane waiting for takeoff, she couldn't help but wonder how a city that looked so beautiful three days ago looked so ugly now.

Puerto Vallarta was everything the brochures said it would be. And Oliver was true to his word. He got the spare room…but it was never used.

* * * *

It wasn't just the rain that had begun to fall, and it seemed like every time she had sex with Oliver it rained. What was up with that? Memories of how she once again had exercised no discipline over her body began to flood her mind. How could she fall for that "I'll get separate rooms; I won't go back on my promise" charade? He didn't go back on his promise…she did.

As they sat on the tarmac waiting for clearance to fly off the island, Oliver interrupted her by saying, "A penny for your thoughts."

It was the first time in a long time he'd said something that she could totally agree with—her thoughts were cheap, and they weren't worth more than a penny. As she reminisced over the past events, she wondered how she got to the point where "no" had been removed from her vocabulary when it came to Oliver. The only words that came from her mouth were "yes,"

"OK," and "uh-huh."

The small yellow streak down her back was now a long yellow streak. And this was only the first leg of the flight. They still had to go through customs before they could board a plane in Houston to go to Detroit. She had done a good job of faking it so far. What difference did a couple more hours make?

Maybe it was time for Karen to move, to truly put all this behind her and start over.

Chapter Eighteen

Lenda knew that airplanes don't wait for anyone. But she took her chances anyway. *How could I mess around and not leave on time? Stupid, stupid, stupid—no, I'm not stupid; stupid is permanent. I'm just dumb. That's only temporary*, she thought. As Lenda got to the curb, she felt the need to pray: "Father, in the Name of Jesus, please, please, please have mercy on me—I *cannot* miss this plane. I *cannot.*"

She approached the attendant and nervously handed him her boarding pass. He frowned and said, "We stop checking in luggage at the curb thirty minutes before flights. I don't think I can do it."

"Why?" Lenda pleaded.

"Because we have to allow enough time to get the luggage from here to the aircraft. I can call and check." He picked up the phone and began to talk to someone. Lenda started praying again. The attendant must have been a poker player because his facial expression didn't tell Lenda anything. When he hung up, his words were music to her ears.

"We have two minutes to check you in here."

"So you'll be able to do it?"

"I think so!" he said, giving her quick wink.

The attendant finished in less than a minute. Lenda almost threw the ten-dollar tip at him to save any seconds she could. She was working with just under thirty minutes, and she still had to get through the airport and to her gate.

When she got to the security line, it seemed to be moving especially slow. But then again, that's what happens when someone's running late. Everyone seems to be moving in slow motion, and no one else is in a hurry.

"Take your shoes off, ma'am," requested the airport security officer.

"My gym shoes," snapped Lenda.

"So, what part of take your shoes off didn't you understand?" the security officer snapped back.

"I understood everything. I'm sorry…I'm just running extremely late, so I'm very sensitive," Lenda explained while removing the shoes.

As the security wand traced her body, she was relieved that no alarms went off. Then Lenda heard someone say, "She's got a computer in the briefcase."

"Send her over here," another voice hissed.

Before the woman could say anything else, Lenda's voice escalated. "What's the matter now? I'm late for my plane."

"What time does your plane leave?" said the security officer.

"12:05!" Lenda was quickly losing patience.

"Don't think you're going to make it!"

"Why am I being singled out?" Lenda snapped again.

"You're not being singled out—you can't have a computer in a briefcase, lady. Computers are supposed to be out, not in a briefcase—you must remove it."

"I'm late catching my plane...please, please..." Lenda begged.

"Then you should've gotten an earlier start! You knew when you left home you were late, so don't expect me to break rules for you. Next time, leave earlier and keep the laptop out!" cracked the security officer.

Lenda reduced all communication to her eyes. She not only wanted to cuss, but she wanted to slap the security officer's face until she was tired. And considering some of her frustrations from the past week, she would be slapping her for a while. Women could be so nasty, and this "thing" standing in front of her deserved the gold medal for nasty!

Lenda's flesh had gone there, and neither she nor the attendant wanted to back down. As the two women locked eyes, refusing to be the one to give in, Lenda heard Holy Spirit say, "Enough, Lenda. Security is right. You should've been on time, and you need to stop acting like you don't know Me."

This minutes-long encounter seemed to be playing out in even slower motion than she originally thought. But common sense prevailed, and Lenda reminded herself that if she wanted to get on any plane this day, an immediate attitude adjustment was necessary.

"I'm sorry. You are absolutely right. I should've allowed more time." Lenda's wave of the white flag produced a self-satisfied smirk on the face of the woman in front of her. Though no words were exchanged, Lenda could hear her say loud and clear, "That's what I thought!"

After her computer and carry-on were returned, Lenda politely put on her gym shoes. In that moment, she realized the Lenda of old, who she thought had died to the flesh spiritually, was unmistakably alive.

With a defeated gait, Lenda decided to run through the

airport. Between huffs and puffs, Lenda asked God to forgive her according to First John 1:9. She also made a decision right then and there: *If I miss my plane, I miss my plane, and it's no one's fault but my own.*

This was her third trip within several weeks. She'd never been late before, so she felt her client would understand. She was determined to represent God well. Up until then, no one would've known that she was genuinely ashamed of her behavior. She was going to make it a point to totally turn her attitude around.

Lenda looked down at her ticket to make sure she was headed in the right direction. Her mind was in overdrive. She wanted to call and let her client know that she was going to miss her flight. After that, she was going to *prayerfully* get on another flight, providing there was one available.

Her mind began to shut down. She couldn't think anymore, so it took her a minute to notice that she was at the gate—and it was full. Were people early for the next flight? She made her way up to the gate attendant.

"Did Delta 696 leave?" she asked the attendant.

"No, it was delayed because of the weather in Houston. We should start boarding in about twenty minutes."

Lenda couldn't hold it. "Hallelujah! Hallelujah! Thank You, Jesus!" Lenda shouted. She didn't care that people were looking at her like she'd lost her mind. She was so happy that the plane was still there.

"Jesus," Lenda looked up, "thank You for keeping this plane here for me!" Lenda found a seat and exhaled for the first time since running through the airport. She also thanked God she wore gym shoes.

There was a man sitting next to her who didn't catch her

attention until he said, "Can I ask you a question?" Looking at his sly smile, she took the bait.

"Sure," she said.

"*So,* Jesus caused the bad weather in Houston so we could take off twenty minutes late? I guess He don't care about people like me who have a connecting flight. You people!" he spewed. Then the man got up in a manner that said, "Never mind, I don't care to hear the answer."

Lenda wasn't even expecting the question, so she just sat there with her mouth gaping—nothing coming out. She didn't know if Jesus had caused the bad weather in Houston, but what she did know was that this flight was delayed because He knew she couldn't wait another three hours to get to Houston.

Right then, she heard Holy Spirit's voice, and she could visualize a smile on His face when He said, "Poor fellow, guess he doesn't know that favor isn't fair." That brought a smile to her face, and her joy returned. The attendant soon began to board passengers.

* * * *

The weekend went by way too fast. After the near debacle going to Houston, everything else relating to the trip was sweatless. Houston was a beautiful city. Lenda had an inkling the taxi driver was purposefully taking the scenic route to the airport so she could relish the drive. She loved the way the expressways were painted pink, and she couldn't help but notice how clean the city was.

Lenda was early when arriving at the airport. She didn't want a repeat of her outbound flight. After going through security, she arrived at her gate with ninety minutes to spare, so she decided to get something to eat and people watch to pass the time. She loved people watching. The things she saw when she watched people, like the lady who elbowed what looked like her husband because he was ogling a statuesque woman in a mini. The man had a look on his face that said, "Why did you do that? I didn't do anything."

Then there was a little girl eating an ice cream cone that looked like the Leaning Tower of Pisa. Lenda began to count to see if she could make it to ten before it dropped on the floor. Seven was the magic number, and the screams came right before the ice cream hit the ground. Her dad was trying to console her, but she wasn't having any of it.

Lenda's eye then caught a couple making out in the airport—really making out. Their display of affection would embarrass the most seasoned bride.

It's one thing to kiss someone, but this was borderline porn. If they were married, Lenda wondered why they couldn't wait until they got home. Maybe *that* was the problem.

As Lenda continued looking at the couple, the woman looked a little familiar. Maybe it was the high heels—Lenda only knew one person who could wear stilettos like that through the airport. *Come to think of it, the shoes remind me of some Karen had,* she thought. *But that couldn't be…*

Before Lenda could finish her thought, she caught a side view of the woman. It WAS Karen! It was Karen and that man, standing in the customs line. *What are they doing in the customs line? Did they go out of the country together?* Lenda couldn't believe her eyes. Karen didn't see her because she was so engrossed in Oliver. *This girl has gone crazy.*

Lenda thought back to Karen's response when she asked Karen to pick her up from the airport. She told Lenda she was working. *Well, I guess you could call what she was doing "work." The question is—what was she working?* Even though it seemed strange that Karen would be working on a Sunday, Lenda gave her the benefit of the doubt, figuring that she had to get ready for Monday or something. *Boy was I way off.*

Karen never saw Lenda, yet they were within a few feet of one another at one point. From the way Karen and Oliver were making out, it didn't seem like they cared who was watching them.

Appalled, Lenda continued her journey without saying a word. *This isn't the right time, but so help me—I will bring this up! Wouldn't it be funny if we were on the same plane?*

* * * *

As Lenda waited for her bag on the turnstile, she was surprised to see so many blue pieces of luggage that looked like hers. She decided to make the effort to attach a flower to her suitcase as soon as she could, or buy luggage that would stand out.

Luggage in hand, she began her trek through the airport. This time, because she was home, she wasn't in a hurry. She paused to people watch again. She was disappointed that Karen wasn't on her flight. She wanted a face-to-face, caught-in-the-act encounter. But it didn't happen.

After checking with her mom and picking up her son from his dad's house, Lenda headed home. Her son talked nonstop about the good time he'd had with his dad. He mentioned something about a basketball game and pizza, but Lenda wasn't listening. Her thoughts were back at the airport. *What was Karen thinking? How could she go away with a man she hardly knows and one she isn't married to? She's too old for that.* The picture of Karen in those heels making out with Oliver troubled Lenda even more. *How could she sell herself so cheap?*

"Ma, are you listening to me?" her son pleaded.

"Yes, Matt," she lied. "Mommy's happy that you had such a wonderful time." Under her breath, she confessed to the Lord that she had just lied and according to First John 1:9, she repented.

Lying was not one of Lenda's strong suits and even now, she could tell that her son wasn't convinced. The picture of Karen and Oliver wouldn't go away. It all kept playing over and over and over.

Chapter Nineteen

Lenda picked up the phone to dial Karen. This was the third or fourth time she had dialed, only to hang up before the phone rang. Somehow she felt like she was meddling. She thought: *But don't real friends meddle?* She decided to let the call go through, hoping the answering machine would come on. Instead, she got a real voice.

"Hello," answered the bubbly voice on the other end.

"Hey girl," Lenda started.

"Lenda? Girl, I miss you!"

"I miss you, too. Hey, are you free for dinner this week?

"You buying?"

"Do you ever pay?"

"There *you* go with absolutes."

Lenda had to smile; the girl was relentless. "No, I'm not buying, so you can pick a place that will match your budget. And the last time I checked, it was huge!"

"McDonald's," Karen laughed.

"McDonald's it is," Lenda sighed.

"Girl, this must be serious—you never agree to McDonald's." Silence on Lenda's end. "Lenda, is something wrong?"

"We'll talk at dinner. What, McDonald's?"

"Girl, I'm just kidding about McDonald's. How about Southern Fires?"

"That's the one off Jefferson on Bellevue, near Belle Isle?"

"Yeah, that's the one."

"OK, that's cool. How about Thursday at seven?"

"We've got to wait until Thursday? I know you want to talk about something—it's all in your voice. I want to know today!"

"I can't do it till Thursday."

"So can we do six?"

"What's an hour?"

"It's one more hour I don't have to wait for my beating, 'cause that's what it sounds like this is going to be: a good beat down, packaged as a dinner."

"Six it is, at Southern Fires."

"Bye, Lenda."

"Bye, Karen."

"Hey, before you hang up, tell Matt that I have tickets for us to see the Detroit Symphony Orchestra in two weeks. So have him schedule his weekends right."

Lenda assured Karen that she would give Matthew the message.

Karen was still staring at the phone several minutes after the conversation had ended. *I wonder what prompted this,* Karen thought. Karen would probably still be looking at the phone if Jelly weren't scratching at the door. *Poor Jelly.* If she and Oliver *did* hook up, she wasn't sure what would happen to him. Oliver had already made it clear that dogs were not allowed in the house. Was he really worth her dog?

Why did she vacillate so much? Lenda touched a nerve when she got on Karen for putting Jelly away when Oliver came over. *After all, I don't do that for anyone else. Why him? Why not stand up for what I want? Why do the needs of others, especially men, always prevail?*

It was Monday, and Karen had to wait until Thursday. She wasn't kidding when she said the little dinner sounded like it was going to be a beat down. It reminded her of when she was a little girl and her mother would call on the phone to tell her she was going to whip Karen when she got home. The wait was unbearable for her as a little girl and nothing had changed—this wait was also going to be unbearable. *But I know Lenda enough to know if she said Thursday, no sense in calling her to get together sooner 'cause it won't happen,* she concluded.

* * * *

Lenda was kind of surprised at Karen for reading her on this. *I just hope she doesn't call me to try to schedule an earlier time,* Lenda thought. She needed to talk to God about this one. Karen was so fragile in her eyes. She wanted to make sure she didn't offend her. But no matter how she put things, it was still a very delicate subject that probably wouldn't be taken well. *Lord, help me to talk boldly to Karen and not allow her tears to sway me. Help me to love on her, but still help her see what she's doing is wrong.*

* * * *

Soul food restaurants were not Lenda's favorite. She always questioned if the greens were really clean. However, this place was better than most. As usual, the line was long. The wait was going to be at least twenty-five to thirty minutes because Southern Fires didn't take reservations. Lenda didn't mind waiting, but Karen would most likely fuss if she got there before they had a chance to be seated.

The wait didn't turn out to be so bad. And Lenda was grateful to be seated before Karen arrived. She even had time to determine from the menu what her choice would be for the evening. However, the selection was difficult because everything looked so good. But she decided to go with the marinated chicken breast and for her two sides, she was going to have the collard greens and macaroni and cheese. She knew she'd need an extra day of exercise to make up for the meal, but she didn't care.

Lenda deliberately requested a table near the back, just in case the tears came. That way, everybody wouldn't be looking at *her*. If she had a dollar for every tear Karen cried, they both would be millionaires.

Lenda was looking so intently at the menu that she didn't see Karen come in. Suddenly realizing her presence, Lenda stood to give her a hug. Lenda couldn't help but notice the heels; they were the same ones Karen had on at the airport. She abruptly thought: *Why would anyone in their right mind wear high heels every day?* Perhaps that thought was birthed more out of jealousy because she couldn't wear three-inch heels for one hour—let alone a day. Maybe she was jealous in a nice kind of way.

"So what's going on?" Karen broke out.

"Well hello, how are you?" Lenda said.

"Girl, we can forget all the pleasantries. What's up?"

"Why does something have to be up—why can't I just yearn for a dose of Karen?"

"Talk that junk to someone else. What's up?"

Lenda was rescued by the waitress.

"May I get you ladies something to drink?" said the waitress.

"I'll have a Cranberry Nantucket Nectar," Lenda said.

"And I'll have one as well, but make mine Kiwi Berry."

"Oh, and please bring me a large water with lemon," Lenda added.

"And a large water for me, please—no lemon. See, I'm a big girl. I drink my water straight. The little baby here has some growing to do!" Karen giggled at the waitress.

"I'll be right back with your drinks, ladies."

Once the waitress was out of sight, Karen looked at Lenda with a frown on her face. "Did you see her uniform?"

"Yes."

"Well, do we tell her or her manager? I don't want someone serving me with a dirty uniform. It looks like cats have been sucking on *it and her hair* all night. Sorry, I want another table and another waitress."

"This time I agree with you, Karen. I wonder why management didn't check her. I know they had to see the stains and white stuff all over her shirt. What does that say for them?"

Just then, the girl reappeared with the drinks in hand, but the straws, even though covered, were positioned under her armpits. With Karen's mouth primed to say the wrong thing, Lenda interrupted and asked for the manager. With a baffled look, the waitress complied.

Both Karen and Lenda sat in silence until the manager appeared. *She* did not disappoint them. Dressed in a nice navy suit with a smile on her face, the manager politely said, "Now how can I help you, ladies?"

Lenda and Karen didn't waste any time expressing their displeasure in the young lady's appearance.

The manager apologized and then said, "Ladies, I don't want you to move. You're customers. I'll have someone assist you—and consider your drinks on the house."

Within minutes, they not only had a new waitress whose uniform looked like it was fresh from the cleaners, she was standing in front of them with a smile to take their dinner order—and their drinks had been refreshed.

When dinner arrived, it didn't disappoint them—it was scrumptious. Lenda even managed small talk with Karen while they ate, to avoid the bigger issue.

After dinner and small talk, it was time to order dessert. Lenda went with the strawberry shortcake, which consisted of pound cake and vanilla ice cream, covered with strawberries and whipped cream. Karen ordered the homemade peach cobbler with a scoop of vanilla ice cream.

When the desserts came, they looked too good to eat. The strawberry shortcake had red syrup drizzled in the shape of a strawberry around the edges of the plate. The peach cobbler had orange syrup drizzled around its edges. Presentation meant everything and though they were both stuffed, they pounced on the desserts like a cat who had just seen a mouse.

Karen was so full she actually forgot that this dinner had a purpose. As if she was reading Karen's mind, Lenda cocked her head to the side. Her face registered concern laced with love.

"Remember when I asked you to pick me up from the airport last Sunday?" Lenda was ready to put it all out there.

"Yes," Karen replied apprehensively, scared to fall into a trap.

"Tell me again why you said you couldn't pick me up."

Instantly, Karen lost her appetite for the remaining dessert.

"Let's not play games, Lenda. What is it?"

With her head bowed as if she was about to pray, Lenda began a slow, deliberate recall of the airport scene while twirling her fork in the dessert that was left on her plate.

"I went to Houston for a conference with a client last week and coming back home, something caught my eye. I noticed one very attractive young lady in a pair of stilettos, making out with a man in the customs line. As a matter of fact, they were identical to the ones you have on now," Lenda paused, looking at Karen defiantly as if to say, "You better not lie to me." As she continued, she was surprised to see that Karen was just as defiant.

"My first thought was: 'They need to take that home,' but another thought superseded the previous one because if they were married, they wouldn't have to make out in the airport while kids and adults alike were appalled at the lewd display of affection," Lenda went on, but not as courageous as when she first began. Finally coming up for air, Lenda put her fork down, sat back in the chair, crossed her arms and with a sneer on her face, she began to stare at Karen, waiting for her response.

Karen, with an obvious smirk on her face, locked eyes with Lenda as she held up her right hand and waived for the waitress. Without a word spoken between the two of them and eyes still locked, Karen asked the waitress to bring the check and promised a huge tip if she would expedite the process.

"You're just going to leave? You're not going to say anything?" Lenda blurted.

"Right now, I'm hotter than August. You cooked up this foolishness and served it on a beautiful platter called 'I'm just concerned about you,' and you expect me to eat it!!! I don't think so. My mother is dead, and you don't make a good substitute! Because unlike my mother, I *did* like you up until sixty seconds ago. I'm sure I'll get over this! Perhaps in a week, I'll like you again. I am forty-seven years old, and I don't need your…" Before she could finish, Lenda grabbed her arm and began to dig her fingers into Karen's flesh.

"Then act like a forty-seven-year-old woman instead of a desperate teenager."

The waitress returned, but when she saw the scene before her, she did a Dorothy from Oz: she clicked her heels and disappeared.

"Karen, is that what you think I'm trying to do, be your mother?" Lenda asked.

"Who do *you* think you sound like, Lenda?" Karen replied with a slightly elevated voice. "You and I are cut from two different molds. While I've enjoyed you as a friend for many years, this is getting old," she continued.

"Karen, why are you putting yourself through this?" Lenda pressed.

"Through what? What is it I'm putting myself through? I know you don't want to hear this. But since you brought it up, let me help you with something. My intent in going away was not to sleep with Oliver. But you guessed it, I did. And you know what else? I enjoyed it! And guess what else? I'll probably do it again, and again, and again. Is this what you want to hear? And you know what? Before you go there, I will. Does Jesus still love me? Yes, He does! I'm sure He doesn't like what I'm doing, but He died for my sins as well as yours. My sin might be a lack of self-control. But believe me, you are not perfect!

"I'm proud that you've managed to be celibate for so many years. I'll send you some gold stars in the mail. But you know what, Lenda? You sin, too. So don't act all holy—it's not becoming.

"You eat too much chicken. You glut! Remember, sin is sin. I don't police what you eat, even though you need to cut back and eliminate some rolls—and I'm *not* talking about the kind you bake in an oven. I'm talking about the ones around your waist!

"Stop policing my life! You're happy being Chicken-Licking Lenda. And I'm happy to be me!"

Lenda never could have imagined a worst-case scenario like this. She was at a total loss for words. With a last-ditch effort, she could only come up with, "I just don't want to see you hurt. And yes, while Jesus forgives sins, don't you think it hurts Him when you, His daughter, practice sin?" Lenda knew when she said it that it wasn't going to work. She tried again. "Whether you will admit it or not, when you sleep with someone that's not in covenant with you, the guilt comes. And when you're alone, you will feel so bad that you disappointed God. Is it worth all that, Karen?" Lenda said.

"Let me think…yes, Yes, YES it's worth all that!" Karen barked. "And while we're admitting our sins, don't you think it hurts Jesus as well when you eat all that greasy chicken, clogging your arteries, raising your blood pressure? Don't you feel bad when you lay down at night with heartburn from all the hot sauce you've eaten that you can hardly breathe? Don't you think that it also disappoints God that you lack self-control and can't stop eating chicken? Sucking on those bones like a dog. 'Is it worth all that, Lenda?'" Karen mocked.

"Ladies, is everything OK?" asked a man from the restaurant.

"Who are *you*?" Karen demanded.

"I'm the owner. My waitress seems to feel like you need some assistance. Perhaps you've had too much sugar?"

He paused for a response, but Lenda and Karen were still glaring at one another.

"We can provide help if either of you need it." Next to him were two men who looked like they were linemen for the Detroit Lions. It was obvious they were some sort of security.

Finally, Lenda responded, "We're fine."

Ignoring Lenda, he looked at Karen, "Ma'am, do you need any assistance from us?"

"I'm OK, honest."

"You have ten minutes to take care of your bill and exit the premises. If you take longer, what you're saying to us is that you need help, and we'll return with the help you need. Is that clear, ladies?"

"Clear," both ladies echoed.

The men had barely left the table before Lenda thought she'd give it one last try.

"Karen, do you know that you're going to stand before God one day?" Lenda begged, as if this conversation was new.

"Lenda, we're all going to stand before God for lying, gossiping, overeating, and being busybodies. And guess what? To God, it's all the same. Yeah, busybodies and gluttons like yourself will be in the same line as the fornicators," said Karen.

"Lying can't give you AIDS," Lenda said.

"Yes it can! 'Cause if he lies and says he don't have it and he does—there you go!" Karen said.

"Has it ever dawned on you that if all the single women closed up shop, a lot more marriage invites would go out?"

That comment caused Karen to jump up and put on a devious smile. She leaned down to Lenda with an in-your-face gesture. "You know what, Lenda? That never dawned on me," Karen purred with a sinister growl. "It's never going to happen because I for one am not closing up shop! This little confrontation here has helped me make a decision I've been thinking about for a while. I'm going to get a new sign painted for *my* shop. In nice bold letters, it's going to read, 'Open for Business 24/7.' Twenty-four hours a day, seven days a week. Please don't call me, and I won't call you," Karen said, as she sashayed from the restaurant without looking back.

Never in a trillion years would Lenda have imagined that their conversation would have gone this way. Never in a trillion years. She was stunned beyond measure. Lenda thought: *Karen goes to church pretty regularly. How can someone who's that involved in church act like that?*

Lenda was fuming!

Lenda would have bet money that Karen would have felt remorseful and taken ownership that what she had done was wrong. But for her to be so defiant about sin was scary. The sad part was deep down inside, Lenda knew that the relationship would never be the same again.

How *would* they go on? After all, Karen had such special bond with her son. *Was my need to check Karen worth our*

214 | YOU'VE GOT A MAN

relationship? I think not!

The waitress appeared again, and Lenda remembered that she needed to pay the bill. So not only did she lose a friend, she was stuck with the tab.

After paying the bill, the young waitress returned with the leather pouch that had Lenda's change in it. Lenda left fifteen percent gratuity but judging from the waitress's face, it wasn't enough. Then Lenda recalled that Karen had promised a huge tip if the waitress returned quickly. Lenda wasn't in a good mood, thus her response: "My friend told you to expedite the bill; she didn't tell you to return with two goons and a wannabe sheriff. If you aren't satisfied with what I gave you, I can always take back the fifteen percent and then when you have nothing, that fifteen percent will look huge!"

Lenda didn't wait for a response. She stood up and walked out, much like Karen did moments earlier, except Karen had a swagger to her walk; she didn't. And someone other than Lenda had her mouth open in shock—the waitress!

Chapter Twenty

As Lenda pulled into her driveway, she felt like the world had fallen on her shoulders. How did this day end like this? Was she a busybody? Was she supposed to see her friend practicing sin and not say anything? Lenda didn't know the answer to any of those questions, and she wished she had kept her mouth shut and just prayed. *What are friends really for? Tell me, Lord, at what point does a real friend turn her head to a friend's bad behavior?*

As she turned off the ignition and slumped back in the seat, the tears came. "Lord, it wasn't worth my friendship…it wasn't worth it," she cried out. Lenda's son saw her sitting in the car. He went over to the car door to see if she was OK.

He saw the tears. "Ma, what's wrong?" he asked with concern.

"I'll be OK. I just had some words with Auntie Karen. I'll be OK, really."

"Is Auntie Karen alright?" Matthew asked.

"Yes. She's fine."

"Is she crying, too?"

"I don't think so, son."

"You sure you don't want to come in the house? I'll help you."

"No, Matthew. I'm fine."

Matthew turned to walk away, but he came back.

"Ma, I don't like to see you cry."

Lenda opened the car door and held out her arms. Her son hugged her. As he reached in the car door and held her neck tight, she cried some more. After a few moments, Lenda convinced him that she was alright and only needed a few more minutes to sit in the car. She promised that if she wasn't in the house in five minutes, she'd play a game of *Phase 10* with him, even though it was a school night. That got her a "Sweet! Take your time, Ma!" from him.

"Take my time?" Kids will do anything to prolong bedtime, and she knew how much her son loved to play *Phase 10*.

Minutes later, she pulled herself together and walked back into the house. Lenda noticed that Matthew was getting tall and looked more and more like his dad every day. She had enough to do and worry about without getting in Karen's business, or as Karen would put it, "policing her."

Karen was right; she needed to stop eating so much chicken!

Lord, I will call to apologize; please have it in her heart to forgive me, she thought.

Lenda was so blessed. Even with the divorce, she had a wonderful son who loved the Lord and enjoyed going to church. Lenda had never had any trouble out of him. He was a good son—very respectful, and just a wonderful young man. She had a nice job and for the most part a good family. Why did she see the need to counsel people? It wasn't her profession.

She should have been writing a letter to her brother. It had been weeks since she'd seen him because of traveling and her schedule. In all honesty, she really hadn't seen him since their breakthrough. But she had called him a couple of times.

Her sister had been taking her mom to see him, and Lenda was getting some much-needed rest. But she missed her brother.

Looking up, she heard herself say, "Lord, if You can restore the relationship with Karen, I'll leave the counseling to You and the ministers You ordain."

Before this happened, she wanted to invite Karen to Thanksgiving dinner at Queen's, but that wasn't going to work. She decided to have Queen do it.

While walking through the house, she could almost hear Karen saying, "Please don't call me, and I won't call you." Well, if Karen really felt like that, the bright side would be that Lenda wouldn't have to worry about someone coming to her house in the middle of the night 'cause she's having man trouble and eating her Oreo cookies.

Who was Lenda trying to con? She loved Karen and knew that if this did break up the relationship, it would hurt—and it would hurt a lot. Lenda made a decision right then and there: *Whatever it takes, I'll make it right.* Suddenly she heard a voice say, "I'm glad you said that." Lenda knew that it was the voice of Holy Spirit.

"Holy Spirit, I know You're not happy with me right now. I know I could've handled this better, and I'll make it right."

"Well, not only will you make that right, I have a question for you. Why did you not contribute to the donation for Diane when the envelope was placed on your desk at work?"

Lenda's first thought was, *How did You know?* But that was dumb, because Holy Spirit knows everything.

"Holy Spirit, no need in me skirting the question. It's because she's mean. You know it, I know it, and everybody else knows it! She never speaks to me and when she has to for work reasons, she always writes a note. She's very difficult to work with."

"Lenda," Holy Spirit continued, "you still didn't answer My question. Why didn't *you* give? You say you love God with your words. You're quick to point out someone else's sin. Why didn't *you* give? Anybody can love someone who loves them, but you must love when the person seems unlovable. You must forgive when you don't feel like it. Jesus commanded it, and I'll uphold it.

"So this is what I want you to do. When you go back to work on Monday, remember that five dollars you *thought* about putting in the envelope? Now you'll add an extra zero. Go to the bank, get money, and put fifty dollars in the envelope. And you will tell no one that you put fifty dollars in it. Also, when Diane comes back from lunch on Monday, you will have a sealed card on her desk with a smiley face on it. Can I depend on your obedience, Lenda?"

"Yes, Sir."

"Good night Lenda; sleep well child," said Holy Spirit.

"Holy Spirit, I know You can read my thoughts, so I need to say this…I'm going to do what You said when I go to work. But You and I know that what You've asked me to do is hard. But I really can't think like I want to 'cause You'll know what I'm thinking. So I thank You for letting me say the little I've said."

All of a sudden, she felt a pout coming on. "How did the conversation go from Karen to Diane at work?"

"Lenda."

"Yes, Sir."

"Remember, You've got a Man, and My job is to make you better. That's what real men do. They make everyone around them better."

"Yes, Sir."

People always told Lenda that God didn't talk to them. After this conversation, she was convinced even more that He *did* talk. But perhaps like tonight…they don't like what He's saying, so it's easier to say He's not talking than to do what He says. *I'd better quit thinking, 'cause again, He hears my thoughts.*

Lenda felt like Holy Spirit was smiling at her. She smiled back. Now she was *really* wide awake. Where was she before this conversation came up?

Back to Karen. She knew nothing was worth the friendship between them. Besides, her son loved Karen. He confided in Lenda early on that he didn't want to call her Miss Karen. He felt Auntie Karen was much more affectionate. They agreed that Auntie Karen sounded better, so he called her that. He would be so hurt if this intense fellowship came between them.

Sometimes Lenda felt like he loved Karen more than her. They could sit and laugh for hours. He would not be happy to know what happened. So Lenda decided she wasn't going to tell him anything else about it.

Chapter Twenty-One

Karen couldn't remember the last time she allowed herself to get so upset over words.

I can't believe Lenda had the audacity to dig her fingers into my arm. Lord, I almost lost it! I am a grown woman! What makes her think she can reprimand me like a child? Friends shouldn't get that carried away.

You really need to talk to her! She claims she talks to You every morning. Could You gently tell her next time that she needs to mind her own business and get a real life?

I just wonder if our season of friendship is over. Lord, I don't bother anyone, so why do people feel the need to bother me? What a night!

Karen continued her silent tantrum for another ten minutes and finally, Holy Spirit spoke to her. What He said was startling.

"Karen, you need to love yourself."

"I do love myself," Karen spoke aloud.

"No, you don't. If you loved yourself, you wouldn't do and say certain things."

"Oh, you're talking about the twenty-four-hour sign?" she wondered. "You know I didn't mean that, Holy Spirit. I was

222 | YOU'VE GOT A MAN

so mad I wanted to say anything that would upset and yes, even hurt Lenda like she was hurting me. I wanted to see her mouth wide open. And it was open!" A brief smile appeared across Karen's face, but it quickly disappeared because she could feel Holy Spirit wasn't pleased. She knew her actions were grievous to Him.

Now she had two of her favorite people mad at her, Lenda and Holy Spirit. The funny thing was that sometimes it was so difficult for her to hear from God. But either He was speaking very loudly tonight or because she acted like such a butt, maybe she was more sensitive to His voice—and the feeling was still there.

*　*　*　*

Karen had showered and got into her bed, but she couldn't sleep. "Thanks a lot, Lenda!" she hollered. "Thank you! Thank you! Thank you!" She had to deal with the kids at school the next day, and she needed her rest.

As she lay in the bed tossing and turning, she finally picked up the remote. Nothing good was on, so she turned on the Trinity Broadcasting Network. She didn't watch it all the time. But when she couldn't sleep, it lulled her right to sleep. And she would wake up hours later, turn the TV off, and sleep the rest of the night.

The preacher staring her in the face this night wasn't a regular, but he was cute. Karen looked up as if she saw someone staring at her with hands on hips. "WHAT? He *is* cute, Holy Spirit," she laughed.

The preacher's words suddenly caught her ear.

"What Jesus is saying to us in Ephesians, the fifth chapter and the fourth verse, is we need to watch what we say. The Word of God says here in the Amplified Bible that we shouldn't let things like silly and corrupt talk or coarse jesting come from our mouths.

"In other words, don't joke around and say stuff you don't mean. Somebody made you mad, so you went off! The Word says it's not fitting or becoming for that kind of talk to come from our mouths."

Karen's eyes rolled again. *Where is the remote? I'm looking at and hearing Lenda in a man's body,* she thought. While she was trying to find the remote, the minister continued.

"And even though I didn't intend to go here, I believe somebody watching by television needs this verse. Look at the verse above four. The third verse says, *'But immorality (sexual vice) and all impurity [of lustful, rich, wasteful living] or greediness must not even be named among you...'* Who are the named among you? He's talking to a select group of people, the body of Christ!

"Listen to me if you're watching by TV. Jesus did not die on the cross so that you could practice sin, sleeping around when you say you love God. Stop it now! Stop it now! Your very life depends on it. Cut off the relationship if it's not of God."

Karen shot straight up in the bed; she wasn't feeling Trinity tonight.

Click!

Even though the TV was off, it was too late; those words resonated in Karen's head. Even Jelly, who was sitting quietly in the chair next to Karen's bed, was sitting up straight. His ears were pointing as if to say, "I heard that, too."

Lord, was he talking to me? This is just too coincidental. I mean, the Scripture on saying things you really don't mean and the fornication bit. What did he mean by saying my very life depends on it?

Karen's stomach was churning like she was getting ready to ride a roller coaster. Actually, her stomach had been acting up quite a bit lately. Maybe it was time for a checkup.

Jelly was making noises, too. He knew something wasn't right, as dogs have keen senses.

Eventually, Karen drifted off to sleep.

* * * *

Karen was so sleepy that she didn't think she'd make it till the bell rang. She was thankful that Thanksgiving break was around the corner. She needed a break from the kids, her friends, *and* Oliver. Before she could gather herself, the door flew open—security was trying to keep two female students apart. Some sort of mayhem had broken out.

"HEY! HEY! HEY! Stop it! What's wrong with you, Ashley?" Karen shouted.

"That @%#&! better stop *&%$#@! with me!" Ashley yelled.

"Shut up before I pour a bottle of soap down your mouth!" Karen screamed.

"YOU…"the other girl started.

"NOT another word! Ashley, you better not utter another word!" Karen shouted even louder.

The kids in the main office were giggling until Karen rolled her eyes at each one. They dropped their heads and got quiet.

"Put *her* in the back room, and take Ashley to my office!" she directed the security officers.

"I don't want to hear a sound out of *anyone* or you *all* will have detention for a week!" Karen said.

Karen walked to her office with a purpose and couldn't

wait to slam the door.

"Ashley Collins…what's wrong with you?" Karen demanded.

"Miss McDonald, she started it," Ashley cried.

"Started what? What could she have started to make you want to fight? You're an A student getting ready to graduate next year. Do you need this on your record? You want me to suspend you until January?" Karen paused. "Why, Ashley? You're one of my best students! Why?" Karen pressed.

"You won't give me a chance to answer you," Ashley whined.

"Answer me! And it better be good!" Karen said.

"She called my momma a name!" Ashley said.

"'She called your momma a name,'" Karen mocked in disgust. "What did she call her, Ashley? Never mind, don't answer that 'cause it doesn't matter. Is your momma what she called her?"

Ashley hung her head and began to cry.

Karen put her arms around Ashley and began to stroke her hair while she cried.

"Miss McDonald, I don't like people talking about my momma. You know my momma walks with a limp, and they were talking about her. I love my momma, and I don't want people saying things about her," Ashley continued to cry.

"Ashley, look at me. Don't allow the words of other people to cause you to lose your cool and act up. That other girl is failing. A three-week suspension won't hurt her. On the other hand, it *will* hurt you because you're trying to get a scholarship.

"Let people say what they want, but don't ever lose your

temper and act in a way unbecoming to a young lady. I have you come in here and help me because I want you to excel. I see a young woman with great potential; don't allow somebody who is on the verge of getting kicked out of school get you in trouble. Do you hear me?" Karen asked.

"Yes, ma'am," Ashley got out between sobs.

"Promise me that you won't allow other people to control you," Karen pressed.

"I promise," Ashley said.

"Sit here while I write out this report." When Karen finished, she handed Ashley some tissue and put ten dollars in her hand. "Stop by McDonald's on the way home and treat yourself."

Ashley's face lit up and as she stood up to leave, Karen could tell something was on her mind.

"What is it, Ashley?"

"I love your signs."

"What signs?"

"The ones you have hanging all over your office. I read them every time I come in here. They encourage me."

Karen felt low. When she heard Ashley say signs, her thoughts went to the night before and what she had said about hanging a sign on her body.

"I'm glad you like my signs."

"Especially those two."

"Which two?"

"That one by Benjamin Franklin that says, 'Remember not only to say the right thing in the right place, but far more difficult still, to leave unsaid the wrong thing at the tempting moment.'"

"Ummm," Karen responded.

"I should've done that today. And look at that one Miss McDonald. It's by Benjamin Franklin, too. That one is really for me: 'By failing to prepare, you are preparing to fail.' Know what I'm preparing for?"

"No. You need to go on to class, Ashley," Karen said.

"I'm preparing to be just like you. All the girls want to be like you! I mean, I love my momma and I want to do some things like her, but I want to be just like you when I grow up! You're pretty. All the boys have a crush on you. You have nice clothes, and you always look like you just stepped out of a fashion magazine. We all dream about being like you when we grow up!"

"See you, Ashley. Don't be like me; be who God wants you to be. Don't focus on the material; look on the inside." Karen lowered her voice when she said God because according to the Detroit Board of Education, people weren't supposed to talk about God at school. *That's what's wrong with these kids now. They need to put prayer back in schools. Clearly they can see what's happened since they took it out! We have a bunch of kids who don't respect authority or themselves, and only prayer will save and change them,* she thought.

Ashley snapped Karen back to the present moment. "But that's just it. We know you love God, too. You're the complete package, Miss McDonald. You're who keeps some of us coming to school. We want to see you…see what you have on…see your smile and hear you encourage us. Nobody encourages us like you, Miss McDonald. We're not stupid. We know when you counsel us it's from the Bible, but you just can't say Scripture and Bible."

With a proud voice, Ashley continued, "Know what I want

for graduation?"

"What, Ashley?" said Karen.

"One of your signs, so I can hang it in my room and look at it whenever I want. Plus, it'll remind me of you!"

"Bye, Ashley," Karen said, playfully pushing Ashley out of the door.

Karen closed her door and softly hit her head against it.

"Ashley, Ashley, don't be like me…please don't be like me!" Karen silently yelled. "How can I counsel her, when the very thing I told her not to do, I did?"

"Lord, why? First the TV preacher, now Ashley. Who's next?"

Karen heard a still, small voice say, "Get it together, and there won't have to be a next."

* * * *

Karen pulled up in Lenda's driveway and called Matthew on his phone.

"Hello," Matthew answered.

"Hey Matt, Auntie's in the driveway. Come on out," Karen said in her Matthew-only voice. She loved that boy like he was her very own. That's why she was going to make sure his college fund was paid in full.

Even though Lenda never said anything about her finances, Karen knew it was rough for her. She didn't want to see Matthew suffer because of Lenda's divorce. He was the closest thing to being the child she never had. She thought: *Why have money if you can't share it?*

Out of her bedroom window, Lenda watched Matthew run to the car. She could see him give Karen a hug. *Guess she's still mad at me; she usually comes in and raids the cookie jar. I hope we get it right before Thanksgiving,* she thought.

"Auntie, you and Ma still mad?" Matthew asked Karen.

"What are you talking about, baby?" Karen said with as much innocence as she could muster.

"Well, when you guys had dinner a couple of weeks ago, she was sitting in the car for a long time. When I came out to ask her what was wrong, she was crying and said the two of you had some words."

"Is that what she said?" Karen asked.

"Maybe it wasn't those exact words, but it was something like that."

Silence.

"Matthew, sometimes people don't agree with one another and get angry, but it doesn't mean they don't love each other. They just disagree."

"But I thought you could disagree and still like each other."

"I just said that disagreement doesn't mean you don't love someone."

"Yeah, but can't you love someone and not like them?"

Karen thought for a minute. She had to be on it when she answered.

"I guess you can, Matt."

"Do you still like her?"

"Of course I do!"

"So why didn't you come in just now? You never come to pick me up without coming in and fussing with her about the cookies."

Karen stopped at the red light and looked over at Matthew. He was so handsome—and so innocent and perceptive. The car behind them began to blow the horn—the light changed, but Karen still didn't know what to say.

"Matthew, sometimes adults just need some space. And they need nephews like you who will help them stop acting like children. Thanks, baby."

"What I do?"

"You helped Auntie see that she was acting like a spoiled little child. Ready for the symphony?"

"Yes. I hope they play 'The Imperial March' from *Star Wars*!"

"So do I!"

* * * *

The symphony was everything they thought and more. After a late lunch at Fuddruckers and a drive around Belle Isle, Matthew was knocked out. She was so glad they played Darth Vader's theme. It made Karen smile to see the grin on Matthew's face. It even made Karen smile to know that Lenda also took Matthew to see the Detroit Symphony Orchestra. Her heart went out to children who never got the opportunity to hear them.

Twitter, Facebook, and all that other social media stuff has its place, but balance is key. Kids need to and should be exposed to finer music. These concerts are free, Lord. All parents need to do is register, but most that I see and come in contact with can't pull themselves away from what they think is important to them to spend quality time with the gifts God has blessed them with. TV is used to babysit rather than educate.

Some of our kids don't stand a chance. Oh God, the kids should be my focus and not my sex life or lack thereof. I'll get it together. I'm too old to be doing some of the stuff I do.

Chapter Twenty-Two

Lenda was in the fridge pulling out Thanksgiving Day leftovers. She enjoyed leftovers more than she did the actual Thanksgiving dinner. All was quiet, and the extra days off work only reminded her of how blessed she was.

Matthew was in his room playing video games. While the food was heating, she began to set the table. This was going to be her first one-on-one meeting with Karen since the major blowout. She wasn't nervous about it, but she was anxious.

It helped that they were together over Claudette's house for Thanksgiving. Claudette cooked. Lenda was glad she had invited them over because Ken and Quintella had an eleventh-hour change of plans. This year marked the first that they didn't have a big dinner. Since Ken was planning to take Quintella away before Christmas, they chose to spend Thanksgiving with their immediate family.

But it still worked out for the rest of them. They all had a nice time sitting and playing games and enjoying each other. It was especially great that Matthew got to be around two other men. Even though Lenda wasn't fond of the one, she was grateful that Matthew wasn't spending Thanksgiving with all ladies. He got to watch the football game with men, and he didn't have to answer foolish questions asked by unlearned women about the game and its rules.

As Lenda finished her last preparations, she thought about how happy she was for Claudette and her new friend Christopher. But when it came to Karen and Oliver, she couldn't get past the fact that she didn't like him. She attributed her feelings to knowing that it wasn't a "holy" relationship like Claudette and Christopher's. She felt like he was treating Karen like "low-hanging fruit"—pick it, eat it, and then eventually go after what you can't grab.

While it was nice to see Karen happy, Lenda couldn't help but think…*at what expense?* Since she didn't have concrete evidence of anything, she asked God if it was jealousy, or if she was being judgmental; she needed to be sure. However, the same answer kept coming up…he simply wasn't the one. His actions, though they seemed genuine on the surface, were selfish. In Lenda's estimation, Karen was nothing more than his latest toy.

It also didn't help that every time Lenda and her mother were by themselves at Claudette's, her mother would whisper, "You next in line, baby. God's moving the man line, and you next! I can feel it in my bones—yours is right around the corner!" *Mothers and their children,* Lenda thought.

Lenda was also finding it hard to keep focused periodically because she kept thinking about her brother and what he was eating in prison on Thanksgiving.

"I'll be glad when he comes home. That's one day I'm going to go all out and cook him the best dinner imaginable. I'm believing Annie will come, too," Lenda said, talking to herself.

Lenda missed her sister at Thanksgiving dinner, but she only said, "I have other plans."

"Lord, but back to Karen—I don't know if we got along so well yesterday because of all the people or because Karen has really forgiven me," Lenda added.

Thanksgiving Day had been the first time they had been in the same room with each other. When Karen took Matthew to the concert, she only waved when she dropped him off. She thought a wave was better than nothing. But the fact that Karen actually accepted her invitation to come over for leftovers was huge.

Lenda figured she probably agreed because she really didn't consider them leftovers. Her meal was cooked, but no one ate it. So technically, they weren't *real* leftovers. She could thank her mother for that.

Ethel always taught Lenda that no matter who invited her for Thanksgiving, she should cook her own dinner. That way, when she got home, she could enjoy her own turkey and dressing.

Lenda thought for a minute: *I have never once had a Thanksgiving where I didn't fix my own complete dinner. Even when Mom invites me, I still have my own dinner prepared at home.*

Lenda stepped back and looked at the table. It was so pretty.

"My set is old, but it looks good," Lenda said, staring at the brown ribbed Sango plates with shades of black. They were simple but elegant as they rested on the gold chargers. The brown and beige layered napkins encased in the beaded napkin rings that were trimmed in gold only made the table look that much more sophisticated.

She had to laugh because the bronze goblets were purchased at the dollar store. Lenda could remember the day she saw them; she couldn't believe they were that striking. If she had a nickel for every person who complimented her on them, she could treat herself to something really spectacular.

And the flowers—they were the icing on the cake.

"I can always depend on Wesley Berry Flowers to come through for me," Lenda gushed.

She went with a mix of fresh flowers in luscious shades of raspberry, lavender, and pink, snuggly arranged in a lavender glass vase. Lenda knew what was appealing to the eye, but names of flowers told her nothing. She had to actually see them. The card read, "Pink roses and alstroemeria, raspberry sinuata statice, and lavender carnations…" They were gorgeous.

Lenda intended to give the flowers to Karen after dinner, but she was having second thoughts. She was thinking about keeping them.

The entire sight was fit for a queen. And they *were* queens!

With everything in place for Karen's arrival, Lenda took the opportunity to see what Matthew was doing.

Simultaneously, Lenda knocked and opened Matthew's bedroom door.

"Hi Ma," Matthew dragged.

"'Hi Ma,'" Lenda mocked. "Don't sound so happy to see me."

"Ma, why don't you wait until I say come in?" Matthew protested.

"'Cause it's my house; I pay the bills, so I don't have to wait," Lenda teased.

"Then why do you knock? Why don't you just open the door and come on in?" Matthew continued to protest.

"Because that would be rude," Lenda answered with a smile.

"My friends' parents don't ever go in their rooms,"

Matthew said as he moved out of the way for her. He knew what was coming, so he didn't wait for Lenda to ask him to move over.

"Bad mistake for them," Lenda came back.

Lenda went over to the computer and began to drive the mouse without asking. She went to the Internet browser and clicked on the drop-down. She then hit the favorites and checked out his history.

"As usual, very good," Lenda said, giving Matthew a playful thump upside the head.

"What? I could never do anything bad. You come in my room too much."

"It's called Parenting 101," Lenda said.

As Lenda got ready to close the door, Matthew got up enough nerve to ask.

"Ma."

"Yes?"

"Can I eat in my room and watch TV? You and Auntie Karen are gonna be talking that girl stuff. Do I have to listen tonight?"

Lenda thought for a moment. Matthew had his head turned to the side like a puppy waiting for a treat. She decided to throw him one.

"Yes, you can!"

"Sweet!"

"Is 'Sweet!' all you know to say?"

"Nope, it's not all I know, but it's the way I feel!" Matthew grinned.

A familiar knock was at the door. Matthew tore past

Lenda and made a beeline to the front door. Without looking, he opened the door and welcomed Karen into the house.

"Boy, I told you about opening the door without looking," Lenda said.

"I knew it was Auntie," Matthew said.

The girls looked at each other, burst out laughing, and hugged longer than was comfortable for Matthew. He waited his turn to hug Karen, and the girls began their usual banter. As always, he took Karen by the hand and led her to his room. They closed the door, and all Lenda could hear was laughing. Matthew never took her hand and led her to his room like that. These were the times she was jealous, in a healthy way, of the relationship he and Karen shared.

Perhaps she had that kind of relationship with him because she was a counselor. After all, she was trained to deal with teenagers. It was anybody's guess.

Lenda hung up Karen's coat, and she went back into the kitchen.

About fifteen minutes later, Karen appeared.

"Girl, your table looks fabulous!" Karen commented.

"Well, when you're entertaining a distinguished guest, it calls for something extraordinary," Lenda said.

The look in Karen's eyes said, "You're still my girl!"

*　*　*　*

After dinner, they sat by the fire so they could really talk.

"Didn't we have a ball yesterday?" Lenda began.

"We did. Oliver even commented on how nice everything was."

"You really forgive me, right?"

"Girl, that's so old. How could I not? If I hadn't, that would've told me that we really weren't friends in the first place."

"So, did you go shopping today?" Lenda asked, glad they were over the major hump.

"Girl, I don't go out there with those crazies. Poor Claudette don't have a choice. I bet she's still at the store."

"So what's up for Christmas, are you going to go to Queen's this year?"

"Nope, I already told you. I go home for Christmas to see my aunts, and that's a tradition I don't break."

"Karen, you would so enjoy their annual Christmas party."

"Who wouldn't enjoy their parties? They're so elaborate and elegant, like something out of a fairy-tale book. No, I'm going home," Karen replied.

"You love to go home, don't you?" Lenda said.

"Yep!" she lied, partially. *I do like to go home, just not at Christmas,* she thought.

"What's so special about Natchez?"

"It's just a beautiful town to me. Let's see…you've got the Mississippi River and its bridge, which connects to the state of Louisiana. The connecting city is Vidalia. We have this little place called The Malt Shop. Every time I go home, I go there every day, sometimes twice a day! I gain five pounds every time I go home."

"Does it just sell ice cream stuff?"

"No, girl. It's like an old-fashioned, good, fast-food restaurant. They have burgers, curly fries, and malts. They are delicious! And the price is right."

"Is it fancy?"

"Naw, girl! It's as old as the hills, and it looks like it. But the people are friendly, and the service is great. You'll have to see for yourself one day! We even have several of the old antebellum homes…"

"What are those?" Lenda interrupted.

"They are the plantations of the 'Masters,' the grounds where slaves lived and worked."

"Shut up!" Lenda said.

"Girl, yeah. Natchez is full of them. It's interesting that they call them 'antebellum,' which means something belonging to a period of time around the American Civil War. The black people in town don't like going to them at all. But they're major attractions in Natchez, big moneymakers for the South. People, those mostly dipped in the vanilla batter, come from everywhere by the busloads every year in the spring-time, and the city puts on the ritz.

"Then we have the home of President Thomas Jefferson, which is not far from Natchez. And guess how many high schools we have?"

"You can count them?" Lenda asked, surprised.

"Yep—we have, I think, three or four high schools. I've been away so long I can't remember. We have two hospitals, one movie theater, and we have one traffic light."

"Karen, you never shared any of this with me."

"You never asked," Karen laughed. "For some reason, I also love our street names…Homochitto Street, Magnolia Way, Ann Holden Lane.

"Oh, I forgot to tell you…if you ever go with me, or when we go…" Karen looked straight into Lenda's eyes with a "we *will* go one day, girlfriend" gaze. "We can eat at Catfish Walk. That's what I call it—other people call it Cock of the Walk.

But girl, they have the best catfish you ever want to eat. Make yo' tongue slap your tonsils. Let's see, I'll even take you to Natchez Under-the-Hill."

"Wait a minute. Back up to Catfish Walk—do they *just* serve catfish?"

"Noooo! Girl, any kind of seafood you can eat—they have it! A lot of people complain about the staff, but I don't pay them any attention. I love that place."

"OK, so go back to the Under-the-Hill thing. What's that, girl?"

"Rumor has it that it was the home of some of the worst outlaws to ever live in Natchez. It's where the ladies of the night hung out. Outlaws would sell slaves. I'm told it was a playground for the wicked, shameful, and corrupt. It sounds a lot like the city of Detroit."

"That's not funny, Karen—don't talk about our city," Lenda said with a serious tone.

"It's my city, too! OK, back to Natchez. They have souvenir shops. It's just a fun place to visit. You'll see."

"I would love to see the city—it sounds like a lot of fun."

"It is!" Karen's voice lowered. "It is."

Lenda was having a wonderful time with Karen. She loved hearing about all the things from her past that they had never talked about before. But Lenda noticed that Karen's eyes had a faraway look when she talked about Natchez. She had a sneaking suspicion that Karen's past was filled with tainted memories. She was almost sure of it.

"What time is it?" Karen asked.

"Why?" Lenda yelled playfully. "Where do *you* have to go?"

242 | YOU'VE GOT A MAN

"You're not meddling, are you?"

Lenda softened immediately, "No, no, I'm just enjoying your company. But if you need to go, let me get your coat."

The girls laughed, and Lenda made her way to the closet to get Karen's coat. Inside, she was yearning to put in a dig about her leaving. She wanted to ask if she was going to see Oliver, but Holy Spirit was gently suggesting she keep quiet and say nothing.

The Scripture she memorized after the fight was helping her in more ways than one. She kept rolling Proverbs 10:19 from the Contemporary English Version of the Bible around in her mind: *"You will say the wrong thing if you talk too much—so be sensible and watch what you say."* If only she had memorized that verse before the confrontation. *Better learned late than never,* she thought.

Lenda walked Karen to the door, but she hated to see her go when they were having such a good time.

When Karen got to the door, they hugged—both had tears in their eyes. It was Karen that broke the silence.

"I refuse to allow the enemy to come between us ever again…I love you too much, girl," Karen said.

"And Holy Spirit is helping me keep my mouth shut and stay out of people's personal space that I've not been invited into," Lenda admitted.

Suddenly Karen's hands extended into the air and she shouted, "Hallelujah! Thank You, Holy Spirit!"

Lenda laughed and hugged Karen again. She was too choked up to speak, and she didn't want to cry. But she did manage to say, "Call me when you get home."

"I will," Karen promised.

After Karen pulled off, Lenda went to check on Matthew;

he was sound asleep with the TV on. She went back to the kitchen and began to clean off the table. She thought of another Scripture that she read from the Amplified Version of the Bible, Proverbs 21:23, which says, *"He who guards his mouth and his tongue keeps himself from troubles."*

"That Scripture is so true. God, You ain't never lied," Lenda softly said.

She did learn several Scriptures after that incident with Karen, and they helped her understand why the blowup happened in the first place. It was her own lack of spiritual maturity. She was too quick to judge, not just Karen, but so many others. But none of that mattered anymore because she was growing and in her heart, she never again wanted her flesh to get so out of control that she would override Holy Spirit and ignore His counsel...never again.

Just keep your mouth shut, Lenda, she reminded herself. *You have enough to do with just your family, like going Christmas shopping so you won't be out there at the last minute buying gifts and spending money you don't have!*

Chapter Twenty-Three

Being married to a prominent attorney isn't easy, Quintella thought. *It's a wonderful life. But like anything else, it has its ups and downs. It seems like I entertain more than I want to, because it comes along with my "wifely duties."*

Quintella was thankful when Ken told her that he was planning to take her away before Christmas. While most people are shopping for their kids at Christmastime, Quintella is usually shopping for Ken's kids: his office personnel. As the years progressed, he had become adamant about giving out gifts and bonuses at a lavish Christmas party. The parties were an enjoyable time for those in attendance, but they had often been very stressful for Quintella. Even though he would give her permission to hire as much help as needed, the responsibility and success of each party rested solely on her shoulders. Ken would disagree with that, but it was the truth.

"Holy Spirit, You've helped me in the past, so I have no doubt that You'll help me this year and in the years to come. I'm just thankful for an opportunity to get away and rest before the storm," Quintella declared.

Quintella couldn't help but smile at Ken's mother's comment during Thanksgiving dinner. The whole scene was fresh in her memory as she turned out the lights in their bedroom.

* * * *

"So you and Ken are going where?" Ken's mom asked.

"Ken is taking me to Doral Golf Resort and Spa, Ma," Quintella proudly replied. She had always called Helen "Ma." Neither Quintella nor Ken liked the mother-in-law, father-in-law thing.

"I never thought I'd see the day when black folks took golf vacations," Ken's dad replied.

"Black people can do things now that they never could do before. We've come a long way, Dad," Ken replied.

"But if you're taking Quintella on a vacation, Ken, your mother would think you'd be going somewhere like Hawaii or something," his dad jabbed.

Helen continued to intrude, "It seems to me, even though you my baby, like this yo' vacation, not hers. So how do you answer Momma, 'cause Barbara and Carnell won't ask you that, and neither will yo' daddy, but yo' momma will?"

"His daddy won't ask 'cause it's not his daddy's business. I haven't bought a bag of peanuts or put a dollar down for the trip, so I don't have no reason butting into their, I repeat, *their* business," Ken Sr. replied.

"I'm his momma. I got rights."

"Naw, you don't have no rights up in here…" Ken Sr. added.

"Dad, Mom, come on. We've had a great dinner, and we're going to have a greater evening. Trust your son. He knows what's best for his wife. And since I have the floor, let's stop saying black folks and white folks. Let's say those dipped in the chocolate batter and those dipped in the vanilla batter. It has a nicer ring, and it takes the edge off race."

"Now where did you get such a stupid idea from, son?"

Ken Sr. asked.

"Last I checked, nobody told the employment office that. They still have African American, black, Caucasian, and white on their applications. If it's good for them, it's good for us. I know you live in a multicultural society and your firm is mixed. But y'all done gone to another level. Dipped in chocolate batter…what are we now? We done gone from apes to cakes," Ken Sr. laughed, along with the other parents.

"I agree," Helen said.

"I also agree with your dad, son. We agree to disagree. We still black folks, and they still white folks," Carnell said. "It's not racist, son, just fact."

"OK, no argument from me…we just thought we'd introduce y'all to something else," Ken replied to his father-in-law. "But to answer your question, I got that 'stupid idea' from your daughter-in-law. She came home with it one day after a dinner with her friends," Ken shared.

"Son, that's your first mistake. When a group of women are out and they come up with ideas, you just ignore them. Women talk all day, and they come up with some crazy stuff. You don't copy them! Right, Carnell?" Ken Sr. asked.

"You know I'm not going to answer you, especially now that I found out it was my daughter and her friends who came up with the idea. Change my answer—I think it's a good idea," Quintella's father replied.

"Back to this so-called vacation," Helen interrupted. "It reeks of 'yo' trip' instead of 'y'all trip.' Son, taking your wife to a golf resort is like buying her a pressure cooker for a Christmas gift," Helen pressed. "It don't sound like fun to me. What you say, Quintella?"

"Ma, I'm grateful to have a husband that will plan a trip. I know lots of women who will be sitting home doing nothing in a couple of weeks," Quintella said. "I on the other hand will be on a plane with my husband, getting away from it all."

"That's my baby," Ken purred.

* * * *

I'm his baby alright, Quintella thought. She cut the light out in their bedroom and forced herself back to the present. *We'll see after the plane lands if I'm really his baby. I pray the voices of our parents won't prove to be right. This place better offer up more than an eighteen-hole golf course—or, as Ken puts it, several eighteen-hole golf courses. I'll see next week if this is Ken's trip or our trip.*

* * * *

"Well, what you think? Come on. On a scale of one to ten, what do you think about it so far?" Ken asked.

"Ten plus, honey! Are you sure this is a golf course? It looks more like Paradise Island!" Quintella exclaimed.

As they stood waiting to be checked in, Quintella began to take in the beauty that surrounded her. There were more exotic trees on the grounds of this resort than on the whole Grand Bahama Island. What an oasis in the middle of Miami.

"Follow me, sir and madam," a voice called from the distance. Waiting to take them to their villa was of course, not a limo, but a golf cart. As the driver snaked the grounds, Quintella was amazed at the splendor of it all. She already knew she didn't want to leave.

Once they reached their suite, Quintella marveled at its luxury while she unpacked. There were wooden plantation shutters with a lightly colored finish. She ran through the room like a little child, looking at all the amenities. The balcony had a breathtaking view overlooking the famed Blue Monster, which is home to its signature fountain. Elegance, elegance, elegance.

The grass was so perfectly manicured that it looked more like a blanket that they could pull over their heads. The flowers strategically placed around the edges in various shades of pink and purple looked more like an embroidered hem. Quintella wished that for a moment, only one moment, Helen could be there to see what she saw.

"Babe."

"Yes, Ken?"

"Slip into something comfortable because I've made reservations for us both to have a full body massage, and I don't want us to miss our appointment."

Quintella did as he asked. She didn't want to miss a single morsel of what he had planned. It only took her a millisecond to get changed. And then they were out the door.

As they walked the grounds holding hands, her husband began to talk to her as though they were newlyweds. He shared his dreams for their future, and she shared hers.

When they reached the spa, their senses had no idea what awaited them. The fifty-minute, side-by-side body massage was a gift from heaven. Initially they were staring goo-goo eyed at each other while their massage therapists worked on them. But before each knew what was happening, they had lapsed into a peaceful state of calm.

"Ken?"

"Mmmm."

"Can we stay here forever?"

"Mmmm...I was going to take you to dinner. How about if we get room service instead?" Ken slurred.

"Sounds good to me," Quintella mumbled.

*   *   *   *

Sitting on the balcony, realizing that this was their last night at Doral gave her a feeling of nostalgia that hugged her thoughts like a glove on a hand. Quintella had talked with her mom earlier that day. It was snowing in Detroit, and the temperature was twenty degrees. It brought Quintella sheer joy to announce that it was seventy-one degrees in Miami, where palm trees were blowing in the wind. She had hurried to get off the phone; Quintella wanted to enjoy every minute and every second that remained of what they now called their second honeymoon.

Ken was out on the "green," and she couldn't have been happier as she sat on the balcony taking in the views while reading the book *Too Blessed to Be Stressed* by Dr. Suzan D. Johnson Cook. It was such an appropriate read.

Doral has turned out to be just what I needed. It's amazing how we resist the very things God wants to bless us with, she thought. Quintella was now able to fully admit to herself that this wasn't a place she desired to visit. When Ken first announced that they were going to Miami to stay at the famous Doral Golf Resort and Spa, she initially thought he only wanted to go for himself, to play golf.

Even when Helen voiced what she was thinking, Quintella wouldn't allow herself to admit that she had felt the same. She vowed never to disrespect or say anything other than something good about Ken in front of his parents. She found out early on in their marriage that when couples disagree and share intimate details with family members, the family members never forget. She knew that months later, when they are loving each other again and have forgotten about what was said, the parents wouldn't—hence her decision never to share her negative feelings with them. She decided that she would only talk to God because He was the only Person who could change them and do something about the situation.

She also found out early on that some of the things she blamed on Ken were really her fault. And some of the things Ken blamed on her were his fault. They only got into trouble when they would take on an argument instead of going to God. Doing that wasn't pretty, so they made it a point to pray first and then discuss later.

Quintella believed it was the primary reason why their relationship was so good. God saw how they covered and protected one another. And she knew that because of it, God's favor was on them as a couple.

"Now, as I sit here, I repent for even thinking that this trip was all about Ken. The landscaped art that I've been blessed to be surrounded by these past four days has done nothing but comfort me. Sitting in awe of Your beauty, Lord, I promise You that I've made a decision to move on with my life. No longer will I blame my husband and myself for foolish decisions we made in our youth. The devil's foothold has been broken, and I'm a free woman.

"I've got a good man, God! A really, really good man. I didn't say perfect, but good, and I thank You for giving him to me. Continue to bless the fruit of his hands, Lord. Continue to surround him with godly men and women full of wisdom that will protect him and the business You've entrusted to him. Give him favor every place his foot treads. Keep him safe in Your arms, Jesus," Quintella affirmed aloud.

Quintella allowed her thoughts to go to their dinner the night before. For the most part, they ate in silence, with the exception of tender touches every now and then. It was a silence that wasn't uncomfortable, but one filled with peace and a wonderful assurance of their love for each other.

Their dinner table was by the window, which had another breathtaking view of the Blue Monster. That fountain would mesmerize any well-traveled person. It was a postcard-ready view and sitting with Ken, looking into his eyes was an experience Quintella would never forget. The whole experience made her feel like a new bride instead of someone celebrating twenty-five years of marriage.

"Lord, I've also learned more about golf in these four days and how it mirrors our relationship with You. I've always tried to keep up so that I could sit and watch it with Ken," she added. Her thoughts went back to prior discussions she had with Ken about golf. He shared with her how he felt it paralleled their relationship with Holy Spirit.

"Well, your caddy is there to help you navigate through the golf course. He doesn't make you take his advice. You can choose to ignore him or see him as a viable partner, as he shares his wisdom with you on what club to hit and how far you need to hit it. He'll tell you which way the wind is blowing and so forth. Our Friend, Holy Spirit, is also our Helper. He'll tell us things we need to know to help us navigate through life. Like a caddy, He won't force His advice on us. But if we're smart, we'll take His advice, which could keep us out of the bunkers of life," Ken explained.

Ever since the game of golf was explained to her like that, her interest in it escalated. And she never looked at it like she did in the past, which made this trip all the more interesting.

There were five golf courses on the property. Ken wanted to play three, but that didn't happen. She was glad because it meant they'd come back. "Next time, I'll welcome the experience and won't come emotionally kicking and screaming," Quintella said with a smile.

Quintella knew that it had been time to "pay her water bill" over twenty minutes ago, but she couldn't pull herself away from the view. Now nature was no longer calling, it was screaming. After her run, she stopped to get a bottle of water from the fridge. She had to laugh because even on vacation, she made sure she washed all the bottles of water that were stocked in the fridge.

Her eyes rested on the flower arrangement Ken had sent to the room before they got there. Next to the arrangement was a basket loaded with her favorite treats. *How I got such a good man when my sister got such a buzzard is beyond me!*

Chapter Twenty-Four

Lenda and Matthew's ride to prison seemed longer because of the circumstances. Her heart had finally warmed to the point where she gave in to Matthew's pleas to see his uncle after she shared his whereabouts. Inside, she felt like her family was finally coming together, and she was thankful. *Only God could do this!*

Matthew religiously wrote to his uncle before the visit. Lenda wanted to read the many letters they had shared, but she knew in her heart that this was the one time she shouldn't pull rank as his mother. No, she knew that her brother was a good man who had followed the wrong crowd. He had more than paid for his mistake, and it wasn't her place to imprison him emotionally.

She also knew how much Matthew loved his uncle. And in many ways, it was his unconditional love for Ernest that made Lenda reach out to God to help her love her brother again. It was a sheer miracle how God had answered her prayer. She knew it was Holy Spirit who suggested she bring Matthew up for a visit around the holidays. His first visit to see his uncle since he was incarcerated. She laughed to herself as she recalled the earlier conversation with her mom.

* * * *

"What? You're taking Matthew to see Ernest! I can't believe it," she yelled with tears in her eyes. "What made you do it, Lenda? What made you do it, baby!"

"See Mom, I told you Holy Spirit was working on me. I thought it would be a wonderful Christmas gift for Ernest, and it'll be good for Matthew."

* * * *

Lenda couldn't help but think about all the years she lied about Ernest's disappearance from the family. It was difficult for Matthew because they were very close, and he had always loved his visits from "Uncle."

And as time progressed, Lenda knew she had to deal with the obvious. She knew there would be questions, and Matthew certainly had many on their ride. And she was prepared for them—only because of prolonged prayer with Holy Spirit. But her mind got stuck on one question in particular.

"Is Uncle a bad person?" Matthew innocently asked.

"No. Uncle is *not* a bad person. He's a good person who did a bad thing and hung out with not-so-nice people," she responded, in faith. Lenda wasn't convinced that her brother was all that innocent. But over time, she made peace with the knowledge that he was a good person who did something very bad. And now he was paying the price for that.

It took Holy Spirit to remind her that many times we put people in emotional prisons. We try them in the office for mistakes they make, and we never forgive them. We don't talk to them over the water coolers because we've put them in our *own* imaginary prison, and they must serve their time. Or we imprison a relative who may have said something out of order at a family function, and we sentence him or her to a year without contact. She had learned so much from spending time with God. Those lessons were priceless and had made her a better person.

* * * *

"I can't wait to see his face when he sees that child! I never thought this day would come!" her mother shouted in their earlier conversation.

"Mom," Lenda's voice lowered. "Well…uh…I'm not taking you with us," Lenda mumbled with her head also lowered.

"What…why? Why?" her mother repeated.

"Because I want this to be special for Ernest…I'm taking a book, and I'm going to let the two of them talk. He gets thirty-minute visits, and I think it only right that he not have to share it with three people. Please understand. I've been so mean to my brother in many ways. I've judged him. Held back my love for him. There were times during the visits before God dealt with me that Holy Spirit prompted me to hug Ernest, and I didn't. In my own way, I had him in my own little prison where I withheld my love from him 'cause I wanted him to pay. I was mad at him. Those days are over. I just want to love him and do good toward him. I think a visit from Matthew will lift his spirits for the holidays. After all, he was alone on Thanksgiving. He didn't have turkey and dressing with the family. I just want this to be special. Will you please understand, Mom?" Lenda asked, as she twirled a lock of her mother's hair in her hand.

"Baby, I do. For once, I do, and I won't be selfish. Let the boy go and spend time with his uncle." Lenda felt it was a miracle.

* * * *

Those thoughts warmed her heart. Coming back to reality, she briefly looked away from the road to look at Matthew; he had fallen asleep. *I'll wake him up in about fifteen minutes,* she thought.

Lenda began going over a checklist about the visit in her head. She had told Matthew about security and possible dog sniffing. She told him about doors being locked and shut. She told him the visit would go by quickly, and they would have to leave when told to. She told him that he couldn't ask the guards for "five more minutes" like he does when she tells him time is up for any other activity he's involved with. Looking up, Lenda quietly petitioned her "Man." *Is there anything I've failed to tell him?* She felt confident that all bases were covered.

"Matthew, wake up. We're here," Lenda said, as she softly shook Matthew's shoulders. "Wake up, Matt."

To her surprise, he jumped up and yelled, "We're here? I can see Uncle."

"Yeah, you can see Uncle."

As they parked and walked toward the entrance, Lenda's eyes were glued to Matthew, watching him take in the environment. With his head moving from side to side, he took in the sights and sounds of his uncle's residence. There was not an ounce of apprehension, rather an excited anticipation of what was to come.

Out of nowhere, a sense of guilt rushed through Lenda's body. She had never brought Matthew because she thought he'd be depressed and down. His reaction quickly proved her wrong. *That's what happens when we think and don't allow God an opportunity to work out situations,* she thought.

Lenda was also excited because Ernest didn't know she was bringing Matthew. She only told him that she had a surprise for him. As far as Ernest knew, it could have been clothes or one of his ex-girlfriends. In her heart she knew Matthew was the last person he'd expect.

Lenda remembered something she'd said during one of their long-ago visits, before her heart was softened. Ernest told her he had added Matthew's name to his list of visitors and before he could get it all out, Lenda blurted, "That's one visitor you can remove 'cause I'll never bring him up here and subject him to the humiliation of being searched and the invasion of his privacy." The hurt look in her brother's eyes was just as fresh as it was years ago. So she was eagerly anticipating the look she'd get today when he saw him.

As they cleared security and got ushered into the bustling visitation room, Lenda silently prayed that there would be no inappropriate displays of affection. She wanted the visit to be perfect. What she hadn't prepared herself for, was the reunion of Ernest and Matthew.

When Ernest came through the security doors, he looked almost fashionable. His normal prison outfit was missing. He had on a T-shirt and jeans. Matthew didn't care that others were in the room. He bolted toward his uncle in full speed, like a horse coming out of the gate when the bell rings, screaming, "Uncle, Uncle!" It felt as though silence blanketed the entire room and time stood still. Ernest was crying and so was Matthew. Over and over, all anyone could hear was Matthew saying, "Uncle, I missed you, Uncle." Now Lenda was crying. *Great! So much for what I thought would happen.*

The two of them finally got to Lenda. She gave her brother a big hug and a smile to match. Words weren't necessary. Their eyes clearly told the whole story. They couldn't embrace for long because Matthew was pulling at Ernest and firing questions at him like a machine gun. Lenda may as well have been a picture on the wall because for the next twenty-five minutes, she was nonexistent.

She was an outsider who had been given the wonderful gift of witnessing Ernest and Matthew catch up on years of missed opportunities to share intimate fellowship with one another. The book she brought was never opened. This was a better book—a personal and up-close tearjerker that only God could write. She laughed and cried at their conversations and antics. Matthew was showing Ernest various new handshakes, playfully shaking his uncle's shoulders whenever he didn't get one right.

Lenda watched intently as Matthew would look over at her to see how far away she had stepped when he wanted to whisper something in Ernest's ear that he didn't want her to hear. She wasn't jealous, just happy. She was overjoyed about the whole experience. Her only wish was that the time could be extended.

As other visitors got up to leave, she feared the time when the prison guard would come and tap them on the shoulder, bringing this heartwarming reunion to an end. But as the guard approached them, to her surprise, he said, "You got ten minutes." All Lenda could do was lift her eyes and silently thank God for extra favor.

Ending the visit wasn't as painful as Lenda had imagined. Ernest and Matthew shared one of the new handshakes, which took a full minute to complete, and then her brother began to walk toward her as she walked toward them. What Ernest whispered was music to her ears. "Thanks, sis, thanks," he said between tears. All she could whisper back was, "You're so welcome."

Leaving the visitor lounge, Matthew walked backward because he didn't want to take his eyes off his uncle. When he was no longer in view, Matthew looked at his mother with joy and sadness. Lenda knew what to say to make him smile: "I'll bring you again, promise."

* * * *

There was plenty of chatter in the car going home. Matthew opened up and told his mother things she never knew were on his mind. They weren't just about his uncle, they were about everything. Before Lenda knew it, she was pulling into their driveway. Lenda couldn't wait to tell her mother about the visit. She was going to be so happy!

Lenda was convinced: there was nothing sweeter than answered prayer.

Chapter Twenty-Five

Lenda allowed her hands to rest in the dishwater. She began to think about the day's events and the Christmas party at Ken and Quintella's house the night before. As usual, it had been elegant. Ken and Quintella made sure everyone knew that "Jesus was the *real* reason for the season." Ken would call out names, and each person would have to go to the Christmas tree. Right in front of it was a manger with Baby Jesus in it. All of the gifts were in and around the manger, and everybody had to dig to find their gift amongst the life-sized shepherds and wise men. She initially thought it was a little over-the-top, but it grew on her each year. When Lenda asked him about it, Ken explained, "Lenda, when people receive gifts from me, I want them to be reminded of the greatest Gift of all."

This year, seeing Baby Jesus in the manger wrapped in all His gold garb made Lenda smile. And her gift was right near the feet of Baby Jesus. It was grand! But she missed Claudette and Karen's presence, understanding that they wanted to be with relatives and their new beaus. She loved that God had come through for Claudette. So far, Christopher was all that Claudette believed him to be, and Lenda was truly happy for her.

Christmas was always busy for her. *It seems like I have no time for myself,* Lenda thought. *Funny, I never noticed this when I was younger but now that I'm grown, I wonder where the time goes.*

Lenda and her mother had made a standing decision right after her divorce to have an early Christmas breakfast, exchange gifts, and spend some time with Matthew before he'd leave for his dad's house.

This Christmas saw a change in the pattern—a very good change. It was the first time in years that her sister Annie joined them. After breakfast, they sat, talked, opened gifts, and made the most of their time together. Lenda was especially overjoyed when Annie took their mom home to spend some time alone with her. That was such a relief. It meant she no longer had to feel guilty since her mother wasn't going to be by herself.

She firmly believed that everything could be so much easier if all siblings pitched in as their parents got older. She knew firsthand the burden some families put on one person was just plain wrong. Parental visits should be shared, and Lenda was happy that Annie was stepping up to the plate. Her assistance ensured that the rest of Lenda's day could be worry-free. And very shortly, she'd be able to spend some time by herself, enjoying her home.

Her thoughts were interrupted by her son's voice. "This is the part I hate," Matthew said, coming over to kiss her on the cheek. It was customary for him to leave for his dad's as soon as the gifts were exchanged.

"Ma, can I tell you something and you won't be mad?"

"No, Matt. I won't be mad."

"If I ever get married, I'll never get a divorce because I hate leaving you by yourself on Christmas to go to Dad's. Every year, I hate leaving you more and more."

"Oh, don't feel like that. I'm never alone, son."

"I know, Ma—you got a Man."

Lenda was kind of startled. Did she detect some traces of sarcasm in Matthew's voice?

The horn blew, indicating that her ex was outside. "Ma, I love God, but I really wish He would send you a real man," Matthew admitted in a worried tone.

Lenda playfully hit him on his derriere, and he looked at her as if to say, "Ma!" She opened the door and waved at her ex. She was happy that they were truly cordial with one another. Shutting the door, Lenda closed her eyes and prayed, "Father, in Jesus' Name, please allow my son to enjoy his dad, and his dad's wife and children. May they honor You this Christmas season. I thank You, Father, and according to Ephesians 4:29, I pray that no unwholesome talk comes from their mouths, but only what is helpful for building each other up. May my son witness nothing but love in that house. May peace prevail, and may You be glorified, in Jesus' Name. Amen."

Now that the house was empty, Lenda returned to her kitchen to clean it up and get it back in order.

* * * *

With the last dish done, it was lights out and off to the bathroom. It was high time for her new Christmas-evening tradition: run a hot bath with one of her favorite fragrances, pull back a new set of sheets, and sit and thank God for all He'd done that day.

Then she'd snuggle up with a good book. *Oceans Apart* by Karen Kingsbury was her book of choice, and she was looking forward to reading it. After all, it had been on The New York Times Best Seller List for quite some time.

The book had also been sitting on her shelf, unread, for a couple of years. She'd bought it when it first came out, but she never had a chance to read it. Like all the other good novels that were collecting dust on her bookshelf: she decided to brush this one off and actually read it.

She had heard it was a book about forgiveness, which seemed to be the theme that ran through her life this year. Her brother, her sister, Karen, herself, not to mention the people at work. Why not close the year out by reading a novel about it?

As Lenda ran her bath, she added some Trésor bath gel. As the hot water hit the gel, the bathroom began to fill with the familiar smell. She stood still for a moment, taking a deep breath to really get a good whiff of the now-fragrant room, Lenda lifted her hands and proclaimed, "God, thank You for allowing me the luxury of a hot bath."

Lenda was truly grateful because she knew on the other side of the world, people would do anything to be able to run hot water and take a leisurely soak. Just then, she realized that she'd left her rose petals in the fridge. *Is it worth the trip to go get them?* Lenda answered the question as soon as it came into her head. *Yes, it is. Besides, I paid good money for them.*

Out to the kitchen she ran, opened the fridge, and immediately saw the clear plastic bag with the assorted colors. As she made her way back to the bathroom, she recalled the first time she used rose petals in her bath water.

She had stopped at the florist to get a single rose but couldn't decide on what color she wanted. It was a toss-up between yellow and pink. When the florist asked, "Why the dilemma?" Lenda proceeded to explain that she was only getting one because she was going to use the petals in her bath water. To her surprise, the florist explained that they sold rose petals by the bag. She urged Lenda to purchase a multicolored bag and enjoy both colors, along with some additional ones. That was years ago, and she'd been enjoying the experience ever since.

Lenda couldn't help but think about what Claudette told her when she saw the rose petals in her fridge, and had heard her explanation about why they were there.

"Girl, you're a living 'Lendarella.' You're proof that Cinderella was for real! I ain't mad at you, but what you pay for those rose petals? You could come to my shop and buy something that would last a lot longer!" Claudette laughed.

The truth of the matter was that she *did* feel like a princess. She didn't see why she shouldn't treat herself like one. Plus, her Man took good care of her. Even though the petals were a bit expensive this time of year, Lenda had come to the realization that she was well worth the price.

After her bath, Lenda felt refreshed. It was a good sign that she would at least crack the book open. Once she got all lotioned up, she decided to kneel that night for her prayers. Lenda couldn't think of the last time she had kneeled—it was probably when she was looking for a shoe.

She prayed for everybody, which took more than forty minutes. She envisioned how fast the last week in the year would probably go, and she mentioned how she wanted to see each of the girls again before the year was out.

She knew there was a slim chance that she'd see Claudette because she went to a different church. But seeing Quintella with Ken at their church was pretty much guaranteed. Karen was still out of town and wouldn't be back until New Year's Eve—to go to that party!

She prayed that they could all catch up after the first of year. Lenda could respect that everyone wanted to do their own thing. She had made plans to visit her brother. Ethel, Annie, and Matthew were all going to make this trip. Lenda also prayed that his gift package would arrive before them. She sent him some thank-you cards, masculine stationery, and a Sudoku puzzle. She couldn't wait until he got that. After Matthew's first visit, he had insisted that Lenda not leave him out anymore unless they visited on a week when he was with his dad.

When she got ready to get off her knees, Lenda had to hold onto the bed because she had been down there so long. "You're amazing, God. You never hold us to any formality. You just wait and when we decide to talk to You, You're always there. You don't care if we're sitting in a chair, riding in a car, or brushing our teeth. You patiently wait because You desire to spend time with us. What a God You are. You always give us Your undivided attention!" she proclaimed.

Sitting on the edge of the bed, Lenda couldn't help but go into her thankful mode. "Father, I remember it was months ago that I felt so hopeless. I remember so vividly how I sat in Andiamo's not knowing what my financial future would be. I never thought in a million years that you would bless the fruit of my hands so much so that I sit here today so much better financially than I was that short time ago. Even though I'm not where I want to be, You've blessed me with unexpected income from people I never expected to receive from.

"When You told me to resurrect the consulting business I had on the side, I thought it would take at least a year to see profits. But in three sessions, You blessed me with money that left me speechless. To hear the president of that company say to me, 'In three sessions, you have done what others couldn't do in a year. I'm compelled to give you this bonus and to thank you for turning the attitudes of our employees from *can't do* to *can do*. May this small token of our appreciation help you to understand our gratitude,' had me in awe.

"Small token! I wanted to holler when I opened that envelope, but I didn't want the people on the plane to be alarmed.

"Lord, I know that I've had seasons of complaints to You. But when I look at my life, the small storms don't outweigh the larger picture of beauty that You've graced me with. I love my life as a single person. I'm happy that I found out early that you don't need another person to make you happy. Happiness is not found in someone else. It's found in Jesus and Jesus alone. I'll never forget the quote I read by Mother Teresa years ago that said, 'You never know Jesus is all you need until Jesus is all you've got!' And yes, while it would be nice to marry, if I never marry, I'm still going to be happy and satisfied. A little disappointed to be honest, but I'll still be joyful. It's because I've finally learned that true happiness is not found in things, or people.

"Thank You, Lord, for my trip that's coming up in February. You've blessed me to travel to so many places and see so many things. I found out through You that it's fun going on a trip with just me. I don't have to argue about where to eat, I choose where I want to stay, and I enjoy other cultures. Thank You for my health, Lord, that I'll be able to continue to experience all of the beauty that's in the earth."

Life was certainly in full bloom for Lenda. As she pulled the covers over her chest, she was now ready to read.

Once she got started, she was breezing through the chapters. She was ecstatic that she was finally making progress. The tenth chapter was as far as she could go. She took a look at the rest of the book and realized she still hadn't gotten to the halfway mark yet. "I guess I'm done reading," she mumbled as she reached for the lamp and turned out the light.

"Good night heavenly Father, good night Lord Jesus, and

good night Holy Spirit—I'll talk to You Three tomorrow. And angels, thanks for protecting my home and all that belongs to me. You do good on your assignments." *Wow! Where did that come from? For some reason, I never think about my angels. I never acknowledge them, even though I know they're here for me,* she thought. Perhaps it was her enormous sense of gratitude that made her want to include all who were responsible for the overflow of goodness that she was experiencing in her life.

Chapter Twenty-Six

New Year's Eve service had always meant a lot to Claudette. But this year, the meaning was intensified because she had Christopher. He decided to go to church with her, and he genuinely enjoyed the service. As they walked to the car afterward, they would periodically turn to each other and smile. It was definitely something special when two people didn't have to talk—just walk and smile.

It had been almost three months, and the relationship was as fresh as ever. She was cautious, however; such a short amount of time was nothing to get that exuberant about, but things were certainly going in the right direction. And when a person gets past forty, it doesn't take six months to know if the relationship is going anywhere.

Christopher was such a gentlemen. Snow had begun to fall near the end of the service. "Is your scraper in the back?"

Claudette mumbled, "Yes."

As Christopher looked through the window into the backseat, he took Claudette's keys and opened the door so she could get in first. Then he opened the back door and got out the scraper. He motioned for her to wait a minute, while his long arms reached in the car. He then put the key in the ignition and started it up, stepped aside, and closed the door.

He smiled through the specks of snow on the window.

Claudette watched him through her rearview mirror as he cleaned the snow off the back window, after which he cleaned the windows on the passenger side—he continued gliding around the car as if he were waltzing with a woman. When he got to the front, he made a funny face in the snow on the windshield, which made Claudette laugh. He was about to erase the face, so she blew the horn.

"Leave it!" Claudette yelled while rolling down the window.

"How will you drive? You can't see," Christopher laughed.

"I'll ask Holy Spirit to help me," Claudette pleaded.

Christopher didn't give a response; he wiped the face with the scraper. Windows cleaned, he opened the back door and put the scraper on the floor. When he shut it and came back around to her rolled-down window, she had a frown and pouting lips.

"What's wrong?" he asked with genuine concern.

"Mr. Meany wiped the cute face off my windshield," Claudette sulked, speaking in a voice like hurt child.

"I'll see you tomorrow at three o'clock. And don't forget to drive like someone is following you: don't speed up to clear a yellow light—'cause you'll make me run a red one!" Christopher laughed.

"OK," said Claudette, still talking in her childlike voice.

She waved good-bye and waited until he quickly cleared off his windows, got in his car, and flicked on his headlights before leaving.

*　*　*　*

Claudette didn't even know how she got home. Her mind

was so preoccupied with her thoughts that it was as if the car was on autopilot. Not once in the time they'd known each other had Christopher tried to pull a fast one. Claudette was pleased to find out, during one of their many marathon conversations, that he also had a desire to marry without having premarital sex.

His goal to glorify God on his wedding day really shocked Claudette. Although happy, she couldn't believe that men past forty-five still had moral goals.

They both promised to keep the physical at bay until married. She thought about how she had met him at one of her lowest points. *God so knows how to take care of us.*

Claudette was amazed that he never wavered in his position to follow her home when their dates kept them out after one o'clock in the morning. It didn't happen often, but tonight had been one of those nights. He even understood when she suggested they drive separately to church because she wanted to get there an hour earlier to get seats.

As she pulled into the driveway, with Christopher following closely, she noticed that he was smiling, as usual. He sat there until she got in the house and turned on the porch light, which is something else he'd ask her to do on nights like this. They decided it was best that he not get out of the car and walk her to the door. That's because they'd done that at first and instantly realized it was the perfect place to wait for a kiss. They weren't falling for any of the enemy's traps. A kiss was like Lay's chips—nobody could have just one. And so, for them, safety equaled Christopher staying in his car after one in the morning.

Now it was her turn to watch *him* drive away. Claudette had the perfect view from her front room. She so loved living in a cul-de-sac. She knew if a car was parked there it better get out soon or neighbors would be calling one another to see if they knew the owner. For as long as she could, Claudette watched until Christopher's taillights disappeared completely into the darkness. *What a guy!*

Claudette began to think back on the New Year's service. The pastor said he believed that this would be the year God would answer prayers that people thought He'd forgotten. That sentence alone had set off a roar in the sanctuary that lasted for about two minutes. It reminded Claudette that oftentimes she thought she was by herself and that everyone else's prayers had been answered. But when she saw people respond like they did at service, she realized that it wasn't just her, but many others who were all just trying to live the Christian life the best they knew how. It seemed that most of them were also waiting for God to show out in their lives.

Minutes later, the phone rang. Claudette realized she was still sitting on the sofa, staring into space. As she ran to answer it before voice mail picked up, she hit her baby toe.

Answering the phone while simultaneously letting out a yell, Christopher asked in a caring voice, "What's the matter? You need me to come back over there?"

"No, I hit my baby toe!"

"How'd you do that?"

"Running to answer the phone."

"Were you busy?"

"No, just thinking."

"Thinking about what?"

"About some things Pastor said tonight."

Sounding disappointed, Christopher pretended to pout. "And I thought you were thinking about us."

"I was. When Pastor said this was the year for unanswered prayer, I thought that meeting you was like the answer to a prayer I thought God had forgot about. I pinch myself every time we're together. Am I scaring you?" Claudette asked.

"No. I can recall, though, a time in my life where that *would* scare me. But I'm so ready for a relationship like ours; all I can do is thank God for His faithfulness," Christopher confessed.

"Well, I'd better hit the sack if I'm going to wow you with my cooking tomorrow," Claudette said.

"Yeah, I can hardly wait to taste your food—I hope I won't leave looking for a fast-food place," Christopher teased.

"Please! Your thoughts will be: 'Why did she wait so long to feed me?'" Claudette bragged.

"Hey, does Jeopardy come on tomorrow?" Christopher asked.

"That's a good question. It's a weekday—I'll find out. Know what?"

"What?" asked Christopher.

"This time last year I didn't think something like this was possible...I mean, I *thought* it was possible, but I really didn't *think* it was possible. Know what I mean?" Claudette confessed.

"I know. I thought the same thing. Sweet dreams, baby," Christopher said.

"Sweet dreams," Claudette replied.

Claudette could hear Christopher gently putting the phone in the cradle. She chose to hold hers close to her heart. This relationship felt so good, so right. She couldn't help but think to herself: *Funny, I remember saying that I was through with men. Lord, if there is anything about this brother that I need to know, reveal it to me now because I'm getting too deep into this!*

* * * *

Christopher sat staring at the phone. Sitting in church on New Year's Eve next to a woman he really cared about. Being in a relationship that was going into its third month, and he wasn't even tired of talking. Christopher was overwhelmed by the woman God had placed in his path. If he were a kid, three months wouldn't be long. But he was a grown man, so he knew even at three months that they had something real, something special.

Who would've thought that a run to unlock a car door would turn into something so good? Lord, I never said it before, because after that last woman I was determined to live the rest of my life alone. But it's nice to have a real woman to talk to. What's even nicer is that she listens to me. I've never expected a woman to agree with everything I say. But to not listen is unacceptable. Most women I talked to before Claudette had a response before you could finish talking, but this women really listens, he thought.

Christopher began to express his feelings aloud. "God, I believe in my heart that she's the one. But as I've told You before, if You see something that I don't—please reveal it to me. She's showing me a side I like; I pray that it's the real Claudette and not someone she wants me to believe she is.

"Lord, the most miserable thing in life that I've experienced is living with someone who constantly wanted to butt heads with me. She was always right, and I was always wrong. I'm encouraged by Claudette's willingness to allow me to follow her home when we find ourselves out after one in the morning. But on nights like tonight, I care enough about her that I don't want her out in the street going into a house that late by herself.

"You know some of the women I've dated. When I suggested that I follow them, their attitude was, 'I'm grown; I don't need you following me home like I'm a kid! I'm a big girl; I can take care of myself!' Neck rolling, finger pointing, eyes popping. That's so unattractive in a woman. Lord, I can't speak for all men. But for me, when I see that, the relationship is over! It's in the history books. When you're almost fifty, you're too old to be raising a child in a grown woman's body."

As if an afterthought, Christopher looked up and added, "You know what I really like? She respects me. She's not condescending, and she doesn't raise her voice. She knows how to get her point across, and she knows when to let go of a discussion. Even if she brings it up another day, she knows when to let it go. And she lets it go!"

Christopher continued to talk to his Buddy. He was about to bring the conversation to an end when he thought of one last thing. "God, it doesn't hurt that she likes to watch Jeopardy. I could forgive her for not watching sports, which she *will* watch with me, even though she doesn't understand everything. But Jeopardy, that's a plus!"

Christopher got up to get ready for bed, but he stopped in his tracks and looked up. "Holy Spirit, I'm so glad I have *You* to talk to. One who doesn't tell secrets. One who doesn't call me 'soft' because I'm falling for a woman. Thank You, Holy Spirit! The world says that a dog is a man's best friend—not here! You are my Best Friend—my Buddy!"

It was at this point that Christopher raised his hands and began to go into praise mode. He thanked God for letting him see another year. He thanked God for his mom. He prayed and thanked God for the many relationships in his life.

After he was done praising God, he was ready for bed.

Yet something on the inside said Holy Spirit wasn't through talking. Christopher felt He was about to reveal something to him about Claudette, and he was more than ready to receive His godly counsel.

Chapter Twenty-Seven

As was customary with Lenda on New Year's Day, she made herself a cup of hot chocolate and began to read the newspaper. It was always interesting to find out what happened on New Year's Eve night. It never failed. Somebody always got hurt by a stray bullet. *What a dumb tradition, and I wonder who started it anyway. That's what gun ranges are for! Why point a gun up in the air and shoot? Just let a balloon go up in the air with a positive message on it like, "Stay blessed and be a blessing to others,"* she thought.

Lenda began to peruse the paper, "Wow, the first baby born weighed thirteen pounds and six ounces. Ouch! I'll say it for you *and* your momma, little one: you are one big baby!" Lenda said.

Lenda leisurely turned page after page.

"Get out of here! The ball didn't drop in New York because of technical difficulties—somebody's head is going to roll," Lenda continued. She was picking up speed now, curious about the next headline when her eyes fell on a small paragraph with the header: "Woman Killed When Stray Bullet Enters Home, Interrupting Partygoers."

"See, I knew it. There's always an innocent person hurt. I wonder who the poor soul was," Lenda added.

She relaxed and continued to read—still intrigued by this story. She couldn't help but think of how this woman's family would feel when they heard the news. She felt compelled to pray for them. She strongly believed Christians shouldn't just shake their heads when they read a terrible story in the newspaper. Just like when she heard ambulances, police cars, and fire trucks, Lenda would pray for the people she read about in the paper, even though she didn't know them. Lenda put the paper down and began to pray.

"Father, in Jesus' Name, I pray for the lady who lost her life at that party last night. Comfort her family and children if she has them. Help them to get over this tragedy. Please send people across the paths of her relatives and friends to comfort them. May they somehow find the person responsible and bring him to justice, in Jesus' Name. Amen."

As she finished the prayer, she thought about last night's church service and wished that Karen had been there. The message had been uplifting and so appropriate. She sat with Ken and Quintella, but she couldn't take her mind off Karen. She only prayed the party was worth it.

* * * *

As their pastor encouraged them about "new beginnings" and began the countdown, she witnessed Ken and Quintella kiss and share an intimate moment. Looking at them, she wished that she had a date.

Her feelings shocked her. For some reason, couples kissing and sharing intimate moments didn't usually bother her on New Year's Eve. She searched her heart to find out what was different. Possibly it was because their already-small circle had gotten smaller. Now she was the only one who wasn't dating.

Claudette had a good man. Karen had a man, even if he wasn't the ideal man. Her son was with his dad, so she didn't even have him to keep her company. And after the service, she had to get in her car alone and head home to be alone, again.

Normally, Holy Spirit loomed large for her on New Year's Eve. But tonight was different for some reason. If she were honest with herself, she'd acknowledge that she felt lonely. Even though there were thousands of people in the church laughing and talking, in the midst of it all, she felt alone. Lenda managed to smile and laugh with the rest of the people, but tonight, unlike other New Year's Eves, it was all a show.

* * * *

With the paper falling to the floor, Lenda was brought back to the present moment and reminded that she still needed rest. "Well, that was last night. Thank God today is a new day!" Once she had gotten home from church, turned on the TV, and watched all the drunks and the hoopla from New York, she was fine. *Funny, there was no mention on TV last night that the ball malfunctioned.*

I'd better get up and start dinner before Mom and Annie get here, she thought. She knew she'd also have to fry some fresh chicken later for Matthew. She couldn't understand why he would come home late in the evening from his father's house and eat like his dad hadn't fed him, when she knew he had.

Lenda was about to cut up some cabbage when she thought she heard a knock at the door. She decided she was hearing things, but as she continued to cut the cabbage the knock became louder. "This year I'm going to get the doorbell fixed," she mumbled as she walked to the front door. She wasn't expecting anyone yet. Her mother and sister were due for dinner at four o'clock, and Matthew was due after that. Since it wasn't anywhere near four, she couldn't imagine who it could be.

Lenda looked through the peephole. It was Karen's friend,

Oliver. *What is he doing coming to my house at eleven in the morning on New Year's Day? And where is Karen?* Lenda's thoughts were flying as she opened the door.

"Happy New Year!" she struggled to get out with a smile. She still couldn't figure out what he was doing there. Then she took a closer look. His eyes were red, and he looked disheveled.

"Are you OK?" she asked, even though she assumed he was drunk.

He mumbled something that was incoherent. When she asked him to repeat himself, he continued mumbling. "She's gone," Lenda heard through the mumbles.

"What are you talking about?" Lenda demanded, with her voice slightly raised.

"Shots were fired at the party, and one hit Karen in the head," Oliver uttered between sobs. "They said she died immediately…I'm so sorry…I'm so sorry," Oliver blubbered.

If her life depended on it, Lenda couldn't recall the minutes that followed. She just stood in shock, trying to process what she had just heard. When she finally spoke, Lenda heard herself say, "Where is Karen's body?"

"She's at the morgue. I loved that girl. You believe me, don't you?" Oliver pleaded.

She wanted to slam the door in his face. Lenda didn't know how long she'd been standing in the doorway, but her body was now frozen from January's blistering cold.

Oliver continued to share the evening's painful events. He told her how the police came and determined that there was no foul play. Oliver had them send her body to the morgue because he didn't know what to do.

So by the time Oliver had arrived at her door, he didn't

have the strength to do anything else. He now needed another person, namely Lenda, to take over from there.

"Thank you, Oliver. I'll be in touch," she said between her own tears.

Lenda closed the door and leaned on it for strength. Her body slowly slid to the floor as she openly sobbed. One question remained: *What next?*

* * * *

The remainder of New Year's Day was very dark. She was thankful that her sister came by early to see if she could use help with dinner. Annie ended up making the entire dinner, and she kept their mother from asking Lenda all sorts of questions that she didn't have answers for nor that she cared to answer.

It was Annie who called Quintella and Claudette. It was also Annie who suggested that they call Karen's aunts in Mississippi to break the news to them. And it was her sister who called her ex to get him to keep Matthew another day so she could muster up enough strength to tell him what happened to his beloved Auntie Karen.

The next day, Annie called in and took the day off work to stay with her. It was Annie who fixed her tea, rubbed her hair, turned her bed down, and put her to sleep like a child the night before. She had never been more thankful for Annie and the relationship they were now developing.

As soon as Matthew got home and found out, he made Lenda go get Karen's dog, Jelly. Out of the three of them, neither she, Quintella, nor Claudette had thought about Jelly. Despite Lenda's usual disdain for animals, there was no way she was going to leave Karen's baby home alone. Lenda had the presence of mind to call Ken to see if she could legally enter Karen's house under the circumstances. He assured her that it was OK since Karen willingly gave her the key and access in case of an emergency.

And when Lenda put the key in the door lock, unlike past times, an eerie feeling attached itself to her.

Once Jelly got to Lenda's house, his behavior was odd. He whined for a while, and Lenda made a mental note to call the vet. She surmised that Jelly sensed something had happened to Karen, and that he must be going through a grieving period of sorts.

It was a good thing for Jelly and Lenda that he had a relationship with Matthew. After all, Matthew loved to spend time with Jelly whenever he came by Karen's condo with Lenda or hung out there with Karen on his own. So right now, Jelly and Matthew needed each other. But Lenda didn't know what was going to happen when she told him that keeping Jelly was *not* an option for keeps. *I'll deal with that at a much later date,* she thought.

Lenda also reflected on the prayer she had prayed on New Year's Day. She still didn't know for sure if the article she'd read was about Karen because it said they couldn't release any details until the next of kin had been informed. But what she did know was this: you never know who you're praying for in emergencies. Just pray because you could be praying for yourself.

Claudette kindly offered to host Karen's aunts once they got to Detroit, but they wanted to stay in Karen's condo on the river. So Claudette planned to take them there after feeding them dinner at her house on the day of their arrival, which was scheduled for the following day. Karen had already made it clear to her aunts that if anything ever happened to her, she wanted to be buried in Detroit—not Natchez.

The girls provided hotel information for the rest of the relatives. Only Karen's aunts were going to stay at Karen's condo.

Chapter Twenty-Eight

Having a sparkling-clean house to entertain out-of-town guests who came to attend her best friend's homegoing was bittersweet. Claudette could not deny how nice her house looked. Even Christopher commended her on its appearance. Christopher, however, had already decided to get her a maid if they got married: she just kept too much clutter for him.

Claudette was able to get the same cleaning lady who cleaned her house to clean Karen's condo. The lady didn't have as much to do at Karen's place because Karen was immaculate—her condo looked like a page out of *Architectural Digest*. The cleaning lady mainly had to the change sheets in the bedrooms and do some light dusting and vacuuming—unlike her house, where major cleaning was needed.

Claudette couldn't wait to see Karen's aunts. She remembered how much Chunk and Thelma loved their niece. When she talked to them over the phone, they kept saying, "Never in a million years did we think we would bury her. If anything, we thought it would be the other way around."

"Chunk once said, 'The only way you're going to get that gal away from Detroit is for one of us to die!'" Thelma remembered.

Both of Karen's aunts were sweet. Claudette was honored

to have the responsibility of caring for them. They were two sisters who were stunning for their ages. And they were a couple of comical characters who could easily have their own TV sitcom. Claudette was looking forward to seeing them. Christopher agreed to pick them up from the airport with her. Tomorrow was going to be a long day.

* * * *

After Claudette and Christopher took Karen's aunts to the funeral home to make arrangements, all Claudette wanted to do was sleep. It had been a grueling day, and it didn't help being at Karen's condo, knowing she'd never be there again.

Karen's aunts refused to buy new clothing for her to be buried in. And even though Claudette wanted her in a brand-new outfit, the aunts were adamant that it wasn't going to happen. Claudette offered to give them a new outfit from her shop, but the request was denied.

One of them commented, "That girl has more new clothes in her closet than you have in your shop." Claudette couldn't remember which aunt said it and although a slight exaggeration, it was partially true. The girl did have a closet full of clothes with tags still on them. Some of them had even come from Claudette's store.

Claudette and Christopher got up from the couch and began to walk toward Karen's aunts with their arms outstretched. "Aunt Thelma and Aunt Chunk, can we do anything else before we leave?" Claudette asked.

"Y'all done enough!" they both replied.

"I'll be here tomorrow—ten o'clock sharp—to pick up my girlfriends," Christopher teased.

"We'll be ready, boyfriend!" Thelma replied.

Laughter was good during hard times. Claudette was

surprised that Thelma and Chunk refused to ride in the family car provided by the funeral home. Claudette even told them they would ride in the family car, too. But her aunts insisted that they wanted to ride with Claudette and Christopher.

Claudette grabbed Christopher's arm, as the chilly winds from the river tore through their clothes. It was a very blustery day for January 7, and Christopher's arm did a good job of shielding some of the wind.

"You're a charmer. You know that, don't you?" Claudette told Christopher through chattered teeth.

"Are you that cold?" Christopher asked.

Claudette's teeth wouldn't cooperate. The chattering was uncontrollable. "Yeeeessss!" Claudette replied.

Christopher put his arms around Claudette as he teased, "Come here—let Daddy keep you warm."

Christopher's arms felt good. It had been a long week, and Claudette was feeling weak. Once they got in the parking garage, Christopher pulled Claudette to him and held her. This was not good and Claudette knew it, but she stayed in that position longer than needed. Finally, Christopher broke the silence. "Let's go get in the car."

As they walked through the huge parking garage and got to Christopher's car, Claudette pointed to the back. Christopher thought she needed something. When he opened the car door, she jumped in the back.

"What are you doing? I'm not Hoke, and you're not Miss Daisy," he teased.

"Right now, it's safer back here than being up there with you," Claudette replied.

Christopher totally understood and didn't even debate the issue. He gently closed the door, got in the front, and pulled out of the garage, headed toward Claudette's house.

* * * *

Lenda was never so glad to hear a choir shut up! All of
the emotion was really getting to her. She decided to read the
program for the fifth time. Aunt Chunk was about to read the
obituary. *Lord, help her do this,* Lenda thought. *Why do people
feel obligated to do something they emotionally can't handle just
because they feel it honors the deceased?*

Lenda knew from the Bible that people who died were
either rejoicing because they were with Jesus, or they were
weeping and gritting their teeth because they were burning
in hell. As far as she was concerned, they were not interested
in, nor did they care, who said what at the homegoing service.
She knew these services were for the living—not the dead.

As Chunk slowly made her way to the podium, she was
crying before she got out of the row where she was sitting. It
was not looking good.

Lenda remembered the conversation she'd had with her
a couple of nights before. Before she positioned herself to
spring into action and come to Chunk's rescue, she gave her a
minute.

But Chunk was breaking down badly. Lenda thought she
had received her cue to save her. Yet as she stood to take her
place, the unthinkable happened. Chunk looked at her and
screamed like she was in a horror movie, "Stay where you are;
I can do this! I can do this for my niece!" Lenda shrank back
down in her seat in embarrassment and couldn't believe this
was the sweet, gentle woman who sat and laughed with her all
night long. *My goodness, death can bring out the worst in folks,*
Lenda thought.

Karen's high school kids showed up in droves. They gave

a touching tribute. But what moved most of them was when a charming young lady got up to read a poem she wrote, titled "I Want to Be Just Like You!" It was Ashley. And when she was done, there wasn't a dry eye in the building.

What hurt Lenda most was that Oliver didn't even show up. He was too concerned that everyone would be looking at him and blaming him for Karen's death. And to that, Lenda said, "If the shoe fits, put it on and tie it tight!"

*   *   *   *

The homegoing service seemed like it was eons ago. But it was only Friday, and the service had been on Wednesday. Claudette smiled when she thought about Christopher. He had been such a great help, chauffeuring around Aunt Thelma and Aunt Chunk. He said he'd actually enjoyed their company, and it reminded him of why he was glad he was a man and not a woman.

He said Thelma and Chunk talked nonstop, like an out-of-control train with no brakes. They were both vying for Christopher's attention, and he couldn't keep up with all their questions. Claudette was just glad he was so understanding about their limited time together since Karen's death. Claudette was looking forward to dinner tonight with the aunts, Lenda, and Quintella. She loved hearing their stories, and she wanted to know more about Karen. There was so much she didn't know, and having the aunts there was a lot like having a piece of Karen there, even if it was temporary.

"Let's see…I need to have Lenda call that real nice place she told me about in Greektown, next to Fishbone's. Tomorrow is their last night in town for a while, so we have to send them off with a bang," Claudette said aloud. Claudette and Christopher had done almost everything up to that point. She felt the least Lenda could do was plan was the final dinner. After all, she was grieving, too!

* * * *

Claudette felt like a tourist. Chunk and Thelma wanted to ride the People Mover, so it was her job to ride with them while Quintella and Lenda went to the restaurant to wait for their table at Sweet Potato Brown's. The food was to "live for," and Claudette thought it would represent Detroit very well.

Because they were from the South, Claudette thought it would be nice to show them some good old-fashioned Southern hospitality and affirm that Detroit could put their feet in some Southern cooking, too!

Claudette was jolted from her thoughts, "Girl, this train ain't going in the river is it?" Thelma shrieked.

Claudette laughed as the People Mover went from Cobo Hall to the Millender Center; the train did appear to lean toward the river, so Claudette could understand Thelma's concern.

"Can we get off this thing? I've seen enough!" Thelma hollered.

"Thelma, you need to sit back and enjoy the ride. This is fun," Chunk added.

"You wouldn't know danger if it stood in front of you with a red suit, white hat, black tie, and a gun pointed at your head. So you can be quiet! This thing is squeaking and rocking like a roller coaster," Thelma continued. "Y'all can stay on here, but I'm about to get off and get me a cab."

"Aunt Thelma, so where you gonna go once you get off? 'Cause me and Chunk are going to stay on the People Mover," Claudette laughed.

With her hands on her hips and a stare-me-down look, Thelma responded, "It doesn't matter. I'll be off this poor excuse for a train before it falls into the water! I bet you that!"

Chunk lovingly looked at her sister. With one sister already in the grave, it was so nice that their relationship was solid.

Thelma had always been the feisty one. Even as little girls, Thelma would beat up the boys, while Chunk would bat her eyes and smile. As Chunk laughed at Thelma's little tirade, she couldn't help but notice that her sister looked especially jazzy today. How she kept her slim figure was a mystery. She ate a pint of ice cream every night and at age seventy, a size 2 was still too big for her.

Me on the other hand, I seem to find all the pounds Thelma loses, including those from her nightly ice cream binges. All I gotta do is smell something, and the pounds seem to jump on me. Thank God my weight is in all the right places, Chunk thought. At least that's what her man told her as they boarded the plane. She could hear his voice as clear as when they left, "I don't know how I'm going to make it without my luscious pumpkin." Luscious was a good description. Yes, she was seventy-two, but she looked pretty good herself. And she was ready to get back home to "Sweetie!"

"What you sittin' over there smiling about like you crazy or somethin'?" Thelma asked.

"I'm thinking I'd like to go around this People Mover another time just to irritate you," Chunk giggled.

"Open this door! Y'all let me off! Do you hear me? Open this door!" Thelma yelled as she stood at the exit door.

Chunk playfully yelled, "Don't pay my sister no attention, y'all…she just got out the hospital…she's harmless," Chunk joked as they got up to exit the train.

Claudette couldn't stop laughing; these ladies didn't act

a day over forty. It was so refreshing to see two sisters who obviously loved one another have so much fun.

"How far we got to walk?" Thelma squawked.

"Not far—as soon as we reach the bottom of the steps, we're there." Claudette tried her best to console the ladies.

Greektown put on its Sunday best for Thelma and Chunk. Everything sparkled. The streets were clean of debris, and even the pedestrians appeared to be all cleaned up.

Claudette had to admit, Lenda and Quintella were good at picking restaurants. *I guess if I worked for a large corporation like Lenda and eating out was a perk that I enjoyed frequently, I would probably know where all the good restaurants were, too. And it would also help if I had a husband who is a lawyer and my primary job is to entertain him and his clients,* she thought.

"Well, this is a snazzy place," Chunk admirably allowed the words to roll off her tongue.

"Forget snazzy! I'm hungry, so I hope these folks can cook," Thelma chimed in. "A pretty restaurant with lousy food is like a pretty woman with no sense or class! Not good!"

When Lenda and Quintella saw Claudette and the ladies, the both stood to embrace them before they sat down.

"How was the tour and ride?" Quintella asked sincerely.

"Don't ask," was the simultaneous response from Thelma and Chunk.

"Is this another pretty place, or can these people cook?" Thelma demanded.

"Oh, they can cook," Quintella assured her.

"Hush, Thelma," Chunk said. "Wait and taste the food before you start ranting and raving!"

"This past week has been difficult for me. Burying my

baby was something I never thought I'd do. If only her mammy had thought about what she was going to do instead of messing up the lives of those she claimed she loved. I just never thought my next trip to Detroit would be to identify my niece at the morgue."

As Thelma looked around the restaurant, she was quite pleased at the décor. She was even impressed with the waiter. This was the first restaurant she had been to that had a waiter who actually took her napkin and placed it in her lap. He even talked like he was from a royal family. And he was quite handsome, too. Thelma wanted to ask him what he was doing waiting tables. It seemed like such a waste to her that he was doing that for a living. She thought he should have been working in Corporate America or something, but she decided not to say anything. After all, it could have been a second job. And for all she knew, maybe he did work in Corporate America. And even if it was his only job…he was working, and she needed to stop judging.

Everyone gave their orders without much fuss. Thelma, however, didn't disappoint the group.

"Can I give you a suggestion, sir?" She could be charming when she wanted to be.

"Take some of these entrées off the menu. This is too much! 'Cause if you give people too much to think about, it'll take too long to make up they mind. Y'all should just put a couple items on this menu. Are you listenin' to me, sir?"

With a look of respect and admiration, he replied, "Yes, ma'am. I'll share your concerns with management. Would you like more time to peruse the menu?"

"No, I've perused it enough," Thelma mocked.

Gentle snickers broke out around the table.

"I'll have the Stuffed Caesar with Petit Croutons, and hold the anchovies. And I'll also have the Pan-Roasted Sea Bass and some sweet tea." With a nod and a smile, the young man was gone.

* * * *

As Lenda looked around the table, she had to admit that Karen's aunts were adorable. She regretted that the evening would soon come to an end.

"Dessert anyone?" Quintella teased. A unanimous "yes" rang out.

Once the waiter came back to the table, everyone placed their dessert orders. As soon as he left, Thelma was the first to speak.

"Look at y'all big-butt heifers ordering chocolate cake and pound cake. You need to be ordering Weigh-No-Mo' Brownies and Slim-for-Life Tortes."

Lovingly, Chunk replied, "You ordered chocolate cake."

"I need it. You DON'T!" Thelma teased.

More laughter.

Thelma made a face, "I'm really having fun with y'all. I hate it took my baby dying to bring us together."

The mood instantly changed from festive to somber. "We always thought some man would sweep her off her feet, and we'd be able to come up here for her wedding. The girl was beautiful, and y'all know it. The last time I talked to that girl I asked her if she had a man yet, and she said she did. I was so happy. But when I asked his name, she said it was Jesus. That girl would've been forty-eight this year, and she was still going around telling folks that Jesus and Holy Spirit were her Men. I don't understand it. It's like no real men are walking around up here in Detroit. From what I can see in this restaurant, it doesn't look like there's a shortage—they all look good to me." Thelma was talking so much she didn't see the sad faces around the table.

Lenda didn't know that Karen had referred to Jesus as her Man. It seemed like she had always had a real one. Lenda was drawn back into the conversation.

"Lord knows she would've never, ever, ever married in Natchez had she found a real man."

Inquisitively, Claudette asked, "Why would you say that, Aunt Thelma?"

"Too many bad memories," Thelma replied.

"What was so bad about Natchez?" Lenda probed. "Karen seemed to love it!"

Thelma made a face. "You don't think yo' mammy killing herself on Christmas day 'cause she found out her husband had been molesting her baby girl is bad memories?"

Even Thelma wasn't prepared for the open mouths and frozen stares that she faced. "What? Y'all didn't know that?" Thelma asked with an elevated voice.

The girls could only shake their heads with dismay.

"How long y'all been friends?" Chunk asked.

Quintella broke the silence. "More than fifteen years."

"So all y'all talk about is Jesus? I love Him, too. But there are other things going on in the real world! How can you be friends with somebody and never know her mother killed herself?"

The words Thelma spoke were like daggers. They echoed so loudly from Thelma's lips that even the waiter heard them. He politely and gently laid each dessert on the table and vanished like Houdini. They were so engrossed in their conversations that they never saw him approach.

"That's why Karen had such a hard time around the holidays. None of you ever noticed?" Chunk asked, somewhat softer than her sister.

Lenda couldn't help but feel like they didn't know each other like they thought. Taking a quick glance over at Quintella and Claudette, she wondered what other secrets were lurking between them.

"But she always went home for Christmas. She would never accept our offers because she said she wanted to go home," Lenda said.

"That gal never came home for Christmas. She wanted to be as far away from Natchez as possible, so that's when she would take these elaborate trips to dull the real pain she felt."

"Karen was molested by her stepfather?" Claudette asked in disbelief.

"*Naw*, her sister was!" Thelma shot back.

In unison, all three said, "She had a sister?"

"No! You know she was the only child, so if I said the baby was being raped, do you need Holy Spirit to interpret that for you? Y'all just too spiritual to be any earthly good! Yes, I'm talking about Karen. Karen's mother found out that her husband, who was Karen's stepfather, had been molesting and raping that child for years, and she was so in love with him that she didn't see it!

"We used to tell her something was wrong because that child never wanted to be near him. But naw, she always accused us of being too suspicious. Then when she had to have a physical for gym…wasn't it gym, Chunk?" Chunk nodded, and they noticed she had tears in her eyes.

Thelma continued like she didn't see the hurt on her

sister's face. "It was only then that she found out what was going on. She confronted him, and it got real messy. See, Natchez only has a population of about 18,000 people. You can be on one side of the town and break wind, and someone else who lives on the other side of town will call you and say, 'You need to say excuse me with yo' nasty self.'

"People are just that close. Everybody knows everybody's business. So when it got out, he was arrested, found guilty and by the way, he's still serving time. But because everybody knew, the guilt was too much for her, and she took a shotgun Christmas morning and blew her brains out. Karen got up to open gifts, went looking for her mammy, and found her. She came running down the street and got me. We called the police, and that was the worst Christmas ever. I really didn't grieve my sister's death until a few years later because I was so mad at her."

By now, the tears were streaming down Chunk's face. All the desserts sat untouched, and the ice cream was a melted mess. All eyes were on Thelma as she continued to talk in a matter-of-fact way. Quintella slipped some tissue to Chunk, and she wiped her eyes.

"See, Chunk is still not over it. What my sister did was selfish, and we're still feeling the effects of her impulsive act. It was plain selfish. First of all, if you want to kill somebody, kill *him*. He's the one who brought all the pain. And then, why do it on Christmas when you know your child's gonna be the one to find you? So I refuse to cry anymore over her selfish act.

"I told Chunk years ago to let it go. See, all y'all probably have these holy ideas about heaven. When you die you want to see the face of Jesus and the streets paved with gold. Look, when my time is up and I step through the Pearly Gates, I'm going to ask Jesus to hold His thoughts for a minute, and I'm going to find my sister and whip her behind! And you know what? Jesus ain't gonna even stop me 'cause He probably wanted to do it, but His love for her won't allow Him to.

"I'm going to go down in history as the first woman who entered heaven and started a brawl—now you write that down in yo' little Bible note-taking books."

While Thelma came up for air, the rest of the group was stunned to the point of complete silence. There were simply no words.

The waiter reappeared—impeccable timing. As hard as he tried not to listen to the conversation, it was his job to stand close to the table and serve. He didn't know what to say. "Can I wrap the desserts to go? I'll make sure I give you fresh ice cream." Thelma gave him a look that said he should leave them alone, and he politely turned and walked away. Nothing else needed to be said.

"I'm just curious, do you heifers talk about anything other than church and Jesus? This should *not* have been a revelation for somebody you considered yourself close to. What do y'all heifers talk about when you get together?"

If Quintella noticed anything about Thelma, it was that she liked to use the word "heifer" a lot. But even she knew better than to check her about it.

"It's not that we only talk about church, Aunt Thelma. Because we don't get together that often, when we do, it's too much to discuss in such a short time."

"So, this friendship that you've had for fifteen years, is it superficial?" Thelma inquired.

Chunk knew Thelma never bit her tongue about anything, cuing her to step in. "Thelma, it's not the time, and you don't have a right to talk like that. These ladies brought us to this nice restaurant, and they've shown us a good time. I think it's time we lighten the conversation."

Normally, Thelma would go head-to-head, but even Chunk was surprised that she let it go.

"OK, let's talk about something y'all know. Tell me something about Jesus," Thelma shrugged, as she sat back in her chair waiting for a response.

They all sat dumbfounded. As terse and feisty as Thelma had been, what she spoke was the truth. No way should they have called themselves friends for more than fifteen years if all of this came as a surprise.

The worst thing about finding out about Karen and her mother was that they could do nothing about it now. They could only regret that a hole had been in their relationship and that they'd lacked the ability to share truth among each other.

*   *   *   *

The girls really didn't want Thelma and Chunk to leave. Quintella promised that she and Ken would have them over for dinner when they returned to clean out Karen's condo. Christopher and Claudette took them back to the airport.

"Make sure you keep that man, baby. Like the catfish in Natchez, he's a good catch!" Thelma joked. They gave each other a group hug, and off they went.

Even though Thelma and Chunk were safely on their way back to Natchez, there was a lot of unfinished business to take care of.

Chapter Twenty-Nine

What's that? Lenda's head snapped when she was jarred by a sound. She had to calm down enough to be still. She needed to identify where the noise was coming from. *There it is again!* This time, Lenda's heart was racing like an uncontrolled locomotive. She didn't know if she should make a mad dash for the door.

"Calm down, Lenda," she whispered to herself. *If I can pinpoint where the noise is coming from, I can run toward the door and slam it shut.* She even thought about calling out to her son and asking him to come sleep in the bed with her. But he would never hear her; he was a sound sleeper. And what excuse would she give? A grown woman afraid of the dark! Maybe she could say, "Your mom is scared. I need you to stay with me so I can cut off the light and go to sleep."

No, she couldn't do that.

Once again, the noise enveloped the room. With tears welling up on the inside, she whispered, "Holy Spirit, what's that noise?" A gentle voice responded, "The cracking noise you hear is coming from the glass of ice water you brought to your room. Remember, you put it in the freezer first, and the ice was in a big chunk. Now the ice is melting because of the water and making noises as it falls to the bottom of the glass." Trembling, Lenda slowly turned toward the nightstand as if shc expected to see someone.

Again, she heard the noise. But it was accompanied by a thump. "It *was* the ice melting!" she exhaled. More noise came, but Lenda could tell it was just the larger pieces of ice falling to the bottom of the glass. Lenda was now convinced that it was only the ice. Why did she doubt what Holy Spirit said? He was God, and she wasn't.

While Lenda's blood pressure returned to normal, she couldn't help but think about Chunk and Thelma's visit. She had been edgy since they left, especially after the dinner conversation. That's the real reason why she couldn't sleep! And that's why she was hearing noises all night long. The last couple of weeks were catching up with her. Even though the Scriptures said to be *"anxious for nothing,"* Lenda realized that she was carrying stress around like a ten-pound bag of potatoes, with no relief. Lying awake proved to be a waste of time, too. Hearing noises—what a joke. She knew by the sweat that her hair had turned back. She could feel it. The light that beamed directly over her head was giving off too much heat. Now she would have to get up early and straighten her hair again.

She wanted to cry, but she was mad. How many years had Karen kept all those secrets? God had given her friends. But for whatever reason, she chose to go it alone. It was a trick of the devil, but she wasn't going to take this lying down. A meeting with Quintella and Claudette was in order. All secrets would be exposed! *A friend is not a true friend if you can't tell the truth and be honest about what's going on in your life. If they're real friends, we should be able to be honest and still love each other. It's crazy to think that after fifteen years of friendship we can't be transparent with each other,* she thought. Then Holy Spirit reminded her of some secrets she hadn't shared. He also brought to her attention that she needed to rely on

Him instead of her intellect.

Lenda repented. She sat back in her bed and began to think about the goodness of God. Her gratitude caused her to dwell on all the wonderful things God had done for her. That settled it: the cat was going to be let out of the bag. Lenda wanted to be the first to reveal her secrets. She planned to tell them about Ernest being in jail. Yes, she was embarrassed that he was in jail, but she was not going to let the enemy win any longer. It was going to be revealed. "Thank You, Holy Spirit—once again, You're not only The Man—You're *my* Man," she proclaimed aloud.

She felt better already. The light that brought temporary consolation from the darkness was now being turned off. The One who was always with her prevailed in the fight and brought the comfort she needed. Lenda fluffed her pillow, the tears and anxiety were gone, and she could smell sleep like hot homemade rolls being baked in the oven.

Chapter Thirty

Lenda had mixed emotions about dinner. She wrestled with the thought of it being too soon to meet. But considering the timing, they were late in getting together. They should have officially met in January, but it was unanimous that January wasn't a good time for any of them. Besides, it wasn't like they hadn't seen each other then, regardless of the circumstances.

It was the end of February. They all decided that if they didn't do it now, it very well may be never. Emotions were still running high, and no one was ready talk about Karen without crying. There was a possibility that the place they chose would help.

Rumor had it that the jazz band at this restaurant was extremely talented. One of the guys played an electric violin. Lenda's friend told her that when he played, the violin talked. She said their music was a mix of contemporary jazz and Christian favorites.

As Lenda looked at the clock, she decided that she had better get moving or she would be late.

* * * *

Quintella was determined that she would not cry tonight. They needed to heal, and her prayer for the past week was for the Lord to strengthen them and allow the healing to take place. Ken interrupted her thoughts as he kissed her forehead: "Have fun tonight and don't allow the enemy to steal your joy. He can only take it if you give it to him."

Quintella stood up and gave Ken a big hug.

"Thanks for allowing me to go out to have fun with my friends. Some husbands forbid their wives to go out, especially with single women. I really appreciate you for trusting my choice of friends."

"You make good choices when choosing friends. Why should I interfere? You always take care of me. A healthy marriage doesn't exclude outside friendships."

This time, she kissed him passionately.

"Keep that up, though, and I'll lock the doors and kidnap you."

"That sounds like a good idea."

Ken playfully hit her on the butt and winked at her. If she was going to leave, Quintella needed to go now.

*　*　*　*

Claudette was looking forward to dinner. Their first real dinner without Karen was going to be the hardest, but she knew their friendship would weather the storm. They discussed having an empty seat in honor of Karen, but that idea was quickly dismissed. A booth was going to work just fine.

Claudette reflected on how before Karen died it always seemed like there was a group within their group. She and Karen, and Quintella and Lenda. But Karen's passing had brought everyone closer, and it was as if they were tighter than ever before. Claudette didn't know what to expect at this dinner, but she had a good feeling about it nonetheless.

* * * *

Lenda, Quintella, and even Claudette arrived at the restaurant on time. Everything started out pretty tame. They exchanged greetings, placed their orders, and began enjoying the entertainment. The food was really good, and the music was better. During intermission, a verbal bomb was dropped.

"Hey, I feel the need to tell y'all something. Remember when Karen's aunts were here and they shamed us because there was so much we didn't know about her? I think it was Aunt Thelma who said something like 'real friends share.' Well, I have something that I have not been truthful about for fear that I would be looked at in an unfavorable manner."

With her head down and a napkin in hand, Lenda began to roll the napkin over and over, which was a sure sign of her nervousness. After what seemed like hours, she looked up with determined but teary eyes and continued her story. "I told y'all five years ago that my brother moved to another state, and we had a falling out. Well, that wasn't the whole truth. My brother did move, not to another state, but to the state penitentiary. My brother has been incarcerated all this time. We had a falling out, not so much because of what he did, but because of the pain that his actions brought on my mother.

"My brother got caught up with the wrong people. They robbed a bank, and he was the lookout person. He got five years. I was too ashamed to tell the truth, so I've been lying all this time. That's the reason I'm not available to do things most Saturdays, because I take my mother up to Jackson to visit him."

As she came up for air, Quintella broke the silence by reminding Claudette to close her mouth because the gnat that had been circulating the booth was sure to find a home inside.

Light laughter filled the table, but everyone was speechless.

"Maybe tonight wasn't the best night to let this bobcat out the bag, but I was tired of hiding the truth."

Claudette put her hand over Lenda's hand and earnestly replied, "Girl, you should've told us. Your brother being in jail won't change how we feel about you."

Quintella reassured her with more of the same. "What kind of friends would we be not to support you? We could've driven with you and kept you company along the way. Or given you a break by taking your mom."

"As I said before, I take Mom, and I've been known to take my work with me to help time pass. You don't know how good it feels to share this with y'all. It's been difficult. I must tell you that for three of those years I probably actually saw my brother maybe six times.

"For a while, I couldn't even stomach him because of Mom. I think they locked up a piece of her heart when they locked him up. I've seen her age, and it hurts. But you know what? Last year I began thinking, is God pleased with the way I treat my brother? I went through lots of emotions, but my prayer was that God would heal my family, and He did.

"So much happened, but my relationship with my sister changed along with the one with my brother. God convicted me about my self-righteous attitude, so I turned over a new leaf. I made a decision to forgive my brother and love him.

"As a result of my decision, we've enjoyed sweet fellowship that we've never enjoyed before. When Karen died, I realized that if you guys really loved me, I could share this dark side and still be accepted."

Quintella stood up and hugged Lenda. "We're friends for life and even if *you* robbed a bank, I'd still love you, have Ken represent you, and stick with you until you were a free woman again."

Claudette also stood and hugged Lenda, expressing her love and support. They all took an oath that there would be nothing—absolutely nothing—that could come between them. Losing Karen was a heartbreaker; they were not about to lose each other. They were friends for life!

Chapter Thirty-One

Lenda had just returned from another successful consulting trip. If business continued like this, she was on target to quit her real job as a coordinator for General Motors and go into consulting full time. She had called her mother three times between the airport and home, but she still hadn't answered. Annie had gone out of town with a friend, so Lenda had trouble reaching her.

The last time something like this had happened, her mother had knocked over the phone and didn't realize calls were not coming through. Lenda dismissed the thought of going to check on her. It was Thursday night, and she was happy that her ex decided to keep her son that whole week. Her plane had been delayed because of the weather, so she was extra tired.

She couldn't get her mother off her mind, but she reasoned that her mother's phone was probably in another room. She planned to call her on Friday, after she ran some errands. The only thing she wanted to do was take a bath and get in the bed.

She hardly remembered when her head hit the pillow.

* * * *

Friday was a busy day, and it was eight o'clock that night

before Lenda thought about her mother again. *Something is up because Mom always calls me to confirm when I offer to pick her up for church.* Lenda felt uneasy. She dismissed her feelings and went to bed. Calling her on Saturday morning would give them plenty of time to discuss the Sunday pickup.

*   *   *   *

A piercing sound interrupted Lenda's sleep; it took a moment for her to realize it was the alarm clock. As she looked at the dial on the clock, Lenda decided to set the clock for an hour later—her errands had taken a lot out of her. She readjusted the clock and pulled the covers over her head. It seemed only seconds later that the old familiar buzzer rang again. Like a magnet being drawn to another magnet, her fingers found the snooze button. After repeating this act several times, Lenda finally got up. She moved zombielike into the bathroom and realized that this was the first time in a long time that she hadn't talked to her mother for three whole days.

Lenda immediately dialed her mom, ready to ask forgiveness for not calling for so long. No answer. Lenda made a mental note to have her mother to check the phone every now and then. The fact of the matter was that she had to go over there. It wasn't like her mother not to answer the phone.

After showering, she was sitting, putting lotion on her legs when she thought she heard Holy Spirit speak to her. He said, "Call Quintella and Ken and have them come take you to see your mom." Lenda frowned. That couldn't be Holy Spirit talking to her. That was a dumb. "I can't do that anyway," Lenda blurted. *Why would I call Quintella and Ken this early on a Saturday morning to take me to see Mom? Where did that dumb thought come from?* Lenda dismissed the thought and continued to get dressed. She would be at her mother's house in ten minutes, and it wouldn't be soon enough. An eerie feeling was bringing her down quickly.

As Lenda was leaving out of the door, the phone rang. A sigh of relief swept over her. It had to be her mother, wondering why they hadn't talked.

"I'm walking out the door, Mom," Lenda teased as she picked up the receiver.

"Sorry to disappoint you, but it's not your mom; it's Quintella."

"What are you doing calling me at nine o'clock on a Saturday morning?"

"You know, I asked myself that same question. Please don't think I'm crazy or anything. But Holy Spirit woke me up this morning, and I couldn't go back to sleep. I kept thinking of you and your mom. Of course, I prayed. Is everything alright?"

"Funny you should ask," Lenda replied as she slowly sat in a chair. "It's weird, girl. I haven't talked to Mom in three days, and she's been heavy on my mind. I tried calling my sister; she's out of town—and I couldn't get her either. I have this depressing feeling hanging over me. Even this morning, I heard a voice that said to call you and Ken to have you come get me to go to Mom's house. Isn't that strange, girl?"

Quintella was noticeably silent.

Lenda continued, "I mean, I even said out loud that I couldn't do that. Call you and your husband to go with me to Mom's—PLEASE—no way was I calling you!"

Now Lenda really felt uneasy, because the voice on the other end was not responding. "Queen, are you still there?" Slowly, Quintella responded. "You know what, Lenda? I really called you because I felt strange this morning. Why don't we come get you, and the three of us can go with you to pick up your mom? Maybe Holy Spirit doesn't want you to drive for a reason. We haven't seen her in a while, and we could all go out to breakfast."

After trying several times to change her mind, Quintella won. She and Ken would be pulling up within twenty minutes. Shaking her head, Lenda decided that twenty more minutes wasn't going to make that big of a difference. While she waited, she was able to make good use of her time. She went back into the bedroom to make the bed.

All three of them were on their way to Lenda's mom's in *less* than twenty minutes. Ken was breaking every speed limit, and Lenda couldn't figure out why. Actually, none of them knew why the events of the morning were so out of the ordinary. But since they were together, they agreed that breakfast at the Original Pancake House was in order after they picked up Lenda's mom.

*   *   *   *

Quintella forgot how nice the neighbors kept their yards where Lenda's mom lived. The flowers placed in everyone's flower beds looked more fake than real because their lawns were so beautifully landscaped.

Lenda tried calling her mom again so they wouldn't have to wait. Still, no answer. She had lost her key just before this last trip, so she would have to depend on her mom to let them in.

"Mom isn't expecting company, so be prepared to wait," she warned. They parked in the driveway and took the quick walk to Lenda's mom's front door. Lenda knocked and called out her mother's name. Again, no answer.

This was starting to get very creepy.

"Don't they have a block club?" Ken said.

"Yes, they do," said Lenda.

"Well, let's see if the president can help," Ken said.

"OK, I think she lives over there," Lenda said, pointing across the street.

The three of them must have looked odd walking down the street to the president's house, because they passed one of her neighbors and he looked at them like they were from another planet.

When they arrived at her door, Lenda was thankful someone was home. Usually, the block club president was good about keeping an eye out. Her mom had mentioned how serious she was about their street. "Thank God you're here," Lenda exhaled.

After explaining their dilemma, the president mentioned that she hadn't seen any activity at her mom's house in a while. She thought that maybe she had gone out of town. She told her that Lenda's mom had left a spare key with her, in case of emergency. "Let's go," she commanded.

The four of them made their way back to her house. Once they opened the door and stepped inside, a foul odor was noticeable. Ken put his hand over his stomach and stopped walking. Before he could tell Lenda and Quintella to wait, the president blurted out, "Smells like somebody has died or something," holding her place in the doorway.

Brilliant woman, Ken thought.

Ken knew in his spirit that something wasn't right.

The smell hit them like a ton of bricks. Ken pulled at Lenda's coat to stop her, but he couldn't. Lenda rushed past the smell to search the house, with Ken and Quintella closely behind her. No one was prepared for what they saw.

Chapter Thirty-Two

Sitting in the chair in her bedroom was Lenda's mom with a piece of paper in her hands. Her eyes and mouth were open, and she was stiff as a board. Lenda didn't recognize that the voice of the woman she heard screaming was her very own. She could only stand there in terror, as Ken went over and put his hands on her mother's eyelids and closed her eyes shut. Everything after that was a fog. Lenda believed life couldn't get any worse than this.

* * * *

When the police arrived, Ken answered most of the questions. They were satisfied with the responses, so they instructed them to call the funeral home to pick up her mom's body. The police gave them a six-digit code for the funeral home. The number allowed the funeral home to get the body and bypass the morgue. Ken handled everything. His status as an attorney certainly came in handy that day. All Lenda could do was sit in the arms of Quintella and cry and answer any questions that Ken had. There were questions about insurance, which funeral home to call, what family members to notify, and so on.

Before it was all said and done, Lenda's mental chatter began. *Mom was better than this! How could she go out like that, all by herself?* And once again, her brother was to blame.

* * * *

The funeral director finally arrived to take her mother's body. Lenda was sitting wide-eyed, staring out of the window. Ken and Quintella were walking around the house praying. It was only two o'clock in the afternoon. But to Lenda, it felt like weeks had passed. By now, she had so many questions for Ken. "Why were parts of Mom's body stiff? Why did the house smell so bad?" Ken explained that rigor mortis had set in. When Lenda asked what rigor mortis was, Ken explained that it was a state where muscles become stiff after death and then begin to revert after three days. Then they decompose and become soft again anywhere after three more days.

Lenda deduced that her mom must have died Wednesday night. That's why she was able to pry the paper from her mom's hands because the rigor mortis had begun to wear off, and her mom's body had begun to decompose—thus the reason for the stench.

It was a letter from Ernest that was in her hands. It said that Ernest wouldn't be home for Easter. Lenda's mom usually reminded her to refer to Easter as Resurrection Sunday— Lenda would always forget because Easter was easier to say. Just last week her mother told her, "I think it's so significant that Ernest is coming home just before Resurrection Sunday. It's like things have been dead, but God is raising up the dead things just like He raised Jesus from the dead." Lenda didn't quite see it that way, but then her mother always had a different view of things when Ernest was involved.

The letter explained that there had been an altercation at the prison and until it was determined that Ernest was not at fault—he had to do more time. The letter stated that it could be another four months, but it wouldn't be much longer than that.

Lenda knew the anticipation and excitement her mother had been feeling just knowing that her son would be released soon. Her mom was making plans as if a new baby was arriving. Even though the medics said they would have to wait until the autopsy was done, it looked like she'd had a heart attack.

Lenda couldn't help but think the news that Ernest wouldn't be home for the long-awaited homecoming was too much for her mom. She thought: *Why did he have to write and tell her that?*

The funeral director motioned to Ken. He wanted to explain that they had to remove the body and cover up Lenda's mom in what looked like a body bag, but it wasn't. Ken went back over to Lenda to tell her what was about to happen and suggested that they go in another room until everything was done, but Lenda would have none of it. She wanted to witness everything, a decision she would later regret.

Other than prayers and sobs, no other sounds were coming from the house. About an hour after her mom's body had been removed, Lenda broke the silence. "I'm going to make my brother pay!" When she spoke, her words spewed venom. "He's going to pay big time for what he did to my mother!" Just then, Lenda's eyes locked with Ken's. From there, she looked at Quintella. She could tell both were pleading with her to calm down before she did something stupid. But they knew that now was not the time to try to tell her that it wasn't her brother's fault. A mother's love ignores logic and common sense. Yes, sometimes that love can cause physical illness and perhaps, in this case, death. No one really knew. It was no use saying anything because Lenda wasn't hearing anything from anybody.

* * * *

Lenda didn't sleep well. "Why, Why, WHY?" Lenda moaned. She could smell the crisp winds that signified the arrival of spring. She went to sleep with her window open, and the breeze was as refreshing as a cool glass of water.

If I could only turn back the clock just a week—not a month, not a year, just a week. Long enough to visit Mom and maybe sense something was wrong. Perhaps I could see that she wasn't feeling well. Just a week and I would be able to remove the wounds that now cause my soul to bleed! Just a week before, all was quiet. Life was peaceful—breathing was easy, Lenda thought.

Chapter Thirty-Three

Lenda was thankful that Claudette had come over, even in the midst of her protesting. Claudette won, and Lenda was glad she had. Fending phone calls and shooing visitors from the door allowed Lenda the time she needed to get a quick nap, awake, and reflect again on the worst day of her life thus far.

She couldn't help but think about her sister. Lenda knew she would take it hard, but she wasn't prepared for the screams that ripped through the very core of her soul. Annie blamed herself for not spending more time with their mother. She blamed herself for being out of town. It had been three days, and her sister's tears had not subsided. Lenda didn't have another tear to shed—only hate for her brother.

Just think—it was just last year that I wanted everything to be right. I thought we could somehow pull the family together, forget the past, and move on. Mom was ecstatic that we all seemed to be moving in the right direction to restore the brokenness that had plagued our family and kept us from having healthy relationships.

Not anymore! If I never see my brother again, it will be too soon, Lenda raged in her mind.

"Ken? Sorry, I didn't see you standing there," Lenda apologized.

"I know, didn't want to interrupt your thoughts. Can we talk?" Ken proceeded with caution, not looking forward to the conversation he needed to have with Lenda.

He and Quintella had already been warned not to bring up the name "Ernest" again. But Ken had to take a chance that the Lord had softened her heart in the last three days.

"Lenda, I need to talk to you about a sensitive subject."

"Ken, as good as you and Queen have been to me, there is nothing off-limits but one subject, and you know what that is."

Ken cleared his throat, "I'm sorry, but it *is* about your brother."

Eyes that were sad but soft quickly turned to ice.

"Please," Ken pleaded. "Please just give me five minutes. "

Lenda's eyes didn't move, nor did they soften again. Clearing his throat, Ken proceeded very carefully. "Lenda, if your brother is going to attend the service…"

"Stop!" Lenda interrupted. "Since when do they allow murders to come to their victim's funeral?"

"Lenda, he's not a murderer and she was *his* mother, too."

"She may have been his mother. But he has done wrong by her ever since he was birthed into the world, and I for one will not entertain the thought of his presence at her service!"

"Lenda, with all the respect that's in me, you used to tell us about the good times you had with Ernest. He hasn't been wrong all the days of his life. Even a broken clock is right twice a day…cut him some slack. What happened to the mended relationship?"

"It cracked when I saw my mother dead in a chair alone, where she had been for three days or more!"

"Lenda, I love you like a sister…"

"And I love you like a brother, or should I say better than my brother?"

Choosing to ignore her comments, Ken carefully proceeded.

"Lenda, death has a way of bringing out the worst in people. Even sane people go off. But most settle down after a day or two. Won't you let him come?"

"So let me make sure I have this right. You want me to be responsible for a prison inmate?"

"I want you, in spite of everything, to forgive your brother for whatever you believe he's done and allow him to attend his mother's service. I'll be responsible for getting him to and from the service. The warden will let me do it as long as we pay for the escorts."

Surprised by Ken's persistence, Lenda asked, "Who's going to pay for the escorts?"

"I'll foot the expense, Lenda. I checked with the prison and up until this last little offense, which was not your brother's fault; the warden says your brother was an exemplary inmate. They have proof that he was just protecting himself from someone who was jealous of him and attacked him. He was only protecting himself."

"Exemplary inmate—what an aspiration! He embarrassed my mom while she was living. Don't you think she deserves some dignity in death? Put it this way: if he gets here, so be it. But it won't be with my help, *and* I won't be held accountable for what I'll say to him if I decide to acknowledge that I even know him. What made me even think I could love him again? How did I get duped into forgiving him and reaching out to him?" Lenda hissed.

Ken was having second thoughts about getting in the

326 | YOU'VE GOT A MAN

middle of family drama. He just didn't want Lenda to make a mistake that she would regret for the rest of her life. He decided that he'd pray some more and ask God to help him make the right decision for everyone.

*   *   *   *

Ernest's mind had been cluttered with mixed emotions since he received the news of his mom's death. He was thankful that he had befriended an officer who broke the news to him with dignity. But it didn't ease the pain; it just made it bearable. He loved his mother and at the same time was very much aware of how he had hurt her during a moment when one bad decision changed his life forever. What puzzled Ernest was why Lenda hadn't called him. Perhaps she was just overwhelmed with pain.

Ernest knew they were just mending their relationship. His hope was that this would somehow draw them closer. He decided he needed to pray. "Father," he paused and looked up as if someone were standing in the cell with him, "You have helped me to deal with the pain of loneliness and rejection. I'm not asking for anything for me, but I'm asking that You comfort my sister Lenda who has had the burden of being a father figure to me and my sister. Lord, it's been hard on her these past five years. I'm just asking that You comfort her as she makes plans to bury our mom. Strengthen her, and please make sure You surround her with people who will help her during this time. Lord, unless Annie has changed—she's so emotional—allow her to be in control of her emotions so as not to put any undue stress on Lenda. Help her carry some of the load, in Jesus' Name. Amen."

What else could he pray? He knew that the brunt of everything would be on Lenda. It always had been. His baby sister didn't have the know-how to do stuff like that.

He couldn't wait until he was out of jail. He planned to get a job, somehow, and show Lenda just how much he'd changed. Prison had been a cruel eye-opener. But the past five years had really helped him to grow up.

He knew that people on the outside made fun and said cruel things about inmates and their newfound relationship with Jesus. But being behind bars didn't mean that he didn't need to make good choices. *You can stay by yourself and think about all you're missing. You can join a gang and still be worldly. Or you can make a decision that even though you may be locked up, you can commit to Jesus, turn your life around, and be free mentally. For me, the only choice was Jesus—and I'm glad about it.*

His thoughts were interrupted when the guard told him he had a visitor. Strange, he wasn't expecting his sister, and none of the friends he supposedly had before prison ever thought about him. *Heck, a visitor is a visitor.*

As Ernest approached the visitor lounge, his smile widened when he saw Ken. He remembered that Ken was a lawyer and figured Lenda must have sent him there.

They embraced like brothers. After which, there was an awkward moment of silence. "I'm sorry about your mom, Ernest," Ken offered.

"Me too!" Then a horrible thought came like lightening. "My sister's OK, right?"

"Yeah," Ken assured him.

"OK, so what brings you here?"

"Well, I came to tell you that I've arranged for you to attend your mother's service."

Overwhelmed, Ernest broke down and cried like a baby for about five minutes. There was nothing in the law books that taught Ken how to handle his reaction. Ken just gave him some space and a "man pat" every now and then. Finally, Ernest came up for air.

"Man, I thought I wouldn't be able to go."

"You know you'll have to have cuffs?"

"Yeah," was all he could muster. "How will that look, man? I mean, the last thing I want to do is bring more shame on my family. I've caused so much grief, Ken."

Silence.

"My sisters are OK with this right?"

"I wouldn't be here if they weren't," he lied. Ken would have to remember to repent once he got in the car. It was a flat-out lie—but partially true. Annie wanted him to come. But Lenda, that was another issue—and she was the *Christian*.

"Listen, Ken, how about this? Is it possible I could go in real early, see my mom, and sit in the back? Or if the church has a balcony, could I sit up there? I want to be out of the way—hopefully, no one will see me. I just wouldn't want the attention drawn to me and the cuffs, man. I think it would embarrass my sisters, even though they would never say anything to me."

Ken couldn't believe what he was hearing—he and his sister thought alike, only his assessment was a lot kinder than hers. But then he *could* believe it. Ernest had a good heart; Ken figured he had probably gotten mixed up with the wrong crowd.

"I could arrange that," Ken replied. "The church has a balcony. I can get one of the brothers from the church to sit with you."

"Will you explain it to my sisters?"

"Yeah, I can do that." *More lies,* Ken thought.

"Man, you don't know what this means to me. It's bittersweet, though. I thought the next time I'd see my mom outside of the prison would be when I got out. I pictured hugging my mom, and I was looking forward to sitting around the kitchen table talking about old times. Guess it'll have to wait until I get to heaven with her."

They talked another twenty-five minutes. Ken caught him up on what was going on, avoiding his questions on exactly how they found her. Ken never told him the real story. Ken brought him up to speed on his nephew and finally ended the visit.

Ken stood up to leave. He had to get back, and this had gone better than he thought. He had prepared a statement on how Ernest would have to stay in the background, but he didn't have to use it. *Thank You, Holy Spirit.*

"Thanks again, man!" The bear hug Ernest gave almost cut Ken's air off.

"Don't sweat it, man. If the shoe was on the other foot, I have no doubt you'd do the same for me."

* * * *

Ken had been an attorney for two decades, and the sound of prison doors closing still sent chills down his spine. *Most people who are free don't even think to thank God for their freedom. We take so much for granted. It's not pretty being locked up with only a few hours each day to stretch. The price we pay for our mistakes,* he thought.

Ken got in his car. For some reason, he was besieged with thoughts of gratitude. Life was better than good and if he could share some of the blessings God had given him, then that was even better. He was reminded of the lie. Looking up to God, he confessed, "Lord, was it wrong to withhold the

330 | YOU'VE GOT A MAN

truth so someone wouldn't have to feel the pain of knowing that his sister held him responsible for their mom's death, even though it wasn't his fault? Did that lie hurt anyone? Was I supposed to tell an already-hurting man that his sister now hates him and never wants to see him again? Please forgive me if I was wrong."

Ken sat for a moment, smelling the leather of his brand-new Cadillac DTS. Black on black with wood trim. The smell of new leather seats and the smooth gentle ride never wore off for a man—at least for him it didn't. Ken turned on his XM radio to enjoy some music on the long ride home.

*   *   *   *

Pointing the garage door opener reminded Ken that he couldn't remember any of the music that was playing in the car. His thoughts and prayers had been on Lenda and her brother's incarceration. He knew Christians, like anyone else, didn't have a magic wand. At times, life is hard for everyone. *But as much as Jesus did for us on Calvary by shedding His Blood…I guess I expect a little more forgiveness from Christians, just a little more.* He prayed that he was doing the right thing. Only time would tell.

Chapter Thirty-Four

~

"I'm done proofing the obituary, and I only found a couple things," Annie said as she handed the obituary to Lenda.

Lenda looked over the changes, and they were minimal. Then she spotted a question mark and wondered if she should ignore it, pretending she didn't see it, or address it head-on. It was so nice to have a good relationship with her sister after all the wasted years of strife. Did she want to chance losing what they now had? If she had learned anything over the past few months, this one thing she knew: you can't sweep family drama under a rug. That dust will work its way back, and you will have to deal with it one way or the other. She made a decision to get it over and done with. She had to deal with it.

"So what's the question mark for by our names?" Lenda asked.

"Well, it says, 'Ethel leaves to cherish her memory, two loving daughters,' and it has our names. Then it says, 'and one son, Ernest,'" Annie paused and looked Lenda straight in the eyes.

"What's wrong with what I wrote? Is there a better way to write it?" Lenda challenged.

"Well, ah…see, it makes me think that her son wasn't loving. Lenda, this is hard for me. I'm so glad that God healed our relationship. Coming to your house having dinners with you. Being able to call you has so helped me. I'm going to church again. It's all because of you. But, well…I love Ernest, and I don't want to leave him out. He's a good person, and I know you have your reasons for not liking him…"

Lenda interrupted, "You don't think he killed Mom?"

"Why do you keep saying that? He didn't kill Mom. If she loved him too much and she had a heart attack 'cause she got a letter from him, that's not his fault. He was just preparing her that he wasn't coming home. Lenda, I never told you this, but do you know why I didn't like you and why I didn't want to be around you? It's because when we were growing up, people always said you were the pretty one. We'd be standing side by side, and people would say, 'What's your name? You're so pretty. Look at your hair, look at your eyes.' I'd be standing right there, almost joined at the arm with you, and they never said anything to me. It's like I wasn't standing there. They even nicknamed you Pretty Gal. Do you how much that hurt?

"When I was little, I felt bad. But I didn't know how to express myself. As we got older, it didn't stop. People would visit and say nice things about you, and it was still like I didn't exist. Neither you nor Mom ever said anything. You know who came to my defense? Ernest. I remember one day, I don't know why we were dressed up, but Daddy said, 'Look at my Pretty Gal. You got beautiful hair like your momma and your poor sister, I don't know what she got.' Do you know how that hurt? But Ernest heard it, and he came and whispered in my ear, 'You're pretty, too!' I didn't know what to say, but it made me feel better.

"After that, when we'd be places and people would say stuff, Ernest would always come to my rescue. One time, we were out shopping and these ladies came up to Mom, some of her friends, and they said, 'That gal is beautiful. Look at that hair and those eyes.' Ernest spoke up and said, 'My other sister is pretty too, isn't she?' They just looked at him as if to say, 'Shut up, boy! You a child; you don't know nothing.' Did *Mom* say anything? Did *you* say anything? That's why I left home at an early age. It seemed like none of y'all thought I had anything going for me. I figured if I wasn't around, I couldn't be hurt. I didn't like you or Mom. Was that fair? Was it your fault that our looks are so different that other people saw value in you and not in me? No.

"Mom could've shut that stuff down, but she didn't. She was so worried about hurting somebody's feelings that she allowed her own daughter to be hurt over and over and over. But it had to stop, and I learned a lot. Sometimes, those who are closest to us are responsible for most of the emotional damage we suffer.

"At some point, we become responsible. We determine if we are going to break the imaginary chains others put around us. I broke them, sis. I realized that it wasn't your fault, and I decided to love you.

"Now when I'm out, if I feel the need to tell some little girl that she's cute, I make sure that all the little girls around her know they're pretty, too. And when I see people try to do to other little girls what was done to me, I'm quick to step in and say, 'You're pretty, too! What a darling dress.' And then I check whoever is with me and I tell 'em, 'Didn't you see that other child standing there? Don't tell one she's pretty and not say something nice to the other one.' And you know what I've found? It's ignorance. People don't even realize they're doing it.

"So, my sister, if Mom loved Ernest 'to her death.' It's not Ernest's fault, and you shouldn't hold him hostage emotionally for her death. Let him out of your prison. He's served enough time.

"Was it Joseph's fault that his father Jacob loved him more than the other brothers in the Bible? They tried to kill him, but it wasn't his fault, just like it's not Ernest's fault that Mom loved *him* so much. I guess Joseph's brothers, like me, got tired of their parent's favorite child, and they conspired to kill him. I, on the other hand, just ran away. Maybe we ought to get some T-shirts for the next family reunion that say, 'We will not be like the Genesis 37:4 brothers.' That'll give people something to think about and read.

"Why are you looking at me crazy? Don't ask people what they think; they just might tell you. I'm not bitter; I didn't cry one tear telling you how I felt. God knows I cried enough in my lifetime. But with Mom gone, we're connected now. I don't want to spend the rest of our lives as the mediator between you and Ernest. I can't handle that. We have enough enemies in the streets; we don't need to be fighting between ourselves.

"Maybe you should've left me in the world. Naw, God has brought about a change in me these past months, and I'm grateful. So much has been lifted off of me, and I won't allow anyone to throw garbage on me anymore.

"Now, back to this obituary. Can we reword it?"

Lenda went from looking at Annie to the obituary, and then from the obituary to the floor. She could hardly see the obituary for the tears that filled her eyes. She didn't know what to think or what to say. She wasn't prepared for the full-blast, verbal and emotional fire hydrant that had burst open in her dining room, forcing out old feelings of hurt and rejection of which she was unaware. She could only respond by mustering a meager, "Let me see…I'm sure we can come up with something."

Walking away from her sister to stand at the kitchen window, she felt weak in the knees and welcomed the support of the sink. Her eyes looked out of the window, but her heart and mind were on Annie. She moved over to the counter to write something else on the paper.

Meanwhile, Annie just stood in her same spot, unable to move. Minutes later, words came.

"Annie, I made the change. How about this? 'Ethel leaves to cherish her memory, three loving children: two daughters, Lenda and Annie; and one son, Ernest.' What do you think?"

"I think you did good, girl. I think you did good."

Annie turned, walked in the kitchen, and gave Lenda a hug that transmitted the breadth of her love. It was welcomed and returned, and neither were in a hurry to break the physical contact.

"Let's go get something to eat," Lenda blurted.

"OK, but I have a taste for chicken," Annie said.

"Sounds good to me!" Lenda agreed.

*   *   *   *

"Why is it when you eat you get sleepy?" Annie asked.

"I don't know," Lenda replied while throwing the empty food containers in the garbage. "I just know if I don't clean off the table and get this stuff up, it'll sit until tomorrow. I think it's more what you eat that makes you sleepy than just eating. If we had eaten an apple we probably wouldn't feel like we need a nap. But chicken, mashed potatoes, bread, and sweet tea. Not to mention the portions," Lenda laughed. "That's what makes you sleepy."

"OK, now did we forget anything?" Lenda asked Annie.

"Girl, you thought of everything. I didn't know Mom loved the movie *Imitation of Life*. I liked it, too. But I thought only Hollywood could have a carriage with horses pulling the casket. Never would I have imagined doing it for Mom. Folks are going to think a star has gone."

"She *was* a star…Hollywood just didn't know it!" Lenda lovingly joked.

"So what are we going to do about all the requests for Mom's stuff? Aunt Ruthie called again. She wants to make sure she gets her pearls," Annie reminded Lenda.

"You know what? I'm so tired of people asking for stuff and Mom's not even in the ground yet. I think it's so disrespectful when relatives and friends call to beg for stuff! I've never done that. Have you?"

"I haven't. But again, people are different," Annie said as she shrugged her shoulders.

"Well, I think the three of us should decide who gets what. Don't you?" Lenda asked.

"I think so," Annie replied so thankful that Lenda said "the three of us."

"And I'm in no hurry to do it. Are you?"

"No, I'm in no hurry," Annie replied, silently hoping they would do it once Ernest came home.

Lenda looked at her sister with disgust, "If they mess with me, and if left up to me alone, I wouldn't give them a thing! Anything we don't want and anything we don't feel led to give, I'm boxing it up and donating it to The Salvation Army. Calling folks asking for stuff and we're trying to plan her services. That's some dumb stuff. Well, tomorrow is going to be a long day. I'm glad you decided to spend the night. I'm ready for a bath and my bed."

"Yeah, I'm just glad I didn't have to do this alone. I'm also glad we got our relationships right before Mom died. She was so happy seeing us all get along," Annie said.

"So am I. I'll let Matt go in the bathroom after you. You'll see firsthand the drama of waking a teen in the morning."

"I can hardly wait, even though I don't think my nephew is as bad as you say. But I'll take your word for now and see for myself tomorrow."

* * * *

Lenda wasn't sleepy. Tired yes, but sleepy no. She was glad that Ken pushed to bring her brother down. She'd been thinking about all the things Annie had said, as well as Quintella and Ken. They were right. There was no need for her to continue to harbor ill thoughts toward her brother. It was time to forgive again, and she was up to the task. Maybe she, Annie, and Matthew could get there early and go up in the balcony and hug Ernest. *Thank You, Lord, for helping me. What a shame it would've been for him to attend and go back to jail without a touch from me. Certainly he would've known something was wrong. Like my sister said earlier, no need for me to hold him hostage emotionally.*

"God, this forgiveness thing, when will it end?" She was asleep as soon as the words left her mouth.

* * * *

Lenda spared no expense for their mother's homegoing service. As the family car pulled up to the entrance of the church, the horse-drawn carriage looked like a piece of heaven. Lenda was pleased with how beautiful the obituary booklet turned out. She hoped her brother got one of the bottled waters to take with him that had their mom's picture with her name, date of birth, and date of transition on it.

Lenda was even more pleased as they were ushered into the church to see all the people. It was standing room only. The altar was lined with marvelous flowers. *Mom died alone.*

And the way she died left a bad taste in my mouth, but I'm glad that her final departure is so majestic. Of course, it was easy to spend money on it when it was hers to spend. The insurance policy that she carried on her mother was more than enough to buy the extravagant extras. Not because she felt guilty, no, because her mother deserved to go out like this.

The long walk down the middle aisle of the church was almost over. The open casket was upon them. Lenda decided earlier that she wasn't going to look at the shell lying there; she chose to believe that her mom was in the arms of Jesus and that the body lying there was not her mother, but the suit that carried her spirit when she was alive.

Annie, however, didn't share Lenda's same reasoning. Holding Annie's arm, Lenda could almost feel her coming apart at the seams—all she could do was pray. Lenda felt the instant peace of Holy Spirit come over her. Annie looked and, miraculously, was able to turn and leave the casket without breaking down. "Thank You, Jesus," Lenda heard herself whisper as they walked to their seats on the front row. Before sitting, it was as if a traffic light stopped them. Both looked up to the balcony to see their brother standing, looking back at them. Matthew was so close to Ernest; they looked like they were conjoined twins. Lenda was trying so hard not to be judgmental anymore. She wasn't quite there yet. Lord knows she was trying, thanks to Annie. She couldn't quite wave, but she did give a nod. Annie on the other hand blew him a kiss with her lips as they turned to be seated.

The next thirty minutes, the family hour, flew by. Both of them shaking hands and greeting friends. Some asking, "Where's your brother?" And the sisters would say, "He's here somewhere."

Finally, the casket was closed and the service was about to begin. Lenda was so thankful for her church. She wondered how people made it during times like these without a church. But if they didn't know the difference in churches, they couldn't know what they were missing. The ministers assigned to the family were there to support them from day one. She was thankful that one of them sat with Ernest. He promised to talk with Matthew before and after the services. At one point, when they were closing the casket, Ernest yelled out, "I'm sorry, Mom! I'm sorry, Mom!" Lenda sat paralyzed in her seat; she couldn't even look up in the balcony. She was afraid she'd fall apart.

Annie turned and looked toward the balcony and cried more. Lenda felt comforted knowing Matthew was sitting with his uncle; she could just see him putting his arms around him, comforting him. When Matthew asked if he could sit with Ernest, she didn't hesitate to tell him it was OK. Especially when he said, "You'll have Auntie Annie, your friends, and other relatives. Nobody will be up there with Uncle. Can I? Please, please!" How could she say no?

Members from the Comforter Ministry lined the church with tissue boxes in hand. The choice of music brought consolation. But as nice as everything was, Lenda was physically and emotionally drained and would be extremely thankful when it was all over.

Chapter Thirty-Five

What Aunt Thelma said when she and Aunt Chunk came up for Karen's homegoing service was now starting to get to Claudette. She had been thinking about the notion that friends who couldn't be honest with each other really weren't friends.

Claudette and the girls shared so much, and she felt like a hypocrite every time she was around Quintella. God only knew how tired she was of hiding the truth. Quintella even said it herself: "We should love each other enough that we can talk about uncomfortable things." Did she really mean it? Claudette felt like a felon who was hiding from the police. Whenever she and the girls were together, she thought she would be arrested verbally at any given moment.

When Lenda confessed about her brother, they all took it well. No one judged her because her brother was in jail. Everyone was sympathetic and couldn't believe that she had hid it for all those years.

Claudette made her decision: it was time to confess and pray that the judge—in this case, Quintella—would grant amnesty, and the friendship would remain intact. She felt better already. The load she had carried all this time was just too heavy, and she was tired of carrying it.

Claudette quickly picked up the phone before she could talk herself out of it. As she dialed Quintella's number, her hands began to shake. But she ignored her feelings.

"Hello," came the relaxed voice on the other end.

"Hey girl, whatcha doin'?"

"Claudette, is this you?"

Claudette could feel the smile through the phone; her prayer was that she would still be smiling when the dust settled.

"It's me."

"Girl, it's so good to hear your voice. What's going on?"

"Well, I wanted to know if you and I could meet for lunch."

"Lunch with you would be wonderful. When and where?"

"You're the one with the husband; what's his schedule like?"

"See, that's why my husband loves you. He said you always protect our time together; that's what he loves about you. Let's see, he has a trip next week, and he'll be gone for a week. Can it wait, or do you need to see me now?"

"No, next week is good. Say, Friday? There's this new little place downtown called The Woodward. It's so cute, girl. You'll love it."

"Next Friday it is. What time?

"Six o'clock."

"Six o'clock it is. Girl, this is a treat to dine out with you! I'll look forward to our time together."

As Quintella put the phone back in the cradle, she was pleasantly surprised by this spontaneous invitation. But she was a little curious. She hadn't had dinner alone with Claudette in over a year. While she was happy Claudette had called, she couldn't help but think something was up. *Maybe she and Christopher have set the date. Naw, that would be much too early. They haven't dated a year,* she thought. But that would be one wedding she couldn't wait to attend!

Quintella and Ken had prayed that God would send Claudette a husband who would love and care for her, and Quintella truly felt like Christopher was the one. Before she could think about it, her hands were raised in the air and shouts of hallelujah poured from her lips. It overwhelmed her when God answered prayer, and no one but Quintella and Ken knew that this was one more thing she could check off their list.

*   *   *   *

Claudette felt better, but the weight of the burden resting on her shoulders was still there. It felt good knowing that it would soon be lifted. But it crossed her mind that she called Quintella without asking Holy Spirit His thoughts on her pending confession. Claudette looked up as if someone was standing with her and said, "Holy Spirit, why do we move forward with our plans and never ask Your opinion? We just move ahead and ask that You bless our plans. Why do we do that? It's no wonder stuff gets messed up." No answer came; Holy Spirit was quiet on this one.

Claudette hoped she was doing the right thing by moving forward. But she abruptly decided to table her thoughts about seeing Quintella; she was about to spend time with Christopher. That was all she wanted to focus on.

Claudette began to polish her nails to ready herself for her date; she questioned whether her urge to tell the truth had anything to do with the success of her relationship with

Christopher. Why now? What truth serum had she swallowed? Whatever it was, she must have overdosed. This stuff was powerful.

* * * *

As usual, Christopher was on time, and she was ready. She learned fast that nothing could dampen their plans as much as her running late. Christopher had strong feelings about making other people wait. That was one argument, she decided, that just wasn't worth spoiling a nice evening.

Driving to the restaurant, she couldn't help but think about how God had blessed her. The longer she was with Christopher, the more handsome he became. He was still a gentleman after all their months of dating. She kept waiting for the *real* Christopher to show up. And each time they were together, his actions only confirmed that the real Christopher was always there and had nothing to hide.

Dinner was good. They talked for hours; this conversation was deeper than their last. Then it seemed as though they sat silent for days. Finally, Christopher broke that silence.

"So, it's been about six months—and there's something I want to tell you."

Claudette laughed.

"What's so funny?"

"Haven't you figured out by now that I laugh when I'm nervous?"

"What's to be nervous about?"

"Well, you want to tell me something. You're getting nervous, and so am I."

"Claudette, I know church says to wait a year before you get really serious. I'll wait that year, but I want you to know that I want to spend the rest of my life with you—not as your friend, but as your husband."

More silence.

"Did you hear what I just said?"

She laughed again.

"Still nervous? If anyone should be nervous, it should be me. I'm about to give a woman I've only known for six months access to all of my money! I'm the one who should be nervous!"

"I would love to spend the rest of my life with you."

They both sat, looking into each other's eyes. It was clear they didn't know what to do. It wasn't the most romantic script, but they didn't care. They both had just acknowledged that the two of them would do life together—and treasure every moment forever.

Claudette lightened the mood by playfully hitting Christopher on the arm with her fist. She couldn't help but feel hard muscle through his shirt, and she had to cast aside thoughts of having those muscles wrapped around her.

As they continued back and forth with idle chitchat, the waiter came by to announce that the restaurant would close in less than half an hour; he wanted to know if he could bring them anything else. When he left, they laughed and agreed that it was just a nice way of telling them to continue their conversation at Starbucks. Continuing their conversation sounded good, but they both knew it was time to call it an evening.

* * * *

On the way home, Christopher planned to walk Claudette to her front door. He also decided to kiss her.

346 | YOU'VE GOT A MAN

Inside, Claudette could feel that this night was going to be a challenge. Too many things had happened. They had prayed, so she was ready—or so she thought.

When they reached her house, he got out—as planned—and walked her to the door. Standing there, with just the right light shining on Christopher's face, she saw the affection he felt for her. They were holding hands, and it seemed like little bolts of electricity were moving through her body. She wasn't naive. If she was feeling like this, she knew he was feeling the same—and more. As they dropped hands, Christopher looked at her, and she looked at him; it was apparent what they were thinking. The prospect of him leaning in for a kiss was more than Claudette could stand. How long had it been since she had a real one? It had been years. Her lips began to water. Sensations of euphoria left her feeling out of control. *See, this is why God says this kind of stuff should be between a man and his wife,* she thought. To add insult to injury, Claudette had to pass gas. What timing! As she tightened her buttocks to silence the sound, she remembered that it wouldn't block the smell. To avoid embarrassment, she laughed and pushed Christopher away from the front door. She managed a sorry, "I enjoyed the evening. You better go now, or it's going to be difficult to keep our promise to each other!"

Being the gentleman that he was, Christopher smiled, oblivious to what she was really feeling and proceeded to walk down the sidewalk, turning to give her a sheepish grin. Christopher hadn't walked five steps before Claudette let one loose that smelled like a rotten boiled egg, and that's putting it mildly. She continued to wave, with a fake smile on her face. She relaxed only after her door was closed. Leaning against it, she raised her hands to praise God for two reasons. One, they escaped the passion trap again and two, Christopher wasn't there to inhale the smell. She didn't know which one she was more grateful for. Then she thought about it: *God, did you send the gas so we wouldn't get in a situation we weren't ready for?*

No answer.

It was funny that someone her age was so concerned about Christopher smelling her gas. Although it's a natural thing to expel intestinal gas, Claudette was absolutely terrified. Only time would tell when she'd feel comfortable letting one go in his presence.

After kicking her shoes off inside, Claudette thought for a moment and couldn't remember when she had felt so good. Everything was going right. Even though she had recently buried her best friend, the man of her dreams said he wanted to spend the rest of his life with her. It was a complete reversal of emotions, and she felt life couldn't get any better.

Looking at the phone, Claudette noticed the flashing light, signaling some voice messages. She hesitated, not wanting anything to spoil the moment. As she checked her voice mail, a cheerful voice in the first message began to speak. The mere sound of that cheerful voice caused an influx of anxiety. It was Quintella; she called to remind her of their pending lunch. Claudette quickly deleted it; she regretted hearing the message. It was as if someone had poured a bucket of ice on the beautiful warm evening she had just experienced.

The more she thought about the phone call, the more convinced she was that she was doing the right thing. Quintella was excited about seeing Claudette and was only calling to confirm lunch. Claudette was feeling a lot of things—and excitement wasn't one of them. Holy Spirit still had not answered her about whether she should be doing this. Perhaps His thoughts were, "You didn't ask Me; you've made up your mind, so I'm staying out of it." Claudette silently prayed that this wasn't the case.

*　*　*　*

Lunch was turning out great. Quintella was happy to hear about the proposal, even if it wasn't the typical "on bended knee" version. She made Claudette laugh when she said, "I know who the matron of honor will be—that's not even up for discussion."

Confirming, Claudette told her the choice for a matron of honor was a no-brainer. She was looking right at Quintella.

"That's what I'm talking about, and I'm honored to stand with you, 'cause God knows how Ken and I have prayed for you," Quintella said.

More small talk and laughter ensued. While Quintella enjoyed her brownie topped with ice cream, Claudette felt like she was about to lose the dinner she had just eaten. Was it the impending wedding? Is this why she felt she had to have a clean slate?

"Girl, this has been wonderful, but I'm curious. Was there something you wanted to tell me?" Quintella inquired.

"Well, now that you've asked…there is something I want to talk to you about." She thought: *Just say it!*

"Remember our last dinner, when we began to reflect on secrets we had kept from one another because we felt like our relationship would be ruined?" Claudette began.

"Yeah, like when Lenda told us about her brother and we all loved on her."

"Yeah," Claudette said warily.

"Girl, is there something on your heart? It can't be that bad, and you know there's nothing you can say that'll make me love you less."

Claudette was having second thoughts; perhaps this wasn't such a good idea after all. She proceeded with caution.

"Remember the affair your brother-in-law had, and you thought I knew more than I was telling you?"

Quintella not only sat up, she edged closer to the chair.

"Yes."

"The girl...was me," Claudette hesitated. "I'm going to give you the short version of the story."

Claudette quickly began to rattle, "It started with lunch. Your brother-in-law and I had to come up with money-saving ideas for the company. We didn't finish our proposal, so we scheduled another lunch. At some point, we stopped talking about work and began to talk about personal things. I'm not going to tell you what we talked about because it involves your sister, and I'm already embarrassed by telling you *this*. The only thing I can tell you, Queen, is that it wasn't planned. It just happened, and I have lived with and suffered for this mistake for far too long. I felt compelled to come clean, but this was something I wanted to keep between us."

When Claudette stopped talking, she hadn't noticed that her head was down during the whole confession. But when she lifted her head with tears in her eyes, she wasn't prepared for the look she saw in the eyes of her friend. As she waited for Quintella to speak, she prayed that what she saw was a misread. Minutes went by and no words came. Finally, Claudette spoke.

"Aren't you going to say something?"

"For once, I'm speechless. I really think it best I remain that way," Quintella said as she raised her hand to motion for the waiter.

"Are you ordering something else?" Claudette asked.

"No, I want the bill because I've got to get out of here!"

Claudette put her hand on Quintella's hand but as soon as she did, Quintella pulled away.

"Queen, please say something," Claudette pleaded. "Do you know how hard it was for me to open up and tell you this?"

Quintella became much more animated in the way she waved her hand.

Claudette tried again to touch her friend; this time the deadly stare told her not to repeat her actions.

"Oh, you want me to say something? OK, I'll say something. I knew that you knew something. But never in my wildest dreams did I think that what you knew would be anything like this. This is one secret I wish you had kept to yourself! What, you think because you spilled your guts that I will just forgive and forget? You went to bed with my sister's husband! You knew he was married, and you knew it was my brother-in-law. Did you care? Nah! You wanted a man so bad that you almost ruined a marriage. You slut; get out of my face!"

With that, Quintella got up from the table and hurried out of the restaurant. Claudette wanted to run after her, but the waiter came with the bill. Claudette gave him a fifty-dollar bill—more than enough to cover their meals—so she could run out to try to catch Quintella.

When she got outside, Quintella was waiting for the valet to get her car. Claudette ran up to her and ignored the crowd behind her.

"Queen, you called me a slut! What's the matter with you?"

The valet was holding Quintella's door open. As she

hurried to get in her car, she briefly stopped and turned to Claudette, who was quickly shadowing her.

"Quit while you're ahead. I was nice when I said slut!"

"Did you hear anything I said?"

"Yeah, I heard everything you said." Then she looked at the crowd of people who were waiting to get their cars: "Y'all better hold on to your man, 'cause married or not, here *she* comes."

With her last outburst, Quintella slammed the car door and pulled off, almost hitting the attendant, even though her target was Claudette. Horrified, Claudette looked at the crowd with her mouth open. As one could expect, the ladies had a look that said, "Don't even think about looking at my man."

Bypassing protocol, Claudette gave the attendant her ticket and asked how quickly he could get her car. She didn't care that she had just stepped in front of all those waiting.

* * * *

Quintella was driving so fast that she almost hit another car as she pulled out in traffic. The woman driving laid on her horn longer than normal. Quintella looked in the rearview mirror and saw that the car was inches from hitting her on purpose. *Sorry…forgive me…I didn't mean it! You don't know what just happened to me,* Quintella thought. The driver behind her was relentless—pulling beside her, giving her the finger, and continuing to lay on her horn. Quintella ignored her. She was the one acting like a maniac, and she had kids in the car! Ken told her stories about what could happen when road rage occurs.

Finally, both cars had to stop at the light. Quintella noticed out of her peripheral vision that the woman seemed as though she was going to sideswipe her car. Enough! Queen rolled down her window to give her an earful, but she wasn't prepared for what happened next.

* * * *

Claudette didn't remember getting on the freeway; she didn't even remember walking in her front door. All she remembered was falling on her bed and crying herself to sleep.

Chapter Thirty-Six

Ken couldn't wait to get home.

The attendant's voice came over the microphone loud and clear: "Attention please, we will begin boarding Flight No. 727 for Detroit. We are now boarding first class and elite."

Ken got up, folded his paper, and proceeded to board the plane. When he got to the cabin door of the plane after walking down the Jetway, Ken did what he always does every time he gets on a plane. He paused briefly, put his hand on the plane, and prayed: "Heavenly Father, from nose to tail and wing to wing, the Blood of Jesus covers this plane. Thank You, in Jesus' Name. Amen."

The prayer only took seconds. Then Ken put his carry-on up top and exchanged pleasantries with the folks on either side. Quintella always marveled at the way he felt comfortable talking to anyone. He really liked people. Perhaps his profession had something to do with it.

Ken finally took his seat in first class and pulled the paper out again when the man next to him said, "Excuse me young fellow, can I ask you something?"

"Sure," Ken replied.

"What was that you were saying to yourself when you got on the plane?"

"Oh, that's the prayer I say whenever I fly."

"Really?" responded the gentleman.

Ken could tell this was going to be a soul-winning flight. During the next three hours, Ken and David, as he soon learned this gentleman's name to be, became good buddies.

They ate. Ken had bottled water, and David had a drink of another kind. Then, when Ken sensed that it was the right time, he popped the question.

"David," he whispered in a soft voice so no one in first class could hear. "If this plane were to go down right now and none of us made it," Ken paused because he saw the fear in David's eyes. "Don't worry, man. That's not going to happen. But if something like that happened, where would you spend eternity?"

"Wow! I never thought about it!"

"There are only two choices, heaven or hell. Where would you want to go?"

"I'd want to go to heaven," David responded.

"Well, would you like to be sure right here and right now that if anything ever happened you'd be heaven bound?"

"Well…yes, I would, Ken."

"Let me show you something." Ken could feel the adrenaline flowing. It always happened like that when he knew he was about to get someone saved. Ken pulled out his iPhone, opened his Bible app, and showed David Romans 10:9–10. "This Scripture says that if you confess with your mouth, the Lord Jesus, and believe in your heart that God raised Him from the dead, then you'll be saved. Do you believe, David?"

"I believe," David replied.

"Then make this confession of faith—say it with your

mouth and believe it in your heart, and you'll be saved—
assuring you of your seat in heaven. So repeat after me…say, I
believe…." Ken began.

"I believe," repeated David.

"That Jesus is the Son of God."

"That Jesus is the Son of God."

"I believe He died for me, but that He is no longer dead."

"I believe He died for me, but that He is no longer dead."

"I believe He has risen as He said."

"I believe He has risen as He said."

"Dear Lord Jesus, come into my heart and save me now."

"Dear Lord Jesus, come into my heart and save me now."

"I confess with my mouth…"

"I confess with my mouth…"

"And believe with my heart…"

"And believe with my heart…"

"And according to Your Word…"

"And according to Your Word…"

"I am born again!"

"I am born again!"

"Woo-hoo!" shouted Ken as he began to high five David.

"It's that easy, man?" David asked.

"It's that easy. Man tries to make things hard. Jesus loves
us so much that He made this real simple. Look, God knows
your heart and if you truly believed and were sincere, then it's
that easy," Ken said.

"With all my heart, I believed," David replied.

"Man listen, if you were home alone reading your Bible and read these verses and said that confession with no one in the room but you, you would get the same results. You'd be saved, sitting in a room by yourself. God is just that faithful. If you find it in the Word, you can count on it!"

"I want you to do something, though. You got a smart-phone?" Ken asked.

"Yeah," David replied.

"Go to today's date and type, 'Today is my spiritual birthday. According to Romans 10, verses nine and ten, I was born again.'"

Small talk ensued, and Ken encouraged him to get into a good Bible-based church. He gave David his card. Both men promised to keep in touch.

Once they exited the plane, they talked a little more, and then they made their way over to wait to get their luggage from the turnstile.

David got his and left.

Ken was so happy that he wanted to run through the airport but in his best interest, he decided not to. He thought about the Scripture in the Bible that says the heavens rejoice over one soul. He thought: Is it *John 15:10?* He couldn't remember but he knew one thing, there was a party going on in heaven at that moment. Ken was ecstatic!

He now began to think about his wife. Ken didn't know what it was, but he missed her more this trip than he usually did. He couldn't wait to see her. He wondered what would be waiting for him when he got home. Whenever he was away for more than five days, Quintella always greeted him with a nice surprise that included dinner—and it ended with passionate lovemaking. Ken was ready for it all.

With his luggage in the car, Ken realized that when he looked up the Scripture for David, he turned his phone off but never turned it back on. Once on again, he saw that he had three missed calls and a couple of text messages…all from Quintella. *That's not like her to try to reach me like that when I'm flying. The text messages don't say it's an emergency, but I better call her,* he thought. Ken dialed the home and cell numbers, but no one answered. *Hmmm, interesting.*

* * * *

When Ken put the key in the door, he could smell dinner. Was it spaghetti? Where was Quintella? Ken was used to her meeting him at the door. But he found her in the family room, reading.

Quintella got up from the sofa and went to meet Ken when he entered the family room. She wanted to pounce on him, telling him everything that happened both with Claudette and that crazy woman in the car, but it wouldn't be fair to him. So Quintella put her arms around Ken and gave him a kiss.

"Hi honey, welcome home."

"On a scale of one to ten, that kiss was a five; don't a brother deserve at least a seven? After all, I've been gone more than five days."

"The seven-scale kiss will come later."

"Think you'll warm up to a ten by the time we hit the bedroom?"

"Maybe," Quintella laughed, wishing the events the day before weren't still dragging her down.

Ken could tell she was rattled about something before he even asked, but he had learned something: he needed to be ready to hear her story when he asked, and he really wasn't ready to hear it. After giving it a second thought, he felt it would be better to get it out right then.

"OK, what's wrong?" he asked.

"Nothing."

"Come on, babe. It's been a long trip, and I want all of you—not seventy-five percent, which is what I have now. Spill it!"

"I had a really bad falling out with Claudette. The friend-ship is over."

Ken looked at Quintella to see if she was telling the truth, and he could tell she was. "How can that be? What, a fifteen-, sixteen-year friendship is over? Nobody got murdered, did they?"

"Ken, that's not nice."

"I wasn't looking for nice; you love that girl like a sister, and to tell me it's over just doesn't compute."

"How about you sit down and let me explain?" Quintella asked.

"Can I make a request?" Ken said.

"What's the request?" asked Quintella.

"I've been gone a week. All I've been thinking about for the last twenty-four hours is you. All I could think about was holding you and having you rub my hair, among other things. I didn't anticipate this drama between you and Claudette. So please, baby, can you give me the 'Reader's Digest' version?"

As soon as he said that, Ken wished the words had never come out of his mouth. Quintella's face reinforced the fact that it wasn't good.

Getting up to storm out of the room, she turned and asked, "When we go to bed tonight, do you want the 'Reader's

Digest' version then?!"

Standing alone in the family room, Ken couldn't help but wonder what he did. Asking for a short version of a drama-filled story seemed like a good idea to him. It was clear that she was really wound up about something. *What could be that bad?* Wisdom told Ken to go after Quintella and apologize.

He followed her into the kitchen. As she heard his footsteps, she began to walk faster so he couldn't catch her. The game was on. With Quintella on one side of the kitchen island and Ken on the other, the game of chase began; he would go one way and she the other.

"Queen, I'm sorry. Please, let's start over. Give me the long version, will you? However long it takes, I'll listen. I promise. Really, baby. I didn't know it meant so much to you."

By then, Ken had caught Quintella and pulled her close to him. He locked her in his arms and kissed her forehead. "I'm so sorry. Please tell me the story and don't leave out one iota."

Quintella looked at Ken and could tell he meant every word he said. She took him by the hand and led him back into the family room, where she sat on one end of the sofa and motioned for Ken to lie down and put his head in her lap. She began to recount the painful details of the story. Every now and then Ken would interrupt with a, "No stuff—not Claudette?" But by the end of the story, it was evident that Ken was disappointed with her response. His whole body language changed. He held her hands, stopped her from rubbing his hair, sat up straight on the sofa, and looked at her with disbelief.

Quintella could feel an intense fellowship coming on, and she was ready. If this man thought that he was going to side with Claudette, against his wife, he wasn't even prepared for what was about to happen. When Quintella finished speaking, she waited for Ken's response, hoping that he wouldn't go where she thought he might be headed.

"Queen, I'm surprised at you," Ken said as he now stood, looking down at Quintella. Seeing her defensive attack coming, he raised his hands and pleaded with her to let him finish.

"You have been friends with Claudette for too long to react like that."

Quintella stood to face Ken: "I've been friends with my sister more than forty years!"

"That's not the point. I can imagine how you feel, but don't you think it was difficult for her to come clean? Why did you have to call her a slut? And why did you announce to the world, 'Hold on to your man, 'cause she'll take him'?" Ken mimicked as he walked and talked.

"That's not what I said. I said, 'Y'all better hold on to your man, 'cause married or not, here *she* comes.' I said it then, and I'll say it again!" Now Quintella was prancing around the room.

"Listen to you—you don't even sound like my baby."

"Excuse me for reminding you, but that man she had an affair with *was* and *still is* my sister's husband!"

"Your sister is no saint! She's had your brother-in-law on a reward/punishment system for years. She's even bragged about it to you. Don't think I don't hear her when she comes over here and teases you, saying, 'He want some again—don't you ever get tired?' I hear your response when you say, 'He's my husband. I love him, and I enjoy loving him and making him happy.' You think she gets the hint? Naw, she comes back with: 'Who you fooling? Y'all been married too long to be carrying on like that. Listen, if he was my husband, he'd be lucky to get it twice a week, and that's only during the holidays.'

"That, my love, is why we are having this discussion now! Your sister better get a clue before she wakes up one day and his clothes are missing from the closet.

"No man wants to feel like a cash cow. That's why you hear about men that seemingly—out of the blue—leave their wives. It's not something that happens overnight! It's not even about another woman all the time. One day he'll wake up and decide he'll no longer live with a woman who's not interested in him, or one who disrespects him.

"The man realizes that for years she's only been concerned with where they live, what schools the kids go to, paying the bills, keeping up with the Joneses. Some men have never had their wives sit down with them after five years of marriage and say, 'Honey, how can I be a better wife to you?' Or 'Honey, is there anything I can do to help you achieve your goals?'"

Quintella interrupted by yelling, "Maybe he should ask her how he can be a better husband!"

"As I was saying…the man looks at the years of disrespect. The constant headaches, or the outright 'don't even think about it' attitude when he tries to approach his wife after an argument. And then one day he says, 'I don't have to take this.'

"So when he makes the decision to leave, he then decides, since I'm going to leave, let me get a young woman while I'm at it."

"You act like all women do that!" Quintella yelled louder.

Exasperated, Ken put both hands on his head and crossed them. With his elbows close to his temples, he tried to calm down. This time when he spoke, his voice was elevated even higher than before. "Did I say all women? No! You aren't like that! I'm just giving you an example of what goes on in some homes! My prayer is that it's not many, but even if it's one— and we know it's ONE!"

Quintella was screaming, "YOU'RE TALKING ABOUT MY SISTER!!!"

Ken decided to yell even louder, "WHY ARE YOU BLASTING ME WITH YOUR CANNONS!!!" Then he decided to lower his voice, "If it's one family, it's one too many! I say praise the Lord it was Claudette he had his little fling with because if it were anyone else, she would've stolen him away from your sister. And she wouldn't have gotten a second chance. I'm sure Claudette didn't plan on having an affair; you and I both know she's not like that. Her conscience probably kicked in…"

"Conscience!" Quintella yelled.

"What would you prefer, Queen? The Holy Ghost kicked in?"

"Oh no! I wouldn't insult Holy Ghost, 'cause if she had listened to Him this never would've happened!"

"Queen, why you acting so holy, like we ain't never done nothing wrong? Let me say this again: under *no* circumstances, at *any* time, is it *ever* right to sleep with someone who's married. Am I clear?" Ken continued without getting an answer. "Wait a minute. Let me rephrase what I just said. Under *no* circumstances, at *any* time, is it *ever* right to sleep with someone you're not married to. That goes for single or married people. But you need to practice what you preach. We all need to practice more forgiveness. And back to your sister, you need to wake up and stop looking at her through rose-colored glasses! Your sister is a nut! She don't even deserve her husband—he's a nice guy stuck with a nut!"

"I didn't know you hated my sister!"

"I don't hate your sister!"

"You called her a nut!"

"And she is, but I like nuts! I like pistachio nuts. I like almonds and cashews, and I like your sister. But trust me on this one—she's a nut. Think she's learned her lesson? Just the other day when they were over here, your brother-in-law joked about going to bed with an aspirin in his hand and a glass of water. He said he told his wife, 'Baby, this is for your headache.' And she told him 'Headache! I don't have a headache.' And then he said I smiled and told her 'Good, then it's going to be a great night!' And she still pushed him away!

"We all laughed, Queen, but I asked him later when we were alone in the kitchen clearing the table if he was really joking. He said he wasn't.

"That's messed up, Queen! She didn't learn anything—still up to her old tricks. I'm just glad I got the right sister!

"But I tell you what—the next time your sister comes over here, really listen to her and notice the pounds of disrespect she dumps on her husband. Don't take my word, just listen to her.

"I'm not trying to minimize what Claudette did. It was wrong, really, really wrong, but don't you think it was difficult for her to fess up to you?"

Quintella had tuned Ken out.

"You're not answering me," Ken said.

"What do *you* think? I tried sharing something with you that hurt me to the core, and all you can do is take sides with the other woman! It's like my husband left a week ago, and another man came home in his place."

Ken walked over to Quintella with his arms open to embrace her; she moved away.

"Oh, it's like that?" Ken asked as he stepped back.

"Ken, how can you be so insensitive? I hope you *really* like spaghetti because that's all you'll get tonight!"

"Well, since it's like that, I don't even have a taste for spaghetti; I'm going to find me some real food! Later!"

Ken grabbed his keys and slammed the door leading to the garage; Quintella was in a state of shock. She couldn't remember when she and Ken had ever argued like this—it was a first!

* * * *

Ken didn't back out of the garage; he flew out of the garage. He was so mad he didn't know what to do. Then Holy Spirit said something to him.

"It's not about you and Quintella, Ken; it's about the man that was saved on the plane. The enemy still doesn't like people getting saved. Calm down and go back home."

* * * *

Quintella was fuming. *Claudette slept with my sister's husband, and now it's her fault that I'm arguing with Ken,* she thought. The more Quintella thought about Ken's response to the issue, the hotter she got. "Well, since he doesn't have a taste for spaghetti, maybe the garbage disposal will have a taste for spaghetti," she murmured.

On her way to the kitchen, Quintella spotted Ken's house shoes, which she happily kicked like a soccer ball. It felt so good that she went back to the other one and kicked it, too. One went one way, and the other one went in another direction. *I hope he can't find them when he comes home.* In the midst of her grumbling, Holy Spirit was talking to her and trying to calm her down but sadly, she ignored Him continuously.

By the time she reached the kitchen, she heard Holy Spirit's voice again, "Queen, you need to cool down and stop the tantrum." But she was on a roll and wasn't about to stop. She grabbed the pot of spaghetti and looked for a big spoon.

"He don't have no taste for spaghetti," Quintella mocked as she flipped on the garbage disposal. She turned on the water, grabbed the big spoon and as she heaped spoons of spaghetti down the garbage disposal, she began to sing to the tune of "Jingle Bells":

> *Spaghetti gone, spaghetti gone*
>
> *Spaghetti down the drain*
>
> *Oh, what fun it is to see*
>
> *Spaghetti gone away, hey*

As she reached for another spoonful, she heard Holy Spirit remind her of the Scripture in Proverbs 12:15. His voice was so gentle when He said, *"The way of a fool is right in his own eyes: but he that hearkeneth unto counsel is wise."*

Feeling like someone else was holding the spoon, Quintella put it down and looked up to say, "Why? Why?" Then she began to cry. The next twenty minutes were extremely revealing. During that time, Holy Spirit really ministered to her. He helped her to see why she was in the wrong.

Holy Spirit was able to get Quintella to completely snap out of her rage. She looked in the pot—it was still half full. She was directed by Holy Spirit to look at the mess in the sink. She started to clean it up *and* be a big girl and finish dinner. She made a tossed salad and garlic bread. She decided to make a fresh pitcher of lemonade. Ken loved her lemonade. People teased him when he told them that Quintella didn't use a powdered mix; she used real lemons.

Once Quintella finished, she headed upstairs when she heard Holy Spirit say, "Why don't you go find the house shoes and put them back in the family room?" Quintella had to laugh; she had been looking forward to Ken running around the house trying to find the slippers, especially the one she kicked so hard it landed behind the TV—he would have never found it. She chuckled and pulled the big screen from the wall and thanked Holy Spirit that the TV stand was on rollers.

She finally made her way upstairs to take a bath. As she prepared to get in the tub, Quintella noticed that Ken had been gone for two hours. She wondered what could be keeping him out so long. While she didn't want to go to bed mad, she didn't want to be the first to apologize this time. Despite Holy Spirit telling her she was wrong, she still believed he should have taken her side. And she couldn't shake that "nut" thing. Besides, they had already been separated for all those days he was on his trip. This definitely wasn't how she had envisioned their night turning out.

Quintella began to run her bath water. She pondered which fragrance she would use. Would it be one of Ken's favorites?

Why couldn't she stay mad at him? The answer came immediately; it was because from the time they married, they made a decision never to go to bed angry, under any circumstance. But this time was different; she couldn't remember when it was this bad. She decided on one of Ken's favorite fragrances, Amber Romance. While she didn't agree with their advertisements of half-naked women in provocative positions, she did enjoy Victoria's Secret's bath products as well as their lingerie.

Quintella looked at her watch again; no sign of Ken. *Wonder where he is? Oh well, I'll enjoy the bath and go to bed.*

If he doesn't get home, I won't have to apologize, she thought. Quintella felt the tug of Holy Spirit; He was grieved at that thought. "Sorry, Holy Spirit; I'm still in the flesh," Quintella confessed.

While the water ran, Quintella sprayed the sheets with Ken's favorite perfume and pulled out one of her nice gowns. Walking back in the bathroom, she stopped to peek through the blinds.

"Still no sign of my man…oh well," she said. She puttered around some more and decided to go ahead and enjoy her bath. Before stepping in, she got her tea lights and placed them around the cabinet—far from the bathtub. Because they were battery operated, she made sure they were not near the water. She decided to listen to Tim Bowman on her in-wall CD player; this was not a night for CeCe. She added some milk flakes to the water and then slid down into the wonderful mix. Her skin was hollering, "Thank you, Queen!" Yes, it did feel good. Her favorite track came on, and she couldn't help but reflect on how good God had been. She was so grateful for her beautiful home and all the conveniences one could only dream of. Other than a baby, there was nothing she wanted but Ken.

In spite of this spat, Quintella knew she had a wonderful husband who she wouldn't trade for anything. She loved him more now than she did when they got married. She was overcome with thanksgiving and began to verbalize her gratitude to the Lord. She told Him how good He had been to her. She was so involved with what she was doing that she didn't see Ken standing in the door, sheepishly looking at her. Startled, she gasped softly.

"Sorry, baby. I didn't mean to frighten you. It seems you're enjoying yourself. Want me to leave?"

"No, I just didn't hear you come in."

"Baby, I'm so sorry that I allowed someone else's problems to become ours. Forgive me for being insensitive. I can't take back some of the things I said. Some I feel strongly about, and I don't want to take them back. But I could've handled the whole situation differently."

"Yeah, 'cause you didn't let me finish telling you what else happened to me," Quintella said.

"What happened, baby?" Ken asked with exuberance.

"After I got my car from the valet and pulled out, I was so mad that I cut this car off. The woman driving went berserk! She was blowing her horn, speeding up next to the car like she was going to sideswipe me or something. Ken, she was acting a fool! At first I was mad; then I got scared, but then I got mad again. So, the light caught us. She pulls next to me so close that I thought she was going to take the side of the car off. I rolled down the window, and guess what she did?"

"What, baby?"

"She had her kids throw a whole bucket of greasy, slimy, spit-covered chicken bones in my face. I mean bones they had been sucking on. They threw them in my face and sped off!"

"You lying, baby?"

"Ken, are you making fun of me?"

"No, I'm sincere. Then what happened?"

"I started crying."

Ken knew there was something he needed to say, but he didn't want to interrupt the moment. Still, he had to. What he had to say might sound like a reprimand, and she didn't need that right now. After all, he felt a makeup coming on. With caution, he proceeded, "Baby, when you saw the car speeding up alongside of you in your rearview mirror, did you not think to call on your angels?"

"Ken, honestly, it happened so fast that I didn't," Quintella responded. Ken was thankful that she heard his heart and took it like he meant it. "Baby, I'm so sorry I wasn't there to protect you," Ken said.

Quintella didn't know what to say. She knew he was concerned and remorseful. She actually wanted to bring up her sister again, but anything she said could fan the flames. Besides, she really didn't want to argue, so she just played with the bubbles. By now Ken was sitting on the ledge of the tub. This was one time she wished he wasn't so fine. He looked like a little boy seeing a naked woman for the first time.

"That's a lot of water for one person. We really need to conserve our water bill as much as possible."

Quintella laughed out loud and kept playing with the bubbles. On purpose, she lifted her leg in the air and pretended to write on her leg with bubbles.

"What are you writing?"

She decided to tease him some more; she looked at Ken, arched her eyebrow and in a low sultry voice, she answered, "It says, 'Come on in, the water's fine.'" Ken jumped up like a jack-in-the-box and in record time, he had removed his clothes and positioned himself behind her in the tub. Quintella was laughing so hard she couldn't control herself. No one could have guessed that they'd nearly come to blows only two hours earlier!

* * * *

Ken was hungry. An hour had gone by, and he didn't want to wake Quintella. He was a big boy and could fix his own food. He'd thought about Quintella's spaghetti the entire time he was gone. Ken knew he wasn't up to going out for food. He'd been really mad, so he was just saying stuff. He'd just needed to get away. Actually, Ken had always wanted to poll married couples to see how many of their arguments were about relatives. If he were a betting man, he would say a good half.

"Where are my house shoes?" he whispered to himself.

Growing up, Ken developed a habit of needing to wear house shoes. He didn't like walking around barefoot. He remembered they were in the family room. Quintella teased him all the time that she was going to hide them one day and not tell him where they were. It almost happened this night. He made a mental note to buy another pair.

Ken made it back to the kitchen. The fridge was packed. "Thank You, Lord. My baby made me some lemonade." He found the spaghetti. Now all he needed was a small pot to heat it up in. Some people called him old-fashioned, but he didn't play the microwave thing. He didn't like how it could make the food *seem* like it was hot and by the time he sat down to take a bite or two, it was cold. Not Ken—he wasn't the one. By heating it up in a pot on top of the stove, he didn't have to worry about cold spots.

When Ken took the top off the spaghetti, he couldn't help but question why Quintella had made such a small amount. She knew it was his favorite, and he could eat it for days without get tired. *Why did she use such a large container for such a little bit of spaghetti? Women, I can't figure them out,* he thought. But he was thankful. Some men he knew got canned spaghetti. This woman knew better: no canned spaghetti for him. Quintella knew how to set it out for her man; that's why he took such good care of her. There was nothing he wouldn't do for his wife. Nothing.

While the spaghetti was heating, Ken got a bowl for his salad. *Instead of poking fun at us, her nutty sister should take some lessons. Lord, You and I both know she is a nut; I won't take that back,* Ken thought.

As Ken sat and ate, he was thankful that he'd left when he did. Driving always calmed him. It gave him an opportunity to talk to his Buddy, Holy Spirit, and talk to Him he did.

Queen always says, "I got a Man." Well, I've got a Friend who understands my woman, Ken thoughts continued. Ken was grateful for the counsel he received while he was in the car from Holy Spirit about their disagreement. And his promise to the Lord wasn't just lip service. He would never allow things to get out of control like that again.

As Ken looked at his plate, he wished he had heated up more spaghetti. He only had one fork full left. He took the small piece of bread remaining and like an eraser on a blackboard, he used the bread to erase every trace of spaghetti sauce on the plate. Then he threw back his head and opened his mouth and dropped in the piece of bread, followed by the fork full of spaghetti. He was one happy man, a far cry from a few hours ago.

* * * *

As usual, Ken got up at 4:30 a.m. to have his personal time with the Lord. He was so thankful that early on he and Quintella decided to do separate devotionals. They did try doing it together, but Queen couldn't get up at four-thirty, and waiting until six just threw him off.

His goal was to get out of the house every morning by a quarter to seven to beat the traffic. So, they settled on having their own time with the Lord and coming together once a

372 | YOU'VE GOT A MAN

YOU'VE GOT A MAN

week to have a joint study.

After Ken finished reading his devotional and relative Scripture, it was Ken's habit to read the chapter of Proverbs that corresponded with the day. Ken always read from the Amplified Bible because it did just that, amplified the text. Today was the twenty-first, so Ken began reading Proverbs 21. He paused at verse nine, which read, *"It is better to dwell in a corner of the housetop [on the flat oriental roof, exposed to all kinds of weather] than in a house shared with a nagging, quarrelsome,* and *faultfinding woman."* He looked up and said aloud, "Holy Spirit, I didn't say that. You did. But I can tell you from experience that You are so right."

Ken spent another five minutes thinking about yesterday's events, amused by his thoughts. As he finished reading, he really laughed when he got to verse nineteen. It read, *"It is better to dwell in a desert land than with a contentious woman and with vexation."*

"Well, I guess this won't be the shared devotion for me and Queen this week. Holy Spirit, You are my Friend, and I'm glad we can share this because it is truly a 'man thing,'" Ken quietly confessed, laughing at the Scripture he'd just read. The Bible was true but funny, and Ken found much comfort in reading God's Word.

Chapter Thirty-Seven

OK, Holy Spirit. How did this thing snowball out of control? Last month when we met for dinner, we all said there was nothing any of us could do that would cause the others not to love us. We all said we would be friends for life. Lenda even shared with us about her brother. Quintella was the first to hug her and ask why she didn't allow us to support her. We said that our secrets were safe with each other. We talked about how we wished Karen had trusted us and told us about her past. We felt that if she had told us she might be alive now. Karen probably knew our friends better than I did.

Let's see, she called me a slut, wouldn't talk to me, and humiliated me in front of other folks. Holy Spirit, where did I go wrong?

Once again, she didn't hear anything.

After emerging from her thoughts, Claudette reached for the phone and hit one on her speed dial. She felt Lenda was the best with handling these situations, so she had to talk to her.

"Hello," a sleepy voice answered.

"Were you sleep?"

"No, I answer the phone like this all the time," Lenda moaned.

"I'm very sorry to disturb you," Claudette's voice trembled on the other end.

Lenda sat straight up in the bed. "Hey, Claudette? This is you, right?" Lenda asked while trying to gather herself. "I'm sorry, girl. What's wrong?" And like a violent regurgitation, it all spilled out. All Lenda could do was shake her head in bewilderment.

Minutes later, Claudette paused for a brief moment and continued to verbalize her pain. Though it seemed like it took forever for Lenda to come up with a response, all she could muster was a, "Girl, I don't know what to say other than I love you. I really love you, Claudette. We'll get through this." After that, they held the phone even longer before Claudette asked, "Why did Queen feel the need to hurt me like that?"

"Claudette, if I could answer that question, I'd be rich. Girlfriend, betrayal is the worst, and I know you feel betrayed right now. But she'll come to her senses—and I know she'll call and apologize."

"Lenda, she looked at me like she hated me. It's like she wanted to spit in my face. I've never seen that side of Queen."

"Claudette, I know what I'm going to tell you is difficult, but you've got to put this whole affair behind you. You've suffered and repented, and carried your mistake for far too long. Let it go, girl. You asked God to forgive you, and He did. I don't have a heaven or a hell to put anyone in, and neither does Queen. I don't judge you. God will speak to her. It would be a waste of our time to sit here and try to figure out all the whys. My humble suggestion is that we move forward from here. God has blessed you with a wonderful man. Let it go, really."

"Can I ask you another question?"

"Sure."

"I asked Holy Spirit before I confessed this thing, and I prayed; He never told me not to do it, so why did things go so terribly wrong?"

"Claudette, just because Holy Spirit didn't answer you didn't mean for you to *do* it. God always answers His children; sometimes we have to wait for the answer and that's when we miss it, because we don't want to wait. But you know what? We don't even need to go there; it's over and done."

"Lenda, I love you. Thanks for being a real friend." Claudette gently put the phone in the cradle and thanked God for Lenda. She really was a friend.

* * * *

"So much for sleep," Lenda mumbled. "Goodness, how could I be friends with these people for so long and wake up wondering if I know them at all? If I had the strength, I'd go over to Queen's and give her a royal beat down. The girl must've clocked out. I can understand her shock and pain, but she went too far." Yes, Lenda was saying all of this in the comfort of God alone. She continued, "Lord, I know what Claudette did was wrong, but why is it I don't feel sorry for Queen's sister? That girl is crazy! She disrespects her husband in front of everybody, *and* she talks about him. No, Holy Spirit, I will not go there, and I apologize to You for what I just said. The marriage bed is holy; there are no justifications for adultery. I'm sorry I went there."

Lenda looked at the phone, but it was much too late. It was just as well; she really needed to think about what she would tell Quintella. *What's that Scripture? It says something like "instead of trying to get the splinter out of your neighbor's eye, get the telephone pole out of your own." That must be the Amplified Version. Let me look that one up,* she thought. Lenda went straight to the bookshelf that housed *Strong's*

Concordance.

"Let's see, I'll look up the word splinter…well, that's not in there. How about telephone? That's not in there either. Holy Spirit, what's that Scripture?" Then she heard Holy Spirit whisper to look up beam. "Beam, it says, is in Matthew 7, verses three, four, and five." Lenda walked across the bedroom to get her Bible. "What does Matthew 7:3 say?" As Lenda read verses three through five, she decided to memorize these Scriptures so that when she confronted Queen, she'd have her stuff together. This was not the time for Quintella to come back with something like, "You don't even know where the Scripture is located that you're trying to quote. Talk to me when you get your stuff together."

"Oh yeah, I can hear her now, so I'll have my stuff together. I've been around her for so long. But Holy Spirit, why does she feel the need to make those closest to her feel so bad? Yeah, that was a rhetorical question, Holy Spirit. I just need to go to bed and go to sleep. I can't wait to get in her face," Lenda confessed.

"Why?" she heard a voice say.

"Huh?" Lenda replied.

"Why get on Quintella?" the voice of Holy Spirit continued.

"'Cause she's wrong. Why crucify somebody because of a past mistake?"

"You crucified your brother. What about him?"

"Yeah, what about him?" Lenda murmured.

* * * *

Lenda didn't know a lot, but she knew Quintella was wrong. Just hearing the pain of betrayal from a friend only confirmed her decision. Lenda decided to go to her grave never telling her brother how she had blamed him when their mom died. She realized that her feelings were baseless, and she wasn't going to bring any guilt on him by her hands. She couldn't wait until 8:00 a.m. to call him. She didn't know what she would say, or how she would explain her prior abrupt absence and lack of support. But she knew that saying she was sorry would be a great start.

Chapter Thirty-Eight

Ken wasn't used to sitting on the other side of an attorney's desk. This was definitely different. They all had been summoned to the lawyer's office, and all they knew was it was about Karen's estate. Lenda, Claudette, Ken, Matthew, and Jelly were in the room. Noticeably missing was Quintella. As she had put it earlier when talking to Lenda, "Ken can be our representative; I think it best I not be there." Lenda was sad that all her efforts to bridge the relationship between Claudette and Lenda were for naught.

A tall well-dressed man in a navy suit, white shirt, and navy and yellow tie entered the room. "Greetings everyone, I'm the attorney for the late Karen McDonald. Thank you for clearing your schedules to attend this briefing. Normally, we don't have people get together in an attorney's office anymore. Nowadays, the executor in charge just makes sure all of the beneficiaries involved get what's rightfully theirs. I was named the executor by the late Miss McDonald, but her request was that I bring you all together. So in keeping with her wishes, I've assembled you here. I've already talked with her aunts, so now all that's left are all of you, her friends here in Detroit. She asked me to preside over her estate because she didn't want anyone to accuse Mr. James here of any wrongdoing, since he's also named…" His voice seemed to fade, but it was only because Lenda tuned him out.

Over the next fifteen minutes, he went through the arduous task of dividing up Karen's estate. No one really knew the wealth she had amassed because each person was given a sealed envelope. Ken had told her earlier that if people really want to find out about someone's estate, all they need to do is go down to probate court and ask, as it is public record.

Ken was clearing his throat to get Lenda's attention because the attorney was right in front of her with her envelope. "This is for you and your son, Matthew."

"Thank you," Lenda heard herself say. It still didn't seem real that they would never see Karen again, even though months had passed since she was murdered. And it didn't help that they never found the person responsible.

Why Karen decided to do what she did the way she did it, they would never know. Lenda would never go poking around probate court trying to find out what everyone got. She simply felt a sense of gratitude that she and her son were named in Karen's will.

There was even an envelope for Jelly, but it was given to Ken. Jelly, how was she ever going to tear him apart from Matthew? Yes, it was the right thing to do after Karen's death to go get him, but she still wasn't too keen on keeping him.

After Jelly came to live with them, Matthew promised Lenda that he would clean up after him, and he had. He promised her that he would keep his area clean, and she wouldn't have to do anything. And he had kept his promises there, too. The dog was no trouble. But she hadn't grown up with a dog, and she still couldn't fathom having a dog around all the time.

Matthew even took Jelly with him when he went to visit his dad on the weekends. Lenda was hoping that he would grow on her, but that never happened. Looking at Jelly sitting in Matthew's lap, she was afraid that she had already lost the battle.

"Thank you for coming. This concludes our meeting. Are there any other questions?" Lenda finally tuned back into the attorney's voice. Heads around the table shook from side to side, agreeing that no questions remained.

"Consider yourselves dismissed." And with that, they all began to shake hands and voice pleasantries to those in attendance while leaving the office.

Claudette walked toward Ken, not knowing how she would be greeted. Shyly, she smiled at him, and he held his arms out as if to say, "I still love you, girl!" It was such a relief to receive a hug from him. Claudette inquired about Quintella, and Ken only said with a smile, "She's good…just thought we both weren't needed here." Claudette knew otherwise; Quintella really didn't want to see her. She wondered if they would ever speak to each other again.

* * * *

When they got home, Matthew could hardly get in the house before he was asking Lenda to open their envelope. She told him she would after he took Jelly out and she got a chance to take off her coat and get into some comfortable clothes. Playfully, Matthew rolled his eyes and mumbled something unintelligible but respectful.

Seated on the sofa with envelope in hand, one would think they were in a library because it was so quiet. Matthew intently looked at his mom. "Hurry," he insisted.

Lenda's hands shook as the letter opener ripped through the envelope. Her eyes immediately went to the numbers and zeros. *I'd better read this out loud 'cause this can't be real,* she thought.

Lenda slowly began the task of reading their portion of Karen's will. "Now that I've taken care of my friend and she won't have to worry about money for a while, it's time to bless my baby. Matthew, I pray that you'll never have to get this blessing via letter but just in case you do, please know that you're the child I never had. I love you so much, and I want you to be successful. Success comes at a price. The price you'll pay is that of a student who will have to choose between fun and books. You'll have to say no more than yes to friends who want to party rather than study. Always, always, choose to study because it will pay off. I don't want you working jobs at ungodly hours, and I don't want you to have to use your time standing in line for free assistance. So, I have left you enough money to pay for four years of college, with enough cushion built in for clothes, food, inflation, and a little fun. It's only for four years, so stay focused and finish in four years. You can do it because God has blessed you with a wonderful mind. Use it. If it takes you longer to finish, that's on your momma and daddy. If you want to go longer, that's on you. Just know I love you, and I want only the best for you because you deserve it…" Lenda's voice trailed when she caught a glimpse of the big grin on Matthew's face as he looked at the dollar amount on the sheet of paper.

"Ma, where did Auntie Karen get so much money?" Matthew asked, bewildered.

"Just be grateful and say thank you," Lenda said with tears in her eyes. She would never repeat what Karen's aunts said about it being blood money.

"When you go to bed tonight and say your prayers, thank God, thank Auntie Karen, and be grateful, Matt, 'cause she didn't have to do it."

Excited, Matthew didn't want to wait, "Can we pray now, Ma? I don't want to wait until I go to bed!" he proclaimed.

"Sure, Matt. Let's pray."

Lenda and Matthew stood facing each other. With hands held and heads bowed, Matthew began to pray.

"Heavenly Father, in Jesus' Name, I thank You for this wonderful gift of money from Auntie Karen. Lord, I believe Auntie is with You, and I think she hears me, too. So thanks, Auntie! I didn't know you had this much money. But Lord, back to You. Thank You for allowing my mom and Auntie Karen to become friends. If they never became friends, I wouldn't be standing here thanking You now. Lord, give me friends in life, 'cause good friends help you get through the hard times—and we've had some hard times, my mom and I. But because of You and friends, we've made it. Lord, I'm not thanking You today just because of the money, but I'm thanking You more for the memories of Auntie Karen. The times we went to the symphony, McDonald's, Cedar Point, and all the secrets I told her that she never told anyone. Lord, when You give me my friends, help me to be a friend to them like Auntie Karen was to us. I know I said it already, but thanks again for the blessing, in Jesus' Name. Amen."

"Oh Matt…" was all Lenda could get out before hugging him.

Never in a million years would she have thought that Karen would leave her so much money. It was enough that she had cared so much for Matthew, but to bless him in the way she did—it was overwhelming. What Karen gifted to Matthew made what she had given to her mother for Ernest's attorney's fees look miniscule. It's like she got quadruple for her trouble. Lenda thought: *The Bible says that God will give us double for our trouble. I got way more than that!*

Yeah, they were going to be OK. Not only she and Matthew, but her sister, her brother, Claudette and maybe with time, Quintella. Yeah, they were all going to be OK. After all, she had a Man—and so did they!

Remember the poem in the beginning of this book?

I finally figured it out…
When and if something gets ahold of me,
And it's something I cannot see,
I'll remember that its grip only comes,
When I fail to spend time with You Three
God the Father, God the Son, and God Holy Spirit—
Yeah!

—Gloria P. Pruett
10/6/12

Questions for Book Clubs

1. Karen obviously didn't have a good relationship with her mother—how does one get over such hurt?

2. What did you think when Karen was in the mirror convincing herself that it was OK to fornicate?

3. If you look at the body of Christ as a whole, who do you think represents the majority: Lenda, Karen, Claudette, or Quintella?

4. Women: Have you ever dressed up at night in a special gown, combed your hair, and put on some perfume to read your Bible? Men: Have you ever cleaned up, put on some aftershave and pajamas, and then talked to God? Why or why not?

5. Should Lenda have confronted or comforted Karen about her sin of fornication? Why or why not?

6. Do real friends turn a deaf ear to bad behavior? Why or why not?

7. If you were Claudette, would you have confessed the affair to Quintella? Why or why not? Why didn't she pray about it?

8. Have you become cynical, believing that there are no good men/women out there like Christopher/Claudette over the age of forty-five?

9. If the girls felt so strongly that Karen shouldn't go to a worldly party, should they have prayed more, or done more, for her?

10. Are you harboring unforgiveness about either of your parents that you could make right? What about with your siblings or friends? Is it anything you feel comfortable discussing with the group? If not, when you are alone, ask God to help you talk about the issue; know that the cleansing will lift a heavy load off of you. Remember, you've got a Man in Holy Spirit, and He's always available to talk to you.

OTHER RESOURCES

If you enjoyed *You've Got a Man,* you may also want to read Gloria P. Pruett's non-fiction book entitled:

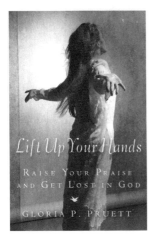

Lift Up Your Hands
Raise Your Praise and Get Lost in God

This book will make praising God an experience so joyful and life-changing that you will get lost in Him. Gloria P. Pruett brings you an easy method to do just that! Follow her as she takes you step-by-step through her new technique that also helps you complete her handy exercise pages.

To order, visit gloriapruett.com